Includes Bonus Story of
Pride's Fall
by Darlene Franklin

Love's Compass

CARLA
GADE

BARBOUR BOOKS
An Imprint of Barbour Publishing, Inc.

Print ISBN 978-1-68322-114-2

eBook Editions:
Adobe Digital Edition (.epub) 978-1-68322-115-9
Kindle and MobiPocket Edition (.prc) 978-1-68322-116-6

All scripture quotations are taken from the King James Version of the Bible.

This book is a work of fiction. Names, characters, places, and incidents are either products of the author's imagination or used fictitiously. Any similarity to actual people, organizations, and/or events is purely coincidental.

Published by Barbour Books, an imprint of Barbour Publishing, Inc., P.O. Box 719, Uhrichsville, Ohio 44683, www.barbourbooks.com

Our mission is to publish and distribute inspirational products offering exceptional value and biblical encouragement to the masses.

ecpa Member of the Evangelical Christian Publishers Association

Printed in the United States of America.

Chapter 1

May, 1875
Del Norte, Colorado Territory

"Imagine having to bear a mark like that for the rest of your life." Eliana Van Horn thrust the *San Juan Prospector* into her father's face as they ambled down the boardwalk of the thriving supply town at the base of the San Juan Mountains. "The tattoo on her chin, how dreadful—and there's nothing that can be done about it!"

John Van Horn peered at the picture from beneath his spectacles. "Yes, Olive Oatman, the Indian captive." He drew his mouth into a tight line and stroked his graying beard. "Everyone has some kind of mark."

Eliana held her head high against the Colorado mountains. "Yes, I know." *All too well.*

Her father loosened his tie, which seemed to be constricting his neck, and cleared his throat. "You've seen that engraving before. That photograph has been in circulation for nearly a decade. Amazing that she's still in the public interest after all this time."

"The article says that the editor of her captivity narrative has died. Apparently, through the years, her husband bought and destroyed every available copy of *The Captivity of the Oatman Girls*. She no longer lectures and wears a veil to cover her tattoo when in public."

"Yet, her picture will continue to tell the story even if the books are gone. Photography does create a permanent record, for good or gain," Papa said.

Eliana pulled the newspaper back and curled it around her chin. Was it right to perpetuate this woman's shame, wrought by the natives? Photography had its merits, but should it have limits as well? And what about the indelible mark etched on her soul? As for the book,

Eliana still possessed her own copy and had been intrigued by the tale for years. Utmost, that despite the atrocities Olive suffered at the hands of her captors, she saw God's hand of mercy when she was kept from starvation by a kind Indian woman. It was then that Olive learned to chide her hasty judgment against all the Indian race.

Eliana also hoped to keep from making hasty judgments. She knew for some, it was enough to be judged simply for the color of their skin. Dare she liken it to the prejudice she received as a woman? Some people wanted to make their mark on the world, while others could never hide from the marks they received. But at what cost?

What would it be like to be attacked or captured by Indians? A shiver crawled up her spine as Eliana studied the picture while she and her father walked along. As her father's photography assistant, Eliana was always fascinated by images in print. And she'd much rather discuss photography than Indians. "If I were her, I'd get a new tintype done and have it retouched to make that terrible mark disappear," she said.

"As for retouching, my photography mentor in Ohio is renowned for that process. You know. . ." Papa stopped dead in his tracks and caught Eliana by the elbow. "You're not worried, Sunshine, are you? If you're hesitant about going on the expedition, now is the time to say so."

Images whirled around Eliana's vivid imagination like a zoetrope as she recalled hearing about the attack on the Slack ranch last year. The Utes burned the new resident out and almost started an Indian war right in the San Juans. Eliana peered at the mountain vista and wondered where renegade Indians hid. She and Papa would travel through wild country soon on their assignment for the U.S. General Land Office. She drew in a deep breath of the fresh Colorado air to cleanse her mind from the unwelcome thoughts that had spun into her head.

"I have no reservations whatsoever. We've made many preparations for this trip, and I won't abandon you. It's too important. This is your big chance." *And mine.* "You've already assured me that this is one of the safest times to go." She tilted her head. "Besides, I'm not afraid of—"

"No Injuns allowed!" A voice bellowed from inside the Silver Eagle Saloon. Head over boots, some unfortunate soul tumbled through the swinging doors, whirring past the Van Horns like a windstorm. Eliana's newspaper flew into the dusty street.

Papa steadied and reached out for her. "Are you all right, dear?"

Eliana gasped as she clung to the porch post and attempted to regain her composure. "I'm fine." At least she was until an oversized man stepped out onto the planking, nearly knocking her over again.

" 'Scuse me, miss." The stench of saloon and neglected ablutions clung to him. "Just doin' a little housekeepin'. Don't want no half breeds stinkin' up the place. The owner ain't partial to his kind." He spit into the road, muttered an oath, and tromped back inside.

Yiska Wilcox sprang to his feet. He brushed the dirt from his pants and the pebbles from his calloused hands. He'd been kicked out of places like this before and swore he'd never go in again. A lungful of exasperation escaped his clenched teeth. Things never changed.

A young woman stared at him like a stunned doe. A middle-aged man stood beside her, a protective grip around her waist. He took in the pair with a furtive scan. The man wore a linen duster over his suit and a bowler hat. Assayer maybe. Surveyor possibly. Or maybe another easterner out to make a fortune. As for his companion, she was a lady if he ever saw one—a rare occurrence in his travels. Even in that pretty dress, she carried no highfalutin airs. A natural beauty.

"Beg your pardon, sir, miss. I hope you aren't harmed."

"Not at all." The man surveyed Yiska head to toe. "Are we, dear?"

"We're quite fine, thank you," the young lady said, her bright eyes scrutinizing him.

"Are you all right, young man? You're the one who was tossed out on his ear." The gentleman stooped to pick up the pipe he had dropped.

"Yes, sir." Yiska flicked his hair away from his face and dragged his fingers through his hair. Where'd his hat go? A brisk wind blew a sheet of newsprint toward him, and it clung to his legs like buffalo bur.

"Now, if you'd be so kind as to hand me my newspaper, I'd appreciate it very much," the lady said.

Yiska grasped the paper and spotted the image of the famous Indian captive, Olive Oatman—the chin tattoo the telling sign. Seemed folks never grew weary of recounting the tale. They even wrote dime novels about her. But the sad truth was that the southwest tribe, Apache they claimed, had abducted her and her sister in their youth from a westbound wagon in Arizona and later sold them to the Mohave. He didn't claim to understand such things, though something akin to regret twinged his heart. At least she was eventually ransomed.

The young woman extended her ivory hand, cuffed in a ruffle of lace that poked out from her jacket sleeve. Her eyes met his directly—the color of sagebrush, with a mixture of mystery and curiosity. He handed her the newspaper. When their fingertips touched, she quickly drew the paper into her protective custody. She acknowledged Yiska with a nod and stepped back. Had she felt the tremor, too? Probably just scared—of him.

Yiska tried not to stare at the marks on the young lady's chin. Must be newspaper ink. The man tapped his forefinger against his own chin, handed her a handkerchief, and said in a low voice, "Dear, you've some ink on your chin." Her eyes darted toward Yiska and back again in alarm. And then her face became as red as a Colorado sunset. Obviously mortified, she turned her pretty head, facing the saloon. Men leered from the uncurtained windows, and she spun back around. Yiska scowled at the scoundrels. What was this woman doing out in front of a saloon in the first place?

After her discreet attempt to wipe her face, she glanced up from beneath her dark lashes with a smirk. "I guess you can't take me anywhere, can you, Papa?" Yiska noticed the slight dimple in her adorable chin.

Her father chuckled then sobered. "I certainly never should've let you cross the street with me." The gentleman's eyes shot toward Yiska. He rocked up on his toes, hands deep in his pockets. "Why don't you tell me what happened in there?"

"I went in to get my wages. Wasn't planning to stay. I'm not overly welcome in such fine establishments." Yiska knew there was a defensive edge to his voice. Did it matter anymore?

"Haven't seen you around here before," the man said, "but then we're fairly new to these parts." Yiska hadn't seen them either. The mining supply town had folks coming and going all the time, especially now that the snow was gone.

"I just rode in." Yiska glanced at his borrowed mount tied to the hitching post. "I came to claim my pay from my boss. I was told I'd find him here."

"Looks like you'll have to wait until he comes out."

"He ain't coming out. Not before my silver's all gone." Yiska kicked the dirt.

The man's eyes narrowed. "What's your boss's name?"

"Trask Whiley, the outfitter. I'm one of his guides. Been out on the trail."

"I know him. He's been helping us get settled in the region." The man glanced at the saloon door. "I'll tell you what. I'll go in and talk to him for you. I've some business of my own to discuss with him. You'll have to stay out here, Eliana."

"Surely, Papa. You didn't think I wanted to go in there with you?"

"They might toss you out on your ear, too," Yiska said.

"Ah, the life of a second-rate citizen."

At that, Yiska cocked his head and raised an eyebrow.

Her cheeks reddened. "I was referring to myself, a female. I didn't mean to imply. . ."

Her father cleared his throat. “What’s your name, son?”

“Yiska. Yiska Wilcox.” He held out his hand. The man shook it with a firm grip.

“John Van Horn. And this is my lovely daughter, Eliana Van Horn.”

“Mr. Van Horn.” Yiska nodded. “Miss Van Horn.”

“Mr. Wilcox, I’d be obliged if you would see my daughter safely across Main Street and wait for me right there in front of Gray’s Mercantile. I’ll be out in two shakes of a lamb’s tail.”

The man was confident. His daughter—endearing.

“That’s mighty generous of you, Mr. Van Horn.” Yiska nodded. “And I’d be happy to see to your daughter’s safety.”

“How much pay do you have coming to you?” Van Horn asked.

“Twenty-six dollars, sir. . .and a new hat.”

“I’ll see what I can do. You said your name’s Wilcox?”

“Yes, sir. Yiska Wilcox. He knows me well.”

“Wilcox. . .” Van Horn shook his head and chuckled. “That’s a good old English name.”

“Miss Van Horn, shall we?”

Eliana thought Mr. Wilcox was about to offer her his arm, but he kept a respectful distance. They walked across Del Norte’s main street—she in her new dress and reticule, and he in a buckskin vest with a tomahawk strapped to his hip. Tumbleweeds rolled in her stomach. What was her father thinking? She had never met an Indian before, never mind walked across the street with one. To her surprise he was relatively polite, though a little rough around the edges. Certainly not what she expected. She did have expectations, after all.

“How long do you suppose two shakes of a lamb’s tail takes, Miss Van Horn?” His grin revealed a nice smile, which added to his rather handsome facial features–high cheekbones, broad forehead, strong jaw, dark almond eyes. Not that she noticed.

Eliana laughed. So, he had a sense of humor. "I don't know, probably about the same as two crows of a rooster. Or three moos of a cow."

"Or four screams of a hawk," he chimed in.

"Good one!" Oh, dear. She hoped he wouldn't misconstrue her amusement for flirting. Eliana hastened her stride.

The ground beneath them rumbled. A wagon barreled around the corner, drawn by a team of wild-eyed horses. Dust kicked up in a cloud. Mr. Wilcox shoved Eliana to one side and almost landed on top of her. Their fall nearly knocked the wind from her lungs. She swiped the dust from her lips and groaned.

"Miss Van Horn?" Mr. Wilcox spoke in a concerned tone and gently placed his hand upon her back. "Miss Van Horn, are you all right?"

"Yes, I believe so. . . ."

Some men gathered round, and one yanked Mr. Wilcox up by the shirt. Another punched him in the stomach. Mr. Wilcox doubled over.

Another man pulled Eliana up by both arms, right into his chest. She jumped back. She didn't know whether to thank the man or slap him.

Two men dragged Yiska Wilcox down the dirt street, though he put up quite a struggle. He looked back at Eliana, his eyes dark and wild.

"Wait!" she yelled. "He saved me from that wagon!"

"I didn't see no wagon. Did anyone see a wagon?"

"No, all I saw was that stinkin' half blood attack this pretty young lady here." The man grabbed a lock of her hair. Eliana swatted his hand and stomped on his foot, sending him whimpering away like a wounded coyote.

"What is the meaning of this?" Her father shouted. The men backed away from Eliana. Others peered out from storefronts.

"Papa!" Eliana ran to her father's side.

"Daughter, what happened?" Eliana clung to him. "What's going on here?" he called over her. Eliana shifted behind her father, still holding his arm.

"Don't worry, mister. We hauled that half-breed varmint off to the jail."

"I wasn't aware this town had a jail," Papa said.

One of the men in the crowd smiled at Eliana, exposing several missing teeth. "We're always looking out for the ladies in this town. Yes, siree."

"Ladies?" Someone snickered beneath his breath.

Eliana tugged on his sleeve, "Papa, we must do something!"

"What's all the commotion about, Van Horn?" A familiar voice penetrated the crowd. Trask Whiley. Mr. Whiley held a certain measure of respect from most of the town folk, and he didn't appear to be inebriated. "Get outta here! Git!"

The men went off in various directions, but most of them disappeared inside the Silver Eagle Saloon.

"Now, Eliana, why don't you tell us exactly what happened?" her father asked.

"Mr. Wilcox was escorting me across the street to the mercantile, as you requested, when a wagon came tearing around the corner. If it hadn't been for Mr. Wilcox. . . He saved my life!"

"Where'd they take him, John?"

"To the jail, they said."

Mr. Whiley seemed to note the question in her father's eyes.

"They mean Thatcher's Sawmill."

A dreadful foreboding gripped Eliana. "What will they do to him?"

"We'd better get right over there." Whiley said. "It's their word against his. And I'm afraid it doesn't take much of an excuse to hang an Injun."

Chapter 2

"There are only two reasons a wagon would drive that fast through this little town—one is Indians, and the other is gold," Trask Whiley explained as he drove Eliana and her father toward Thatcher's Sawmill.

Eliana gripped the edge of the seat. Would they get there in time to rescue Yiska Wilcox from certain execution?

"I thought silver was the main commodity in the San Juans," Papa said. "And what of the Indians? There haven't been reports of danger around here lately." He remained calm and collected, but Eliana could tell he was agitated by the way he gnawed on the end of his unlit pipe.

"Precisely," Whiley said. "Silver's aplenty, so when someone finds gold there's a big hullabaloo. As for Indians, the townsfolk think they've got themselves one now."

"He's not full-blooded," Eliana said.

"No matter. His blood's considered tainted by most."

"That's barbaric!" Eliana wrung her hands and frowned. How could the kind act of a stranger turn into such a fiasco? *Dear Lord, please let us get to him in time. Oh, please!*

"It's what some call Western justice, Miss Van Horn." Whiley snapped the reins.

"There's no justice in this at all," her father said. "The man was protecting my daughter!"

Whiley pulled up in front of the San Luis Valley Bank. An old wagon loaded with shovels, pickaxes, and all kinds of miscellany sat parked in front with a pair of lathered horses hitched to the rig. "Stay put. When I come out of there I should have the proof we need to verify your story, Miss Van Horn."

"Then will they let Mr. Wilcox go?"

"That remains to be seen." Trask Whiley jumped off his buckboard and marched into the bank.

Eliana tapped her foot against the wagon floor. Mr. Whiley told them that Yiska Wilcox was one of his best employees. Mr. Wilcox worked as a guide all around the Colorado Territory's southwest. As a Navajo he had great instincts, and as a white, he was more trusted. Obviously that didn't always hold true.

Two men hauled Yiska in the direction of Thatcher's Sawmill, home to the town's temporary jail. His hands were tied behind his back with a rough cord. As they passed a huge saw blade, one of the men slammed Yiska down on the table, putting his head within inches of the moving guillotine—a mock execution. The buzzing noise was deafening, but his heart thundered louder still.

"Get that man off of there!" yelled Ed Thatcher.

The hooligan pulled Yiska to his feet. "You have yerself a prisoner, Thatcher."

"This Injun tried to kill a gal downtown," the other fellow said.

Yiska stood up straight, his face set like flint.

"Is that true?" Thatcher booted Yiska in the shin. "Is that true, I said!"

Yiska gritted his teeth, not giving way to the pain.

One of the other men yanked Yiska back by the hair.

"She was about to get run over, so I pushed her out of the way."

"I see. A real hero, are we?"

"I ain't never seen an Injun who was a hero before." The man tightened his hold, straining Yiska's shoulders back.

"He ain't no real Injun. He's a half blood. Them's worse," the other man said.

"What, did your Injun papa have his way with a white woman? The way I see it, you're following in his savage ways," the one holding him taunted.

The muscles in Yiska's jaw tightened, his eyes an icy glare.

"Here's his tomahawk." His captor handed it to Ed Thatcher. "I wanted to keep it fer myself, but it's evidence. Thought there'd be some feathers and stuff on it. It's pretty ordinary if ya ask me."

"It's a hatchet, you imbecile. He used this on the woman?" Thatcher asked.

"Some were sayin'."

"Take him back to the pit!"

The so-called jail was an old storage room filled with grimy buckets and sacks of grain for the mill's pack animals. As the men dragged Yiska into the cell, a rat scurried off. The brutes held him down while Thatcher secured shackles to Yiska's ankles.

"You can't keep me here. I broke no law," Yiska managed through his clenched teeth.

"We'll let the marshal in Colorado Springs decide about that. He oughtta be coming by a few months down the road. After we notify him, of course."

"If'n we notify 'im," one of them scoffed.

Yiska scrambled back as the ruffians came at him with hardwood planks.

"Go on! You've done your job!" Thatcher threw his hand up and halted them, but not before one of them hit Yiska in the side.

Thatcher closed the door to the pen, locked it, and left Yiska in misery.

Bewildered, Yiksa tried to focus in the dim cell. He rustled his boots in the dirty sawdust, a foul odor assailing him. How'd he end up in this lousy mess? After he rode into town on that ornery loaned mount, he'd learned that Mr. Whiley was down at the saloon, probably frivoling away Yiska's month's wages—buying a little time until he came in from the range. Whiley always promised he'd take good care of Yiska. Said when he gambled Yiska's wages, it was an investment on his behalf—truth being that Whiley didn't always come out ahead. His boss had a lot of sense, except when it came to cards and women. But unlike Whiley, Yiska wasn't one to take a risk.

Of course when he entered the Silver Eagle, he'd got tossed out again on his backside. Didn't it figure that Miss Van Horn—Eliana—had to witness the whole thing? The pretty lady and her father seemed like fine people, not prejudiced like others—a rare thing in these parts. Why couldn't folks see that he was no different from anyone else? He loved the Colorado wilderness, he worked hard, and he appreciated the beauty of a lovely woman like Eliana Van Horn. What was he thinking? He'd never stand a chance with someone like her. Nor did his lifestyle as a wilderness guide give him an opportunity to ever be with anyone. Period. The path he took was a lonely one.

Yiska sighed. But wasn't she somethin'? That Eliana Van Horn looked like an angel that dropped right out of heaven, plumb into the Colorado Territory! She was all sunlight on this cloudy Colorado morning. She looked all fancy and feminine in her bustled dress and matching hat, but he reckoned there was more about her than met the eye. Something radiated from her like a jolt of lightning, striking a connection between them.

Yiska sat on the floor and rested his head against his knees. A few streaks of light made their way through the crevices of the outside wall and fell upon his shoulders. Should he pray to the Great Spirit in his distress, or the Christian God? Whoever would listen.

"I could use a little help here. Please set me free," he whispered. If the gods chose to answer his prayer, he had no doubt in his heart that Miss Eliana Van Horn, her father, and Trask Whiley would be along soon. He wanted to believe that Miss Van Horn was different. She wouldn't lie about what had happened, would she?

"He's taking a long time, Eliana. I'm going in to see what's holding them up." Eliana's father jumped down from the buckboard. "Will you be all right here for a moment?"

"Yes, Papa, I'll be fine." Eliana shaded her eyes with her hand and returned a wave to a woman sweeping the boardwalk in the distance. "If anyone bothers me again, I'm sure Mrs. Sanborn will notice and send some help."

Her father chuckled. "You're right about that." Mrs. Sanborn never missed a thing. She probably knew all about this afternoon's incident near the saloon and certainly helped usher the news all over town by sharing it with the patrons of her café.

"Please make haste, Papa. Mr. Wilcox's life may be at stake." As her father walked up the steps of the bank, Eliana heard a hawk scream. *"Four screams of a hawk." Oh, Yiska.* Before it screamed again she climbed down from the wagon and scooted into the bank after Papa.

They approached the assayer's barred window, where Mr. Whiley hovered over an old man—the miner—who could clear this matter up.

Mr. Whiley thumped his fingers on the counter and looked up at them. "He refused to leave until his gold was counted." So, the man *had* found gold.

"And I promised him a photograph," Whiley added.

"Now?" Eliana and Papa said in unison.

"No. At his claim, after all this is settled."

The miner looked their way with a toothless grin stretching from ear to ear.

"That was the only way I could get him to hurry it up and come with us."

"Very well," Papa said. "If he cooperates I'll even frame the photograph. Where's your claim, mister?"

"I cain't go telling you that until it's registered," the miner said.

Papa shook his head. For years he'd been photographing Colorado mining activities for the U.S. General Land Office. Thousands of ravenous miners and prospectors flooded the mountains and rivers. At one point Papa had even talked to Eliana about staking a claim himself. He wanted to have enough money to send her back East to Ohio to attend finishing school.

"Papa, you have a treasure trove already right there in your camera," she'd said. "And everything I want to know comes from you." He'd always been a good provider, and she wanted to learn all she could from him about photography.

At last the claim was filed. The old miner checked on his horses, paid a boy to bring his rig to the livery, and climbed aboard Mr. Whiley's buckboard. He wore a threadbare shirt and a pair of grimy overalls patched up with old flour sacks. Eliana couldn't help but notice the one that covered his rear with the company's stamp, XXXX. She flattened her lips to stifle a nervous giggle.

Trask Whiley snapped the reins and raced for the mill at the end of town. Eliana covered her face with her hands to keep the dust out of her mouth.

"Howdy, miss." The miner peered at her with a wrinkled grin. "I understand an apology's in order. Didn't see anyone in the road when I came 'round the corner of Main Street. Course, I was going so fast, if I'd blinked I'd missed ya anyway." The unkempt man reeked. Like many others, he'd probably not bathed in at least six months.

Had he just apologized? Eliana thought not.

"Well, Mr. . . ." The wagon hit a bump and jostled her closer to him.

"Cornelius Crawford's the name."

"Mr. Crawford, thank you for agreeing to set matters straight. It would be a shame to have an innocent man pay for a crime he did not commit."

"Wouldn't want anybody to suffer unnecessarily." The corners of the man's weather-beaten face turned downward, making him resemble an old mule. They rode on in silence. A moment later Crawford leaned close to Eliana with a big grin. "Did ya know I'm rich? I'm rich! Now I can find me a wife."

Eliana jumped back. She couldn't get to the sawmill fast enough.

"Whoa!" Mr. Whiley brought his team to a halt.

Eliana, her father, Mr. Whiley, and Mr. Crawford all hustled past the piles of lumber and buzzing saw blades, the scent of fresh-cut aspen filling the air. When they got to the overseer's office, Mr. Thatcher greeted them. "Something I can do for you folks?"

"Where is he?" Whiley demanded.

"I take it you mean the prisoner," Thatcher said. "Don't worry, he's all tied up. Can't hurt anyone where he is."

"Tied up?" Eliana cried. Her father placed his arm around her. She glanced about. In what sort of makeshift jail were they keeping him?

Whiley leaned close to Thatcher's face. "Let me see him. He's my employee—I have a right. And these folks are coming, too."

"Very well. I'm just holding him here until I get the say so."

"Say so?" What did he mean by that? Eliana blinked back the tears forming in her eyes.

They entered a small caged room at the rear of the large building. Mr. Wilcox sat on the floor in the corner, leaning back against the wall, head hung low. His ankles were chained together and attached to a large iron ring on the wall. Heavy ropes bound his wrists.

"Yiska!" Whiley called to him.

Yiska looked up with a great measure of relief and climbed to his feet.

"We got here as soon as we could," Papa said.

Crawford took a step closer and squinted. "I thought you said he was innocent. Why, he's an Injun! Let him rot in there." He turned and started to leave.

Eliana went after him, hands on her hips. "Mr. Crawford! You can't mean that!"

"Ev-er-y word. I've got my principles."

"Please. . . You must tell the truth—that you came around the corner in your wagon."

"Already told you, I didn't see anyone."

Eliana's father stepped forward. "But you did drive your wagon in haste down Main Street."

"Mr. Crawford, you tell the truth now, or I'll. . ." Oh, how tempting it would be to grab that piece of lumber over there and whack him right across the Xs! Eliana let out a deep breath and softened her voice. "Since you are such a dear, hard-working, and honorable man, I know that you would never want harm to come to anyone. Please tell Mr. Thatcher the truth and let this matter be done. Then you can go back to your gold claim."

Whiley pressed in, glowering at him.

"All right!" Crawford threw his hands in the air. "Yes, I drove my wagon down Main Street on the way to the bank." He looked at Thatcher. "The girl said I near plowed her down. Didn't see her."

"Thank you ever so much, Mr. Crawford." She feigned a smile. Papa winked at her, nodding for her to continue. "Mr. Thatcher, Mr. Wilcox saw that wagon coming and was brave enough to push me out of harm's way. When some bystanders saw that we had fallen to the ground, they made a very wrong assumption about Mr. Wilcox. I owe him my life, and he does not deserve to be punished. Now, if you would be so kind as to release this man. . ."

"Yes, ma'am. Grover, get me those keys." Eliana recognized the other man as one who had brought Mr. Wilcox here. Thatcher took the keys and freed Mr. Wilcox from his bonds.

Yiska rubbed his wrists as he stepped out of the crude prison. He met everyone's gazes and rested his eyes on the prettiest of all. "Thank you." If he could, he would devote his life to protect them—protect *her*—from any danger. Until then, words alone would have to convey his gratitude. Yiska raked a hand through his hair and exhaled. He clamped his mouth shut as pain shot through his side. They'd confiscated his hatchet and exchanged it for what felt like a broken rib.

"It is I who should thank you. You protected my daughter, and that means everything to me." Mr. Van Horn offered Yiska a firm handshake.

"Well done, Yiska," his boss said.

Mr. Van Horn reached into his pocket. "That reminds me, I have your wages." He handed him some paper notes and several coins. "I put a little extra in there for you."

"That's not necessary, Mr. Van Horn." Yiska glanced at Miss Van Horn. He would do it all again if he had to.

"Please take it. This has caused you a lot of trouble."

Thatcher handed Yiska his hatchet. "I believe this belongs to you."

Yiska walked through the door without turning back.

Outside Whiley placed his hand on Yiska's shoulder. "How about we all go get something to eat?"

"Me, too?" Crawford asked.

"We're just going to Sanborn's Café for a quick bite," Whiley said. "Since you're a rich man now, you ought to go clean up and take yourself out to a proper restaurant. We'll drop you off at the livery, and you can be on your way."

Cornelius Crawford straightened his shoulders. "I think I will." He turned to Miss Van Horn and wiggled his eyebrows. "Care to join me?"

Chapter 3

Relief washed over Yiska when they finally dropped Crawford off at the livery. Although he was grateful that the man had finally fessed up, Yiska didn't like the way he ogled Miss Van Horn and bragged about his new-found wealth.

As they drove away, the old miner waved his floppy hat in the air and hollered, "What about my daguerreotype? You promised!" Eliana, her father, and Mr. Whiley burst into laughter. Yiska shrugged his shoulders and enjoyed Miss Van Horn's wide smile and dancing eyes.

Whiley parked his rig near Sanborn's Café. Yiska reached up and took Miss Van Horn by the waist to help her down. Her eyes stayed hitched on his while he lowered her to the ground. He winced in pain, but with her looking at him, he soon forgot about it. As he set her down, he hesitated before he let her go.

"Oh, Mr. Wilcox." Her hands remained steadied against his arms, her voice barely above a whisper. "I feel so responsible. Can you ever forgive me?"

"There's nothing to forgive, Miss Van Horn."

"Are you injured?" She took a step back, looking him over, and her cheeks colored.

He hooked his thumbs in his pants pockets. "Only my pride." He held his gaze but wanted to take in *all* of her, from the tousled honey locks peeking out from her hat to her tiny laced boots.

Miss Van Horn glanced at the ground then looked at him beneath dark lashes. In the silence of the moment somehow their hearts spoke, yet there remained a quiet resistance.

"Injun, Injun, stinking Injun!" some mischievous boys shouted out. The rascals disappeared between some buildings.

Eliana shrank back, the spell broken. Her eyes shot to Yiska's hatchet. She said nothing.

"Mr. Wilcox," her father called. He tossed Yiska his hat.

Yiska caught it with both hands.

"Hey, you found it! Mighty obliged, Mr. Van Horn." He dipped his head and put the hat in its rightful place.

As they approached Sanborn's Café, Mr. Whiley held open the door, allowing Miss Van Horn to enter, and then slipped in behind her. He handed off the door to Yiska with a triumphant grin. What was Whiley up to now?

As the troupe entered the café, customers murmured and gave them odd looks. Mrs. Sanborn scurried over and greeted them with all measure of curiosity. "Eliana, dear. I'm glad to see you're doing well. I heard you had quite a time of it today. Almost got run over by a herd of wild horses, and then attacked by an Indian." Mrs. Sanborn eyed Yiska. It was obvious she wondered where *he* fit in to all of this.

Eliana laughed. "I was almost run over by a wagon, but *this* gentleman saved my life." She hoped that would set things straight. What was it like to have to live under a veil of judgement?

Mrs. Sanborn looked at Yiska with astonishment. "Is that so?" Not waiting for a response, she rattled off the day's menu and took their orders.

The pleasing aroma of Mrs. Sanborn's famous pot roast and strawberry rhubarb pie filled the air. She brought their meals to the table herself, serving Yiska last.

"We've much to be thankful for this day," Eliana's father declared. He reached for her hand and lowered his head in silent prayer. Eliana bowed but dared not close her eyes for fear that her emotions of the day would catch up with her. When she peeked up she saw Mr. Whiley busy cutting his meat, but Yiska remained still until her father was done and had tucked his napkin into his vest.

"Do you think we'll see more of Cornelius Crawford?" Mr. Whiley asked with a chortle.

"I believe I'll have to. I've an appointment to keep with him," Papa answered.

"John, you don't mean you'll actually follow through with it?"

"I'm a man of my word, Trask. It was part of the bargain." Papa leaned back in his chair and looked at Yiska. "As a matter of fact, I hope you'll allow me to take your photograph as a small token of my appreciation."

"Photograph? That's what you were laughing about."

Eliana said, "Yes, poor Mr. Crawford called it a daguerreotype. They haven't been used in ages!"

"You're a photographer." Yiska eyed Papa curiously.

"Yes, and Eliana is my able assistant. We have a temporary studio rented on Alpine Street while we're in town."

"Been here long, sir?"

"Not long enough. We were stuck up at our residence in Lake City all winter and had to wait until the thaw to come down for supplies. It's been good work here since the San Juan Secession of '73 opened up the mining again. And now it's safe for folks to settle here with no real threat of Indians."

Eliana almost spilled her appleade. The table grew quiet.

Yiska shifted in his chair. Had Papa offended him? "Well. . .you never know what kind of trouble they'll cause. Probably twice as much trouble as I would." He cracked a smile and glanced Eliana's way.

The men all laughed, and the awkward moment faded away. But Eliana remained quiet. How often must Mr. Wilcox deflect comments like that? Did they hurt his feelings? Could someone like him ever fit in with her circle of friends?

Mr. Whiley stood and patted his belly. "I've got a card game to go finish. John, want to play a hand?"

"You know I'm not a gambling man, Whiley. Besides, I think I've had enough excitement for one day. Don't you agree, Sunshine?"

"Indeed, Papa." Eliana sighed. "You are all heroes, and again I thank you."

"I think you are forgetting someone, dear."

"Am I?" What was Papa going to say now?

"Yes, Miss Van Horn. *You* saved my life," Mr. Wilcox said.

Eliana felt her cheeks warm. Papa put his hand on Mr. Wilcox's shoulder and shook his hand. "Yiska, be sure to come over to my studio someday before you head back out. I won't take no for an answer."

"Miss Van Horn, a pleasure as always." Mr. Whiley cocked his head and grinned.

"Likewise," said Mr. Wilcox with a nod.

As she watched him leave, she sincerely hoped he would come by for the photograph. If he didn't, she might never see him again. And that would be a tragedy.

Eliana settled into her bed that night in the Van Horns' apartment above the photography shop. After reading a passage from her Bible, she placed it back on the nightstand, distracted by thoughts from earlier in the day. For a fleeting moment she had thought, had wished, Mr. Wilcox would kiss her when he helped her off the wagon. What was she thinking? It had been broad daylight, in the middle of town. She barely knew the man, yet her heart sensed a familiarity, a longing. Her attraction to him surprised her. His strong face and dark eyes held warmth and interest, the contours around his mouth revealed character, and his thick, shoulder-length brown hair and russet skin tone told of his heritage. All of it reminded her that they were worlds apart, he an Indian, and she. . .

Eliana turned the wick of the oil lamp back and snuggled the counterpane under her chin. She tossed about, trying to get comfortable. Although she was exhausted, she still couldn't sleep. What began as a simple morning of running errands with her father turned into. . . And then it hit her. She could have died or been seriously injured today. The tears began to flow as she pressed her face into her pillow.

"Thank You, Lord, for protecting me and saving my life," she whispered. "Thank You for sending Mr. Wilcox to be there at the right time. Please bless him." More tears flowed. What if he had died, too, this day? Eliana was certain she would join her mother in heaven. But Mr. Wilcox—what did he believe about the afterlife? More importantly, would he inherit eternal life with Christ Jesus? She would never know unless she saw him again. *Lord, please allow me to see Mr. Wilcox again, to share Your love with him. And if it is Your will. . .* No, *that* she dare not ask.

Yiska moaned as he stood from the bunk in a back room at Whiley's Outfitters and stretched. He hadn't wanted to complain in front of the Van Horns, especially Eliana. They already felt bad enough. Fact was, his captors had roughed him up pretty good. Bruised ribs, black and blue shins, and he ached all over like he'd been trampled by a herd of stampeding buffalo.

After the jail incident three days ago—or had it been four—he'd gone to check on his borrowed horse to discover the old mare had been taken over to the livery. There he found his saddle, blanket, and the rest of his stuff heaped in a pile in the corner of a stall. His saddlebag had been ransacked, but the thief hadn't taken everything. Must have been scared off. Now he'd have to replace some supplies and clothing—all of which he could get from Whiley's store. But his small blanket had disappeared—along with the journal he had wrapped inside. That could never be replaced. His sole companion on the trail other than his faithful horse, it was filled with pages describing the Colorado territory's wondrous landscapes. Yiska wrote what he saw and in his own way mined the beauty of the San Juans without destroying any bit of it. He hoped someday to share the riches he wrote about—the snow-capped mountains, brilliant vistas, valleys teeming with wildlife—with those who might never get to enjoy them firsthand. To him it was worth more than gold. And now it was gone.

Yiska had searched around town, hoping his journal might turn up somewhere. It wouldn't have value to anyone but himself. Maybe he'd find that someone had tossed it away. So he looked around behind an old building near the Silver Eagle, and Grover and one of his buddies attacked him. One held him and the other whacked him in the ribs. The pain pierced his side, and Yiska felt like he would pass out. If a rib or two weren't broken before, they surely were now.

But a surge of adrenaline came from nowhere, and he pushed back with what strength he had and kicked Grover into a pile of rubbish. Yiska turned and knocked his other assailant senseless. He managed to make it back to Mr. Whiley, who had tended his bruises. Now he finally felt like getting up.

He walked over to the washbowl and splashed water on his face. After he shaved, he grabbed the fresh shirt, trousers, and new socks that Whiley had left him. His rib cage was wrapped tightly, but he managed to get himself dressed. Getting his tall moccasin boots on might be another story. As he walked near the door to them, he heard familiar voices.

John Van Horn's voice came from the next room. "I noticed your new sign out there says WHILEY 'AND SONS' OUTFITTERS," he said. "I didn't know you had sons, Trask."

"I don't. But a man can dream." The men laughed.

Yiska never thought he'd see the day that Trask Whiley would settle down. He'd been more than an employer to him—more like an older brother—but Yiska couldn't picture him as a family man. More than likely Mr. Whiley figured marriage could be a good business venture, and sons would help him carry on his name.

Out in the hallway, Whiley cleared his throat. "John, I'd like to have a word with you about your daughter."

Chapter 4

What was on Whiley's mind now? He wasn't sweet on Eliana, was he? Yiska felt like someone had kicked him in the gut all over again.

"What's this about Eliana?" Mr. Van Horn examined Mr. Whiley with a suspecting eye while Yiska peered at them from the partially open door of the small room.

"Where *is* your lovely daughter today?" Whiley asked.

"She's shopping in town with a friend. Then off to Richmond's Mercantile to check on the catalog orders that we placed—photography supplies and such—and to pick up some sundries for our expedition with the Robbins survey. We'll get the rest of our supplies from you." Mr. Van Horn glanced around Whiley's store. Shelves and tables were stocked with tack, tents, blankets, lanterns, guns and ammunition, mining tools, building supplies, and even some Indian trade goods. "Have you ever thought of opening a remote outfit up in Lake City?"

"I've considered it." Whiley nodded.

"Would be nice to get supplies closer to home. We won't be back in Del Norte before we leave, so we're gathering our provisions now." Mr. Van Horn rocked back on his heels and smiled. "Our grand adventure is nigh upon us."

"That's exactly what I'm concerned about, John." Mr. Whiley's face grew serious. "I've heard recent reports of renegade bands of Utes south of here, and I wanted to warn you." Whiley leaned with his elbow resting on the counter. "It's none of my business what you do, but I thought you might want to reconsider taking your daughter along on your excursion. You don't want her to end up like that Oatman woman."

Yiska swallowed hard.

"Trask, I appreciate your concern. But we've already given it a lot of thought and prayer. I know you're not a religious man, but we have peace about it. This expedition is the chance of a lifetime for me *and* my daughter." Mr. Van Horn turned and, as if speaking straight to Yiska, said, "You know, Eliana will dress like a young man, the way she does when we go into the mining camps to take pictures. That way no one will be the wiser."

Yiska's jaw dropped. How could John Van Horn even consider allowing Eliana to go? It took more than a little peace and preparation to be equipped for such a journey. Yiska should know—he'd roamed the southwest for most of his life. He shook his head. She'd be dressed like a. . .

"So be it. I know there won't be any changing your minds." Whiley let out a deep chuckle. "Does the U.S. General Land Office know she's coming along?"

"They know I'm bringing an assistant."

"And here I thought you were an honest man," Whiley teased.

Van Horn stroked his beard. "You know I hired a man to go with me on the survey. I couldn't help the fact that he got the gold fever this spring and left me high and dry. The contract never specified that I report any changes. It was too late to back out, and I have an able assistant. But if they get wind. . . I can count on you to keep this detail in confidence, can't I? You're the only other living soul who knows about it." Van Horn took his empty pipe from his pocket and tapped it in the palm of his hand nervously.

"I won't say a word. But you'd better hope that the Utes don't find her out. John, I'm serious."

"You don't have to warn me about the danger of Indians." Mr. Van Horn's mouth drew into a grim line before he worked his pipe between his lips.

"Well, not only that, I've heard that Chandler Robbins isn't one to put up with any nonsense. Make sure Eliana carries her weight, or he may detect she isn't who she claims to be." Whiley shook his head and shrugged. "I hope Eliana *can* shoot a shotgun as well as a camera."

Withdrawing his unlit pipe, Van Horn chortled. "Don't worry. They don't call her 'Eagle Eye Eli' for nothing."

Whiley looked up and caught sight of Yiska standing in the doorway. Yiska issued an obligatory nod and left, his head ready to explode with all that he'd learned. He bolted for the mercantile. How could a man set both his mind and spirit toward a decision and come up with an answer like that? Bringing a young woman into the wilds on a long expedition was dangerous for many reasons. Mr. Van Horn must not be thinking clearly. What kind of God did he believe in? He didn't understand what it was like out there. But Yiska did. And only one thing could be done about it.

He had to stop her.

After an hour of shopping and fittings for her friend's new gown, Eliana and Alice headed toward the mercantile at last. As they descended the steps at the end of the boardwalk, Alice's dress caught on a piece of jagged wood.

"Oh, I hope it didn't tear!"

Eliana stooped to release the fabric. "No harm done." The corner of a brown, leather-covered book tied with a rawhide cord stuck out from under the steps. "Look here; someone must have dropped this."

"Open it," Alice said. "How else can we discover to whom it belongs?"

The book was filled will all kinds of descriptive writing. "I think it may be someone's journal." Eliana passed it to Alice.

"There's no name. What shall we do with it?" Alice fingered through some of the pages. "We could keep it. It might make good reading."

"We cannot do that," Eliana chided. "What if the owner is looking for it?"

"What shall we do then?"

"I'll take it to the newspaper tomorrow when I go to place an advertisement. I'll ask the editor to place a special ad to find the owner."

"That seems best." Alice handed Eliana the journal.

Eliana placed the mysterious book in her satchel, and they walked on.

"Good afternoon, ladies," said Mr. Richmond as they entered the mercantile.

"Hello, Mr. Richmond. I came to see if any packages have arrived addressed to Van Horn Photography." Eliana's heart flooded with hope.

"I'll go see what we have for you. A delivery arrived a little while ago. Haven't had a chance to sort it yet."

Alice walked over to the sewing notions. "Oh look, Eliana! This lace ribbon matches the lace on your blue dress perfectly. I didn't notice any like this at Mrs. Donnelly's Dress Shoppe. You should get a length of it for your hair."

"Oh, I don't know. I'm on a budget, and I've spent far too much already." Eliana peeked into her reticule to count her money. "I'd better not, at least until I see how much my other purchases will be."

"But, you must."

Eliana laughed, "Alice, you're rather good at spending my money. But despite your good taste, I must wait."

"Very well." Alice walked toward some bolts of fabric as Eliana made her way toward the soaps and toiletries.

A moment later, Alice sidled up her and whispered, "Did you see that. . .fellow. . .back there? He's looking at you. Look at him!"

"Alice! I will *not* look." Eliana spoke in hushed tones.

"Oh, you must. He's so handsome. . .for an Injun."

Eliana clutched Alice's arm. "What does he look like?"

Alice looked casually over her shoulder, pretending to look about the store. "Well, he's, you know. His skin is very tanned. Dark hair, almost down to his shoulders. He's wearing a slouch hat. He has a buckskin vest and a pair of those high suede boots. And he's grinning."

At that, Eliana turned around. She hadn't realized that Mr. Wilcox was actually in the store. Had he heard their whispers, and Alice's giggles?

Mr. Wilcox nodded. Eliana managed a shy smile. Warmth flamed through her cheeks. She turned back to Alice.

"What is it?" Alice whispered.

"Nothing." Eliana worried her lip.

"Nothing? You know him. You do! I can tell. . . . And you like him."

Oh dear, had he heard Alice say that? Eliana looked at Mr. Wilcox again. He was perusing some books in the corner. *So*, he could read.

In hushed tones Alice continued, "Is he the one?"

Eliana croaked, "Yes. How many Indians do you think I know?"

Alice's mother bustled into the store. "There you are, dear, I've been looking all over for you. You were to meet me back at Mrs. Donnelly's shop after your errands. Come now, I need your help with your sister's dress. She's waiting for us there now."

"But Mother." Alice grimaced and heaved a little sigh.

"Come along now. Good afternoon, Eliana. Our family will be by later in the week for our portrait sitting. See you then, dear."

"Yes, see you then." Alice peeked again at Mr. Wilcox and smirked at Eliana as her mother escorted her out the door.

"Is this what you were waiting for, Miss Van Horn?" Mr. Richmond returned, carrying a carton.

Eliana walked over and placed the sundries she had gathered on the counter. "Is that the only one?"

Mr. Richmond checked his ledger. "The rest of your order hasn't arrived yet. Hmm. Coming all the way from New York. These things take time, sometimes even get lost en route."

"Oh, dear! What if our photography supplies don't arrive in time? We must have them before we leave Del Norte."

Oh, Lord, please make the equipment get here in time. To her dismay, Mr. Wilcox stood there beside her, concern on his face.

"Thank you, Mr. Richmond. I guess that's all we can do for now.

I'll pay for this now, along with these items." She glanced toward the lace ribbon, but she had no need of frippery where she was headed. She took the money from her reticule and placed it on the counter.

The proprietor put his hand on the box and held it there. "Before you go I'd like to check the order, to make sure it's correct. It's the least I can do."

Her eyes darted to Mr. Wilcox. "I'm sure it's all here, Mr. Richmond." Maybe she should tell him the contents were personal. But saying so wouldn't be appropriate in male company. Her heart pounded.

"Miss Van Horn, I insist." He opened the pasteboard container and pulled out three men's shirts and a pair of men's trousers. "Let me check it against the invoice." Mr. Wilcox turned his back and leaned against the counter, arms folded across his chest.

"Three cotton shirts, men's size small, sixty cents each. Two dungarees, boys' size large, a dollar twenty-five. Two pair gents' imitation buckskin gloves, one large, one small, one dollar and fifty cents each."

Eliana's cheeks grew warmer as Mr. Richmond continued his relentless inventory. She stared at the clothing and dared not glance at Mr. Wilcox.

"Men's socks, half dozen each, large and small, forty cents each. Suede vest, men's medium, eight dollars and seventy-five cents. Women's hose, size medium, three pair, a dollar thirty each."

Mr. Wilcox muffled a laugh. Eliana ignored him, her entire face on fire.

"Looks like it's all here as ordered," Richmond said. "Montgomery Ward guarantees complete satisfaction or your money back, and I stand behind that policy. But if I do say so, Miss Van Horn, most of these garments are not going to fit Mr. Van Horn. Much too small."

"They are not for him, Mr. Richmond. They are for. . .somebody else."

"A gift? That's mighty generous."

Eliana resisted the urge to bolt for the door. "Well, yes, they are much needed by the person who'll receive them. Please, if you would package them back up again, I'll be on my way. And please be sure to let us know the moment our other boxes arrive."

"Yes, miss, I know you need them before your trip."

Eliana felt as if all her secrets had been exposed, though she knew it wasn't true.

"Trip. Yes. Before we return to Lake City."

Mr. Wilcox turned and faced her. "May I be of assistance, Miss Van Horn? I can carry your packages for you."

The proprietor looked at Eliana and noted her discomfort. He stood a little straighter. "Don't you be bothering her now. If you have some business of your own here, you can stay. Otherwise be on your way."

"Mr. Richmond, this gentleman is no bother at all. In fact, I will take him up on his helpful offer."

"Very well, if you're certain."

"I've never been more certain of anything in my life. Good day."

Mr. Wilcox carried her package as they walked out of the store. My, he looked like he was in pain.

"Do you get treated like that everywhere you go, Mr. Wilcox?"

"Enough."

"But you are only half Indian from what I understand."

"It's the wrong half."

"Well, it isn't right. Just because you look like. . .I mean. . . You don't really look that much like an Indian. It's just your coloring, and your hair. And that tomahawk—your hatchet. . ." Was she so nervous in his presence that she couldn't utter a decent sentence?

"Would it be a *bad* thing if I did look like a full-blooded Indian, Miss Van Horn?"

"Of course it would. It would be bad for you." Her eyes widened. "Especially since you're innocent." Eliana bit her lip. She didn't mean that like it sounded.

"Innocent?" Mr. Wilcox set her packages down on a bench out front and leaned against a post.

She sat down and looked up at him apologetically. "I don't mean to imply that Indians are inherently bad. *All* human beings are sinful from birth. And everyone has their faults." *Haven't I proved my own by muddling up this conversation?* "But for others to assume that you are a savage is simply ludicrous."

"Is it?"

She couldn't read his expression any more than she could see through a Colorado blizzard, but Eliana could tell by his tone that she'd offended him. "Yes, of course. Since I have met you, you've been nothing but courteous to me. You saved my life, for mercy's sake!"

"And you mine. At least you considered mine worth the saving."

"And I do, Mr. Wilcox. You are a valuable human being, despite the way you are sometimes treated. I hope you never forget that."

"Your good opinion of me is all that matters."

A large, scruffy dog ran by with something in its mouth. "You get outta there!" Mrs. Sanborn's husband hollered at the animal and whacked him with a broom handle.

"Did you see that?" Eliana asked. "The poor dog was just hungry. He didn't do a thing!"

Mr. Wilcox's jaw tightened. "Some people can't tell the difference between a good dog and a bad dog."

Eliana clamped her lips together, eyeing him apologetically.

"I'd best be on my way," he said, "unless I can see you somewhere. To Whiley's outfitting company perhaps? Your father was there."

"He asked me to wait for him here."

"All right, Miss Van Horn. It's been a pleasure as always." He tipped his hat.

"I hope you'll come by to have your photograph taken. It would please my father very much if you would."

"Would it please *you*, Miss Van Horn?"

She blushed. Why did he have to be so direct? "Yes, it would, Mr. Wilcox." It would indeed.

Yiska returned to the outfitting company through the front door. As he entered he glanced up at the sign, WHILEY AND SONS OUTFITTERS. He thought of his relief at learning Whiley didn't seem to have it in mind to marry Eliana. Why should it matter to him? It wasn't like Yiska had staked a claim on her.

"Look what the wind rolled in. Yiska, what are you doing up and about? Feeling any better, son?" Mr. Whiley asked.

"Some."

"Saw you up a little while ago. Where'd you go? John and I went to get a bite at Sanborn's. I was going to ask if I could bring back something for you, but you'd disappeared. Brought you a plate anyway."

Mr. Van Horn smacked his lips. "Turkey sandwiches and gingerbread today."

"Sounds great. Thank you." Yiska rubbed his side. "I went for a walk."

"Doc said you need to rest up if you want to fully recover."

Mr. Van Horn raised a brow. "You were hurt worse than you let on."

Whiley scowled. "He had another run-in with that Grover character and his buddy."

"Oh?"

"I was out looking for something that was stolen from me the other day, and I ran into him. Hard. He tried to finish the job he'd started at the sawmill."

"Yiska ended up with a couple of cracked ribs. But he had the last word, so to speak."

Yiska eyed the map spread out on the table. "What've you got here?"

"This is the route for the Robbins survey of the four corners and down the New Mexico and Arizona border. Mr. Van Horn has been assigned as the official photographer for the expedition."

"How'd you come by that deal, Mr. Van Horn? If you don't mind me asking."

"Not at all. I served with Chandler Robbins during the war—Ohio's 86th Infantry. Served alongside James Ryder as well. He's now a famed photographer back East. I was his assistant during the war and for some time at home. That's how I got my start—brutal as it was. When Robbins approached him about the survey project, he couldn't do it but recommended me instead. Perfect opportunity since I already do contract work for the General Land Office regionally."

As the men leaned over the map, Yiska looked on.

Mr. Whiley traced the route and laid out the itinerary. "Once you make your way down the Animas River and through the Ute reservation, you'll cross the border into New Mexico—Navajo territory. You should be relatively safe there." Whiley glanced at Yiska then continued the itinerary. "You'll continue along the Animas until you come to a confluence of three rivers. There you'll continue on the Rio San Juan. You'll be heading west toward Shiprock." He jabbed the map with his finger. "The coordinates are marked here at the four corners quadripoint."

Mr. Van Horn rested his hands on his hips. "What about the ruins? How will I find them?"

"I have them marked here, and here." Whiley pointed to the various locations. "Besides, your guide will know the area well." Mr. Van Horn looked at Yiska and flattened his lips. Why did he look so disappointed?

"Mr. Van Horn, I almost forgot to mention that I saw your daughter at the mercantile when I was out."

Van Horn peered up at Yiska over his spectacles. "Do you happen to know if our packages arrived?"

"From what I gathered, eh, only the clothing order."

Mr. Van Horn frowned. "I see. Well, I promised I'd pick her up with a wagon. I had better get over there now." He straightened as Whiley rolled up a copy of the map and handed it to him. "Make sure you stop by the studio, young man. I'd like to see you again before we go."

"Yes, sir." Why did he feel like he'd be saying his final farewell?

When Mr. Van Horn left, Whiley rolled up the other copies of the map. Yiska turned his thoughts back to the expedition. "It'll be good to get back down to New Mexico Territory again. It's been too long. Does Mr. Van Horn know that I'll be along as the guide?"

Whiley exhaled. "Well, Yiska, plans have changed. . . . You won't be going on that expedition."

Chapter 5

Eliana paused outside the *San Juan Prospector* to enjoy the grand views—the flat plain, grassy meadows, and stunning vista. To the east lay a sandy desert, and to the west the grand San Juan Mountains, full of promise and adventure. She pulled in a deep breath, entered the large sandstone building, and addressed the clerk. "I'd like to see Mr. Wilson, please."

A neatly dressed man entered the front room, wiping ink-stained hands with a clean rag. "Miss Van Horn, it's a pleasure to see you." He examined his fingers. "Having a little trouble with the printing press."

"Are you still accepting advertisements today?"

"Certainly. It's business as usual. Nothing stops the *San Juan Prospector* from going to press."

"I have a few things I'd like to discuss with you," she said with a smile.

"Snivens, show Miss Van Horn to my office while I finish cleaning my hands. Make sure she's comfortable."

Mr. Snivens ushered Eliana into a large office and seated her in a tufted leather chair across from a large mahogany desk. Such exquisite furniture. What would it be like to have such luxury? Eliana only wished Papa's hard work would reap similar benefits. She would like to see him enjoy some measure of comfort in his lifetime.

"Now, what can I help you with today?" The older man settled into his oversized chair.

Eliana placed a paper on the desk. "First of all, I would like to place another advertisement for Van Horn Photography in your paper. Father and I will only be here a little while longer, and we want to make sure that everyone in the community who would like to have their photograph taken will have the opportunity. We are hosting a special on family portraits."

"I'll see to it." Wilson settled back in his chair. "I'm glad you dropped by today. I understand that your father will be heading out to visit The Silver Queen before he embarks on his expedition."

"I take it you mean Silverton?" Eliana asked.

"Indeed, I do. I'd like to get a picture of a Mr. Francis Snowden at the mine. He was the first to put up a cabin and stake a claim in that flourishing town, and he's the only surviving member of the Baker party, who discovered the mineral deposits there. I have a correspondent headed that way to conduct an interview. But a photograph would be a nice addition to the story."

"I'm sure he'd be honored to do that for you, Mr. Wilson."

"Very well, then. I look forward to printing the engravings of the Robbins survey when he returns. You must be very proud of your father."

Eliana beamed. "Oh, yes, sir. I am. But you know that the U.S. General Land Office has first rights to the photographs."

"A mere technicality. I'll handle the GLO." Wilson glanced at the pendulum clock on the wall. "You had something else?"

"Mr. Wilson, I happen to be in possession of an important document. Perhaps you could help me locate the owner. You may already know to whom this belongs." Eliana placed the leather-bound journal on the mahogany desk.

Mr. Wilson arched his brow. "May I?"

"Please do. This journal is filled with pages of very eloquent prose describing the vast wilderness of the territory. And there is no name to be found. I'd like to place an advertisement seeking its proper owner."

Mr. Wilson put on his eyeglasses and examined the book. He fumbled through some of the pages, landing midway. His eyes scanned the page. He cleared his throat and read aloud.

The ravine sings to the tune of a thousand stars above. The night in no way diminishes the glory of this place, but rather illuminates a view that remains hidden in the day. The moon above shines down on white-capped mountains, a beacon urging me to come near. As I travel forward on frozen ground, large flakes cling to my garments and will soon cover the ground like a woolen blanket. My shelter lies near, a cave, and fresh pine boughs for my bed. A flickering spark is all that I will need to ignite a small fire and regenerate the warmth I once felt in late spring. Should an avalanche usher me to an early end, I am grateful for having sojourned under such a majestic and heavenly night.

Eliana sighed. "I regret having intruded on this individual's private world, but. . ."

"Miss Van Horn, you have done a great deed by bringing this to me." The editor held up the journal to the light of the window, the San Juan Mountains visible in the distance. "This world needs to be shared!"

The chill in the air penetrated Yiska's aching ribs through his buckskin coat. He'd hoped to be feeling better by now—or was it Mr. Whiley's announcement that still wounded him? Chilled him. How could his boss refuse to let him go on the survey expedition? Whiley knew that Yiska was more familiar with that territory than anyone else. It was on the Navajo reservation, after all.

Only the other day he'd wondered how he could prevent the adventurous Miss Van Horn from going on the trip. But at least if he was there he could help keep her safe. . .and keep her secret. He'd also get to spend time with her. Of course, she'd be safer still if she didn't go at all.

He hadn't managed to find an opportunity to talk to her about halting her plans for the trip. When he saw how disappointed she'd been about the missing photography supplies, he hadn't had the heart to discourage her further. Instead, when he'd gone back to purchase some new clothing and a journal, he bought her that slip of ribbon. What was he thinking? If he couldn't find a way to talk her out of the trip, how would he ever manage to offer her a small gift? He sighed.

No use dwelling on it. Mr. Richmond's peculiar look at Yiska was punishment enough for his impulsive act.

But perhaps giving her the lace would make her more receptive to considering his concern for her. Obviously she hadn't fully thought about the dangers. Maybe he would be able to speak with her today.

He stepped into Van Horn's photography studio in a store front next to the bakery. From the corner of the room he watched Eliana as she posed her friend's family for a portrait. Alice's mother was seated, and her father stood behind her, hand on her shoulder. Alice and a younger sister stood on their mother's left, while two boys stood on the opposite side by their father. A backdrop of a painted mountain landscape completed the scene.

"Andrew and Angus, you must keep still. If you keep smiling, your faces will be blurred in the picture. Now please cooperate and keep your mouths closed. If you do, I've a gumdrop for each of you."

Yiska had seen those boys before. Weren't they the ones who had called him names in front of Eliana last week? He slipped out and decided to go to the bakery to pass the time until they were finished.

Once he knew they had gone, he returned to the studio with two raspberry turnovers wrapped in a cloth napkin. Miss Van Horn bent over a table with a paintbrush in hand. "Mr. Wilcox, I'm glad you came by."

"I was at the bakery and thought to bring you a snack." He set the pastries on the table.

"How thoughtful. And these are my favorite!" Miss Van Horn walked over to an elegant tea service in the corner of the room. "Do you drink tea, Mr. Wilcox?"

"Yes." He looked at the table where Eliana had been working. "What are you doing over there?"

"I'm hand tinting some ferrotypes. Color adds a little life to their faces, don't you agree? I've some photographs to develop as well. It's been such a busy week. Townsfolk are making sure they come see us before we are on our way again. We won't be back in Del Norte for some time."

Yiska looked around the room. "No, I reckon you won't." A display table caught his attention. He pointed to a celluloid panel with four identical miniature portraits. "What do you call these?"

"Four ferrotypes to a panel are called *bon tons*."

"That's a peculiar name. What do people do with such small pictures?"

"They put them in lockets or in miniature albums like these." Eliana picked up a small, ornate book and opened it to show pages of tiny pictures inside. "The actual photographs are referred to as gems. These show many of our clients over the years who have been gracious enough to let us have a sample."

"Gems. This one is of you." *A beautiful jewel.* On the table beside them, Yiska noticed another picture of Miss Van Horn. He picked it up. As he held it he imagined what it would be like to hold her in his arms. *But why dream something that will never be?*

"That's a cabinet card. Papa took that one of me a few weeks back in the new dress he bought for me."

"I remember that dress. You had it on the first day we met." Why'd he have to say that? Now she was blushing.

"Since you're here, you must allow me to take your portrait—a cabinet card. Don't be shy. People have their pictures taken all the time. Have you ever had yours made?"

"No, can't say that I have."

Miss Van Horn glanced over his outfit and smiled. "Are you wearing new clothes?"

He nodded. Did she think he had dressed up to come see her?

"Perfect. See, you are all dressed for a sitting. You must agree," she said.

How can I say no to such a charmer? "All right. On one condition."

Miss Van Horn tilted her pretty head. "And what, Mr. Wilcox, is that?"

"Do I look like a Mr. Wilcox to you? Please call me Yiska."

"Then come this way, Yiska." She turned her head back over her shoulder. "Oh, and you must call me Eliana."

Eliana had almost spilled the pigments when she looked up and saw Mr. Wilcox—Yiska—enter the studio. How ruggedly handsome he looked in his fringed leather coat. He took his hat off and hung it on a hook by the door, his dark hair framing his chiseled features. And now she would finally get to take his photograph.

Eliana began to move one of the chairs away from the sitting area when Yiska placed his hand on hers.

"Allow me." He gazed directly into her eyes. "All of them?"

"All but one. They can go over there against the wall." As he put the chairs away, she said, "I'm so glad you stopped by today. Papa will be pleased."

"I wanted to see the shadow catcher's daughter again before you left Del Norte."

Eliana's curiosity piqued. "Shadow catcher?"

"That's what Indians call photographers. Will I see your father today?"

"He's in town, but I expect him back anytime."

"Good. He asked that I stop by, but I do have something that I'd like to talk to you both about."

"All right. But now let's get you situated for the photograph. Please place that chair directly in the center of the backdrop."

Yiska positioned the chair per her direction.

"Now, you may sit down."

Yiska turned the chair around, its back facing the camera, and straddled it.

Eliana giggled. "All right then, have it your way. For now."

"That's my aim," he said with a grin.

Eliana tilted her head one way and then the other. "Would you mind, Mr. Wil—Yiska—if I fixed your hair? You have a slight issue of indentations from your hat."

"Whatever you please."

Eliana grabbed a comb from her pocket and proceeded to flatten the subtle bumps. She hadn't realized his hair would be so thick.

He looked up at her. "You could always let me wear my hat."

"No, I think it will be better without it." Eliana recalled the first time she saw him—his hat was missing. In this close proximity, the scent of rich, new leather tickled her senses. How good he smelled. "Yiska, I think you ought to remove your coat."

"That won't be as easy as you think," he confessed. "I'm healing up from a couple of bruised ribs."

"Why didn't you tell me? I let you move those chairs."

"It's not the kind of thing a man likes to brag about."

Eliana could tell by the way he glanced away that she shouldn't press for an explanation. She hoped his injury wasn't from those big-booted ruffians who had taken him to jail.

"No harm done. Now, if you could help me off with my coat, that'd be mighty nice of you."

Eliana stood behind him and carefully pulled the coat as he released his arms from one sleeve and then the other. She laid it down on a chair, her heart aflutter. Gracious. She'd never been so intimate with a man in her life. She looked toward the front door, wishing she could go out and get a breath of fresh air. She walked over to retrieve Yiska's hat from its hook and peeked out the window. What was taking Papa so long?

"What next?"

"Well. . .we must position you for the photograph. I'd rather you sat in the other direction please and place your hat on your knee. Sometimes we like to give our subjects props, and I cannot think of a more suitable one for you."

Yiska adjusted himself accordingly.

Eliana gingerly placed her hands on his sturdy shoulders to square them, his warmth passing through her fingers. Thoughts rushed into her head of the last time she had been this close to him—the day he had helped her down from Mr. Whiley's buckboard, and she thought he might kiss her.

She pushed a loose tendril of hair from her face and regained her bearings. "Now, when I go over to the camera to take the picture, you must remain perfectly still or the picture will be blurred, and we'll have to go through all of this again." She couldn't endure it.

"How do I look?"

"You look very handsome." *Did I really say that?* She was accustomed to complimenting her subjects, but not under these circumstances. Oh, how could she?

Yiska smiled.

Oh, but he had a nice mouth. And his eyes. "Mr. Wilcox, you mustn't smile, or it will ruin everything." She noticed a speck of jam from the raspberry turnover on his face.

"You. . .you have a bit of raspberry on your face." Eliana pointed to his chin. "You know, they used raspberry syrup in the old days to keep the camera's glass plates wet. We mostly use dry plates now."

"Tintypes."

"Yes, although they are actually made from iron."

"I see." Yiska wiped his face, and then again, missing the spot both times.

"No, here." Eliana dabbed it away, blushing.

She turned and hastened to her camera, pulling the black tarp over her head before he could see that her face had probably reddened to the color of that raspberry jam. She wanted to remain there forever, but no. . . . She regained her composure and looked through the viewfinder. "Mr. Wilcox! Please do not smile."

Yiska seemed eager to watch her develop the photographs. His interest in the procedure seemed genuine. Eliana was glad to answer his questions, but she simply couldn't allow him to be alone with her in the darkroom. He waited in the sitting area, and her thoughts swirled so much she could barely breathe by the time the processing was completed.

A short time later Eliana emerged from the darkroom and handed Yiska the finished product.

"Thank you. But I don't know what I'll do with it." Yiska walked over to the display table and picked up the small portrait of her. "How about a trade?"

Eliana's pulse quickened. "That sounds fair." They stood silently for a moment, admiring one another's images.

"Good news!" Papa waddled into the studio carrying a huge box. "Our supplies have arrived! We can leave any day now."

And when they did, apart from his photograph, would Eliana ever lay eyes on Yiska again?

Chapter 6

Trask Whiley watched Yiska count out the boxes of ammunition. Yiska looked up. "Fifteen Henry rifles, eighteen Winchesters, and fifty rounds for each. You could stand to get a dozen more traps. I've written it all down."

"You've got a good head for business, Yiska. Perhaps I should keep you off the trail and have you work here in the store instead."

Although Yiska missed being out in the territory, he didn't mind staying at the store for a bit to take stock of the outfitting company's inventory. "You'll need to increase your supplies of mining equipment, too. They're coming in droves."

"How're your ribs healing up?"

"Much better now, though I can't lift anything heavy yet."

"Glad you can still lift a pencil. You've been mighty handy around here lately." Whiley placed a hand on Yiska's shoulder. "Time to take a break."

They sat on the front porch, sipping cups of strong coffee. Whiley targeted a nearby spittoon. How Mr. Whiley drank and chewed at the same time, Yiska would never know. He kicked back, stretched out his legs, and pulled his hat over his eyes while Whiley browsed *The Prospector* for the competition's advertising.

"Richmond is selling mining supplies now, too. He's got pickaxes and shovels for two bits apiece under my price. What does he mean by underselling me? I'm going over there."

He left *The Prospector* sitting on the wooden bench, and Yiska caught it as it was about to blow away. He looked at the front page, catching a headline—HAYDEN CONTINUES TO SURVEY WESTERN LOOP. Soon enough Chandler Robbins would be making the headlines. Yiska hoped they wouldn't read FEMALE PHOTOGRAPHER CAPTURED BY UTES. If Eliana was going on that expedition, he had to find a way to go as well.

As he flipped through the pages he couldn't get Eliana's pretty face, her bright hazel eyes, and hair the color of a fawn out of his mind. Nor could he remove the image of her lovely feminine form, the way she moved, the scent of lavender that wafted through the air in her presence—or the yearning that he had to explore the territory of her heart.

Another headline snagged his attention. Yiska could hardly believe his eyes. An article had been published under the pseudonym, "Anonymous Explorer." He skimmed it, his pulse rocketing as he read. It was an entry from his missing journal! A glance at the print ending the column told him this was not the first but the second entry from a journal that had been turned in to the newspaper's editor, Mr. Wilson, and that Wilson was eager to make the acquaintance of its owner.

Yiska jumped to his feet, paced the porch, then whacked his hat against the post. This was his prized journal, his faithful companion, and his hope to become accredited as a travel correspondent in the Southwest. He'd planned to submit some of his entries to a newspaper in the East—one which did not have the "benefit" of knowing his heritage. Mr. Wilson would never believe it if Yiska came forward to reveal that the journal belonged to him. He looked at his hat, now all dented. He needed someone who could speak on his behalf. He'd better track down Trask Whiley.

"Now you're talking sense, Richmond." As he went into the mercantile, Yiska found Mr. Whiley "negotiating" with Mr. Richmond. He turned to Yiska. "What is it?" he barked.

"I need your help," Yiska said.

Whiley exhaled and held up his hand. "All right." He looked back at Richmond. "I believe we've come to an understanding." Whiley stomped into the street and started walking. "So what is it? Don't mean to be impatient. He just got my dander up."

❧

"Good afternoon, Miss Alice." Mr. Van Horn said.

"How do you do, Mr. Van Horn? Is Eliana here?"

"I'm right here, Alice." Eliana lifted her head from behind the counter. "I'm packing our supplies." She wiped the perspiration from her forehead. "Your photographs are done. I'm glad you stopped by."

Mr. Van Horn smiled at Alice as he stepped aside to let her enter. "And they came out quite well, I might add. It's getting harder all the time to tell the difference between my talented daughter's photographs and my own."

"She's one special girl," Alice said. "I'm sure going to miss her. Eliana, do you have time for tea at Mrs. Sanborn's café?"

"Well, I don't know. . . ."

"Sure she does," her father said. "I've been working her hard enough."

At the café Mrs. Sanborn served Eliana and Alice a pot of hot tea with some warm apple muffins and a fresh bit of gossip. "That anonymous author in *The Prospector* is the talk of the town. He has all the men hankering to get out into the mountains and all the women practically swooning." The girls giggled as Mrs. Sanborn walked away to serve another table with the same dish.

"I wish you could stay longer." A forlorn sigh escaped Alice's pouty lips.

"We can correspond. Lake City opened a post office. Please don't act like you'll never see me again."

"Perhaps I won't. You'll probably become a famous female photographer and run off with that Indian."

"Alice! Mind your imagination. I'll do no such thing."

Alice's eyes grew mischievous. "You can't tell me that you haven't at least thought of it."

Eliana looked down. Her cheeks must be all shades of red. She looked up at Alice and burst into giggles, quickly covering her mouth.

"I knew it! Your secret is safe with me. And your other one also."

Eliana feigned innocence. "What do you mean?" Could she possibly know?

Alice declared in a soft voice, "Eliana Van Horn, you have been disguising yourself as a man!"

Eliana grabbed Alice's hand. "Shhhh! I cannot believe you know! Please, Alice, you cannot tell a living soul. Papa only agrees to it for my protection." She dared not mention the expedition.

"I won't breathe a word. I would never want any harm to come to you." Alice blotted her napkin against her lips. "Now, how about confessing your undying love for that Yiska fellow."

"Alice, I do not love Yiska. Not in that way. I only care for him as I would any of God's children."

"Is he a child of God, Eliana, or is he a heathen?" Alice asked.

Eliana wished she knew. There was a long silence.

Alice mouthed the words. "Has he ever kissed you?"

"Kissed me? I hardly know him." But she had thought about it. Did that count?

Eliana was relieved when Alice picked up the newspaper that had been left behind on a vacant table. "Oh, look! There's another article by the Anonymous Explorer. Listen to this:

The sand shifts like shadows underneath my tired feet. Though paths are worn before me, some I have trod alone and beckon others to follow. The cliffs rise to tell legends from days of old. And tales anew I write, to share these wonders with those who might otherwise have never known.

Eliana and Alice sighed in perfect harmony. Alice placed her hand against her chest. "Isn't the author romantic?"

"Beyond compare. Now that is one I could spend my dreams on. Yet I can't help but feel that I had a hand in betraying his confidence, by giving over his journal only to see it end up in print. Those reflections are immensely personal." Eliana also felt a pang of guilt that these thoughts had betrayed her feelings for Yiska.

"You needn't feel bad. How do you know that you haven't done the author a good deed?"

"Look here, Wilson. I've known this young man for more than ten years. He's like a son to me. I know, I know—you're thinking a half breed can't possibly write like that. But my own mother schooled him herself when he lived with them. I know firsthand that he can read and write better than I can." Mr. Whiley walked toward the window to cool down and faced Wilson again. "Read just one sentence of any one of those entries, and he can tell you what happened next. He knows all those places like the back of his hand. As a matter of fact, he should be compensated for those articles."

"Here now, Whiley. I've never known you to be a dishonest man. I'll take your word for it." Mr. Wilson looked at Yiska, confounded. "Young man, have a seat."

Mr. Wilson rocked back in his chair. "Yiska, you've captured your audience with the enthusiasm of dime novels. I'd like to print the rest of your journal. In fact, I've already taken the liberty of having it copied. And I'd like to see more. Of course, for now you'll continue to be hailed as the 'Anonymous Explorer.' We've got newspapers to sell."

How this disaster turned into a writing job, Yiska didn't know. And had Mr. Whiley really said that Yiska was like a son to him? After ironing out some of the particulars for his compensation and future publication, Mr. Wilson offered another proposition. "One of my correspondents suddenly came down with the measles. I need someone capable to handle an assignment for me out in the San Juans. Silverton. It's an interview with Francis Snowden." He slid a piece of paper across the desk toward Yiska. "The details are right here. What do you say, Mr. Wilcox?"

"I'd be happy to do it, sir."

Yiska stood and shook Mr. Wilson's hand then turned to shake Whiley's, who offered his support. Yiska would still be a trail guide, but he would now have the added pleasure of writing about what he saw for pay. Things couldn't have turned out better.

Wilson took Yiska's journal out of a desk drawer. "I believe this belongs to you."

Yiska held it with both hands. "Thank you, Mr. Wilson. I feel like I've been reunited with an old friend."

"One more thing. I've hired someone to take a picture of Snowden to accompany the interview. You might even meet up with them out there. Van Horn Photography. Do you know them?"

Chapter 7

Eliana pulled the shawl around her shoulders and yawned as she waited with her father at the station agent's window at Barlow & Sanderson's Overland Stage & Express Line. The mixture of the chilled morning air and her eagerness to be under way perked her awake. She looked forward to going home to Lake City and seeing her friends, though their time there would be brief and busy with further preparation—the expedition now only weeks away. Only one thing lingered on her mind, and soon she could leave that thought behind her.

"Two tickets. Del Norte to Lake City," Papa said.

The station agent motioned to the attendant to weigh the trunk and cartons filled with their photography equipment.

The attendant grabbed the trunk stamped VAN HORN PHOTOGRAPHY. "What's in here, mining tools?" Obviously the man couldn't read.

"Easy with that—it's fragile," said Eliana's father.

"Ain't stamped FRAGILE."

Papa tapped the trunk. "Right there. FRAGILE. Now go easy."

The attendant nodded and moved with great care. Did he think it was full of explosives? No matter. If he dropped that trunk with her father's expensive equipment inside, there'd be an explosion one way or another. Though usually a patient man, Papa's ire would certainly rise if the tools of his livelihood were damaged. He'd spent a good deal on his new equipment, and it was going to cost him a great deal to get it home.

"Two passengers. Eighty miles each. That'll be a grand total of forty dollars and fifty cents," the agent said.

Eliana gasped. But Papa would recoup his investment once he got paid for his work as a technician on the Robbins survey.

The man looked at Eliana over his spectacles then addressed her father. "That's twelve dollars each and twenty-two cents a pound for your extra baggage. You'll pay for your meals along the way. Full meals are two bits each."

Papa retrieved the payment from his wallet and placed several paper notes and a couple of pieces of silver on the counter.

The station agent stamped their tickets and turned to the attendant. "What are you waiting for? Take that baggage out to the Concord. It pulls out of here at five o'clock sharp."

Eliana adjusted her bonnet and took note of the other passengers waiting to board the stagecoach. How many passengers would travel with them? A middle-aged couple and another rather stocky man with several carpetbags stood nearby. The grease in the gentleman's hair would be covered in dust by the time they arrived at the relay station. At least Papa remembered not to apply his own Thompson's Magnificent Hair Tonic for Men today. He looked better without it.

Eliana listened as the woman read the rules of The Barlow & Sanderson's Stage & Express Line from her brochure to her traveling companions. "Are you armed, dear? These rules are quite specific. . . . 'Firearms may be kept on your person for use in emergencies. Do not fire them for pleasure or shoot at wild animals, as the sound riles the horses. In the event of runaway horses remain calm. Leaping from the coach in panic will leave you injured, at the mercy of the elements, highwaymen, hostile Indians, and hungry coyotes.'" The woman's jaw dangled open.

"A necessary precaution, dear. I have my gun right inside my coat."

Papa cupped his pocket watch in the palm of his hand and noted the time. "Let's go, Sunshine."

The woman patted her husband's arm and scrunched her face up to his. "Aw, did you hear that, dear? He calls his daughter 'Sunshine.'" The man humored her with a pasted-on grin.

Eliana's heart warmed. Her father had called her Sunshine ever since she was a little girl. In the years following her mother's passing,

Papa constantly reminded her that she was like the sunshine ever brightening his days. Even though she was now nearly twenty years old, he still called her the endearing name every now and again.

Papa took her by the elbow, and she stepped up into the small compartment of the vermilion-red stagecoach. He handed her his rifle. As she settled in, she pulled Yiska's picture from her reticule to take a quick peek before her father got on board. She couldn't help but wonder where Yiska was now, and if he ever thought of her. Their lives had collided in a providential way, but she had no way of knowing to what end.

❧

"Mornin', Lucky Jim." Yiska loaded his saddlebags into the rear boot and climbed up to fasten the rest of his gear on top.

"What gives us the pleasure of your company, my good friend?"

"Shadow's up at Rio Grande Pass. Came down lame. Figured a bumpy ride on your rig would beat dealing with that loaned mount I had." Yiska smiled. "Besides, I'm nursing a couple of cracked ribs."

"How'd you come by those?" the driver asked.

"Guess I'm not as lucky as you." Yiska finished tying down the rest of his gear.

"Glad to have you aboard this fine day. How's about ridin' shotgun? Lazy Eddie was otherwise detained, so I'm solo today. It'll be an easy ride—no mail or payroll on board."

The large trunk strapped to the top of the coach caught Yiska's attention—Van Horn Photography. He heard the familiar voice of John Van Horn boom through the air like a cannon. "Yiska Wilcox!"

"Mr. Van Horn." Yiska smiled. "Didn't expect to see you here, sir."

"Our supplies finally arrived, and we were anxious to get a move on." Van Horn stuck his pipe into his pocket.

Yiska's mind galloped ahead.

"Eliana is inside the coach. I'm sure she'll be pleased to see you. You *are* planning to ride inside?"

Yiska looked up at Lucky Jim.

"Looks like today's your lucky day, Yiska. You wouldn't want to disappoint that pretty young lady." He winked.

"Now don't be putting ideas in that fella's head," Van Horn said. Sounded like he wasn't too keen on the idea of anyone being interested in his daughter—especially Yiska.

"This whippersnapper would be blind as a bat if he hadn't already noticed that perty daughter of yours. Go on then and get in. I haven't got all day." Lucky Jim's laughter filled the air.

Yiska climbed aboard with a big grin and put his rifle underneath his seat. He took off his hat and greeted Eliana. "Miss Van Horn. Good to see you again." Would she be as happy to see him?

"Yiska. This is surely a surprise." Eliana's cheeks blushed pink.

"Yes, a pleasant one. Your father said you're headed back already. Looks like I'll have the pleasure of your company once again." Yiska leaned back in his seat, quite content to gaze across at her.

Eliana tilted her dimpled chin. "I must say that I'm surprised to see you take the stage. Don't you prefer to ride?"

"I was outnumbered. Doc said I wasn't fit for riding horseback quite yet, and Mr. Whiley insisted I take the stage." *Did Whiley know the Van Horns would be on this stage?* "You can't tell me the ride will be any smoother, but at least I'll get back to my own horse up at Rio Grande Pass a bit sooner. Shadow might not even remember me, I've been away so long."

The door to the stagecoach opened once more. A large man glared at Yiska and growled. "It seems overcrowded in there."

"What do you mean? Let me see." A woman with a shrill voice pushed past the man. "Ooh," she gasped, looking at Yiska with alarm. "They didn't say that wild Indians would be riding *with* us!"

Eliana straightened, her mouth hanging agape.

"Now wait just a minute," Mr. Van Horn said.

The woman ignored them and turned to her husband. "When is the next stage?"

"Not for another week, dear."

"We can't wait that long. Why they don't bring a train out this way I don't know." The woman shook her head frantically. Then in a loud whisper she said in her husband's ear, "I thought you said the Indians were put on the reservations."

Yiska sighed. Some fights were not worth picking, and this was an old one. He tried to keep his voice pleasant. "I'll ride up top, ma'am, if it would make you more comfortable."

"I should hope so." The man folded his arms across his broad chest, frowning.

As Yiska removed himself from the coach, he overheard the woman. "He spoke English, dear. I didn't know they could do that."

Yiska climbed to the driver's box and found a spot beside Lucky Jim.

"So you'll be riding shotgun after all." The burly driver handed Yiska a sawed-off shotgun. "Can't be too careful." Lucky Jim looked straight ahead. "G-long! H'up, there!" He cracked the braided whip, and with a jolt the four-in-hand lunged forward.

Reins threaded through his fingers, the driver guided the horses with gentle but firm control. "We call the reins 'ribbons.' This is how I talk to the horses."

Ribbons. Yiska slid his hand into his pocket and toyed with a piece of lace ribbon between his fingers. Would he ever have the nerve to give it to Eliana? Or to give her his heart? And even if she did return his feelings, how could he ever ask her to live the life of an outcast?

How ironic that Yiska, a perfect gentleman, rode above instead of these ignoramuses. Eliana hoped the crotchety woman appreciated his thoughtfulness, though she knew that was doubtful.

Sixteen miles west and two and a half hours later, the stagecoach arrived at the South Fork relay station in record time, without incident. While the hostlers changed out the horses for a new team, the travelers took their reprieve with coffee and johnnycakes served by the station agent's wife.

"We're going south to Pagosa Springs now," the woman told her. "We'll try a soak in the hot springs there."

How thankful Eliana was to learn that the trio of tourists would not continue the journey northwest with them. The ride from Del Norte had been nothing short of a nightmare. The woman, squeezed between Eliana and the window, had fidgeted almost the entire way and complained of motion sickness. To Eliana's great relief, nothing ever came of it.

The woman's husband and the other gentleman had filled up the opposite bench and shared a flask of bottled merriment, becoming more obnoxious with each passing mile. They had offered some to her father, and though Papa wasn't a drinking man, she couldn't help but wonder if he was tempted if only to put up with the unpleasant ride.

At last, the passengers had dozed off. The couple both snored while their stocky companion's head practically hung out the window. When the man descended the coach, his dusty hair looked like a powdered wig.

At least that ordeal was over.

As the lady departed to board the new coach that had pulled into the station, she leaned toward Eliana and whispered much too loudly, "Be careful of that Indian." Yiska was looking right at them.

Eliana lowered her gaze.

She braced herself as the stagecoach jerked forward and pulled out of the swing station. Papa sat beside her on the padded leather seat, and Yiska now joined them, facing them from the opposite bench. A knife was strapped to his calf. His hatchet hung from his hip. No wonder the woman was intimidated by Yiska's presence.

The rumbling of the wheels and clopping hooves of the four horses reverberated around them. Dusty particles floated through the air. Inside the coach, an awkward quiet descended. Eliana rolled up the canvas curtain and buckled it. As the stagecoach traveled the toll road along the Rio Grande, she took in the lush view of the river and the great expanse of the mountains all around them. Lulled by the rocking motion, thoughts of the land and its people filled her mind.

Through the years, many had fought over the Colorado Territory, but since the treaty with the Utes, whites had flooded into the area to claim the mineral-rich mountains and rivers. She recalled how proud she was of Papa when he was commissioned to make a glass-plate of the Ute Chief Ouray, who negotiated for the Utes' peace. Papa was very impressed by the man. He had told her how the government wasn't upholding its end of the Brunot Treaty. No wonder the Utes were still hostile at times.

Sometimes she felt like a trespasser in the land, yet it was home to her now. What was it like to have one's homeland confiscated? Where was Yiska's home? She thought of her own ancestors and sighed. She sat up straight, her hands in her lap, and addressed her traveling companion. "So, Mr. Wilcox."

He looked at her with his dark, penetrating eyes. "Yiska."

"Yiska." She smiled. "We've already established that you're part Indian."

Papa chewed on the mouthpiece of his empty pipe, and upon hearing her comment almost choked.

"True." Yiska's expression betrayed nothing.

"Your Christian name. . ." Eliana's cheeks grew warm. "I mean, your given name. It almost sounds Jewish. Don't you think so, Papa?"

Papa shrugged.

Yiska appeared amused at her blunder. "It's Diné, Navajo." He picked up his dented hat from the seat and fiddled with it. "It means 'after the night has passed.'"

Eliana eyed him with interest. "You're the first Navajo I've ever met. The first Indian, in fact." She directed her fingers to her chest. "My name means 'God has answered.' It's Hebrew—my mother was Jewish."

Papa tapped his pipe on his knee and stared out the window then cocked his head toward Eliana.

"Jewish?" Yiska raised his brows. "I was under the impression you were a Christian."

"Oh! Yes, we are." She let out a nervous laugh.

Yiska looked askance.

"I've adopted the Christian faith, as did my mother. Her parents died when they emigrated from Germany, and Mama met Papa shortly after that. Friends introduced them to Jesus, and I learned about Him from them." Though butterflies fluttered inside her stomach, Eliana dared to ask the next question. "Do you know much about Christianity, Yiska?"

"Some," he said. "I've heard that Jesus appeared on earth. My mother's people have never seen their gods in the flesh."

Are they his gods, too?

"Can you tell us about them?" Eliana asked.

Yiska dragged his fingers through his hair. "The Diné have many—Coyote, Water Monster, Changing Woman and her twins Monster Slayer and Child-Born-of-Water, and others. Their relationship to the sacred places—the holy lands—is more important, although they are connected."

"So many," Eliana said. "God's son, Jesus Christ, was born in the Jewish Holy Land, Israel. But that land has been taken from the Jews—it's now called Palestine. That's where my mother's ancestors were originally from."

Yiska crossed his arms. Was he thinking of all the land that had been taken away from the Indians?

The mountains rose up around them, and the coach struggled over rocks and ruts. As it ascended a steep incline, it went over a sharp swell in the road and then jerked forward. Yiska's head almost hit the ceiling. Papa's somewhat portly frame kept him situated, but Eliana nearly tumbled off her seat. *O Lord, please don't let me fall on Yiska!* Her father steadied her, and she exhaled with relief. She smoothed her skirt and tried to gather her thoughts—this conversation had its own bumps to deal with.

"Well, the important thing is that regardless of location, Jesus lives in the hearts of those who believe in Him, who turn from their sin and accept Him." Eliana placed her hand on Papa's arm. "Papa is better at explaining."

"All right." Papa leaned back in his seat and took a small pouch of tobacco from inside his coat pocket. "Allow me to present you with a word picture. Take my pipe, for example. If I fill it with tobacco and light it, it will produce smoke." He dipped the pipe into the tobacco pouch and tamped it down. Then he took a match, and with a puff ignited the fragrant hickory-scented contents.

He shook out the match and tossed it away. "By faith a believer becomes a vessel where Christ dwells—the pipe. He will smoke it, so to speak, as the believer lives out His teachings, and in turn the Christian's life produces a pleasant aroma." Papa took another puff and coughed. ". . .and a little smoker's lung, but that's beside the point. Perhaps that's a poor analogy, but it's the best I can do under the circumstances." Papa chortled.

Eliana hoped her father's example resonated with Yiska. Then, from the corner of her eye, she noticed something flicker. She glanced down. Papa's spare neckerchief had fallen to the floor. Sparks threatened to consume it.

"Papa! Your neckerchief is on fire!"

Chapter 8

Yiska stomped out the glowing edges of the neckerchief. "Safe now. Looks like your match never made it out the window."

Mr. Van Horn shook his head in disbelief.

Eliana took a deep breath. "Thank you, Yiska. Papa insists on nursing that pipe, though it's usually empty when he does so." She glanced up at her father and smiled. "But I suppose it served its purpose anyway. At least I hope it did."

"It got my attention." Yiska chuckled. "That was a good. . .picture with words. The Dinė tell stories like that around their campfires." He looked at Mr. Van Horn. "Only they know how to put the fires out."

"For that you owe me a neckerchief, young man," Mr. Van Horn said with a glint in his eye. Then he leaned forward. "Yiska, what about your father?"

"My father was an Englishman. I don't know what he believed." So much of his childhood, most of his memories, remained cloaked in shadows.

"He wasn't a religious man, I take it," Van Horn said.

"I don't know. He gave thanks to the Christian God, but he also talked about the Great Spirit—mostly among the Navajo." Yiska shifted in his seat. The Van Horns listened patiently, their sincere expressions inviting him to share things that he'd hardly ever spoken.

"Pa was a mountaineer, a trader with the Navajo. He died when I was a boy, and my mother and I went back to her people. That was before The Long Walk to Fort Sumner. She sent me away to save me from that fate." Yiska swallowed hard. "She never made it back. I'd gone to live with Trask Whiley's parents, who my family knew. I helped out around his pa's trading post, and his ma taught me how to read, write, and figure."

Yiska stared at his boots for a moment then continued. "Mrs.

Whiley talked about Jesus, and had me read her Bible sometimes. After the war Trask had gone out on his own. I was about sixteen when he came back. He asked me to work for him, and I've been with him ever since." Yiska sat straighter. "As far as what I believe? I'm not really sure."

❧

The stage hastened its speed. Eliana coughed as dust particles filled the air. Tension permeated the small space. *How does one respond to such a revelation?* She yearned for Yiska to embrace Christianity and would love to discuss it further, but she simply uttered a silent prayer and took comfort in knowing that Papa certainly prayed for Yiska as well.

Yiska exhaled, stared out the window for a while, then faced Eliana again. "I never did thank you for taking my photograph."

He was changing the topic of conversation. Had she offended him? Her mood plummeted.

"I didn't see that photograph," Papa said.

Eliana reached into her reticule. "I have it right here, Papa."

Her father inspected the picture. "Very good. Very good indeed. I like the way you positioned him. Suits him well. Your hat was in better shape then."

"Eh, it was," Yiska grinned. He picked up his hat and smoothed some of the dents. "It's seen better times."

"Eliana, I intended for him to keep this." Papa handed the photograph to Yiska. *Papa, no! Now how will I ever get it back?*

"Thank you, sir. She did a fine job, despite the subject." Yiska leaned back and rubbed his cheek with one of his fingers, and the corner of his mouth turned up in a crooked grin.

Eliana glanced away all flustered. *How could he?* An avalanche of thoughts assailed her—taking his picture, combing his hair, raspberry jam—and he was thinking the very same thoughts.

"Yes, and she's a good assistant. Hard worker, my girl." Papa put his hand over Eliana's. "Indeed, she's every bit as talented as I. She has a good eye."

Yiska squeezed one eye shut, and his mouth eased into a sly grin. "Which one?"

Laughter filled the coach. Yiska had such a way of putting others at ease. When they stopped laughing Eliana caught him staring at her. Was he as captivated with her as she was with him?

Papa cleared his throat, "As I was about to say, she has two pretty eyes and a canny ability to see a good shot from behind the camera. I don't know what I'd do without her."

"Or I you, Papa." Eliana hoped she'd never have to know.

Yiska stretched and loosened his bandanna. He took in a deep breath of the clean Colorado air, still feeling the ache in his ribs. The sun was high overhead. The coach had made good time on the drive to the Wagon Wheel Gap home station. Then it had taken twice as long to go the same distance to the next station, due to the rough terrain. The hotel served a hale lunch of buffalo venison stew, buttermilk biscuits, and mixed berry pie. Lucky Jim saw that the horses were changed for a fresh team.

Within half an hour they were ready to continue their course along the Rio Grande. There were no new passengers, which pleased Yiska. While Eliana and Mr. Van Horn enjoyed the view of cattle roaming the hills, Yiska enjoyed watching *her*.

"I believe that ranch belongs to Kit Carson's brother-in-law," Mr. Van Horn said. Kit Carson was responsible for sending the Navajos on their long walk. Yiska wasn't pleased at the reminder. What made him open up the way he did about his past? Did it matter that much that Eliana understand him?

Eliana glared at her father. He took her cue and changed the topic. "The stationmaster told me Wagon Wheel Gap got its name when they discovered an old wheel in the river. They believe it was from Charles Baker's wagon when he passed through here while exploring the area."

"That's interesting, Papa. It reminds me of Mr. Snowden in

Silverton, the last living member of the Baker Party." Eliana looked at Yiska. "Papa will be photographing Mr. Snowden for the *San Juan Prospector.*"

Yiska wanted to ask if she would be there, too.

The Van Horns pulled out their newspapers. "Do you need some reading material, Yiska?" Eliana asked.

"No, thank you. I can't read with all this movement."

"Perhaps I could read something aloud. Would you enjoy that?"

"That sounds fine," he said.

"Oh, I know you will enjoy this!" Eliana beamed. "This is a journal entry penned by the Anonymous Explorer. The *Prospector* has been running a series of them." She began to read with a lilt in her voice.

A multitude of color explodes into the valley on a carpet of lush mountain meadows. Once lying dormant under the cover of winter, hearty blooms and delicate petals display their beauty and fill the air with fragrance.

Flowers have now awakened along quiet streams and rocky places, greeting the wildlife as it enters this blissful place. This romance with nature fills my heart in a way I wonder if any human ever could.

Though Yiska's heart raced, his face remained like stone.

Eliana sighed and folded the newspaper. "Have you ever heard such beautiful words? I can hardly imagine being surrounded by a place so sublime."

"Beautiful, yes," Yiska said. *The words are even more beautiful on your lips. How I wish I could take you there.*

"That was penned by the Anonymous Explorer." Eliana placed the paper on the seat beside her and straightened.

Mr. Van Horn raised a brow. "I wonder what place the author is describing. I'd love to go there and photograph it. Yet it seems he has kept it a secret."

"Oh, Papa, it would be wonderful to see in person!" Eliana's eyes danced.

"Any idea, Yiska?" Van Horn asked.

"It sounds like a valley west of Handies Peak. Northwest of here—in the San Juan forest between Stony Pass and Eureka Gulch."

"Have you been there?" Mr. Van Horn asked.

"Yes."

"Is it as lovely as the writer claims?" Eliana asked.

"More so."

Eliana grew quiet and looked down at her hands, and then met Yiska's eyes. "I have a confession, but please promise not to tell."

Yiska nodded.

"I found a journal on the steps at the end of the boardwalk. I brought it to the newspaper, hoping to place an ad to find the owner. But the editor decided to publish it instead."

Yiska's heart skipped a beat. "Really?"

She nodded. "I felt awful when Mr. Wilson printed it without the author's permission." She placed her hand on the newspaper. "This is art, and the work of a romantic. I hope the author is not terribly disappointed. Though I know I would have been."

"Perhaps it all worked out for the best. Mr. Van Horn, what are you reading?"

Mr. Van Horn peered up at Yiska. "*Scribner's Monthly.* An article entitled 'The Cañons of the Colorado' by Major John Wesley Powell. It's a series of three articles detailing his explorations, with engravings from Hiller's photographs. John Hiller was first hired as a boatman on the expedition, and later Powell hired him as photographer. Goes to show, if you have the ambition. . ."

Eliana leaned over her father's shoulder. "The pictures transport you right there. That's what we. . .you. . .hope to do on the expedition, Papa." She looked at Yiska. "My father is going on a survey in New Mexico."

"He already knows about it, dear."

"Does he?" Eliana's eyes widened, filled with curiosity and alarm. "Yiska, have you been hired as the guide?"

"Well, yes, he was there when I was discussing it with Trask Whiley. And no. Yiska will not be on the expedition." Mr. Van Horn's glare issued Yiska a warning to keep silent about the matter.

Eliana looked again at the *Scribner*. "Papa, maybe your photographs will be published after the survey and circulated in a magazine."

"Sunshine, that is precisely what I hope to accomplish. Photographic documentation would not only serve to educate people, but inspire them to visit such remote places and appreciate God's creation. I would love nothing more."

Yiska's heart swelled. *Dreams so much like my own.*

"I hope you have that opportunity, Papa. And I, too, would love to see my own photographs in print. Alas, I am a woman, and that most likely shall never be." Eliana sighed.

Mr. Van Horn looked at Yiska. "What aspirations do you have, son?"

Eliana tilted her chin toward Yiska, beckoning an answer. He dared not share the nature of his dreams. He tried to disregard the rough grade beneath the wheels of the coach and the rumbling inside that cautioned him to put his growing attraction toward Eliana aside. He could tell they were pulling into the Willow Creek swing station by the slowed gait of the horses hooves.

"Whoa!" Lucky Jim hollered. The timing couldn't have been better.

The quick change of the horses at Willow Creek left Eliana feeling restless. The brief stop provided her a chance to stretch, wash her dusty face, and join the others at the well for a refreshing drink of water. In another fifteen miles, through narrow canyons and slopes, they'd arrive at Rio Grande Pass—only about three hours away, and three hours from saying farewell to Yiska.

She'd hoped she could spend more time talking with him, but a mother and her son of about eight joined them for this length of the trip. Papa assisted them as they climbed aboard and then followed. He turned to help Eliana, but Yiska took her hand and helped her up. Did he plan to ride above with Lucky Jim?

But to Eliana's delight, Yiska climbed in and sat down—beside her! She tingled all over.

"Are you an Indian?" The boy asked.

"I'm a trail guide. . .and a journalist," Yiska said.

Eliana cocked her head and eyed Yiska, mouth agape. He turned to her with a sly grin and winked. Did he mean—was Yiska the Anonymous Explorer?

The boy spoke again. "Oh. I was hoping you were an Indian." His frown of disappointment wrenched her heart.

"Why's that?" Yiska said in a gentle tone.

"I'm part Indian. And I never met a real one."

The boy's mother patted him on the knee and said in a soft voice, "Jacob, please don't bother the man."

"No bother at all, ma'am." Yiska rested his elbows on his knees and met the boy eye to eye. "Jacob, is it?"

"Yes, sir." The boy's eyes widened.

"I'm more than just an Indian, and so are you." Yiska gave a strong nod. "What do you like to do?"

"I like to build things out of wood."

Yiska grinned. "See. Jacob, the builder. I'm pleased to know you." Yiska addressed his mother. "Ma'am, you have a fine young man here."

"Thank you. Mr. . ." Were those tears the woman was blinking back?

"Wilcox. Yiska Wilcox."

"Pleased to meet you Mr. Wilcox. I am Mrs. Stafford." She turned back to her son. "Jacob, please pull your bandanna over your mouth and nose to keep the dust out."

"But, Ma, I forgot it on the table at Grampa's cabin."

"Oh, Jacob." The boy's mother sighed and started to rummage through her satchel.

Yiska untied his neckerchief and handed it to the boy. "He can have mine."

Eliana's heart melted. *Why can't everyone see what a good man Yiska is?*

"Thank you, Mr. Wilcox." The boy took a toy soldier from his pocket and fiddled with it.

"Sure thing. And you can call me Yiska."

Eliana wondered if Jacob reminded Yiska of himself as a child. A boy looking for truth, aching to understand who he was. Similar thoughts crept into her mind about her own heritage. Why did these things matter so? Wasn't it most important simply that the child was loved? She was certain that Jacob's mother loved him. Did she remind Yiska of his own mother? Yet he was an orphan for most of his life. Eliana thought of Mama, and leaned a little closer to Papa in the seat next to her.

The stage bounced over a deep rut and tossed Eliana forward.

"Whoa." Yiska caught her and settled her back in the bench.

Eliana's face flamed as she glanced at him and let out a deep breath. "Thank you."

"Is she your wife?" Jacob asked.

"Jacob!" His mother had stretched her arm across her son's legs to keep him from bouncing about, but she yanked it back and covered her mouth.

Papa's eyes flashed open. "No, young man—she's *my* daughter. Her name is Miss Eliana, she's a photographer, and I believe she was about to take a nap. Isn't that right, dear?" Papa's lips pulled into a tight line. My, but it had been a long day.

Eliana corrected her posture and latched on to her father's arm. He rested his neck against the back cushion and nodded off as the coach rattled along. Yiska leaned back and pulled his hat down over his eyes. Jacob was soon asleep with his head against his mother's arm. Eliana smiled at Mrs. Stafford, wishing they could have some female conversation, but found herself settling against Papa's shoulder.

As her eyes fluttered shut she became more aware of Yiska's presence beside her—the warmth of his leg radiating to hers through her skirts, his muscular arm burrowed against hers, his shallow breathing. Out of the corner of her eye, she saw Yiska tilt his hat and steal a peek at her, but she chose to ignore it. A myriad of thoughts rolled into her mind. Was it wise for her to be this close to him with the feelings she was starting to have? There was still so much she did not know about him. Eliana's swirling thoughts and the rhythm of the coach lulled her to sleep.

A burst of noise jarred the passengers awake. Shots rang out, and the horses bolted. Jacob's mother screamed and flung herself down on the seat to cover her son.

Chapter 9

Everybody down!" Adrenaline surged through Yiska's body at the sound of gunfire. A strong instinct to protect Eliana overcame him, but her father's shielding arms thwarted his effort.

The coach sped up, and he reached across the floorboards to retrieve his rifle from under the seat. Jacob's mother peeked up at Yiska, her eyes full of fright. The boy didn't appear harmed. Mr. Van Horn had found his own rifle and was readying the gun. Yiska peered out the windows on each side to assess the situation. Who was out there? Bandits? Utes?

Shots resounded. Yiska and Mr. Van Horn fired back. A bullet thwacked against the coach. They returned more fire.

"Ma, you're bleeding," Jacob cried. Blood seeped through her sleeve.

Eliana crouched down next to the boy's mother and tried to steady herself on the bouncing floorboards. She pushed the woman's sleeve back farther to try to examine the wound, but the task was impossible during the chase. At least the blood wasn't gushing. That must be a good sign.

She tore off a piece of her petticoat, pressed it against the wound, and wrapped her other arm around the terrified woman's shoulders. "I think it only grazed her arm, Jacob. She'll be all right."

The gunfire subsided. Had the culprits retreated? The coach pitched over bumps and ruts, its speed increasing. Yiska clutched the edge of the seat. Something was very wrong. Was Lucky Jim down? He shouted to Mr. Van Horn. "I think the horses are running on their own. I'm going up."

"Yiska." The concern in Eliana's voice pricked his pounding heart. His desire to protect her overwhelmed him, but they might crash if he didn't do something. Then he remembered—her father had called her Eagle Eye Eli.

"Cover me." He handed her his rifle, and she positioned herself near the window and cocked it.

Yiska hauled himself up to the window's ledge and grabbed hold of the rails above. The wind whipped him, and he clamped his hat tighter.

Another shot echoed. Eliana and Van Horn fired back. Yiska pulled himself on top of the rocking coach and lay on his belly.

He cupped his hands around his mouth and shouted. "Eliana, my rifle." She handed it up to him.

He crawled forward to the driver's box. Lucky Jim slumped on the footboard, the reins caught under his arm. Yiska bent to grab them, and another shot whizzed over his head. He raised his rifle and fired back. Four Utes had come out of hiding, whooping and hollering on horseback as they circled the careening coach. The renegades reared their horses and shot their guns into the air. They left in a flash, their horses kicking up dirt in their wake.

Yiska wedged his gun between his legs. Sweat soaked his brow as he grabbed hold of the reins, and tried to gain control of the runaway team. The spooked horses ran wild over rocks and ruts, rattling the stage like the rumble of an avalanche. Dust filled the air, blinding Yiska's view. He held the reins firmly, but tried to give them enough slack so the horses could guide themselves on instinct—any abrupt turns could tip the coach onto its side. He hoped the wheels of the vehicle were as sturdy as they looked. If he could only get the horses to settle into a normal gait, he might be able to bring them to a stop.

"Yiska," Lucky Jim groaned.

Yiska startled. He'd thought Lucky Jim was dead. Relief eased some of his tension.

"Pull the brake, slowly. The resistance will signal them to stop."

"I'm trying. A branch is stuck in there."

Jim stirred, clamping one hand to his bloody shoulder. "Give me the reins and get it out."

"You sure?"

"If you don't get that brake loose, the horses are going to go right down into that ravine around the bend—and all of us with them."

Yiska gripped underneath the seat and leaned forward. The rutted road sped by beneath him. The pounding of the horses' hooves filled his ears. He gritted his teeth, reached down, and pulled on the tree limb that was wedged against the brake.

It didn't budge.

He fumbled for the hatchet and whacked at the branch, careful not to slice into the brake. At last it broke free and flew downwind. Now he could control the lever. He gripped the metal handle and pulled back, gently at first, then exerting more pressure. Jim propped himself up and gritted his teeth while he pulled on the reins.

The stagecoach slowed its pace, and with the resistance the horses' terror waned. Soon they slowed to a trot. Lucky Jim handed Yiska the reins. "Pull 'em in now. Easy does it."

"Whoaaaa." Yiska pulled back on the reins, increasing the tension against the bits. The hitch chains jangled as the four-in-hand team came to a complete stop, this time with no hostlers to come out to greet them.

"Now lock the brake," Lucky Jim said.

Yiska secured the coach and scanned the timbered foothills that bordered the rugged trail. No sign of their pursuers. He exhaled, muscles relaxing, and hollered down to the passengers. "All's clear. You can come out now, with caution."

❧

Eliana disembarked, shaken by the tumultuous ride. Papa helped her down with rifle still in hand. He also offered his hand to help Mrs. Stafford and reassured her son that she would be all right.

After the coach slowed, Eliana had managed to tie her scrap of petticoat around the woman's arm as a makeshift bandage. If no infection set in, the wound would heal in no time.

"Are you all right, Sunshine?" Papa asked.

Eliana threw her arms around him. A lump formed in her throat. "Yes, Papa. Are you?"

Papa wiped the dirt and sweat from his brow. "It takes a lot more than a little gunfire to upset me."

Anxious to see Yiska, Eliana hurried to the front of the coach where the horses stood, soaked and lathered.

He looked down at her from the driver's seat, a slow grin easing onto his dusty face.

Her eyes moistened. "Are you all right?"

"Yes." He wiped his face with the back of his hand.

Papa walked up beside her. "And what about the driver?"

"Lucky Jim was shot in the shoulder. Help me get him down," Yiska said. "We're still a couple hours from the next station, and his wound needs tending."

The two men helped Lucky Jim down and got him into the coach. Young Jacob held the door open to allow fresh air inside. Eliana ripped more of her petticoat for bandages and climbed inside to take care of Jim. Jacob's mother, though a little pale, waited outside, resting on a boulder with a watchful eye on her son while Papa stood guard.

"You saved us," Jacob said. His wide eyes, full of admiration, looked up at Yiska.

"Well, I had a little help." Yiska turned toward Eliana, his gaze resting on her face.

Something about the way Yiska looked at her made her feel more connected to him with each passing moment. Each experience they went through together brought them closer, strengthening a bond she couldn't understand. Yet, as with an undeveloped photograph, she still could not envision what might yet come.

"Miss Eliana can sure shoot a gun," Jacob said.

"Yes, she can," Papa said.

"Thank you for watching my back." Yiska turned and nodded at Jacob. "The Van Horns make a good team."

He poked his head inside the coach. "How is he?"

"Ask me yourself—I'm not dead," said Lucky Jim. Eliana held back a giggle.

Yiska lifted his chin. "Now I know how you got your name."

"Luck ain't got nothin' to do with it. The good Lord has been watchin' out for me for a long time. Matter o' fact, He was watching out for all of us today."

Jacob piped up. "He was. I know it!"

"How's that, Jacob?" Yiska asked.

"I was praying to Him the whole time. He even heard me over all that shootin'!"

Everyone started to laugh and Eliana's heart warmed. *Out of the mouths of babes.* Perhaps Yiska would see God's hand in his life. *Thank You, heavenly Father.*

"Yiska, are you going to drive the stage to the next station?" Jacob asked. "I'll ride shotgun."

"Oh, no you won't, young man," his mother said.

Yiska ruffled Jacob's hair. "I'll tell you what, you can help me check the horses."

"Sure," Jacob said. "Hey, Yiska. Who was shootin' at us? Indians?"

Yiska looked from Jacob to Lucky Jim. "They appeared to be Utes. Probably just trying to stir up trouble."

Lucky Jim touched his bandages. "Thank you, Miss Van Horn. I'll be getting along now."

Eliana gave Lucky Jim a scolding look. "But you've just been shot. You need to ride back here so you can rest." She checked to see that he wasn't bleeding through his bandages.

"I won't get any rest unless I'm up on the driver's box, miss." Lucky Jim groaned as he sat up. "Yiska, I'm going to need some help up there. You make a fine jehu."

Yiska helped Jim out of the coach then leaned back in. He took Eliana's hand and squeezed it, and then he left. Warmth spread through her veins like a gentle stream that nourished the blossoms in a hidden valley.

❧

Yiska gazed at Eliana as she relaxed in a wooden rocker on the front porch of the log cabin. The building served as the hotel and restaurant for the Rio Grande Pass home station. After the attack, it took them two long hours to get here, fourteen from the time the stage pulled out of Del Norte that morning. It was good to be able to stop for the night in this serene valley. The stationmaster wouldn't have a replacement driver coming in until the morning, and everyone seemed grateful for the reprieve.

A satisfying meal of fried pork, potatoes, gravy, bread, and custard pie had left him feeling quite subdued. As Eliana sat reading, loose tendrils of hair spilled down around her face like a waterfall. The last rays of sun illuminated golden highlights.

She looked up and smiled. "I didn't see you there."

"I didn't want to bother you," Yiska said.

"You're not. Please, sit down."

Yiska eyed the Bible on her lap. "What are you reading?"

"Psalm 138." Eliana looked down and read from the open page, her voice soothing to his ear. " 'I will praise thee with my whole heart: before the gods will I sing praise unto thee. I will worship toward thy holy temple, and praise thy name for thy lovingkindness and for thy truth: for thou hast magnified thy word above all thy name. In the day when I cried thou answeredst me, and strengthenedst me with strength in my soul.' " She placed her hand on the page and glanced up at Yiska.

He answered me today. The thought entered Yiska's mind like an echo calling across a canyon. He looked at the Bible with interest. "That book is important to you."

"Mm. It's life to me," Eliana said. "It belonged to my mother. Papa and I usually read from it after dinner, but tonight his head was throbbing, so I encouraged him to retire early. Maria and Jacob have turned in as well."

"Maria?" Yiska squinted.

"Mrs. Stafford, Jacob's mother. Come to find out, she's my friend Celia's older sister, whom I had never met. They'll travel on to Lake City with us tomorrow." Eliana smiled. "Maria was hurting some from her injury, and she and Jacob were both exhausted."

"It was a brutal day." Yiska shook his head. "I checked on Lucky Jim. One of the stable hands helped the stationmaster remove the bullet. He thinks Jim will be all right. Said you did a good job tending his wound."

"It wasn't the first time. Papa and I have encountered other unfortunate incidents out here."

"I take it this wasn't the first time you ever handled a rifle," Yiska said.

"No. . .but you seemed to know that," Eliana said.

"I guess I overheard something recently about Eagle Eye Eli."

Eliana's face turned as many shades of pink as the color hiding behind the clouds in the evening sky—only she had nowhere to hide.

She buried her face in her hands and shook her head. "I can't believe it. You know I. . . ?"

Yiska smirked. "Yes. . .size small men's dungarees."

"But you do know. . ."

"That you wear the disguise for protection?"

"Yes. And that I'm. . ."

"Going on the expedition with your father."

Eliana threw her head back and moaned. "Why would he tell you?"

"He didn't. I heard him discussing the expedition with Mr. Whiley."

"Mr. Whiley is the only other one who knows. The disguise was a plan to keep me safe when I assist Papa." She rolled her eyes. "You, of all people, had to find out. Did you suspect it when we were at the mercantile?"

"I already knew."

Eliana exhaled deeply. "Well, you might as well tell me. What did my father say when he learned that you knew about it?"

"He and Mr. Whiley discussed it. They decided that it would be unsafe for me to go on the expedition as the guide. They thought I'd give you away. Something about. . .the way I look at you." Yiska had argued the point with them to no avail. *Could it be that obvious?*

The corner of her mouth curved. "You're the guide for the Robbins survey?"

"Was."

Yiska stood and scanned the horizon then turned back to Eliana. "The sun will be down soon. I need to go check on Shadow. He's out in the pasture." He extended his hand toward her. "Come with me."

She stood and placed her hand in his. So delicate and soft. He held it until they'd descended the front steps. Despite the wearisome day, she still looked lovely. Her dark green dress sprinkled with tiny flowers reminded him of a certain valley. *Beautiful.*

"Will you be cold?" he asked.

Eliana adjusted her shawl. "No. This will be fine."

As they made their way toward the pasture, a majestic view of the Rio Grande opened before them. A clearing in a grove of ponderosa pines revealed the winding river below and the sun setting in the distance behind mountains tipped in white.

"How lovely. It's hard to imagine that there are so many wonderful places in the Territory."

"But there are." *And I wish to show you all of them.*

Eliana tilted her head. "You should know, Mr. Anonymous Explorer." A satisfied grin crept across her lips.

Yiska shrugged. "Looks like *my* secret is out, too."

She lowered her lashes then looked up with misty eyes. "I feel awful. I almost ruined everything for you. Your plans. Your dreams."

Eliana. You are my plans. My dreams. He lifted her chin with the tip of his finger and gazed into the deep pools of her eyes. "Everything worked out fine. I have an assignment to interview Mr. Snowden in Silverton? And if I have my facts straight, there's a certain photography assistant that I might get to see there."

Her countenance softened. Was it relief? Expectation? "Now, shhh." He wanted to take her in his arms but resisted. He could almost see the reflection of the sunset in her eyes. "It will be getting dark soon." He took her hand, and they approached a split rail fence. He let out a sharp whistle, and Shadow appeared from a dusky corner of the pasture, galloping toward him.

Black as midnight, Shadow pranced around, shaking his head up and down. He came up to the fence and nuzzled Yiska's face. Yiska caressed his nose and then put his arm around the horse's head and patted his muscular neck. "Shadow, my friend. Looks like they treated you well."

Eliana smiled. "He's a handsome horse. No wonder you're proud of him."

Yiska's smile widened. "I couldn't ask for a better one." He climbed over the fence to check Shadow over. He slid his hand over the mustang's sleek coat and down his legs, inspecting every inch of him.

"How'd you come by him?"

Yiska looked up at Eliana. "He was wild. A rancher up in Gunnison helped me train him." Yiska patted Shadow's haunch. "Well, Shadow, looks like you'll be ready to hit the trail tomorrow morning."

Eliana's face fell. Was she as disappointed as he that tomorrow their paths would take new directions?

"We ought to get back before it's too dark," she said.

"Have you forgotten that I am a guide?" Yiska asked, as they turned back toward the cabin.

" 'Tis true. . .*and* a journalist."

"And a journalist. Thanks to you." Yiska smiled. "When do you expect to be in Silverton? Perhaps I could meet you there."

Eliana's eyes brightened. "Yes. You could conduct your interview, and then we could take the photograph."

"A good idea. . . But I would like to see *you* again, Eliana."

"The one who's responsible for you not getting to go on the survey?"

"The very one." Yiska gazed into her eyes. "I can't help the way I look at you."

"The way you're looking at me now?" She tilted her chin and flashed her dancing eyes at him. "Or perhaps the way you looked at me as I saw you through the lens when I took your photograph. There *was* a certain look you had that day. . .a stifled smile perhaps?"

"Can I help it if you make me smile?"

"That reminds me. You have something that belongs to me."

Yiska thought of the ribbon he had bought for her. How did she know?

She raised her eyebrows. "The picture of you that my father confiscated. It belongs to me, you know. It was a fair trade."

"Ah, but it was given back to me, so now it's mine." A grin eased across Yiska's face. "I'm willing to trade."

"For what?" The look in Eliana's eyes dared him to suggest a worthy exchange.

"For this." Yiska caressed her face with his fingers and with a gentle touch lifted her chin. As he looked into her warm eyes, he sensed her timidity. "Have you never kissed an Indian?"

"No. . .I have never kissed any man."

Yiska enveloped her in his arms and pressed his lips against hers, savoring her sweetness beneath the twilight sky.

Eliana awoke with a start, and her eyes scanned the small, unfamiliar room. The relay station was nothing more than a large log cabin; her bed, a small cot. The room was sparse, with only a washbasin sitting upon a pedestal table and a single chair against the wall—her shawl draped on it—and a horseshoe wedged above the doorframe, for luck.

She jumped to her feet and looked down at her wrinkled dress. When had she fallen asleep? She hardly remembered coming back to the station last night. She was utterly exhausted after the long ride on the stagecoach yesterday. And blessed. They had all been in grave danger. *Thank You for a new day, heavenly Father, and please bring quick healing to Lucky Jim and Maria.*

She rubbed her arms in the morning chill. Thoughts of her time with Yiska the evening before swept over her with warmth. Had he really kissed her? She closed her eyes, and images of his tawny skin, his dark hair, and enchanting eyes looking deep into her own sent a tingle over her skin. She could almost feel his touch. His closeness. She reached for her shawl and recalled how he had wrapped his buckskin coat around her on their way back to the cabin. As she draped the shawl around herself, she imagined the warmth and scent of leather. And of him.

She searched for her reticule to retrieve her comb and make herself presentable before going downstairs. She hoped she would see him again before he left.

She remembered that she'd placed her small bag in Papa's room for safekeeping. As she hurried across the landing to his room, the smell of bacon and fresh-baked bread filled her senses. The stationmaster's wife met her in the hallway.

"Good mornin'. You're in a hurry today."

"Yes, good morning." Eliana saw that the woman held her mother's Bible.

"I was asked to see that you got this. Apparently you left it on the porch last night."

"Oh, thank you." Eliana smiled and took a step forward, eager to be on her way so she could get downstairs.

The woman touched her arm. "That young fella, Yiska, gave it to me before he rode out. Said it was important that you get it."

Eliana turned, her heart sinking. "He's gone?"

"Yes, miss. Pulled out before the sun was up. My husband told him about some men who were in need of a guide." The woman put her hands in her apron pockets and gave Eliana a knowing smile. "Breakfast will be served shortly."

The stationmaster's wife walked away, leaving her alone in the hall. Eliana hugged the Bible and sighed. *Lord, would it be Your will for me to see him again?*

She looked down at the Bible and opened the cover. There inside lay the cabinet card photograph of Yiska. He had returned it. Hope and longing filled her heart. She closed her eyes to hold back the flood of tears that threatened to release.

"There you are." Papa appeared at the top of the stairs, a glint in his eye. "Are you ready, Sunshine? Our journey awaits."

Chapter 10

Lake City, Colorado

It's a miracle that our cargo made it here in one piece," Eliana said as she and her father sorted through the new photography equipment and supplies in the back room of their studio. The small shop was almost a second home to them, as quaint as their clapboard house situated next door.

Papa inspected his new camera with a critical eye. "I was more than a bit worried for a while, but the good Lord saw fit to keep everything intact."

"And us, too." Eliana kissed him on the cheek.

"We won't make any new appointments while we're here, unless it's something important. We already have enough work to keep us busy until we head out again."

Eliana picked up a small carton from the floor and placed it on the counter. "You do remember that Celia is coming in next Monday for her wedding portraits? I still can't believe she's getting married." Eliana glanced up. "I thought she would be one of the last among my friends to settle down—she's so particular. But Thomas won her heart." Eliana sighed.

"Seems rather rushed to me," Papa said.

"The preacher, Reverend George Darley, is coming to town. And if the weather is nice, they'll be married out at Lake San Cristobal."

"How you gathered all this news already mystifies me. We haven't even been back a full day." Papa grinned. "Hand me that cloth, please." Papa carefully wiped the lenses. "You know, Sunshine, one of these days I suppose you'll marry, too. Your mother warned me of such a thing, but I never wanted to believe it. You've become a remarkable young woman before my very eyes."

"It's not as if I'm available for courting. Most of my time is spent behind the camera or in men's clothing. Or both." Eliana shook her head. "It's hard to get a gentleman to notice you that way."

Papa rubbed his whiskers. "Well, I seem to know a young man who's taken notice of you."

Was he displeased? She would ignore the comment. Eliana finished inspecting the thin iron plates. "All of the plates are in fine condition. Now we'll need to blacken them, and then we can pack them up for the expedition."

"I'll japan them myself," Papa said. "I wrote out a list of tasks for you this morning. Now, back to the subject at hand."

"I don't know what you mean. . .unless perhaps you're speaking of Cornelius Crawford?" Eliana laughed. "He's not even my type."

Papa chuckled. "You know whom I'm speaking of, dear."

Eliana lowered her lashes. "I may never see him again."

"If my suspicions are correct, he'll find his way to you somehow."

Oh, how she hoped.

Yiska pulled open the flap of his saddlebag to retrieve his journal and a pencil. This would make a good spot to get some rest and do some writing. The pool of water would provide refreshment for both him and Shadow, and the shade would feel good after riding in the bright sun for most of the day. A little jerky and dried fruit would do for now to curb his hunger, and later he would try to catch some trout.

He sat down on a large rock by the stream. Water flowed into it from a precipice above. Dappled sunlight filtered through the trees, and visions of Eliana's sweet face, her clear hazel eyes, the slight dimple in her chin, and her adorable smile filled him with wonder. Eliana Van Horn disturbed his thoughts, challenged his beliefs, and filled the long-vacant crevices of his heart.

Yiska untied the cord that bound his journal and opened it. From between the pages, he pulled out the photograph of the beautiful woman who had changed his life forever. He'd never given any credence to the idea of sharing his life with someone, yet now she seemed to be the compass navigating his every thought.

He would see her again. Perhaps not on the expedition, and it may not be in Silverton, but he would track her back to Lake City if he had to, just to hold her once again.

Eliana displayed Celia and Thomas's wedding photographs on a table covered with a white linen cloth. She admired how well they had come out—the family sitting and bridal portraits were stunning. But the one with Celia standing behind her soon-to-be groom was Eliana's favorite. Celia wore a beautiful new paisley shawl, which she would someday use for her child's christening.

Eliana imagined how the couple's children and grandchildren would enjoy the pictures and ruminate over their happiness on this occasion, as she treasured the daguerreotype of her own parents' wedding. How lovely Mama looked, and Papa, so proud and handsome. Perhaps she would marry, too, someday, though her heart ached knowing that Momma would not be there to share her joy. How she longed for conversation that only a mother and daughter could share, especially now, when her heart overflowed with so many new feelings. So many thoughts of Yiska.

"These photographs came out lovely, Eliana. Celia will be pleased." Maria Stafford leaned over the table to admire the pictures of her sister's wedding party.

"Oh! Maria, you startled me. Thank you for saying so." Eliana smiled at her new friend. "This family portrait with you in it came out very nice. You photograph very well. I'd love to take a picture of you and Jacob sometime."

"I'm sure Jacob would like that. You've already done so much. It's nice to have a place of our own again after living for such a long time with others. It was very kind of your father to let the upstairs apartment to us."

"I'm glad it pleases you. Why don't you have some tea with me? I was about to take a break."

A short time later, the women sat in wicker chairs on the side porch of the studio, enjoying their tea and the pleasant afternoon.

Maria took a sip and placed her cup back on the saucer. "Where will you be traveling, Eliana?"

"Papa and I have to photograph some of the mining areas, and then we have a special assignment to photograph a prominent citizen in Silverton. It will accompany an interview to be published in the *San Juan Prospector*."

"Your travels sound exciting, but I do hope you are careful." Maria arched an eyebrow. "Although you are rather skilled at handling dangerous situations. Thank you again for helping me with my injury."

"How is your wound?" Eliana took a sip from her porcelain cup.

"It's healing well, thank you." Maria massaged her arm. "It seems like I've been healing in one way or another for over a year now. Losing my husband in a mining accident was more painful than any bullet wound could ever be. But I'm doing much better now and have become stronger for it." Maria took another sip of her tea.

"It must've been very difficult for you," Eliana said. "There are many risks in loving someone, are there not?"

"Do you speak of Yiska?" Maria asked. "I've noticed something special between the two of you."

Eliana felt the roses bloom in her cheeks. "Is it that obvious?"

"Well, Jacob seemed to notice." Maria gave her a gentle smile. "Love cannot be hidden. It even shines in the darkest places. Look at Celia and Thomas—when he became gravely ill this spring, it made her realize how true her feelings for him were. He insists it was her love that pulled him through."

"Yes, but is love enough?" Eliana asked.

"No, it isn't. You must also have faith," Maria said. "In God, and each other."

The two women sat in silence, pondering these thoughts. As Eliana stared at the porch floor, a large boot landed on one of the steps. She glanced up, surprised to see Trask Whiley.

"Good afternoon, ladies." Mr. Whiley flashed a wide grin.

"Mr. Whiley! What brings you to Lake City?" Eliana greeted him with a cheerful smile, despite her reservations about his not allowing Yiska to go on the survey.

"I had some business up this way. Just arrived on the Southern Overland Express. Perhaps I should've traveled here with you and your father last week," he said.

Eliana and Maria looked at one another then shook their heads with utmost dismay.

"No. That would not have been a good idea," Eliana said. "We encountered some trouble on the way."

"Yes," Maria said, "but we had a heroic young man with us who saved us from marauding Indians." She glanced at Eliana and smiled.

"Yiska." Mr. Whiley said.

"You know him?" Maria asked.

"Yes. I'm his boss. . .and his friend. Was anyone wounded?"

"The driver was shot in the shoulder. . .and a bullet grazed Mrs. Stafford's arm."

Mr. Whiley's eyes widened, and he shook his head. "I'm sorry to hear that, ma'am."

Maria nodded. "Thank you. I'm recovering quite well and am thankful no one was seriously injured."

"Forgive me, I've neglected to introduce you," Eliana said. "This is Mrs. Maria Stafford. She and her son rent the apartment above our studio. They moved here from Willow Creek."

"That's down my way, more or less." Mr. Whiley tipped his hat. "Mrs. Stafford, a pleasure."

"Ma, Ma!" Jacob ran up and threw his arms around his mother's neck. "Can I go down to the creek? Ace's pa is going to take us fishing."

"Sure, son, but please mind your manners and say hello to Mr. Whiley, a friend of the Van Horns and of Yiska's."

"Howdy, sir. You know Yiska? He's my friend, too. He saved our lives!" Jacob smiled up at the tall man.

"That's what I've heard." Mr. Whiley grinned. "Any good fish in that creek?"

"Ace said it's filled with trout. You can come with us if you'd like."

Mr. Whiley chuckled. "Maybe another day. I have some things I need to take care of. By the way, Miss Van Horn, where can I find your father?"

"He's out for the remainder of the afternoon, but you can see him at dinner tonight. That is, if you'll come. We'll eat at five o'clock. Maria and Jacob will be joining us."

"Five o'clock then. Ladies. Jacob." Mr. Whiley tilted his hat and sauntered away.

Maria turned to Eliana and whispered, "I didn't know we are invited to dinner this evening."

"You are now. But I'll need your help cooking the meal. I'm much better behind a camera than behind a stove."

"Easy there, Shadow." Yiska leaned back as he led his horse down a rocky crag. He had escorted a small convoy of miners to Cunningham Gulch and now was headed back through Stony Pass. The anxious men he'd guided hoped to strike a silver vein in the hard-to-reach area and somehow managed to haul along some large, steam-powered equipment and other supplies with the help of their burros.

Yiska continued his trek northeast and hoped to arrive at Rose's Cabin within a few days. Miners who flooded the area almost always kept the new building's many rooms occupied. Mr. Whiley had arranged for Yiska to use this stop as a connecting point for his next assignment. On his way there, he would go through the valley that had enthralled Eliana. Though it wouldn't be as colorful as he'd described until after the summer rains, it would provide easier terrain for him and Shadow.

Eliana marveled at the picturesque setting of Lake San Cristobal as friends and family gathered to celebrate Celia and Thomas's wedding. Mountain views surrounded them, and pines towered over them, providing the perfect amount of shade. The wedding couldn't have taken place on a finer day.

Eliana, in her new blue dress, swirled around with Papa to the gleeful sound of fiddles.

"You're a fine dancer, Papa," she said.

Papa's eyes crinkled. "As are you, my Sunshine. I'm going to sit this next one out, but I think I see someone who can take my place." Papa snagged Jacob's arm as he passed by. "Would you do me a favor, young man, and dance with Miss Eliana?"

"Sure, Mr. Van Horn. I won't be dancing with Ma anymore, since Mr. Whiley finally got her to dance with him," Jacob said.

The fiddles started to play again. Eliana took Jacob's hands, and they swung round and round until the music stopped. "Thank you for the dance, sir." She tried to catch her breath.

"I'm going to get some lemonade. Would you like some, Miss Eliana?" Jacob asked.

"That sounds like a grand idea, thank you. Would you bring it to me over at our picnic blanket?"

"Sure. I'll get some cake, too."

"Didn't I already see you with some cake?" Eliana asked.

An impish grin appeared on Jacob's face. "Maybe."

"Well, I won't tell," Eliana whispered.

She made her way to the old patchwork quilt that was spread out under a large pine. Papa leaned up against the tree talking with Reverend Darley, the minister who had performed the nuptials.

"It's such a beautiful day for a wedding!" Eliana beamed. "Reverend Darley, Celia was pleased that you were here to perform the ceremony."

"It was my pleasure. And although this is a grand place for a wedding, maybe by this time next year others will have the privilege of having theirs in a church," Reverend Darley said.

"A church in Lake City? How wonderful."

"My brother, Alexander, the other Reverend Darley, is planning to start one here. He's a carpenter as well as a minister, and he intends to build it himself."

"Excellent! I'm sure many will support the effort," Papa said.

"And what about you, Reverend Darley?" Eliana asked.

"I'm pioneering in the San Juans. My mission is to bring the Gospel to the western slope. There are many new settlements and mining towns that need to hear the Word of God. There are some who haven't heard it since they arrived here. I've preached to men, women, and burros, alike." Reverend Darley smiled, arms resting across his knees.

Eliana tilted her chin. "If there are no churches, where do you preach?"

Reverend Darley held his hands out. "Anywhere they'll listen. I'll sit down with them in the mining camps or call a meeting in a saloon. I meet them where they are, as the Lord does with us."

"It sounds like you're a missionary," Eliana said.

He nodded. "I am. Are not all believers bearing witness to Christ wherever they go?"

Eliana thought about that. There was much truth in what he said.

"Since we are made in His image, I suppose we ought to reflect Him to others. Aye?"

Eliana turned to Papa. "That reminds me of Reverend Mattheson and his enthusiasm for telling others about the Lord."

"Do you mean Harland Mattheson?" Reverend Darley asked. "I believe he is occupied as a naturalist now. Does some work for the government."

Eliana looked at her father in confusion then turned back to Reverend Darley. "Isn't he preaching anymore?"

"Oh, I don't think we've heard his last sermon yet."

Maria and Mr. Whiley walked over, lemonade in hand. Maria sat down on the blanket beside Eliana, but Mr. Whiley remained standing, towering above them like one of the ponderosa pines.

Papa turned to the minister. "Reverend Darley, you've met Mrs. Stafford, Celia's sister. And this is a friend of ours, Trask Whiley, here on business from Del Norte."

Reverend Darley cocked his head. "Del Norte, eh? Gateway to the San Juans. What type of business are you here for, Mr. Whiley?"

"I own an outfitting company and thought I'd investigate the possibility of opening another in Lake City."

Jacob ran up to Eliana, a cup of lemonade sloshing about, and handed it to her, along with a plate of wedding cake. "Here, Miss Eliana."

"Thank you, Jacob. You're a true gentleman."

Reverend Darley looked directly at Mr. Whiley. "You know, I'm about the Lord's business, and I'd be pleased if you'd join us for Sunday meeting tomorrow. I've called a service at the grange. The ladies will pack baskets, and a hymn sing will follow."

Jacob tugged Mr. Whiley's arm, "You won't miss it, Mr. Whiley, will you?"

Mr. Whiley looked down at Jacob, "I suppose it wouldn't hurt any." He glanced at Maria. "You'll be there, I take it?" Now it was Maria's turn to blush.

In a flash, Jacob ran off again to play with some cousins.

Mr. Whiley addressed Papa. "John, about that business we discussed a few nights ago. I've decided to send Yiska on the survey after all. I think it would be in everyone's best interest." Mr. Whiley glanced at Eliana. "The benefits outweigh the risks."

"I've given it some thought myself and am in full agreement," Papa said.

Elated, Eliana refrained from hugging Papa.

"If everything works out," Whiley said, "he'll have an additional role other than being a guide. I got word this morning that editor Wilson at the *Prospector* wants to hire him as a correspondent for the survey."

"What a great opportunity. It's not a conflict for you?" Papa asked.

"Not at all. In fact, I've been hoping he'd get a break like that. It will be good for him."

Maria looked up at Mr. Whiley. "Yiska mentioned that he was a journalist. If he's half as good as that Anonymous Explorer I've read lately, he's bound to make a name for himself." Mr. Whiley, Papa, and Eliana smiled knowingly at one another.

"Did I miss something?" she asked. At that moment, Jacob appeared by his mother's side, faced flushed from play. "Oh, mercy, look at you. I might have to walk you down to the lake and let you have a swim."

Eliana's heart filled with joy for Yiska' good news. She would get to see him again! Her heart raced. She told herself to breathe lest she swoon from all the excitement.

"Mr. Whiley, how do you plan on letting him know?" she asked.

"If I only had a way to get word to him along the trail, maybe at Rose's Cabin, but I can't get out there myself."

"Maybe I could be of assistance," Reverend Darley said. "I'm traveling that way and will be there for a couple of days. Then I'll head down to Silverton as well. Chances are I'll run into the fellow. What did you say his name is?"

"Yiska." Jacob piped up. "He's part Indian, but that's not all he is. He's a journalist, too!"

As the adults laughed, Eliana dared to hope. Could it be that Yiska's dreams would soon come true? And could they ever include her? *Lord, please watch over Yiska, wherever he may be.*

Yiska led Shadow along a narrow path high on a ridge. Mountain walls rose around him, but soon a green valley would be in view, dotted with rocks and streams and colored with purple lupine, red prairie fire, and blue columbine.

As he turned the corner he came upon a pair of yearling brown bears about ten yards in front of him. He laid a hand on Shadow's neck, careful not to make any abrupt moves. "Steady, boy," he whispered.

As the bears came closer he reached for the rifle that hung from his saddle and scanned the area. One of the bears swiped at the other, and a playful wrestling match ensued. Shadow snorted and began to back away. The young bears looked up.

Yiska dropped the reins and cocked his gun, his heart thumping in his chest. The yearlings scampered away. Barely breathing, he waited before resuming his journey. Was the mother bear nearby?

He listened, surrounded by mountain stillness and the sigh of the wind through the pines. Exhaling in relief, he lowered his gun, gathered the reins, and rubbed Shadow's crest to calm him. Shadow pawed the ground, agitated, and attempted to turn.

The yearlings' mother charged toward them, a brown blur on the path. Yiska jerked his rifle up and fired. The she bear leaped for Yiska. She slammed into Shadow's flank then fell dead.

Shadow reared back from the bear's massive weight, neighing shrilly. Yiska scrambled for the reins and flew backward over the edge of the ridge.

He landed on a ledge several yards below in a motionless heap.

Chapter 11

Yiska moaned as he awoke to the damp nudge of Shadow's nose against his face. The horse's reins dangled on the ground. As his vision cleared, he realized he'd fallen from the narrow ridge above. How his horse found his way down and across the wide ledge he didn't question—Shadow's instincts were far better than his own.

Yiska pulled himself up and looked down over the ledge. His rifle lay broken on the boulders below. He felt his hip for his side arm and was glad it was still there. He rubbed his sides and let out a slow exhale. His ribs were still intact. Except for some aches and bruises, he was all right. He sat up and grabbed his canteen from the pack behind his saddle, took a swig, and splashed a bit on his face.

Yiska made his way back up the ridge, Shadow in tow. There lay the lifeless four-hundred-pound bear. He took off his coat and shirt and laid them on a rock. He tossed his hat there with them and wrapped a headband around his brow to keep his hair out of his face. He'd salvage the bear skin and whatever meat he could take with him. Nature would dispose of the refuse, but he'd have to work fast before the scent of blood drew the attention of wildcats or coyotes. He kneeled over the animal, preparing to cut away its thick coat.

Click.

Yiska looked up, sun glinting in his eyes. The barrel of a shotgun stared him in the face.

"I hope you intend to share that with me, Injun." A weather-beaten man in fringed buckskins and a wide-brimmed hat glared at him.

Yiska eyed him carefully. He kept his voice calm. "Put that gun away, and I'll give you what you want. There's plenty here, but I could use a hand."

The heavily bearded man lowered his shotgun. "My name's Bouclier—they call me Buck."

"Yiska Wilcox."

"You Whiley's scout?"

"I am."

Buck eyed the bear. "Looks like ya got yerself a good-sized brownie."

"She almost got me," Yiska said. "I'll take as much as I can, and you can have the rest."

"What are you planning to do with the fur?" the man asked.

Yiska stood. "I might trade it up at Rose's Cabin."

The mountaineer hoisted his shotgun back over his shoulder. "I could take it off yer hands. . .for a fair trade." The man pointed his chin toward his horse and a fully loaded pack mule.

Yiska swatted a fly away from his face. "Lost my rifle over the edge of that ridge."

"Good then. Let's get to work on that beast."

The task complete, Yiska washed the thick, red blood from his arms and chest while Shadow drank from the stream. He cleaned his hatchet and knife and dried them with a bandanna. He strapped huge portions of meat wrapped in oilcloth behind his saddle and helped tie the bear skin to the trader's mule.

"Headin' to Corydon Rose's place, on my way to Ourey," Buck said.

"That's where I'm going, too."

Buck nodded. "Well then, it looks like you've got yourself a travel companion."

So be it.

The men descended the incline and rode on until after sunset, when they decided to stop for the night. Yiska made a fire, and they cooked a supper of fresh bear meat and canned beans. As the temperature dropped, they retreated to the lean-to they'd put up.

Under pine bough shelter, Yiska reclined against his saddle with his Navajo blanket as his cover and new rifle at his side. The howl of coyotes echoed in the distance as he thanked the Christian God that He had heard his call for help today.

Eliana, now dressed as the young man Eli, hummed as she sat on the bench next to Papa. He drove their wagon along the dirt toll road toward Eureka—one of several assignments they had contracted in photographing the mining towns throughout the San Juans. Their white mule, Sampson, pulled a box-covered wagon with VAN HORN PHOTOGRAPHY painted on its sides. It housed a darkroom and temporary shelter for the pair.

"Did you hear Mr. Whiley at the hymn sing? He is quite a talented baritone," Eliana said.

"He carried quite a tune, I'll give him that. He actually knew some of those hymns," Papa said.

"He and Maria harmonized very well together." Eliana smiled at the thought of the unlikely couple.

Papa tugged on the reins and held his head high. "What I really enjoyed was the sound of my lovely daughter's voice."

Eliana smiled. "I do love to sing, and it was wonderful to hear all those people gathered together to worship. I'm glad we'll have a church in Lake City next year."

Papa gave a light snap of the whip. "Come on, Sampson, giddyup. At this rate, it will take us until next week to get to Eureka."

"Mr. Whiley seems quite smitten with Maria," Eliana said. "You never know, they might be the first couple to get married in that new church."

"Trask Whiley married. I've heard stranger things," Papa said.

At last they came to the hill that overlooked the mining town, and Papa pulled the wagon to a stop. Plats of stick houses and log cabins were set in rows near the Sunny Side Mine, built stair-stepped up the mountainside. "This is a good view," he said. "We'll set up here. Then we can go down into the town and get pictures there."

Eliana hopped down from the wagon, tucked her shirt into her trousers, adjusted her suspenders, and checked the buttons of her extra-large vest. She tucked some stray hairs back under her hat. Her shoulder-length hair was tied back with a piece of rawhide. No one could see her here, but it was better to be safe.

Eliana and Papa unloaded their equipment. They set up a stereo camera, which would use wet-glass plates to create stereographs. They'd decided, however, that when they were on the Robbins expedition they'd only use the dry process method. That way there would be no need to develop the pictures in the field, as they would bring the plates home for processing. Nor would they have to worry about glass breaking. Nevertheless, Papa still planned to bring a small, collapsible darkroom, since they would be leaving the wagon behind.

Eliana adjusted the lens of her camera and turned to Papa. "What made you change your mind about Yiska?"

"It troubled me when I learned he knew about your disguise," Papa said. "I thought his knowing would jeopardize your secret."

Eliana flattened her lips and listened.

"I've been able to get to know Yiska better since then, Sunshine. I would trust him with my life. . .and yours. In fact, it will probably be good that he does know—he may be able to help protect you." Papa brushed his hand over his beard. "But I *will* warn him to keep a proper distance from you."

Eliana sighed. She supposed Papa was right, but how she longed to spend time with Yiska. If only someone could get word to him in time about the opportunity to work with the Robbins survey. *Heavenly Father, in Your way, would You please see to it that Yiska will find out? You know, above all, what this will mean to him.*

Men gathered around Yiska and Buck as the trader displayed the bear fur outside Rose's Cabin. Buck hoped to impress the men enough for someone to make a trade. "It's a beauty, ain't it? I traded it with an Injun. Came upon him while he was dressing it and offered to help.

Three brown bears had attacked him. Scared two of 'em off, but he shot this one dead, right before it plowed him off a cliff." Buck looked up at Yiska. "At least that's what Yiska tells me. He's the one who shot it!"

The men eyed Yiska up and down.

"What do you say? Can anyone offer me a fair trade or a nugget of gold?" Buck asked.

A man sidled up to Yiska. "Is that story true, young man?"

"More or less," Yiska said.

"Well then, it's a good thing I was praying for you. You nearly lost your life."

Hands in his pockets, Yiska leaned his weight back on one leg and narrowed his eyes. "Beg your pardon?"

"You heard right. Your name's Yiska, is that right? Yiska Wilcox?" the man asked. "I've been waiting for you. I have a message from Trask Whiley."

Yiska stared at him. "Do you need a guide?"

"No, but I could use a traveling companion on my way down to Silverton. My name's George Darley."

The men walked away from the group and stopped to talk under some trees. Yiska took off his hat and brushed the hair from his face. "What's this message from Whiley?"

"He wants you to go on the Chandler Robbins survey. He said you know the details."

Yiska broke into a grin. "Thank you. That's good news."

"There's more," Darley said.

Yiska cocked his head. "What's that?"

"Mr. Wilson from the *San Juan Prospector* wants to hire you to be a correspondent during the expedition. Mr. Whiley was in full support. Mr. Van Horn thought it was a good idea as well. They both were concerned that you get the good news in time, in case you missed Van Horn in Silverton." Darley smiled. "There was also a pretty young lady there who was hoping very much that I'd meet up with you."

Eliana. Yiska shook the man's hand. "Thank you, Mr. Darley."

"My pleasure." Darley smiled. "They gave me the message, and I've been praying for you ever since."

Yiska blinked. "Praying, you say. I've been doing a little of that myself."

"By the looks of that bear skin, I'd say you'd be crazy not to."

Chapter 12

Yiska traveled with Mr. Darley southwest through the hilly countryside on horseback. How he ended up traveling with a preacher was beyond him. Yiska expected to hear sermons for miles on end, but Darley entertained him with tales of his journeys. He showed genuine interest in Yiska's travels as well. When Darley did mention God, it was in a natural way that didn't bother Yiska. Darley didn't scold the way Trask's father did back when Yiska worked at his trading post. Instead, Mr. Darley spoke of God as an old friend. Someone he respected and trusted. A traveling companion.

High in the hills, the two dismounted to stretch their legs and rest for a bit. They walked to the edge of a bluff and admired the way the mountains hugged the river below. Although some ice still encrusted its edge, the river flowed freely, and the flora hinted summer was on its way. Yiska took off his gloves and stuffed them in his coat pockets. "It's been a mild spring. The weather's on our side."

Mr. Darley loosened his scarf. "Do you remember that fierce snowstorm in May a few years back?"

"Sure do."

"I'll never forget it," Mr. Darley said. "I set out for Silverton across the old San Juan Trail after preaching at Hell's Acre. I went with Gus Talbot, the mail carrier, that day. No different than any other. When we got to Burrows Park, away from the timberline, we had to snowshoe it over the range, since the thaw was late. The clouds gathered, and if we quit walking, we were likely to freeze to death." Darley looked out over the mountaintops, shielding his eyes from the sun. "The snow came down hard. We could barely see to put one foot in front of the other. Both of us stepped right off a steep cliff, tumbled twenty feet down into the gulch. If the Lord didn't hear me call out to Him then, I would've supposed He was deaf."

"I'm beginning to think He does listen," Yiska said.

"I lived to tell about it, didn't I?" Mr. Darley grinned.

"I've asked for His help three times lately—when they threw me in jail for saving Miss Van Horn, when our stagecoach was attacked by renegade Utes, and during my run-in with the bears." Yiska remained quiet for a moment. "Why God would answer me, I don't know. Maybe others were praying and He heard them instead."

"That's an interesting thought. I've often wondered the same thing."

"You? But you're doing God's work."

"True. Though it's not the work we do that gets His attention. It's a humble heart that seeks Him." Darley folded his arms across his chest and looked Yiska in the eye. "He hears us because of His love for us, nothing more. Doesn't matter how loudly we call out to Him. Like when I shouted out during that blizzard. He heard me all right, but I have no doubt He was also attentive to the quiet prayers of a dear old lady who had it on her heart to pray for me during that storm."

"How'd she know you were in trouble?" Yiska asked.

"She saw me travel past her cabin on the old wagon road that day. Being the first woman in these parts, she knew the weather well and noticed how the clouds hung around the mountain peaks to the west. She grew concerned and prayed for my safety. A year later I saw her at a meeting, and she told me she'd never forget that terrible storm. I promptly agreed with her. She said she had it on her heart to pray for me until the storm let up, knowing I wouldn't relent until I reached my destination. I nearly wept when she told me."

Yiska thought about how he almost went on his own trek to Silverton, eager to conduct his interview after helping those miners up by Stony Pass. Had he done so, he would've missed the news about being hired as correspondent for the survey. And, by some miracle, he had survived the bear attack and made it up to Rose's Cabin, where Mr. Darley waited for him. Yet when Darley greeted him he said, *"I've been praying for you, young man."*

Yiska swallowed hard. He recalled the words Mrs. Whiley spoke to him when he left her home. *"God go with you. Remember that He is as close as a prayer."* He'd appreciated the kind words, but hadn't understood what they meant. Now he saw that the God they believed in was real. Perhaps this God even cared for him.

Yiska whisked a yellow jacket from his sleeve. A memory of Eliana the last night he had seen her came to his mind—of her in his buckskin coat. After taking it from her shoulders, he'd wrapped her in his arms and kissed her on the cheek. In turn she whispered in his ear, *"I'll keep you in my prayers, Yiska. Be well."* Her sentiment meant far more now.

The preacher continued. "I've learned it's one thing to call on God in urgent times, still another to trust Him daily on the path of life."

"Mr. Darley, you already *know* how to get to Silverton. Why'd you take me as a guide?"

Darley looked at Yiska as if amused. "Who's to say I'm not your guide for this part of the journey?"

Yiska smiled and shook his head. He looked out over the gorge and upward, holding the brim of his hat. He pointed to an eagle flying overhead.

"Magnificent creature," Darley said.

"They make it look so easy to soar on the wind like that."

"Perhaps it is, given the right conditions."

"Perhaps it is."

Eliana shifted her hips on the hard bench as the wagon jostled down the winding road toward Howardsville. The prosperous town hosted rows of storefronts and a multitude of cabins, unlike most of the other mining towns with merely a spattering of buildings. Papa had stopped whistling hours ago, a sign he was weary, too.

The white mule came to a complete stop. After an arduous trek over crude roads that wound their way around the Arastra Gulch mines, Sampson was exhausted.

Eliana exhaled, climbed down from the wagon, and took hold of his halter, urging him forward with a bit of sugar. "Just a little farther, boy." Once he resumed a sluggish pace, she hoisted herself back up beside Papa.

Although the late afternoon sun hid behind the clouds, she felt rather warm and unbuttoned her coat. Then she sneezed.

"Don't you catch a cold now, Sunshine," Papa said. "We don't need you pulling to a stop, too."

"It's the dust, Papa," she said. Or was it? *Lord, please don't let me get sick.*

Papa eyed her suspiciously. "We'll spend the night here and head down to Silverton the day after tomorrow."

"Day after tomorrow?" Eliana frowned. "We're so close. Shouldn't we be there already?" Sneezing again, she grabbed a handkerchief from her pocket.

"No need to worry. We've plenty of time yet, and Sampson isn't the only one that needs a rest."

"If we must." Eliana worried her lip.

"It's not like my Eli to pout," Papa teased. "I heard the hotel here pays special attention to women. It's unfortunate that they won't know you are one."

"Regardless, I intend to take a nice long bath and wash my hair—what little of it I have left." She reached back and adjusted the short ponytail behind her head. It had been nice to let it grow during the winter, but it was better this way for her disguise.

"Unlike you, seems like each winter that goes by I have less of my own to worry about." Papa chuckled.

"What do you mean? You still have a good head of hair." She lifted his hat from his head and set it back again and laughed.

Papa scratched his beard. "I think it's finding a new location on my chin. Speaking of which, did you bring some extra charcoal to darken your jaw?"

"Yes, Papa. I've thought of everything."

The following day, word got around that a photographer was in town, so Van Horn Photography set up shop in the hotel lobby. Papa spent the afternoon making tintypes for customers. Eliana remained upstairs in her room to nurse her cold—Papa's orders. Checking on her often, he brought her chicken soup and ginger root tea. She passed the time reading her Bible, napping, and dreaming of Yiska.

She awoke the next morning with renewed energy. Her head began to clear. But raucous burros had brayed half the night, disturbing Papa's sleep. The songsters corralled next to the hotel hadn't bothered her at all. Papa had agreed to photograph the town buildings that morning, so Eliana offered to lend a hand.

"But you've hardly had time to recover." Papa yawned.

"I believe I'm more revived than you after that midnight serenade." Eliana ignored further protests and headed to the livery to fetch Sampson and the wagon.

After the productive morning, the mayor treated them to a wonderful meal of roast wild turkey and sweet potatoes at the Hungry Burro—though Papa didn't find the name of the restaurant amusing in the least.

That afternoon, the gradual descent into the valley of Silverton proved much easier on Sampson, and on the Van Horns. Eliana admired the snow-crowned mountaintops and the valley cloaked in green.

"The Silver Queen." She sighed. "How pleasant to meet you, your majesty." *Have you seen my handsome prince?*

Papa left the mule hitched outside the Earl Hotel while he and his "son" took their baggage inside. Eliana didn't mind playing the role but had to keep her awe in check when she saw the splendor of the beautiful hotel where they would spend the next few days.

When they went back outside, a crowd surged down the boardwalk. An old fellow plowed into Eliana. With nothing but a "Pardon me, lad," he continued on his way.

"What's all the commotion?" Papa asked a passerby.

"There's a preacher in town. Called a meeting at the Last Call Saloon."

"It must be Reverend Darley," Eliana said. Would he have news of Yiska?

"That's no place for a. . .for you." Papa caught his near miss when someone walked by. "Bring Sampson and the wagon over to the livery, Eli, and then you can go back to the hotel and relax. I'd like to hear Reverend Darley preach. And I'll find out if he got word to Yiska."

Disappointed, she untied Sampson, climbed aboard, and took the reins. "I'll see you back at the hotel."

After delivering the wagon and mule, she stepped outside the livery and shoved her hands into her pockets. She looked down the road at the mob entering one of the saloons. It wasn't fair that she couldn't go hear the reverend preach, but no reputable woman would dare set foot in a place called the Last Call Saloon. Then again, "Eli" Van Horn could go in her stead. She dusted the dirt from her sleeves and swaggered down the street.

With her shoulders held back, Eliana stepped into the saloon and made her way through the throng of men and unfamiliar odors. Every nook filled with eager men waiting to hear what the minister had to say, whether out of sincerity or curiosity. At the far end of the long room she saw Papa. She'd keep to the rear, well out of his view. She shuffled past men of all ages, some in day suits, but most in work clothes. A voluptuous woman in a knee-length, low-cut dress of red satin and black lace pushed past her. Eliana found a barrel in the corner and hopped up. Even so, she could only get an intermittent glimpse of Reverend Darley as the crowd shifted around her. But at least she could hear the message.

Dice scattered on the floor as Reverend Darley rallied an audience by pounding his fist on a faro table. "Gentlemen, such a fine day to meet with you. I appreciate your taking a break from gambling to hear the Word of the good Lord."

As Darley surveyed his murmuring audience, Eliana scanned the sea of hats before her. She hoped to catch sight of a certain dented one, but she knew it was unlikely that Yiska would patronize a saloon, even if he was in town.

Darley extended his hand, revealing a silver piece. The crowd hushed. "I found this Spanish coin along the Old Spanish Trail. I thought I'd discovered silver when I saw it sparkle in the sunlight. It was silver all right, but I was fooled. What I found was evidence that men have searched for treasure in these parts for centuries." He lowered the volume of his voice, and all paid careful attention. "Folks have found coins and tools left by the Spaniards when they mined these very mountains. Many of those places remain hidden, because they were without the means to mine the lode in this dangerous place. Nor did they want to pay the king his royal fifth." A few in the assembly chuckled. "Indians buried the mines because they valued land more than mineral. Today we have but legends and hearty souls like you."

"Do you know where the treasure is, Brother Darley?" someone shouted.

"I reckon I do," he said, and all the men listened. "Silverton got its name because, although there isn't much gold here, you have silver by the ton." Men raised their glasses and cheered.

"Not so long ago, they called your fine town Baker's Park. Charles Baker's team came here looking for gold but missed the silver altogether."

"That's right, he did, leaving more for us," a voice mocked. Laughter erupted around the room.

"Job said, 'Surely there is a vein for the silver, and a place for the gold where they fine it.' A prospector once argued me on that passage saying the word 'fine' should be 'find.' A prospector always hopes to find hidden treasure. But this verse refers to the found treasure that must be extracted and purified. Many of you know the treasure I'm speaking of. You've heard about it from your youth, but left it back east in pursuit of the San Juan bonanza. What have you forsaken to go after riches that remain hidden, when a greater treasure lies in God's Word?"

The men were silent. Eliana fought her fatigue, not wanting to miss a single word of the message.

"Friends!" Eliana jumped at the preacher's resounding voice. "While you are trying to strike it rich on earth, remember there is a greater lode in heaven."

Eliana sneezed and rubbed the tip of her nose with the back of her gloved hand. To her dismay, when she looked up her gaze fixed on a familiar set of eyes.

Chapter 13

Mutual recognition prompted Eliana to scoot through the side door and follow her acquaintance into the back alley. "Mr. Crawford, whatever are you doing here in Silverton?"

Cornelius Crawford eyed her up and down, perusing her male attire. "I could ask you the same thing"—he snickered—"*Miss* Van Horn."

Eliana's face heated. "Oh please, Mr. Crawford, promise me you will not give my identity away," she whispered. "It's a matter of safety."

"Promise? Like you promised to take my photograph back in Del Norte?" Cornelius chided.

"I do apologize, but I never saw you again, nor did you come see us."

"Suppose you have a point there. Tell me, little missy, what are you doing dressed like a feller? Ya almost had me fooled, 'cept for those pretty eyes of yours."

A deep voice penetrated the still air. "I'd like to know the answer to that myself." Eliana's eyes widened. It was Grover, one of those evil men who put Yiska in jail.

"Out of the way, old man. I have a little unfinished business with the lady." Grover pointed his revolver at Cornelius and slithered toward Eliana, hunger in his eyes. Cornelius scurried down the boardwalk away from the gun.

Eliana inched backward but found herself against a wall. Grover leaned in against her. Her stomach lurched, and she pushed uselessly against his chest.

Thwack! Yiska's hatchet pinned Eliana's attacker to the building by the sleeve of his duster. She ducked out of the way as Yiska jumped the brute and thrust his gun into the man's back.

As he retrieved his hatchet, the man's coat ripped.

"Easy there, that's new," the brute growled.

Yiska grabbed him by the collar. "Put your hands on your head and turn around. Slowly."

Grover. One of the thugs from Del Norte. "Had a feelin' I'd see you again."

Cornelius Crawford reappeared with the law in tow.

"I'll be glad to take him off your hands."

Yiska looked around to find the deputy sheriff behind him, eyeing them suspiciously.

Eliana stepped forward. "Mr. Crawford. This man in the duster is the one who attacked me, is it not?"

"Yes, miss. . .mister," Crawford said.

Eliana smiled. The man had redeemed himself at last. She heaved a deep sigh and pulled her hat lower as the deputy hauled Grover away.

"Thank you, Mr. Crawford. You've done a good thing."

"I may be down on my own luck, but you can count on me."

Eliana opened her mouth as if to speak.

A chorus of "Amens" arose from inside the saloon. Yiska stepped between the pair and ushered them back inside the saloon. He squeezed Eliana's arm. "We've a sermon to finish hearing."

The crowd inside the Last Call seemed even more attentive than before. Reverend Darley did have a convincing way about him.

The preacher continued his discourse. "The wealth hidden in the earth cannot be obtained easily. Men must work to contrive ways to get the hidden treasure into their hands."

"He's got that right," Crawford whispered.

Yiska elbowed him and then caught Eliana's gaze. She immediately lowered her lashes. Despite her attire, she looked every bit as pleasing as he remembered. His heart raced.

"Consider the miners then. Let their courage, diligence, and constancy in seeking the wealth that perishes urge us to seek true riches. The great King Solomon said it is far better to get wisdom than silver or gold. Yet these minerals are sought and grace neglected. Should not the certain prospect of heavenly riches compel us more? Come, your heavenly Father beckons you, His gift of grace waiting to bestow."

Tears streamed down Crawford's cheeks. "Lord, have mercy on this sinner," he whispered.

A chorus of men began to sing a hymn, and others joined in. Yiska watched as Cornelius Crawford and several other contrite souls stepped forward and met Reverend Darley in front of the faro table. Yiska bowed his head in respect as Darley ended the meeting in prayer. When he looked up, Eliana was gone.

Eliana hurried to the hotel and up the stairs to the Van Horns' suite. Once inside, she leaned against the closed door to catch her breath. She flung her hat onto the settee and scrubbed her face at the washstand. In the mirror, she studied her disheveled reflection. How could she make herself presentable? Surely Yiska would come to find her.

Eliana brushed her hair in haste and secured it in a celluloid headband, allowing her locks to hang onto her shoulders. In her private room, she pulled off her boots and rummaged for the one dress she had packed, a light brown gingham. Her lace-up boots were nowhere to be had. Slippers would have to do. She passed through the heavily draped doorway to the parlor, where she plucked a few petals from a fresh bouquet sitting on the center table. She crushed the petals in her palm and rubbed the scent against her wrists and the back of her neck, hoping she wouldn't smell like. . .a man.

No sooner had she plopped down on the settee and shoved her hat behind it, than a knock sounded at the door. She stood, smoothing her dress, and went to greet her company. She opened the door a crack. Piercing brown eyes stared back at her.

"Yiska, please come in. Papa will be here soon." She opened the door and beckoned him into the room as if nothing were out of the ordinary. "I was hoping to see you."

"Were you? Why did you leave the saloon?"

Eliana could feel the warmth creep up her neck. Hand to her chest she said, "You must be having a delusion. Or perhaps you have me confused with someone else."

His eyes narrowed beneath the brim of his hat. "They say everyone has a twin."

"Do they?" she asked nonchalantly. "Let me take your hat. Is this new?"

Yiska took it from his head and deposited it on hers. "Yup. That's about right." He rubbed his jaw with his thumb, indicating with the angle of his mouth that there must be a remnant of charcoal grease still on her face. Instant recollection of the first time they met, when she had newsprint all over her chin, made her face color again.

"Don't do that," Yiska said.

"What?" she asked.

"Blush."

"I'm sorry." Eliana's cheeks flamed even more.

He tossed the hat on a chair. "You know, you are irresistible. . .even dressed like a cowhand."

She swatted the air. "Cowhand?"

Yiska laughed.

"It's embarrassing to have you see me like that." Eliana winced in shame.

A slight curve appeared at corner of his mouth.

"Thank you for protecting me from Grover. I only wish he could have heard Reverend Darley's message. It might have had a positive impact on him."

Yiska shrugged. "Let's hope a little jail time will have a similar effect."

"I'm surprised that you were at the saloon," she said. "As I recall, you haven't a fondness for them."

"The preacher invited me. How could I say no?" Yiska's brow wrinkled. "He's a very convincing man."

"That he is." Eliana walked to the window and fingered the lace curtain as she looked into the street. Hoping for some cool air, she attempted to open the window.

Yiska came up behind her. "Here, let me do that."

As the gentle breeze entered the room she turned to him. "How did you know I was there and in trouble?"

He hesitated. "I prayed for you. Then I heard a sneeze and when I turned around, I saw you in the back. I went to find you, but you'd disappeared. Figured you might have seen me and left out the back."

"I never saw you, though I did see Cornelius. I followed him to the alley to ask him to keep my identity secret. That's when Grover showed up." Eliana cocked her head and grinned. "Did you say you prayed for me?"

Yiska nodded. "I did."

A flood of reassurance washed over her.

"You'll have to get used to the fact that I'll see you in your disguise," Yiska said.

"You're going on the survey!" Eliana's mouth blossomed into a smile.

"I am. Mr.—I mean, Reverend Darley found me at Rose's Cabin and gave me the good news. I hoped I'd find you here and not have to wait until the rendezvous at Animas City."

"I'm glad you found me," Eliana said, her voice barely above a whisper.

Yiska stepped closer. "Like a hidden treasure." He lifted a hand and toyed with her hair. Then he brushed the back of his fingers over her cheek and lower lip with a featherlight touch.

Her stomach tightened and she tried to remain calm. Was he going to kiss her again?

❧

"Look who I found in the restaur—" Papa burst through the doorway holding a tray of dishes with their evening meal. Reverend Darley, behind him, carried another.

Yiska stepped back from Eliana and rushed toward the door

to assist Papa. "Mr. Van Horn. Reverend Darley. How good to see you. Let me take that." He took the tray and set it on the table then retrieved the other from the minister.

Eliana faced the window for a moment, hoping the fresh air would cool her cheeks. Then she turned to greet them. What must he and Papa have thought when they opened the door?

"It is a pleasure to see you again, Miss Van Horn," Reverend Darley said. "Though your father warned me I might find you in different attire. You look lovely."

"That you do, daughter." Papa kissed her on the cheek. He couldn't be too upset.

As she approached the table, the aroma of rosemary and thyme greeted her senses. Generous servings of beef, new potatoes, and a medley of vegetables filled four plates.

"There's enough for four. Are we expecting company?" Eliana asked Papa.

Papa look at Yiska. "I believe he is already here. You're welcome to join us, Yiska. In fact, this plate is for you. George told me you were in town, and I had a suspicion that we'd see you sooner rather than later."

Yiska looked at the mountain of food. "Much obliged. I can't recall the last time I saw such a feast."

"Let's sit then," Eliana said. "Reverend Darley, we'd be honored if you would ask the blessing on the meal."

Following the prayer they ate quietly, enjoying the food. After Papa took his last bite, he removed the cloth napkin tucked in his vest and wiped his mouth. "Yiska, we were concerned that you wouldn't get the word in time to go on the expedition. You must be thrilled to be going on the survey. And, by the way, we're right proud of you."

"Thank you, Mr. Van Horn."

Fearful her emotions would betray her, Eliana lowered her gaze. She retired to the settee and listened as the men continued the conversation.

"God has a way of making divine appointments," Darley said.

"Isn't that right, Yiska?"

"It was good timing meeting up with Reverend Darley. He's been entertaining me with his tall tales all the way down from Rose's Cabin," Yiska said.

Darley placed his hand on Yiska's shoulder. "This young man has a tale of his own to tell. Something about a little meeting with a family of bears."

Yiska recounted his adventure in his humble way. "It means a lot to know that folks were praying for me. Guess that's what spared my life." When his gaze met Eliana's, his eyes glowed with appreciation for her prayers. A quiet understanding grew between them, and a restful peace came over Eliana, inducing her sleepy eyes to close.

"Papa." Eliana awoke as her father covered her with an afghan. She lay reclined on the settee, the room dark except for the faint light of a gasolier. Both Reverend Darley and Yiska had left. When had she dozed off?

"You might want to get up and sleep in your bed. It might be your last time sleeping in comfort for a while. I'm going to turn in now, too. Good night, Sunshine." He kissed her on the cheek.

"I will. Good night, Papa."

He walked toward the bedchambers then stopped and turned back. "God bless you."

"What's that for?" she asked.

"When you sneezed during Reverend Darley's sermon today."

Chapter 14

Yiska, Eliana, and Papa set out at dawn on horses obtained from the Silverton Livery with Sampson in tow, packed to the hilt with provisions and photography equipment. Yiska and Papa had mailed the interview and photograph of Mr. Snowden to the *San Juan Prospector*. Yiska also notified Mr. Wilson that he was pleased to accept his new assignment as a correspondent for the Robbins survey and asked him to inform Mr. Whiley. Now they were on their way to rendezvous with Chandler Robbins.

Hymns of praise flowed from Eliana's joyful heart. Refraining from singing at the top of her lungs, she sang softly, "Fairest Lord Jesus, ruler of all nature. . ."

Yiska's smile flashed in the sunlight as he pulled up beside her on Shadow. "Don't stop on account of me."

Papa rode up beside them. "I'm afraid she's not one to sing for an audience, though my songbird is worthy of one."

Eliana hoped that the shade from her hat would shelter her face from the bright sun that so easily tanned her complexion, as well as hide the blush that warmed her cheeks.

Yiska pointed from the narrow canyon to the tempestuous Animas River raging between the Needle Mountains. "This river is a terrible serpent. Not even passable at some points. We follow it all the way to Animas City. Don't ride too close to the edge. It's too rocky, and there's not enough shade. Keep to the tree line, and it will give us some protection and make the ride smoother."

The river reflected the azure sky on the almost cloudless day. The temperature warmed as they headed farther south. Eliana removed her overcoat and tied it behind her saddle. By noon the small convoy found an embankment by the river under the shade of the tall pines. She was glad for the respite from the struggle she'd had all morning with her ornery mount, Firefly.

After they'd eaten a frugal lunch, Papa put his pipe back in his pocket and checked Sampson's line. "Time to move on, Eliana." He mounted and rode back up the rocky incline.

"C'mon Firefly, you've had your nourishment." Eliana coaxed her willful horse with a firm tug and braced her boots on the stony ground by the river's edge, trying not to slip. She whistled and clucked as she pulled the horse's reins. "Firefly. Git. Git up here!"

Yiska rode out of the shade. "Stubborn," he said.

"That mare or my daughter?" Papa asked.

Eliana turned and looked at the two men. Yiska's grin didn't escape her notice as he rode by on Shadow. "I could use a little assistance here, gentlemen." She yanked on Firefly's halter, but the mare wouldn't budge.

"You're doing fine, dear. She won't obey you unless you learn to handle her yourself."

"Fine." She begged, she pleaded, and to her own chagrin, she nearly cussed. Her face flushed. She glared at the men, daring them to say a word.

Yiska called out over his shoulder, "You'll catch more flies with honey than with vinegar."

"Some old Indian saying?" Her father chortled.

Yiska hiked his chin and grinned. "Something Mrs. Whiley used to say."

"Well, if there were any honey in this forsaken place, I'd give her some," Eliana huffed.

Yiska made some high pitched kissing sounds. Firefly immediately raised her head, dug in her hooves, and came up the embankment—Eliana in tow. Yiska issued a satisfied nod.

"How'd you do that?" she asked.

"Like this." He pursed his lips together once again.

Eliana glared at him and shot a glance at her father, relieved that he was looking away. "Yiska. . ." she whispered, between clenched teeth. "How did you know it would *work*?" She cocked her head. "Some secret way of the Navajo?"

"Let's see. You made every other sound possible. Figured I'd give that one a try."

"Well, thank you. I've more experience with mules than with horses."

"My pleasure." Yiska patted Shadow on the neck and put light pressure on the animal's belly with one knee. The horse turned and proceeded toward the ridge. He trotted ahead to scout out the trail.

"Show off," she muttered under her breath.

Papa let out a chuckle at the exchange and pulled his own horse around. "He's all right in my book. But you'd best mind your manners."

"My manners?" Eliana asked.

"Don't want to stir up any trouble, especially after we get to the rendezvous."

"Would you care to explain?"

Papa pinched his eyebrows to let her know he was serious. "We have a lot of miles yet to travel. Don't encourage him."

Eliana tried to ignore the accusation and let out an exasperated breath. With one foot in the stirrup, she hoisted herself up on Firefly. Papa didn't really think she'd risk the expedition by entertaining notions of romance, did he? With a kissing noise she urged her horse forward.

After a rough twenty-four miles from Silverton, Yiska led the Van Horns to the shelter of ponderosa pines to camp for the night. He dismounted and took in a deep breath of the pine scented air then gathered branches and leaves to prepare a lean-to while Eliana and Mr. Van Horn set up their small canvas tents. They gave the horses and mule some oats and water from the stream. Then Yiska stretched a line between two trees and tethered the animals. He made a fire, and Mr. Van Horn heated some canned hash, boiled some coffee, and offered a prayer of thanks. After they ate, Van Horn read a short passage out loud from his Bible. As they sat around the campfire in the twilight of the early June evening, they listened to the sounds of the rushing river and chirping tree frogs.

"We made good progress today. You both did well when we had to ride up those ridges. The rest of the way will go a little easier." Yiska stirred the fire with the end of a branch. "We should get to Baker's Bridge by late morning."

"How far is that?" Eliana asked.

"About ten or twelve miles," he said. "Then another twelve to Animas City. We should get there by sundown tomorrow."

Eliana let out a deep sigh. "I'll be so glad to get there." She rubbed her legs. "I'm so tired and sore."

Mr. Van Horn tapped his empty pipe on his knee. "You're not used to all the riding. But I'm afraid there'll be much more of it ahead, my dear. The expedition hasn't even commenced." He raised an eyebrow. "Other than that, how are you holding up? I haven't heard any sneezing."

Eliana stretched, issuing a low moan when her body protested. She mumbled as she lumbered toward the river's edge. "I'm fine. . . . It's the other end I'm worried about."

Yiska cocked his head, covering his mouth to smother a laugh.

Van Horn chuckled as he got up, Bible in hand. "I'll turn in now so I can be up for the second watch."

Eliana placed her fingertips on her lips then turned them toward her father, sending him a good-night kiss. "Sleep well, Papa. I'll go to my tent shortly."

Yiska observed the closeness between the two. They meant everything to each other.

"Be sure to wake me, Yiska," Van Horn said.

"You bet." Although they weren't in hostile Indian territory, small parties kept guard. There was always the danger of wild animals or the occasional desperate soul who ran dry while prospecting the river to beware of. Good thing Eliana could handle a weapon.

Yiska wandered to where she stood, her silhouette like a male. But underneath the manly clothes, he knew she was every bit a woman—the woman he was falling hard for.

Eliana took off her hat and untied the cord from her hair, her tousled locks falling around her face. Her hat dropped to the ground, and Yiska picked it up. Their eyes met as he handed it to her, but neither of them spoke.

The firelight, reflected in her eyes and gave the illusion that he could see deep into her heart. He longed to kiss her, passionately, as he did the first time their lips met, but he dared not. He had to train himself to keep a proper emotional distance for the expedition. Maybe when it was over...

A branch snapped. Eliana let out a tiny gasp. Their heads darted in the direction of the noise, Yiska's hand ready at his side. He caught a glimpse of the white tails of deer fleeing into the woods.

Eliana sighed in relief. "Perhaps I'm not cut out for this." She turned and took a few steps away.

Yiska walked up behind her and wrapped his arms around her. With his head nestled over her shoulder he spoke into her ear in a low voice. "Eliana, this is your dream. Every moment, all of it. Even when you're tired or afraid. You're braver than you realize, and you will do this, and do it well."

She sniffed and put her hand up to her face to wipe her tears. She clung to his arms, and her breathing relaxed. There they stayed as one, watching the light of the moon dance upon the river.

When Eliana awoke the next morning before dawn, breakfast was already cooking on the fire, and Cornelius Crawford was serving it up.

"Mornin' Miss...I mean, young man." His whiskered cheeks framed a toothless grin. "I came in last night after you all had retired. I'd have caught up with you sooner, but I got a little off track. Betcha didn't know I'm going on that survey expedition to New Mexico with you."

Astonished, Eliana placed both hands on her hips. "I'm surprised you're leaving your mine behind."

Papa and Yiska emerged from their shelters dumbfounded.

"You didn't say anything about that when you came into camp last night," Yiska said.

Cornelius handed Eliana a plate of beans, bacon, and biscuits. "Told you I was down on my luck. Lost my gold claim in a card game. But since I gave my heart to Jesus, He's been blessin' me and helping me get my life in order. I gave up the whiskey and even got me a job."

"I take it you have a job on the expedition then," Papa said.

"Sure do. I wuz hired as the cook. Providin' I can get down to Animas City in time." Cornelius chewed on a piece of bacon and smacked his lips.

"All this in a matter of a couple of days, Crawford?" Yiska asked.

"You betcha," the reformed miner said.

Papa chuckled. "Sounds like a genuine miracle. Glad to have you along." Yiska choked on his coffee and shook his head.

They rode along at a good pace, making their way through the gorge. Eliana breathed in the fresh morning air and relaxed as she and Firefly fell into a steady gait. Peacefulness permeated her heart as she remembered Yiska's soothing words the night before, and the thought of his masculine arms around her.

Yiska rode ahead to scout then circled around to meet the group. "Baker's Bridge is up ahead."

"That's the bridge Charles Baker and his team built back in the sixties, during the gold boom," Papa said. "I'd like to photograph it if you think we can afford the time."

"We'll cross and rest for a spell. Then you can get your pictures," Yiska said.

Eliana contemplated the narrow section of the river where logs were strewn together from one thick section of rock to another. "Is it safe?"

"It's as safe as it ever was." Without hesitation Yiska rode Shadow across and waited on the other side. Papa followed, Sampson trailing behind him. Cornelius came along next on a coal-colored mule loaded with pots and pans.

Eliana sat on Firefly and urged her to cross the bridge, but the horse seemed frightened of the water rushing underneath. Firefly's hooves clopped up and down on the logs, and then she backed up. Eliana tried to ease her forward once again then increased pressure with her heels.

The horse reared and threw Eliana to the ground with a thud. The force pushed the wind from her lungs and left her gasping for breath.

Chapter 15

Eliana coughed and struggled to resume breathing while Yiska and Papa raced across the bridge. They crouched beside her side as she lay on the hard ground.

Beads of perspiration dotted Papa's brow over eyes filled with alarm. "Sunshine, are you all right?"

Eliana clamped her teeth together and grimaced in pain as she attempted to get up.

"Stay still for a minute," Papa said. "You're awfully pale."

"I'm fine, Papa. Please help me sit." The croak in her voice did little to convince even her.

"How can you be fine? That crazy animal just threw you."

When he hesitated, she grabbed his arm and yanked herself to a sitting position. Pain exploded through her body like dynamite in a cave. She took a shaky breath, opened and closed her hands, and made circles with her wrists. Her body seemed to be in working order. Nothing broken. Deep, pebble-filled scratches crisscrossed her palms. Why hadn't she left her gloves on?

Papa carefully brushed the grit from her hands. He then examined her head, feeling for bumps. "Is that tender? There's a small knot back there."

"It is rather sore, but not too bad," she said.

He patted her legs through her trousers, from her thighs all the way down to her boots. "Can you feel your legs?"

"Yes, Papa. Really, I'm fine." She hadn't seen him this worried about her since she fell out of the old oak tree when she was eleven years old. She'd climbed up to check the view of the pastures and fluffy clouds. If she could have figured out how to carry a camera up with her, she might have been able to take a picture of the nest of baby birds she discovered there.

As her thoughts floated about, she hadn't realized she was leaning back with her head against Yiska until she felt the rumble of his voice through his chest. "Should we move her?"

"Yes. Let's take her over there and make her comfortable," Papa said. *Oh, but Papa, I am comfortable here with Yiska.*

A slight groan escaped her when Papa scooped her up. Eliana felt limp as he cradled her in his arms then set her on a grassy hill and propped her against a fallen tree.

Papa bunched his coat behind her for comfort. She looked around to get her bearings.

Cornelius approached and handed Eliana a canteen of water. "Have some of this."

"Thank you. That's very kind of you."

"Yer welcome. Glad to see yer in one piece." The spry old man went back over the bridge, where he'd left the horses and pack animals tethered to an old fence post.

A shock of alarm ran through Eliana. "Firefly! Where. . . ?"

Papa placed his hand on her arm. "Yiska went after her."

She let out a sigh of relief. "Oh, good. He'll find her."

Minutes later Yiska appeared riding her mount, in full control. *My, he looks good on a horse.* Eliana chastised herself for taking such liberties with her thoughts—that fall must've made her giddy.

She widened her eyes as she addressed Yiska. "You're brave."

"She needs to know she can still be ridden." He leaned down and gently rubbed the mare's neck.

"I know. I'll ride her, if you can please get her across the bridge for me."

"That's what I intend to do. But can you ride? Are you hurt?"

His concern moved her. "I'm just sore. I've come this far, and nothing will stop me from going on that expedition." She remembered Yiska's encouraging words from last night and willed her gaze to show her determination.

Papa handed Eliana her hat, interrupting her thoughts. "Eli Van Horn has spoken."

But the warmth in Yiska's eyes reflected hers, answering her unspoken message. "If you can make it another mile we'll noon somewhere special."

&

Eliana rode Shadow for the next mile, while Yiska remained on Firefly. They came into an area with mists rising up from the ground. A huge mound of mineral-laden lava rock came into view. Steaming hot water flowed from the colorful lump into streams all around it.

Her eyes flashed at Yiska in delight. "Hot springs. The streams flow into heated pools of water. The Utes and Navajo have often fought over healing waters like this. I thought a soak might ease your pain—there's enough brush to give you privacy." His thoughtfulness sent a ripple of warmth through her. If the healing balm could be applied to her aching body she'd be whole. This man was taking hold of her entire being.

"Eliana."

She turned to face him.

"I'll show you where you can soak while Crawford fixes something to eat and I tend to the animals. Your Pa's unpacking his camera."

"Oh, that reminds me. He never did photograph Baker's Bridge."

Papa came up beside her. "That's all right, dear. Seeing you fall like that embedded a permanent image of the location in my mind. Reminds me of the time you fell from the oak tree when you were a child and broke your elbow."

Yiska's eyebrows lifted in amusement.

Eliana retreated to the spring. With the men at a discreet distance, she wrestled herself free from the binding around her chest and took the liberty of removing all but her undergarments. She descended into the therapeutic pool, welcoming the warmth and appreciating Yiska's thoughtfulness. She exhaled as she submerged and allowed the tension to dissipate, the hot mineral water soothing her aches and pains.

Through a small place in the vegetation she spied Yiska sitting on a boulder facing the opposite direction, writing in his journal. Papa approached, and they engaged in conversation. Then Yiska jumped up and stomped his boot. Papa rocked up and down on his toes. What were they arguing about?

Mr. Van Horn had never spoken to Yiska like that before. It took all the self-control he had to keep from raising his voice at the man, but he didn't want Eliana to hear them. The sparks that flew during that discussion could have ignited a stick of dynamite.

He knew her father worried about her. The stress of the day must have hit him, but Yiska had done nothing to deserve the condescending lecture. The man nearly blamed him for Eliana's accident. Mr. Van Horn demanded that Yiska do three things: keep her secret, keep her safe, and keep his distance. He understood Van Horn's implied warning—no romance. But when Yiska reminded him that he already had been seeing to her welfare, Van Horn reversed his tone. "If anything ever happens to me," he said, "I'm counting on you to continue to watch out for her."

The man didn't even have to ask.

At the lower elevation, the four travelers marveled as the range opened up into a beautiful valley dotted with several old log homes. Only a handful of families had lived there since the Baker party wintered there in '61, but more folks were moving in to reestablish Animas City. It thrilled Yiska to see Eliana's excitement. Her father's temperament returned to normal as if they'd never had that discussion.

The sun set as the small caravan rode over the grassy knoll, seeking out the trading post where they would find Chandler Robbins. Finally. They had arrived at the rendezvous.

Eliana climbed down from Shadow's back, a bit stiffly, while the others dismounted. Yiska grabbed Shadow's reins and handed the horses off to a hostler. They headed toward the trading post, where a man sat sketching the sunset. As he saw them approach, the man rose with a chuckle and made his way toward them.

Papa quickened his step and held out his hand. "Harland Mattheson? What in God's green earth are you doing in Animas City?"

Eliana recognized the name. Mr. Mattheson's thick beard, though whiter now, and his limp were also familiar. Although anxious to greet him, she hung back and kept her head low.

Reverend Mattheson slapped Papa on the back. "John, old friend. Chandler told me you'd be going on the survey as the official photographer. That was what finally convinced me to come along. Imagine. Three of us from the Ohio 86th Infantry back together again."

"It's great to see you, Harland. What has it been, seven or eight years?" Papa took Reverend Mattheson to the side and spoke to him in a low voice.

Reverend Mattheson looked at Eliana and grinned, and Papa beckoned her to come near. "Look at you. All grown up." Their longtime friend looked her up and down. "I must say you do look quite different from the last time I saw you"—he leaned closer and whispered—"as a girl." The man cleared his throat. "Don't worry; your secret is safe with me."

"Thank you, Reverend Mattheson. It's good to see you. We've missed you a great deal."

"I go by Mr. Mattheson these days. I haven't had a church for some time now. I've been keeping myself occupied as a naturalist."

"Yiska. Cornelius." Papa called the men over. "Harland Mattheson, this is Yiska Wilcox, correspondent for the *San Juan Prospector*. He's also our guide. And Cornelius Crawford, one of the best cooks around."

Eliana was proud of the way Papa made the introductions—especially the way he made Yiska sound so important.

Mr. Mattheson issued a nod. "Gentlemen. Pleased to make your acquaintance."

"Let's go inside and see Robbins and get you all something to eat.

Though I'm sure it won't be nearly as good as Mr. Crawford's cooking, the owner's wife is serving up a nice stew and fresh bread."

Eliana was glad to see the old friend who baptized her as a girl. One thing she knew for sure—she could trust him to keep her identity confidential. He had at least one secret of his own.

Inside the trading post, Papa saluted Chandler Robbins. "Sergeant."

"Lieutenant." Mr. Robbins returned the salute and shook Papa's hand. "John, it's good to see you after all these years. I'm glad Ryder recommended you when he couldn't get away."

"I appreciate that he did. He gave me my start. Taught me photography right on the battlefield." Eliana listened with interest, as her father seldom discussed his past.

"What about you?" Mr. Robbins asked. "I understand you do contract work for the GLO. They were pleased to have you sign on for the survey."

"I'm doing fairly well. It's hard work documenting the mining areas, but we also have a small studio up in Lake City to serve the community."

Mr. Robbins arched his thick eyebrows. "Hell's Acre?"

"That den of evil is only a remote section of town. The folks in Lake City officially established a fine town last year. There's even talk of building a church."

"Is that so?" Mr. Mattheson asked.

"Yes, George Darley was out recently. In fact, we heard him preach at home and then up in Silverton. He drew quite a crowd at the Last Call Saloon," Papa said.

Mr. Mattheson chortled. "Leave it to George. Can't say that I've heard a sermon in some time. But I've no one to blame for that but myself."

"John, you keep referring to 'we,'" Mr. Robbins said.

"Of course, excuse me." Papa called Eliana over, though she stood only a few feet away.

"This is Eli, my son and my photography assistant. This is Chandler Robbins."

With a nod, Eliana acknowledged the impressive, rugged man. She hoped he wouldn't think her rude for not shaking his hand, but hers still stung from the fall. Besides, she felt it would be proper if he made the advance first, since he was the man in charge.

"Sir, it's a pleasure to meet you. I've heard a great deal about you," she said in a masculine timbre.

Mr. Robbins dipped his chin. "If you're any bit like your father, I'm sure you'll be a great asset to the team."

Mr. Robbins regarded Papa. "Any other children?"

"No, only the one."

"And your wife?"

"I lost her several years ago."

"Must not have been easy raising a kid on your own, but I see he turned out all right." Mr. Robbins turned toward Eli.

Eliana shoved her hands in her pockets, her eyes scanning the gentlemen. Mr. Mattheson looked every bit as uncomfortable as her father. Papa cleared his throat and nodded.

"Watch yourself there!" Heads turned to see a disgruntled man of about thirty, who had been lingering nearby, wipe spilled coffee from the front of his suit.

"Pardon me." Yiska took a bandanna from his pocket and dabbed at the man's chest.

"Don't touch me! Who let this savage in here?" the well-dressed man barked.

Robbins walked up to the pair, and Papa followed. "Hold on now. It's just a little accident," Mr. Robbins said.

"Do you know how much I paid for this suit?"

"I don't want to know. You should have left it in New York City and brought proper clothing." Mr. Robbins made a point of scanning the worn and dusty outfits of the men around him. "Gentlemen, meet Warren Cates from *Atlantic Monthly Magazine*."

Warren Cates straightened as Mr. Robbins made the introductions. Then Robbins eyed Yiska. "I don't believe we've met."

Yiska's eyes shifted to Eliana's father and then back to Mr. Robbins again.

Papa interjected, "This is Yiska Wilcox. He's here to do feature work for the *San Juan Prospector*."

Mr. Robbins looked Yiska square in the face, as if he expected more. Papa continued, "Yiska is also your guide."

Robbins looked Yiska over with a satisfying nod then looked hard at the agitator. "Now hear that, Cates. Next to me, Mr. Wilcox is the most important person on this expedition, and I expect you to treat him as such."

Eliana doubted Robbins normally treated his guides with much respect, but he surely knew how to put Warren Cates in his place.

"I've heard you're one of the best guides around," Robbins said. "I wouldn't be surprised if your travels have given you plenty of interesting things to write about."

Mr. Cates harrumphed.

Eliana restrained herself from boasting about the Anonymous Explorer.

"Thank you. I've read some of your work and studied your maps. Superior detail," Yiska said.

"I appreciate your good opinion. More will be published next year—including this survey of the four corners." Robbins scratched behind his ear. "I'd like to go over the maps with you after you grab some supper, and then we'll all meet outdoors to go over the itinerary."

An hour later the entire survey team gathered around a campfire, fifteen in all.

"My goal is to confirm the coordinates from the Washington meridian and reset the marker at the intersection of Colorado, Utah, Arizona, and New Mexico," Robbins told them. "From there we'll go south to establish the boundary between the New Mexico and Arizona territories."

Eliana listened attentively to every word.

"I emphasize my goal. I've been commissioned by the U. S. General Land Office. All others have been hired on to support the mission. Some of you are joining us of your own volition, like Harland Mattheson, a naturalist, or on assignment, like the journalists Warren Cates and Yiska Wilcox."

Mr. Cates rolled his eyes.

"No one is indispensible, and I'll not hesitate to dismiss anyone who interferes with my progress."

Mr. Robbins looked at Yiska. "Wilcox will also serve as our guide. He has a few words about our journey."

Eliana felt so proud of Yiska; it was hard not to smile at him as he spoke. "We have over three hundred miles in all to travel, and although you can feel the chill in the air tonight, we will leave these mountains for the heat of the desert. We'll follow the Animas River south to New Mexico, where it joins the Rio San Juan. Don't underestimate the rivers. The Spaniards called the Animas the 'River of Lost Souls.'"

Yiska hadn't mentioned that before, and it struck Eliana as both eerie and poetic.

He continued. "But that isn't the only danger we might encounter. It's twenty miles to the border, and most of it is in Ute territory. Stay armed and together. If all goes well, we'll make it into New Mexico by nightfall tomorrow."

Robbins clapped his hands together. "All right, fellas, let's get to bed. We're pulling out at first light."

As the men adjourned, Eliana followed Yiska to tell him she thought he did a fine job explaining things.

Warren Cates got there first. " 'River of Lost Souls?' I heard the river got its name because that's where the Indians buried their enemy's bodies." Cates sneered at Yiska. "Don't go getting any ideas."

"Don't give him a reason," Eliana hissed.

Cates pivoted around. "Indian lover."

She'd defended Yiska again. Now what could she say? "He can take care of himself. But I don't like you carrying a grudge before we even begin the excursion. It's not fair to the team."

Cates started to grab her by the neck, but Yiska's arm flew up to stop him.

"Leave the kid alone and get out of here." The muscles in Yiska's jaw tightened.

Cates contorted his face and tromped off like an irritated mountain goat.

Yiska walked into the darkness without turning back. Eliana did not follow.

At daybreak Eliana and Papa took some photographs of the train of pack mules, wagons loaded with provisions, and armed men on horseback ready to embark on their journey. Chandler Robbins rode at the head of the column with Yiska beside him. She would not get to speak to Yiska to offer an apology until they stopped for a rest, but from what he explained about the Utes, she wasn't even sure that would happen. Eliana yawned as she put the camera back into the pack. She'd tossed and turned all night. She anticipated having trouble sleeping the night before the survey commenced, but all she thought about was the trouble she had made for Yiska. The pressure in her heart squeezed the joy right out of her.

Along the way, Papa and Mr. Mattheson enjoyed catching up on the years. Mr. Mattheson told Papa how he had become a naturalist. Some of his sketches and descriptions had even been published in a scientific journal. The sun rose high in the sky, and at last the convoy stopped to have a meal and rest the animals.

Papa and Mr. Mattheson sat on a log with their rifles propped by their sides, engrossed in conversation while eating their fill of fritters and coffee. Eliana went over to tend Firefly. She petted her nose and wondered if her mount was as sore as she was. Her body still complained from the harsh fall and longed for another soak in the hot springs.

Yiska appeared with Shadow in tow.

"You startled me," Eliana said.

He rested his hand on her saddle. "Have you watered her yet?"

"No. But I need to."

"Come with me."

They led their horses past Papa, Mr. Mattheson, and Mr. Robbins. "I'm taking Eli down to water his horse," Yiska called out.

Papa waved, hardly aware of their presence.

They traveled in silence to a small hill overlooking a wide stream. Aspens offered a shady retreat. Eliana found her confidence and faced Yiska. "I'm sorry. I shouldn't have defended you to Mr. Cates like that."

"You're right. You shouldn't have." She couldn't read anything into his flat tone. Was he angry? Of course he was.

Her eyes stung, but she refused to cry in front of him. "I'm going to take Firefly down to the stream."

"I'll go with you."

She looked back at him. "No. I mean, I need some privacy. I have a few things to tend to. Please keep your back turned."

Yiska's mouth drew into a tight line. "All right. Don't be long."

She led Firefly down the slope and let her drink from the clear mountain water. Eliana knelt down by her, cupped her hands, and took an icy sip. She tossed her hat to the ground, released her straggly plait, and shook out her hair. She would fix it in a moment. She spotted some high bushes nearby and retreated behind them to relieve herself. Now untucked, dare she adjust the bindings that camouflaged her figure?

She removed her neckerchief and unbuttoned down to the top of her underbodice. She knelt back down near the stream and splashed her face and neck, letting the water trickle down her chest. The days were growing hotter, as Yiska had warned. The frigid water and the gentle breeze invigorated her. In a few more hours they would reach New Mexico, where they'd stop for the night. She could do this. It wasn't an easy journey, but she was determined to endure any hardship—including Yiska's disappointment in her, and her disappointment with herself. *Please Lord, let him forgive and trust me again.*

A hard lump caught in her throat as she tried not to weep. Pain intensified throughout her body. She lowered her head and released tears like a torrent.

A shadow flickered across her reflection in the water. She was not alone. Had Yiska come to find her?

A wave of fear assailed her. Eliana turned and gasped—a lone Ute Indian loomed in front of her.

Eliana struggled to get to her feet, but he lunged forward and held her with the sharp point of a knife to her neck. She stared into his black eyes and let out shallow breaths. Where was her voice now?

Chapter 16

Yiska pulled his journal from his saddlebag and fumbled through the pages. A page had been torn out, and Eliana's photograph was missing. The private words that he'd penned about Eliana up in the flowery basin—gone. Someone was up to no good.

Warren Cates. *He knows that Eli is a girl.* Yiska's chest tightened. Blood pulsed through the veins of his forearms as he squeezed the leather tome.

In the distance, Firefly neighed and stomped. Alarm ripped through his body. *Eliana!*

Yiska tore down the hill, boots stirring up dust and stones. Firefly pawed the ground, her nose pointing to the overgrowth. Adrenaline exploded through Yiska's body. He broke through the bushes and found Eliana pinioned against a boulder.

Yiska's breath seethed through clenched teeth as he flung himself onto her attacker. The Ute rolled over and sprang to his feet. Yiska lunged at him, grabbing his wrist so hard the bone dagger dropped from his grip. The Ute seized Yiska's waist and threw him to the ground. They wrestled over dirt and pine needles. Rocks cut into Yiska's shins.

Yiska straddled the warrior, pinning the man's body between his legs, and held his own knife at the enemy's neck. Piercing eyes of hot coal glared at him. *God, help me!*

A strange shift from anger to answer brought Yiska to his senses. To kill the man would bring more trouble. As he kept the Indian pinned to the ground, knife at his throat, Yiska spoke the Piute word for 'trade,' one of the survival words he knew. "*Nararwop*."

His face like stone, the warrior issued a slight nod, acknowledging agreement.

Yiska sliced through the Indian's beaded bone neckpiece. A warning. He jerked his chin, motioning the man to get up.

The Ute stood resolute. The lean and muscular build above his breechcloth and leggings revealed brute strength. Yiska drew his revolver for insurance.

The Indian made a guttural sound as he angled his head toward Eliana, where she hovered on the ground. "*Mamachi.*"

With a sharp jab to his chest Yiska answered. "Mamachi—*My* woman."

Yiska pointed at Eliana's horse. "*Poonggo.*" He inched back and untied Firefly from the large root where Eliana had secured her. He had to appease the oppressor to ensure their safety.

The Indian took a step forward.

Yiska raised his hand, and the Ute halted. Yiska grabbed Eliana's rifle from the scabbard attached to her saddle and placed it on the ground behind him. He released Firefly's girth and tossed the saddle to the ground in one sweep—blanket, pack, and all. Yiska motioned for the Indian to come forward and stepped away from the horse.

The renegade whisked himself up on the mare's bare back and rode away with the force of a sandstorm, echoes of screams trailing behind him.

Yiska released the wind from his lungs and turned to Eliana. He pulled her to her feet and wrapped his arm around her waist as they ascended the steep incline, keeping his ear tuned to potential danger. He took Eliana's saddle and gear, hoisted it up in front of Shadow's saddle, and mounted his horse in one swift motion. Then he stretched his arm to Eliana and helped her up behind him.

She wrapped her arms around his waist and laid her head against his back. Yiska dug his heels into the sides of his faithful mount, and Shadow bolted. After riding a short distance, they stopped in a grove of piñon trees.

Yiska dismounted, placed a firm grip around Eliana's waist, and lowered her from his horse into his embrace.

"Will he return?" she asked.

"No. I'm sure of it. And if there were others, we'd have seen them by now." He stepped back and cupped her face in his hands. The very hands that had almost killed a man now held the one he loved. The mystery of it confounded him.

Eliana's eyes still held fear. "Why didn't you kill him?"

His eyes widened. "Is that what you wanted?"

Arms wrapped around him, she grabbed a fistful of his buckskin shirt in her hands. "No. But a few times I thought it might happen."

"If I killed him, there'd be more trouble to contend with. The Utes take a life for a life. None of us would be safe until they avenged him."

The fear in Eliana's eyes waned and became like dew.

Yiska swallowed hard. "I had to say that."

"That I am your woman?" Hazel eyes looked up at him from beneath her dark lashes.

"Yes."

She wet her lower lip. "Am I?"

Yiska leaned his forehead against hers, and they took in the same air with shallow breaths. As he brushed the hair from her face, he felt her tremble. She was shivering.

Yiska lowered his gaze and noticed a graceful neck and collarbone, soft enough to touch. Her top few buttons were undone. With gentle ministrations he fastened them, one by one. He could almost feel her beating heart, and knew she must feel the pounding of his when she placed her palm against his chest.

The thunder of hoofbeats came upon them, and a small posse of men pointed their rifles straight at Yiska.

"Papa, no!" Eliana cried. Half a dozen men approached on horseback, looking more like a lynch mob than the cavalry.

Papa cocked his rifle. "That's my daughter you've got there. Move away from her."

"That's right, Wilcox. Nice and slow," Mr. Robbins echoed.

"Eliana, come over here." Her father's face was like stone.

Eliana walked up to the cavalcade, no bindings in place and her hair hanging in tangles down to her shoulders. She stood by her father's side. "Papa, you have it all wrong. A Ute attacked. Yiska saved me."

The group of men shifted their attention and scanned the area. A couple of them circled back and kept guard.

Warren Cates rode in a little closer. "That's not what it looked like from here. Looked like Wilcox was the Indian doing the attacking."

How dare he verbalize such an accusation? And in the presence of all these men, already gawking at her.

"Eliana, are you all right?" Mr. Mattheson asked.

Robbins narrowed his eyes, seething.

Eliana nodded toward Mr. Mattheson. Papa kept his eyes on her as he got off his horse. When he pulled her into the safety of his arms, she broke into tears.

Every bit the commander, Mr. Robbins pressed for details. "Where are the Utes now, Yiska? Why didn't you signal an alert?"

"It just happened. There was only one Ute, and I managed to trade Eliana's horse for her release. I'm confident the agreement satisfied him. I didn't want to risk an Indian war."

An odd twinge disturbed Eliana at the thought that her horse was more valuable to the Indian than she was. But what mattered was her value to Yiska. "Gentlemen. Stop pointing your guns at Yiska. He has done nothing wrong. . .or inappropriate. He handled the situation well."

"Do you care to share why we found you as we did just now?" Mr. Cates asked.

"*That* is none of your concern, Cates." Papa scolded.

"I beg to differ. Mr. Robbins, do you care to tell them, or shall I?" Mr. Cates sneered.

Chandler Robbins pulled a piece of paper from his pocket and held it up, along with a photograph of Eliana. "As we all can see, and evidenced by this photograph and the remarks on this paper, John

Van Horn does not have a son. He has a daughter." Mr. Robbins narrowed his eyes at Papa then turned his attention to her. "Your name is Eli*ana*."

Papa looked askance at his comrade. "You knew?"

"I just learned of this a short time ago. I was about to discuss the matter with you when. . ."

The men grumbled. "Well looky here, now we got ourselves some female company," one said.

"Silence," Robbins commanded.

"Yes, sir. I'm sorry, sir." Eliana's face heated with shame.

Robbins spoke through clenched teeth. "Your apology will do nothing to help now. Having a female along puts me in a precarious position, miss, and all of us in jeopardy of harm. We have no choice but to pull out of here immediately and get across the border. We've come too far to safely turn back." Mr. Robbins's eyes flashed at Papa. "And then, Van Horn, I'll decide what to do about your *assistant*."

Yiska kept his distance. Eliana rode double behind her father, and Yiska dared not speak to either of them until the storm blew over. As the team pulled forward, purple mountain vistas faded against the backdrop of looming sienna plateaus. The brilliant sunset of red and orange stretched across the early evening sky—a contrast to the dim mood of Chandler Robbins. The leader of the expedition had spoken little to anyone for the past few hours, casting a dismal shadow over all. At the border, Robbins and his surveyors set up their instruments and marked their first official point while several men stood guard, rifles in hand.

When they crossed into New Mexico territory, a feeling of familiarity came over Yiska. They were now in the land of the Diné, his mother's people—his people. Here on the Navajo reservation, the imminent danger of the Utes had passed. There was little threat of trouble with the Navajo here, and he would wear his headband to signify his kinship, though it would do little to ward off desperadoes. But he had a different force to reckon with now. Chandler Robbins. Yiska scouted ahead, all the while contemplating his and the Van Horns' fate.

He spotted the caravan headed toward him and trotted up to meet them. "Mr. Robbins, I found a place to spend the night in the shelter of some bluffs about a couple miles south."

Robbins rubbed the back of his neck. "How far is it to Aztec from there?"

"Twenty-five miles."

"All right. We'll spend the night up here. Lead the way."

Yiska shifted in his saddle. "Mr. Robbins. . .about today."

Robbins's lips drew into a line as straight as the Colorado–New Mexico border. "It's been a long day, Yiska. I'll speak with you and the Van Horns in the morning."

"Yes, sir. In the morning."

❧

The surveyors had already taken the measurements this morning, and the convoy of wagons and animals was all lined up and ready to go. But the entire cadre of workers sat in front of the campfire as Mr. Robbins paced back and forth.

Eliana bit her lower lip. Obviously, public humiliation was part of the punishment for her crimes.

"Yiska, let me get this straight. You knew about this arrangement all along?" Mr. Robbins asked.

"Yes, sir."

"And as the guide on this survey you didn't see the need to fill me in?"

"No, sir. I mean, sir, I wasn't concerned," Yiska said.

"And John, did you notify the GLO about the gender of your photography assistant?"

"It wasn't required on the application," Papa said.

"But you knew it was assumed that she—he—would be a male."

"That is typical, but I found no place to specify." Papa clamped down on his lower lip.

"Without my knowledge—or anyone else's for that matter—that we had a female in our company, you put not only your daughter but all of us at risk." Robbins smacked his hat against his thigh. "Confound it. There shouldn't have been a need to know in the first place."

Mr. Mattheson cleared his throat and signaled Mr. Robbins with his pointing finger. "Chandler, I also knew."

"You're kidding me." Robbins laughed in disbelief. "No, I suppose you're not." He continued to pace. No one uttered a sound. "Is there anyone *else* who knew about this. . .other than Mr. Cates, who made a point of finding out?" Robbins's eyes narrowed at the man.

"I knew, Mr. Robbins," Cornelius Crawford said. "I promised not to tell. For her own protection. You wouldn't have wanted me to go back on my word. The good Lord wants us to be honest."

Mr. Robbins scratched his head and muttered. "Honest."

Eliana's face heated. She was next.

Mr. Robbins walked right up in front of her. "Miss Van Horn. Eliana—Eli. Very clever."

"Thank you, sir," she gulped.

Mr. Robbins crossed his arms. "No. Don't thank me. Just tell me. What on earth did you think you were doing?"

"I intended to assist my father with his photography on a survey expedition with the esteemed Chandler Robbins." She held her chin up. "I've been my father's right hand man. . ." A nervous guffaw escaped from her lips, but then she found her composure. "I've been helping him for years. He needed my help when he got the government contract to photograph the mines. He hired a man to assist him on this expedition. But he thought he had better prospects in the San Juans than on a desert survey. The disguise was for my protection."

"Are you quite through, Miss Van Horn?"

"Yes, sir." Eliana winced. "And please call me Eliana."

The creases in Robbins's forehead deepened. "Did my outfitter know about this scheme?"

Yiska spoke up. "I'm afraid so. Only recently."

Robbins threw his hands in the air. "Well, folks, looks like we're outnumbered. Unless anyone objects, *Eliana* will remain on the expedition."

"What about Wilcox?" Warren Cates protested.

"What *about* Wilcox?" one of the assistant surveyors asked. "He's been working twice as hard as you."

"He certainly has," another voice called out.

Eliana stood. "Indeed!" She defended him again. She covered her face in her hands and sat down, unable to look at Yiska.

Mr. Robbins let out a sharp whistle. "Settle down, or we're all going home. I'm paying you by the mile, not by the day. Time is money. And time is wasting." Robbins parked his foot on a boulder and leaned his elbow against his knee. "Now, although Eliana has proven that she is a capable member of this team—she even puts some of you to shame, I might add—I expect you all to treat her like a lady. No disrespect. Keep a proper distance. And let her do the work she came here to do."

He eyed Papa. "Does that sound fair?"

"Yes. Thank you. You won't regret it." Papa gnawed on his pipe.

"Eliana, is there anything else you'd like to add?" Mr. Robbins asked.

She offered a weak smile. "Well, I think we ought to be on our way."

Mr. Robbins shook his head and grinned. "The lady has spoken. Get ready to pull out."

Eliana's heart swelled. She was on an important survey expedition, not as Eli, but as Eliana Van Horn. A woman on an official government survey. Who'd have ever thought that possible?

Chapter 17

Aztec Ruins, New Mexico Territory

Yiska scanned the stone ruins from the outer edge of the encampment in Aztec, the remnants of pueblos left behind by an ancient tribe. As he fiddled with a dry blade of grass between his teeth he thought about the struggle to survive, only to have it all come to ruin—like it almost had for him yesterday. And to continue on, not knowing what still might crumble around him, and have the strength to stand. Must the motivations of one's heart always succumb to external elements? Would his?

Eliana's father ambled up to Yiska. "Impressive site. The masonry is astounding. It must have taken a long time to build."

"Some say it was built in the twelfth century, and here we stand admiring it." The ancient ones had disappeared with little to mark their existence but the sandstone rubble. What kind of legacy would Yiska leave? He had no home. No family. All he had were the words he wrote, which would leave little more of an impression on this world than Shadow's hoofprints in the sand.

Mr. Van Horn cleared his throat. "I'd like to speak with you about yesterday."

Yiska nodded and tossed the blade of grass to the ground. "All right."

"Tell me, what you were doing with my daughter by those pines?" Van Horn rocked back and forth on his heels. His mustache shaded the tight line of his mouth.

"I was, eh, buttoning her shirt." Yiska held up his hand. "She was shivering—in shock—and her shirt was undone."

Mr. Van Horn scowled. "Did the Indian do that?"

"I think she had, down at the river," Yiska said.

"Why was she alone?" Mr. Van Horn asked.

Yiska shrugged his shoulders. "She wasn't, not really. But she needed privacy. That's when the Ute found her."

"Regardless, it wasn't appropriate for you to. . .be so familiar with her." Mr. Van Horn glared.

Yiska looked back with a blank stare. Would Eliana's father rather that Yiska left her undone? It was no use reasoning with the man. He was rightfully upset.

Van Horn loosened his neckerchief and took a deep breath. "I hope you'll forgive me. I've been hard on you lately. My concern for Eliana. . . Well, I never did thank you." He extended his hand and offered Yiska a firm handshake. "You saved my daughter's life again and risked yours in the process."

"There's nothing to forgive. I'm glad I could help."

"Seems like you're always there when she needs you." Mr. Van Horn's mouth tightened. "I can see that you care about her."

Yiska looked down at his boots and contemplated his next words. Then he looked straight into her father's eyes. "She's a fine woman, Mr. Van Horn."

"You just remember what I said. If anything ever happens to me. . ." Mr. Van Horn wrinkled his brow. "I trust you, Yiska."

Why did this man keep talking like this?

"There you are." Eliana appeared, still dressed in men's clothing. But her hair hung down around her shoulders, and her face beamed like the sun. "Are you ready, Papa? I've got the cameras all set up."

"You didn't have to do that all by yourself," he said.

"I'm anxious to get started. Mr. Robbins and his crew are already at work, and everyone else is busy at their own tasks."

Yiska slid his hands into his back pockets. "Well, I guess we're slacking then."

"Good morning, Yiska." Eliana gave him a shy smile.

"Mornin'."

"Thank you again for. . ." She let out a little sigh. "I keep getting myself in trouble. But that's about to change. I'm feeling much more confident now."

Her father placed his arm around her shoulders. "Glad to hear it. Now let's take those pictures of the landscape, and maybe Yiska will help us explore the ruins."

Eliana stood in awe of the acres and acres of ancient dwellings laid out in a massive U-shaped configuration with hundreds of contiguous rooms. After taking an array of exterior photographs of the great Aztec Ruins, they met up with several of the others in the huge circular-walled structure in the center of the courtyard. Yiska remained behind, where she last saw him leaning against a wall of stone, pen and journal in hand.

Warren Cates's bravado bounced off the sandstone bricks in the open coliseum. "Remarkable. This place must have belonged to a wealthy leader. I could see myself living here if I were one of the Aztecs."

"Actually," Yiska said as he climbed through one of the openings, "this is a *kiva*, a ceremonial chamber like the smaller ones outside. These rectangles in the floor were baths, and this was a fire pit."

Mr. Cates's chest puffed out. "I read in one of the Natural History Museum publications that the Aztecs kept a continuous fire burning in hopes to bring back their Eternal King, Montezuma."

"That may be true, but the Navajo believe that these and other ruins like them belonged to the Anasazi—the ancient ones, or enemy ancestors."

Cates swiped his hand along his forehead, mocking the traditional Navajo headband that Yiska had worn since they entered Navajo land. "I suppose you can trust this uneducated half breed above esteemed archaeologists." He looked around at the group smugly.

"You do know then, Mr. Cates, that anthropologists are now consulting with the Navajo and other tribes, like the Paiutes, to quantify their theories," Mr. Mattheson said.

"Well, it's neither here nor there."

"I beg to differ with you," Papa said. "We have much to learn from the past. About ourselves. The future."

How unusual for Papa to speak this way. He seldom looked back, but lately he had spent much time in conversation with Mr. Mattheson, reminiscing she hoped, discussing the reason Mr. Mattheson had left his calling. Papa positioned a camera and took a few photographs of the interior of the chamber.

"Mr. Cates, do you have any experience with cameras?" Eliana asked.

"As a matter of fact, I do. I've learned a little about photography during my tenure with the *Atlantic Monthly*."

Eliana eyed her father, who stood near Mr. Mattheson and Yiska. "Well then, perhaps you wouldn't mind taking a group photograph of the four of us. Then I'll be happy to take one of you, of course."

Mr. Cates acceded. "Ah, yes, of course."

Yiska and Eliana explored the many rooms of the immense stone fortress, talking as they climbed over piles of rubble, ancient steps, and dim passageways. Van Horn and Mattheson had returned to camp with Sampson, who had faithfully lugged their equipment to the site. The fact that her father entrusted Eliana to Yiska's care meant a great deal to him.

"Why do you think these dwellings were abandoned?" Eliana asked.

"One can only speculate. Drought maybe? Depleted resources. Maybe even war. There are other ruins similar to this. One is just ten miles south of here. And sixty-five miles farther, there's a much larger ruin in the Chaco Canyon," Yiska said.

"Larger than this?" she asked.

"Ten miles wide. The dwellings rise up five levels with grand arches and ornamentation."

Eliana tilted her dimpled chin. "How do you know so much?"

"I've met a lot of people in my travels, and I read as much as I can. I wish I could take you there. You could take pictures and show them to the world. You'd become famous."

Eliana laughed. "And you would write all about it and become known to all as an expert journalist. You would no longer be the Anonymous Explorer, but the esteemed Yiska Wilcox."

He stood a little taller and suppressed a smile. "I do know this—the correspondent who writes about the Chaco Canyon ruins will make quite a name for himself. Mr. Robbins was good enough to give us time here while the animals rest today, so I guess we'll have to be content exploring the impressive Aztec Ruins." And perhaps to discover the unexplored territory of Eliana's heart.

They turned a corner and entered a long corridor of rooms connected by a passageway of successive doorways. Eliana grabbed Yiska's hand. "Come on, let's see." As they approached the doorway, she slipped her hand out of his, ran ahead, and ducked behind a wall.

Yiska caught up with the mischievous explorer, finding her with hands pressed against the wall behind her, taking in heavy breaths amidst intermittent giggles. He trapped her against the cool stones, one hand on either side of her, and tried to catch his breath. After a moment they both relaxed, but he didn't move his arms. Nor did she object. Yiska leaned toward Eliana and placed his mouth upon hers, the timeless moment blazing like the hot New Mexico sun.

He pulled away from her, his heart racing like a herd of wild horses. He forced himself to withdraw from her intense gaze. His eyes locked on a spot in the stonework behind her. "Fingerprints."

Eliana blinked. "What?"

"There are fingerprints of the builders in the mortar, right there." Yiska pointed his chin.

Eliana turned to look, still enclosed in the prison of his arms. He wasn't ready to release her just yet.

"Imagine, after all these years. Someone has left a permanent mark." Eliana turned back around, back still against the wall.

She tilted her head up, and Yiska admired the graceful arch of her neck. He stroked the smooth skin with a feather-light touch, following her gaze to the ceiling. "Those are original timbers, still in place after all this time." Leave it to him to spoil the mood, prompting her to slip down under his arm and make her escape.

Eliana skipped away, passing through a few doorways. Yiska followed at a slower pace. Let her play her game—he intended to win. But as she passed through the next doorway, Cates jumped into her way, blocking her path.

"Out of the way," Yiska commanded.

"I just want to have a word with the pretty lady." Cates feigned innocence. "What are you doing spending your time with a novice like him when you could enjoy this fine day with me?"

Yiska put his hand on his hatchet. "You don't know who you're up against."

"Don't threaten me, Wilcox," the weasel said.

"I'm not speaking about me. It's Miss Van Horn that you need to worry about."

Eliana turned back and flashed Yiska a smile. She put her hands on her hips. "Let us pass, Mr. Cates. We have work to do."

After dusk Eliana and her father finished processing photographs from the day using their small portable darkroom under the shelter of their tent. Eliana opened the door flaps to let the remainder of the evening light in. "I almost forgot to mention, we found Anasazi fingerprints in a stone wall today."

"That's a remarkable find. It's unfortunate something like that is too small to photograph," Papa said, wiping his hands on his canvas apron. "Harland found an ancient relic."

"I'll have to take a look when I'm done." Eliana went outside and sat on a stool at a worktable and wiped the dust from the equipment. "I'm so glad you allowed me to come on this expedition, Papa. I'm discovering so much about the world and myself." Foremost in her mind, the discovery she had made today about her feelings for Yiska. The warmth that spread from her toes all the way to her cheeks when he'd kissed her had taken her by surprise—and she hadn't even been blushing at the time. Was this what it was like to be in love?

She looked up and pushed the hair back from her face. "You seem to have enjoyed rekindling your friendship with Reverend Mattheson. I mean, Mr. Mattheson."

"*Reverend* Mattheson is correct. His faith has been tested, but he'll come around."

Eliana smiled. "I'm so glad to hear that." When she completed her task, she put the supplies away. "I think I'll go take a look at that old relic."

"Were you talking about me or my artifact?" Mr. Mattheson chuckled as he poked his head outside his tent door.

"There's the old fossil now." Papa grinned.

"Papa told me about your discovery." Eliana looked with interest at the small box he held.

Mr. Mattheson sat down at the table with Eliana, took an object out of a box, and held it up. She took a close look at what appeared to be a ladle. "How fascinating. The painting on it is beautiful. Do you think there is any significance to the design?"

"I'm no expert, but there may well be." Mr. Mattheson cocked his head and grinned. "That's quite an astute remark. Reminds me of my wife. Essie used to look beyond the obvious for the deeper meaning in things. She would have enjoyed knowing you." His eyes lingered on Eliana's face.

A moment later Mr. Mattheson stood abruptly and almost dropped the piece of pottery. Eliana wrapped her hands around his to steady his grip.

"Thank you," he said. "It would have been a shame if it had broken. Some things cannot be repaired." As he wrapped the piece in several layers of cloth and placed it in the box, Eliana had the distinct feeling that he was thinking of something—or someone—else.

She rose from her seat. “Papa, we haven’t been keeping up on our evening Bible reading, and today is Sunday. Reverend Mattheson, perhaps you could read for us and share some of your insights.”

“I don’t know about that. It’s been a long time,” he said.

Eliana folded her hands and rested them on the table. “Please, it would mean so much to me.”

A look of defeat crossed his face. “I’m not worthy. Never really was.”

“Are any of us truly worthy to do what the Lord asks of us? You taught me that when I lost Josephine,” Papa said.

“I remember. You weren’t feeling up to the task of parenting alone. But you’ve done a splendid job, my friend.” Reverend Mattheson smiled at Eliana.

“You said the Lord would equip me for the task, and He did. He’ll do the same for you,” Papa said.

Reverend Mattheson took Eliana’s hand, “How can I complain? I’m ashamed I didn’t initiate the idea myself, being the Lord’s Day. God knows I need some nudging, and you were just the one to do so.”

“She *has* been known to get her way,” Papa chimed in. “And I’ve heard that our heavenly Father has a way of bringing us back around.”

Eliana knew her father meant his own time in the wilderness as a young man, and his friend’s role in bringing him back to the Lord. If not, what would have become of her?

Papa placed the Bible in front of his friend.

“That’s Mama’s Bible,” Eliana said.

Reverend Mattheson wrinkled his brow and shook his head. “Then I’m definitely not worthy. But as you said, it’s the Lord who equips us. Even this broken vessel.”

“Good evenin’.” Yiska sauntered up to the table. “I hope I’m not interrupting.” He lowered a glance toward Eliana.

She offered him a small smile.

“You’re right on time,” Papa said. “That is, if you’d like to spend a few minutes with us while Reverend Mattheson reads from God’s Word.”

Yiska arched an eyebrow. "Reverend? I guess God equips anyone. No disrespect intended. I just never would have guessed."

"That's not to my credit. But coincidently, we were just talking about how it's our heavenly Father who makes us worthy, not ourselves."

Yiska sat down. "I do think I might be ready to hear what He has to say about that."

The early morning sun greeted Eliana the following day, her heart full of praise. As they followed the river southwest, Mr. Robbins and his surveyors stopped for frequent measurements. This provided much opportunity to document the sublime landscape of sandstone arches, juniper-dotted deserts, and multicolored plateaus. Seeing Papa enjoying himself so much made her heart overflow with joy.

But the news Papa gave her that morning mattered most of all. Yiska had accepted Jesus as Creator and King. He had spoken with Papa and Reverend Mattheson at length about his questions after she had retreated to her tent and prayed.

He now understood the reality that Jesus was no mere man, but a divine being—God's only begotten, who was with His Father from the beginning of time and appeared to the world in the flesh. The Son had at last risen in Yiska's heart.

She couldn't wait to see Yiska, but he'd been detained with Mr. Robbins and his crew all morning.

Papa set up his camera overlooking a wondrous gorge layered with vivid earthen hues. The crisp, flattened tops of the plateaus contrasted with pointed mountaintops that were but a faded shadow of blue in the distance. On this side of the canyon, enormous sandstone rocks rose up around them, creating interesting places to explore.

Yiska walked up to the bluff and greeted Eliana. "Beautiful."

Upon hearing his voice, she turned around. "Yiska. It is a beautiful world. I thought my eyes had beheld all its loveliness in the San Juan Mountains, but here I see a new kind of beauty that I never even knew existed."

"That's exactly how I feel today."

Eliana continued to stand several feet away from him, though never feeling closer, simply admiring Yiska and what the Lord had done in his life. What He had done in her own, for she, too, was growing in faith every day. Some days flowed smoothly while others raged over rough waters, but through it all the current brought her closer to the Lord. She couldn't imagine that anything could spoil the joy she felt that moment.

Several feet ahead she spied Papa. He gradually backed away from his camera, gauging the perfect view, and stepped near a towering bank of rock.

A movement on the precipice above him caught Eliana's attention. She shaded her eyes just as a pile of rocks shifted.

A medium-sized boulder rolled off the crag and crashed down on Papa.

"Papa!" Eliana screamed as she flew to his side, Yiska right behind her. Reverend Mattheson dropped his sketch pad and hurried toward them.

Papa lay on the sandy ground, bleeding from a gash in his head. The boulder was in pieces near him, stained with blood.

"I'm right here, Papa." She cradled his head in her lap as tears poured down her face. "I love you, Papa."

Reverend Mattheson hovered over him, gripping her father's hand. Nothing else could be done.

A small stream of blood trickled from the corner of his mouth. Papa took a shuddering breath and spoke his last words. "Tell her."

Chapter 18

Sobs wracked Eliana's body as she leaned over Papa. *How could this happen?* A few moments ago he was enjoying his life, only to have it end in a flash.

Yiska's gentle hands helped Eliana to her feet. She fell into his embrace, releasing her grief and shock with a flood of tears.

After a moment, she turned to Reverend Mattheson, her hands still on Yiska's chest. "What did he mean? Tell me what?"

The man's eyes filled with compassion. "We can talk about it later, dear."

"No. I want to know now."

Yiska's warm hand stayed on her back. "Are you sure?"

A sob caught in her chest, and she tried to breathe. "Yes. I need to know."

Reverend Mattheson handed her a handkerchief. "Let's go over there and sit."

Yiska wrapped his arm around her waist and led her to the shade of ancient piñons, where she sat on a large boulder.

Reverend Mattheson covered the body of his longtime friend and joined them. "Robbins and the others need to know," he said to Yiska.

Yiska set his hand on Eliana's shoulder. "Will you be all right?"

"I'm in good hands. Thank you." She squeezed Yiska's hand and held it to her face before releasing it.

As Yiska walked away, he glanced back over his shoulder. Eliana's heart warmed to know his concern for her. She folded her trembling hands in her lap and bowed her head. She could find no words to pray but was thankful that her heavenly Father would hear the groaning of her heart.

"What did Papa want me to know?" She looked into Reverend Mattheson's ashen face.

"Perhaps it's best to wait until you are less upset," he said.

"I may already know." A look of surprise jolted his face. "Is it that he was not. . .my father?" Eliana clutched her stomach and took slow breaths.

"I don't understand," Reverend Mattheson said. "John said he never told you."

"He didn't. But when I was fourteen I found a letter you wrote to him, thanking him for adopting me. You asked him never to tell me about the circumstances of my birth—that my life would be ruined if I knew." Eliana turned away, the floodwaters threatening to flow once more.

"That was after I learned your mother died."

Eliana brushed away a fresh tear. "Papa was my father in every way that mattered. I didn't want anything to change. He was all I had."

Reverend Mattheson buried his face in his hands. He looked up and shook his head. "You've lived with this for all these years, dear girl." He wiped beads of perspiration from his forehead. "I never should have placed this burden on him. Nor should you have ever had to know."

"Burden? Is that what I am?"

Reverend Mattheson's face blanched. "No! You are not a burden. The only burden was my ill choice. I've carried around regret for my selfish decision ever since I made it." The man sobered. "I should have raised you myself. You were my wife's child."

Bile rose in Eliana's throat and she swallowed hard. She took a few deep breaths and walked over to Reverend Mattheson's side and sat with him on the large rock. "Don't say that. I was blessed to have Papa as my father. You gave me two amazing parents." A lump formed in her throat. "Though, if you had raised me, I'm sure you would have been a wonderful father as well."

"John Van Horn was a far better man than I will ever be. He took you into his arms as an infant and accepted you as his own without hesitation. He and Josephine loved every inch of you. She was a fine mother, as my Essie would have been."

Eliana sniffled, trying to restrain her tears. "There's more, isn't there? Tell me what happened."

Reverend Mattheson let out a deep breath and set his hat in his lap. "We were on our way west—Esther and I, your parents, and several other families. I was called to preach at the township we were headed to. The wagon train was attacked by Comanches. We managed to fight them off. But Essie. . ." He balled his hands into fists and turned his head aside, taking heavy breaths.

"You are not my. . ."

Reverend Mattheson's mouth formed into a grim line.

"Comanches." Eliana placed her fingers on her lips as tears pooled in her eyes, and she fought the nausea away. *I'm half Indian. Like Yiska.*

Reverend Mattheson stood and paced. "When we learned she was with child, I promised it didn't matter, that I'd accept the baby as my own. But when she died in her travail, I could barely face my life without her and could not comprehend how I would ever care for an infant." He looked at Eliana as if to gain her understanding.

"The infant who caused her death." Anger vied with compassion, creating a storm within her.

Reverend Mattheson rushed up to her. "No. You were an innocent babe. It was the Indian I blamed."

My father. But a small voice spoke to her heart. *Beloved, I am your Father.*

She looked up toward the bright sun and heaved a deep sigh. "Go on. Please."

"John and Josephine had always wanted children of their own. I placed you in their care and had them promise never to reveal the shame of your true parentage."

"Shame." Eliana swallowed. The Voice spoke again, quiet and sure. *Those who look to the Son will not be ashamed. Look to me, daughter.*

"I continued my sojourn west and pastored that little church, but your parents settled in Missouri. I could only bring myself to visit a few times. You looked so much like your mother it hurt—so selfish of me." He gazed at Eliana for a moment with misty eyes. "Her hair was much lighter, and her eyes were blue. But your smiling eyes and that little dimple in your chin. . . You have her generous heart and feisty spirit as well."

Eliana let out a little whimper.

"The truth ate at me through the years. I was living a lie. It was I who bore the shame. I should have protected Essie. Kept my promise to her."

Eliana took a deep breath, trying to take it all in. "I'm sure you did everything you could."

Reverend Mattheson choked up. He turned away and looked into the distance, his hands plunged deep in his pockets. Before he turned around, he pulled out a handkerchief and blew his nose.

Eliana rose, compassion also rising within her for this hurting soul. "The last time I saw you, you baptized me."

"Yes, when you were twelve. It was my last baptism. After that, I realized what a hypocrite I was and left my days as a pastor behind me. Though it did little to appease my guilt."

"Reverend Mattheson." Eliana sighed. "I've always respected you. I don't hold your choice against you. You did well to place me where I could be best cared for—with a loving mother and father who longed for a child. But you gave me a heavenly Father as well, who has met my every need. And He will also meet yours, if you allow Him to."

Reverend Mattheson laughed and shook his head. "No wonder John called you Sunshine. Even now you are a shining light."

Eliana stepped toward her would-have-been father. "Would it help if I told you that I forgave you long ago? I wish I'd found a way to let you know. You and Papa carried an unnecessary burden on my account." Tears trickled down her face.

"Sweet child." He pulled her into his arms, and together they wept.

❧

Yiska stood among the circle of men, hat in his hands, as Reverend Mattheson spoke at Eliana's father's grave.

"In John's last days, he had a chance to explore and photograph some marvelous sights, including the Aztec Ruins. The remarkable fortress of many rooms amazed him. But none of it compares to the wonders he is seeing in glory." He opened his Bible but did not read from the pages—he spoke the words from his heart. " 'In my Father's house are many mansions: if it were not so, I would have told you. I go to prepare a place for you. And if I go and prepare a place for you, I will come again, and receive you unto myself; that where I am, there ye may be also.' "

Yiska believed these words and rejoiced that this faith gave Eliana hope and courage, although her sadness was unmistakable.

When the service ended, Yiska enfolded her in his arms. If he could only absorb her pain the way his shirt soaked in her tears.

The somber caravan proceeded a few miles to Farmingtown, at the confluence of the Animas, LaPlata, and San Juan rivers. Eliana now rode her father's mount.

Once they had set up camp, she retreated to her tent for a nap. Sometime later Yiska found her sitting alone by some low bushes.

"They call that Indian paintbrush." He pointed to the red flowers protruding from the sandy ground.

"Mmm. They're so pretty," Eliana said.

Yiska looked into her sleepy eyes, a little puffy from crying. "Would you like some company?"

"Please."

He sat on the ground. "Mr. Robbins tells me we'll stay all day tomorrow and leave the next morning."

"I'd prefer to keep going, but I know the animals need to rest," she said.

"He also needs to replenish supplies at the trading post and pick up the new sandstone marker for the four corners."

"I'm planning to complete this expedition. . .for Papa."

Yiska nodded. "I expected you would."

They sat in silence for several moments. Then Eliana looked at him with wide eyes. "I haven't told you about my conversation with Reverend Mattheson."

"You don't have to. Unless it would help."

Eliana nodded but said nothing until Yiska took her hand and gave it a gentle squeeze. "Reverend Mattheson's wife, Esther, was my real mother. He gave me over to the Van Horns when she died at my birth."

Yiska lifted his eyebrows. "Mattheson is your father?"

"That is what I believed. But, no. A Comanche warrior is." Her eyes shifted away.

Couldn't she bear to look at him? "Eliana. This must be a shock."

She bit her lip. "When I was fourteen years old, I discovered a letter from Reverend Mattheson to Papa revealing that I was adopted. I never told a soul."

Yiska retracted his hand. "Why didn't you tell anyone?"

Eliana looked back at him, her gaze intense. "I was ashamed. . . and frightened." She let out a deep sigh. "I didn't want to lose my Papa. I didn't understand the things the letter hinted at. I was foolish not to tell him. Something like that could have never changed our relationship. He will always be my father."

"What about your true heritage, Eliana?" Yiska asked.

"Essie Mattheson was also a Christian Jew. She led my mother to the Lord."

"And you are part Indian. Like me. Is that what you're ashamed of? Why you never told me?" If so, she would always be ashamed of him. The thought pierced him like a poison arrow.

Eliana looked at Yiska dismayed. "What do you mean? I'm not ashamed of you. Or myself. I didn't know who my true father was until today, or what had happened to my real mother. I'm disturbed by the horrific circumstances. I can't even think about it." She buried her face in her hands and wept.

"Eliana, forgive me. I never should have said that. I was afraid that this knowledge would make you despise me. . .and yourself. I couldn't bear that."

Eliana's tears flowed freely. "I could never despise you, Yiska. You are an honorable man." The corner of her mouth curved. "Even if you are a half breed." A whirlwind of laughter and tears mixed together. She leaned her chin on her clasped hands.

Yiska enclosed her hands in his and took in her sweet, precious face. "And now we know that the shadow catcher's daughter is also a half breed. A Comanche, you say?"

"Yes, and that's all I will ever know of him. But what is more important is that Papa loved me as his own, and I him."

Yiska look deeply into her eyes, her heart. "Your eternal heavenly Father knows all about *you*, and how you feel right now. At least, this is what I am learning."

"You're a good student." Eliana smiled.

Yiska pulled her close. "I've had an excellent teacher. She's quite the taskmaster."

After picking at her dinner, Eliana joined Yiska and the others who gathered on the porch of the trading post with their coffee. She sat to the side looking in the direction of the converging rivers, listening to their camaraderie and storytelling. Even so, she felt alone—until Chandler Robbins approached.

"Eliana, I'm sorry about your father. He was a good friend of mine back in the infantry. But now I'm in quite a quandary. You're no longer under his protection, and it's highly inappropriate for me to have a single woman in such a situation on this expedition. As you know, I've already gone against my better judgment to keep you with us, although you have proven yourself, and I don't regret it."

"Then let me stay."

"This goes beyond all protocol. I'm sorry, my hands are tied."

Mr. Robbins looked at Reverend Mattheson, and his eyes narrowed. "Harland, you'll have to marry her."

Everyone quieted.

Reverend Mattheson's brow wrinkled. "Marry her? She's like a daughter to me."

"I know that. I mean you're a man of the cloth. You'll have to perform a marriage ceremony."

Eliana stood and stomped her boot. "I am not going to be forced into a marriage, Mr. Robbins. How could you suggest something so absurd?"

"Hold on now. Women have married for far less important reasons. If you can't find a suitable match among the men here, then you'll have to go back or wait here for us to return. And the latter is not advisable."

Eliana scanned the cadre of bachelors, all who averted their eyes. But there was one man that she'd consider as a husband—and he was looking right at her. Her face prickled with heat.

"If you won't marry, then I'll have to send you home. And there is only one person capable of seeing you back safely." Mr. Robbins looked directly at Yiska.

"No." Eliana planted her hands on her hips. "I cannot ask Yiska to give up his goals on my behalf."

"Eliana, I'll take you, if that's what you want," Yiska said.

She shook her head. "I don't want." *What I want is to. . .*

"Please calm down, Eliana," Mr. Robbins said. "Like the three rivers, it looks like you are faced with your own confluence of choices."

Mr. Robbins was right. The rivers flowed from various directions and she, too, must decide which way to go. She only wished someone else would make that decision for her.

"Walk with me," Yiska said.

He took Eliana by the hand and headed toward the San Juan River, where he found a place for them to rest. The setting sun filled the horizon with vivid pinks, oranges, and reds. The colorful array reflected on the water, though nothing compared with Eliana's beautiful soul.

"It's so serene here. I wish I could capture it and put my thoughts to rest." Eliana faced Yiska. "I don't want to go back. I've made such progress with the photography on this trip. I want to see the project through. For my father. For me." She lowered her chin. "Is that selfish?"

Yiska shook his head. "Not at all. I understand. I have goals of my own to see through."

"And I would never want you to compromise them for me."

"I hope that won't be necessary." Yiska took some sand in his hand and let it sift through his fingers. "You know, Navajo healers create sandpaintings to help in times of grief and decision making. They draw a picture with different colored sands to reveal an answer for the troubled soul."

Eliana propped herself up with her arm. "Perhaps this Navajo can help me find a solution."

"I know you are seeking the path of God. Has He given you any insight?"

She shifted on the dry grass. "Some."

"Is marriage not an option?"

"Who would you want me to marry? Mr. Robbins? Warren Cates? Cornelius?" Eliana stifled a giggle.

Yiska did not laugh, and his stomach tightened. "I don't want you to marry any of them."

Her eyes widened. "Good, because I will only marry the one who loves me, the one whom I love."

The two sat in silence for several moments. Yiska drew a heart in the patch of sand in front of them. Eliana looked up at him, her hazel eyes dawning with understanding. She placed her hand over his and retraced the heart.

One heart.

Eliana whispered, "This is what the Lord has shown me, but I knew not how to ask."

"You don't need to ask. My heart already belongs to you, Eliana. I want to be your husband and journey through this life with you."

Crystal tears streamed down her cheeks. Yiska placed his hand behind her head and laced his fingers through her soft, full hair. The tender kisses that he placed on her lips mingled with her tears of joy and relief.

"We will marry tomorrow, if you'll have me. We can tell Mr. Robbins in the morning."

Eliana placed her hand on his face, and it warmed him down to his boots. "I love you, Yiska Wilcox."

"And I love you, Eliana. I think I always have."

Eliana glanced down at her shirt and trousers. "I suppose it's a good thing that I have my gingham dress along."

Yiska planted a kiss on her forehead. "You'll be lovely." Then he reached into his pocket and pulled out a piece of lace ribbon. "I've been meaning to give this to you for a long time now. Maybe you can wear it in your hair for our wedding."

"Yiska, it's beautiful." Eliana examined the lace. "This is from the mercantile in Del Norte. Don't tell me you've had it since then."

Yiska gave her a sheepish grin.

Eliana threw her arms around his neck. "Yiska Wilcox. Now *you're* blushing."

Chapter 19

How could a woman sleep the night before her wedding, the very day her father had died? But in the untamed southwest, deserts became sandstorms, reservoirs became raging rivers, iced peaks released avalanches, mountains buried treasure, and life went on. The rising sun greeted Eliana as she emerged from her tent and greeted the new day.

She yawned and stretched her arms high into the sky. Having slept some, she at last relinquished her struggle when early morning light brightened her tent. She sat outside and read Mama's Bible for over an hour, finally turning to the family record in the front pages. John Van Horn, father. Josephine Leman, mother. Eliana Esther Van Horn, daughter. Now she knew. Not only was Essie—Esther—Mama's best friend, but Eliana's middle name honored the mother who gave birth to her.

She turned the page. Deaths. She needed to enter Papa's death record. Her heart burned with sadness at the thought. The following page revealed a blank marriage certificate, and her pulse quickened. Reverend Mattheson would fill this in for her today when she became Mrs. Yiska Wilcox. Eliana Wilcox. She liked the sound of that.

"Miss Van Horn. Eliana." Warren Cates stared at her.

Eliana startled. "Really, Mr. Cates, must you always sneak up on me like that?"

"I have a solution to your dilemma," he said.

She closed the Bible in her lap. "Mr. Cates. . ."

"Hear me out. Come with me to Chaco Canyon and be my photographer. We will fully document the area and make a grand name for ourselves. Imagine the notoriety. You'll be published in the top scientific journals. You'll be the first woman photographer with that type of acclaim. Think of it!"

"I will have to decline, Mr. Cates. I've made other plans." *I would not marry a scorpion like you in a million years.*

"What could be more important than an opportunity like this?"

"My wedding," she said.

"You've no need to marry. You can create your own renown. You and I will make a team. And then we'll see."

"I'm marrying for love, not for opportunity."

Mr. Cates' face creased with frustration. "Are you intending to marry that half breed?"

Eliana stood and crossed her arms. "I'm marrying Mr. Wilcox."

"For love?" Cates laughed. "What could he know about. . . Let me put it this way, Eliana. If you don't come with me, his short career will be over before it even begins. I will smear his name all over—" Cates grabbed Eliana by the arm.

Yiska, Mr. Robbins, and Reverend Mattheson walked up behind Cates. Yiska twisted the man's arm behind his back. "That'll be enough, Cates."

Mr. Robbins jabbed his finger in the man's chest. "Let me put it to *you* this way. You're off the expedition and going back the way you came. And if you dare make one disreputable remark about this fine correspondent, the *Atlantic Monthly* and every other magazine will have a full report from the government to discredit anything you write regarding any of the territories in these four corners, or anywhere else for that matter. Do I make myself clear?"

Warren Cates scowled and spit on the ground missing Yiska's boots. "Yes."

Mr. Robbins gave him a push. "Pack your gear and go."

Yiska wrapped his arm around Eliana, and Reverend Mattheson came alongside them. "I believe we have a wedding to plan."

Yiska bathed and readied himself for his wedding. He put on clean trousers, a fresh shirt, and combed his hair—deciding not to wear his headband. Then he knelt down and prayed to his Maker to help him to fill the role of a husband in a way that would bring honor to God and give joy to his wife.

At the trading post Eliana waited for him with Reverend Mattheson, Chandler Robbins, and the rest of the survey team.

Yiska greeted her with a wide smile. "I've come to collect my bride." She had pinned the strand of lace in her hair. He took the end of it between his fingers and whispered in her ear, "You are beautiful."

A Navajo weave scarf adorned her gingham dress, and she had fastened a silver concha at the neck. She must have purchased them from the trading post.

Cornelius handed her a fist full of desert flowers—Indian paintbrush, larkspur, fiddlenecks, and others. "Every bride needs a bouquet."

"How thoughtful. Thank you, Cornelius." Eliana then eyed Yiska and pointed to the spot where her camera was all set up.

"Mr. Robbins has agreed to take a wedding photograph of us after the ceremony. That is, if you don't mind." Yiska recalled the day she had taken his picture and captured his heart forever.

Reverend Mattheson walked up to the two of them and placed a hand on each of their shoulders. "Are we ready?"

Eliana hesitated. "We have no rings."

He reached into his pocket and held two gold rings in the palm of his hand. "This is your father's wedding band. I thought you might need it." He smiled at Yiska.

Eliana looked at the smaller one. "And the other?"

"I've carried this with me for nearly twenty years. It belonged to my wife. . .your mother." Mattheson choked. "I'd be honored if you would wear it."

Eliana pressed her hand to her chest, and tears welled up. "The honor will be mine." She reached out and hugged him.

Yiska and Eliana led the procession down to the river's edge, where they pledged their lives to one another. After they exchanged rings, Reverend Mattheson handed Eliana an earthen vessel that Yiska had obtained at the trading post. "It's a Navajo wedding vase," Yiska said.

She studied it with curiosity. "It has two spouts."

"The bride and groom each drink water from it to symbolize two souls drawing spiritual nourishment from a single source." His eyes penetrated hers. "Our source is Christ, the river of life. He is the sun in my shadows, the light that brightens the shadows of my past. And He has blessed me with you."

"And me with you." Eliana took a sip from the vase, her glistening eyes upon him. She handed it to Yiska, and he drank from the opposite spout.

Yiska gazed at her, memorizing the moment, the way he felt with the late afternoon sun shining down upon him. . .them.

Tears of joy streamed down her cheeks and trailed over her lips. Yiska brushed light kisses over her moist mouth, sealing his love for his bride.

Eliana knew her face was as bright as the crimson sunrise when she exited her wedding tent with her husband the morning after they celebrated their holy matrimony. How wonderful it was to lie in Yiska's strong arms that night, reflecting on the joy of their marriage. But today was a new day, and the team would make the final leg of the journey toward Wilson's Peak.

The heat of the day as they rode through the desert would have been unbearable, if not for the light breeze coming off the San Juan River.

Yiska pointed to a huge, jagged rock formation protruding out of the sand several miles away. "There it is. Wilson's Peak. Some call it Shiprock, saying it looks like a clipper ship. But the Navajo called it *Tse` Bit' a i`*, 'rock with wings.'"

"I can see how it got its name." Eliana looked at the mysterious pinnacle and thought of how strange her life had become. Would they live in her house in Lake City? Could she keep the photography studio? Did Yiska want a family? "What else do you have in view, Yiska? I mean after the expedition. Will you continue to work for Mr.

Whiley as a guide?" What would become of her if he was gone for many months?

"I plan to make a home for my wife. For my children. Mr. Whiley is thinking of opening a second store in Lake City. He might let me run it, and I could also write for one of the newspapers. I have some money saved, so I hope we might keep your house and your photography studio."

"Oh, Yiska. Your plans are wonderful. It sounds like you've given them much thought."

"That's what a man does."

"And a woman."

Yiska rode Shadow closer to her, leaned in, and planted a kiss on her lips.

When they arrived near Wilson's Peak in the late afternoon, the surveyors set up their equipment and spread out in a triangular formation at points surrounding the pinnacle. It took quite some time to complete their measurements and document the astronomical coordinates. Eliana set up a camera on its stand to photograph the massive rock and the landscape of low plateaus and interesting formations.

By nightfall the team had settled down and gathered around the campfire. Rich blues and reds cast a luminous glow in the cloudy evening sky, creating an eerie backdrop against the great winged rock. Eliana missed Papa. She could imagine him sitting there chewing on his empty pipe, gazing up at the brilliant colors.

Cornelius slapped his hat against his leg. "Take that!" He looked up, all eyes on him. "A sand spider."

"The Navajo believe that killing a sand spider can make one bald," Yiska said. He leaned over to Mr. Robbins as he pointed to Cornelius's balding skull. "He has killed too many sand spiders." Laughter echoed into the night.

"You know so much, why don't you tell us about that fearsome rock over there." Cornelius nodded toward the silhouette of the pinnacle.

"All right," Yiska said. "A long time ago, the Diné were saved from their enemies after praying to their gods for deliverance. The ground rose, and they were transported into the east and lived on top of the rock. One day during a storm, while the men were away working the fields, lightning split off the trail, and only the sheer cliff remained. The women, children, and old men left on top starved. Their bodies are there to this day. It is forbidden to go there, so no one can stir up their ghosts or rob their corpses."

"That's a cheerful tale," Cornelius snickered.

Eliana hugged her coat around her and inched closer to Yiska. "Do you know any other Navajo legends?"

"There is another one of a large bird named Picking Up Feathers. He was the child of Diné gods, Sun and Changing Women. He lived on top of the peak and fed on human flesh. Each day he flew to Where the Mountain Went Out on Top to get men"—he leaned into Eliana's shoulder—"but never women. He now lives in the Sun's house."

"I'm glad to hear that. I wouldn't want him to come down and take you away from me so soon," she said.

Mr. Robbins stood and stretched. "All right, time to call it a night. Remember, we're more exposed out here, so we'll tighten our watch. And as you can tell, the temperature will continue to drop during the night."

Eliana smiled. She had Yiska to keep her warm.

Robbins continued, "We'll pull out at dawn and head north to Darling's Line to locate the four corners marker." He looked over at Yiska. "Oh, and thanks for the stories, Yiska. Let's hope they won't give us nightmares."

Four Corners – July 10, 1875

The next afternoon Eliana marveled when they reached the Colorado–New Mexico border in such good time. She was excited to finally see the original marker that Ehud Darling set in 1868. Mr. Robbins and his crew would install a new monument in its place, a seven-foot pillar of hard sandstone, and Eliana was here to document the historical occasion. She set up her camera, this time with Yiska's assistance. She thought it best to begin instructing him on how to handle the equipment. She'd need his help for the many hundred miles that awaited them as they continued south to survey the boundary between the Arizona and New Mexico territories.

"Is this where you want it?" Yiska asked.

Eliana turned around and checked the position. "Perfect. Thank you." Beyond him she noticed Chandler Robbins talking to his assistant surveyors. He seemed disturbed, and his hands flailed in every direction as he spoke.

A few minutes later, Robbins called the team together to explain the situation. "The marker is in the wrong location. According to my modern instruments, Darling fell three miles east of the proper intersection. It looks like we have to go a little farther west."

The teams loaded up and went on, and Chandler Robbins at last located the coordinates of the 37th parallel and 109th meridian from Washington.

Eliana held her camera on the site as Yiska helped some of the men lower the marker three feet into the ground while others kept watch with their rifles. The marker was set exactly in the place where the four territories intersected. Perhaps someday they would become states in this wonderful, wild land.

As the sun displayed its vibrant colors, Mr. Robbins and the survey team headed out to set up camp. Yiska helped Eliana load her photography equipment onto Sampson. And then he took her by the hand and walked her up to the marker for a closer look.

"Mr. Robbins etched the exact coordinates here, and the name of each territory on the sides." Yiska pointed to each one. "Utah, Colorado, Arizona, New Mexico."

Eliana looked with interest at each side of the square column. She tilted her chin and suppressed a smile. "There's only one problem, husband."

Yiska placed his hand on his hat and squinted. "What is that, wife?"

"You must decide where to kiss me." Eliana circled around the tall stone. "Here, here, here, or here?"

"That's no problem at all. I will kiss you in each territory, here and everywhere else on our journey."

"And I will hold you to that promise, my love."

Under the canopy of an Indian paintbrush sky, Yiska kissed Eliana. Again. And again. And again. At that moment Eliana knew the memory of this day would remain engraved on her heart forever, the perfect reward for the shadow catcher's daughter.

Dear Reader,

Love's Compass is my debut novel from 2012, originally titled *The Shadow Catcher's Daughter*. What an adventure it has been! I hope you enjoyed traveling along with Eliana and Yiska on their romantic journey as much as I did. Though their story is fictitious, the actual 1875 survey of the Four Corners was real, so I decided to have my characters tag along. Using the latest technology at the time, surveyor Chandler Robbins set the boundary for the corners and discovered the earlier survey at Shiprock, NM, was incorrect. A recent controversy indicated that the monument may not have been correctly placed as measured from the Greenwich Prime Meridian. But prior to 1912, and at the time of the 1875 survey, coordinates were measured from the Washington Meridian (about 3 miles difference). This is inconsequential, however, because the border between the states, as determined in the Robbins's survey, was accepted as the legal boundary. Today's monument is exactly where the state lines intersect.

When reading about Chandler Robbins I discovered that he served with photographer James F. Ryder in Ohio's 86th Infantry during the Civil War. Ryder is famed for capturing the war with his camera; thus I decided to make him John Van Horn's mentor, which in turn connected the three men as old wartime companions. Ryder stated once that what he saw through the lens of the camera was "faithfully reported, exact, and without blemish." That is how our heavenly Father sees his children. I do hope you believe how precious you are to Him.

I have a few other "real" characters like Mr. Wilson and Mr. Snowden in my story, but my favorite secondary character is Reverend George Darley. He was known as "missionary to the San Juans" and really did preach in saloons! He and his brother built the very first church on Colorado's western slope in 1876. For more information about the research involved in this novel and to learn more about George Darley's extraordinary adventures, please visit me online at carlagade.com.

If you liked this story please leave a review for me at Amazon.com and like my author page on Facebook. I hope you will enjoy the bonus story, *Pride's Fall*, by Darlene Franklin which also takes place in the Four Corners.

Love & Blessings,
Carla Gade

New Englander **Carla Gade** writes from her home amidst the rustic landscapes of Maine. With eight books in print she enjoys bringing her tales to life with historically authentic settings and characters. An avid reader, amateur genealogist, photographer, and house plan hobbyist, Carla's great love (next to her family) is historical research. Though you might find her tromping around an abandoned homestead, an old fort, or interviewing a docent at an historical museum, it's easier to connect with her online at carlagade.com.

Pride's Fall

By Darlene Franklin

Chapter 1

Mesa Verde, Colorado
June, 1899

Standing Corn waits at the entrance to her home on the cliff, gazing across the valley floor, looking for a sign that her promised, Killdeer, has returned from the hunt. She hears the call of the horn, announcing his return. Three short blasts followed by two longer blasts announce a successful foray, with plenty of food. The tribe will eat well tonight.

She rushes to the circle of elders to celebrate Killdeer's return. The women of the tribe grab bells and drums, and together the people go out to meet the men returning from the hunt.

Standing Corn sees Killdeer, the skin of the mule deer draped across his shoulders, leading the hunt party. The remaining hunters carry poles loaded with deer and pheasant and other trophies of the hunt. The juice of berries runs down Killdeer's beardless face.

Killdeer stops the procession in front of Standing Corn. He points to the bounty of the hunt, brandishing his bow and arrow. She lays an admiring hand on his muscled arm before she clasps her hands together and lifts them to the sky, showing her appreciation for his prowess. The expression on his face doesn't change, but he opens a pouch around his neck and hands her a necklace made of the teeth of a wolf. She clasps it to her breast and then holds it high for everyone to see. Cheers erupt from the crowd.

So far, so good. Rex Pride had climbed to the second level of dwellings built into the side of the cliffs. From here he could see the panorama of action taking place below him. He had never worked with untrained extras before, let alone a group of Indians. They found their marks; it should work on film.

He focused his eyes on Muriel Galloway, the actress playing

Standing Corn. In person, she was an ethereal beauty, with hair dark and luxurious enough that she didn't need a wig to portray an Indian princess—only a hairdresser—although her pale skin required heavy makeup. When he watched the rushes of today's film, he feared she would fade into the background and hold little more interest than the dull-eyed women trudging around her.

He'd invite her to watch with him. For an artist who demanded as much of herself as Rex did of the entire crew, she'd feel keen disappointment if his fears proved well founded. Instead of drawing every eye to her when she was on screen, she was lost in the crowd. From this height he gained some perspective. Crowd scenes often presented problems. A frown creased his face. Muriel rarely needed guidance, but she could do better. She must do better—exaggerate her gestures a little more. He'd work out the close-ups with camerist Benny Gruber later.

Women returned from the fields, holding baskets of corn in their arms and crossing directly in front of Muriel, cutting her off from the camera.

Rex raised his voice. "Cut!" Assuming Benny would relay his command, he climbed down the ladder at breakneck speed.

❧

"Cut!" Rex Pride's voice rang out high above the milling crowd of extras hired for the scene. Muriel scanned the area, locating him scrambling down the ladder.

Muriel sought the coolest spot she could find—a bit of shade underneath a canopy set up over the refreshments—and accepted a glass of lemonade from Frederic Fulton. Fred played the role of Killdeer in their current film project, *Ruined Hopes.* "What bee got in his bonnet? We didn't finish the scene."

"He'll tell us soon enough. I suspect it was me." Muriel resisted the urge to wipe away the sweat gathering on her brow. Smudging her makeup would result in time needed to repair the damage and make Rex more frantic. "He's going to tell me that I didn't project my emotions enough."

Rex Pride of Pride Productions demanded perfection. He was difficult, make that impossible, to work with, but no one understood the new medium of film better. Her time working with him had turned out to be everything she had imagined and more.

"We've got to do it again. You there." Rex called over Sarah, the Navajo woman who coordinated the extras. "What was that group of gatherers doing coming between Miss Galloway and the camera? They ruined the whole shot. We have to do it again from the top."

Sarah's face didn't reflect any umbrage at Rex's tirade. The actors endured Rex's demands because he was the best in the business film industry. But why would people with nothing to gain except a few seconds of exposure on a movie they might never see accept the abuse?

Something flickered in Sarah's impassive eyes as she nodded. "I will tell them." The extras clustered around her and listened intently.

"And you." Rex's voice brought Muriel's attention back to him. "Muriel, you are not on a stage. You are acting in front of a camera, and you must draw the camera's eye to yourself. If you cannot make the transition to film, stick to the stage."

Muriel bit back the retort on the tip of her tongue. *This is not my first film. My last film was well received.* "I will make adjustments."

Rex clapped. "Places, everyone." He scrambled back up the ladder while everyone returned to their places on the open ground.

Filming in the wilds of southwest Colorado represented a risk compared to working in a studio. Before they began working, Rex had shown them Thomas A. Edison's 1898 documentary, *Indian Day School,* filmed entirely on location in Isleta Pueblo, New Mexico. He had convinced Muriel at least that the authentic cliff dwellings would make *Ruined Hopes* unforgettable.

"Lights." Rex's voice boomed from above. Benny signaled his readiness. "Camera!" Another signal.

Muriel sank into Standing Corn's mind and assumed her pose, waiting for the return of Killdeer.

"And. . .action!"

They made it through the scene without interruption before Rex called "Cut."

Muriel breathed a sigh of relief. Unless Rex wanted to film the scene again, always a possibility, they had finished the day's filming. She wanted to watch both versions later to see what worked better about the second run-through.

The extras must have agreed that the day's filming had finished, since they streamed away from the staging area in groups of two or three. Their work was done; they didn't have to look at the film or memorize more lines or listen to Rex's criticism, as she did.

Rex climbed down the ladder and shouted, "Come back! We've got to do it again!" He motioned for Sarah to bring them back while he took one of the hunters aside. "Brent, you've got to make it look like you're carrying hundreds of pounds on that pole, not the paper-mache you have. Muriel, move your hands away from your eyes so that we can see your facial expressions better. And Helen. . ."

Muriel took a seat in one of the many rooms located along the base of the cliffs and accepted the drink that Sarah handed her. She wished she could remove the heavy makeup caked on her face, but that wouldn't happen until Rex was satisfied with the scene. Judging from his lengthy instructions, that wouldn't happen anytime soon.

Muriel didn't think she would ever grow tired of gazing at the cliffs. An entire civilization had once existed in these strange homes built into the rocks. Some of them were higher than the tallest building she had ever seen, the Tacoma Building in Chicago. She studied the honeycomb-like dwellings and prayed for God's peace in the middle of yet another difficult day on-site with Pride Productions. The call of "places, everyone" drifted in her direction. Most of the extras had returned, although she could see a cluster of people walking in the direction of their village.

She stood and prepared to go back out into the heat. Rex was striding toward her. The man was a perfectionist, a harsh taskmaster—a genius. He demanded only the best, and a film with Rex Pride would guarantee her pick of any role she wanted to play in the future.

If she survived the filming.

He was shouting by the time he reached her. "Miss Galloway."

"Muriel." Any other way was impossible.

"Other directors may allow you to dictate the pace of production, but I am not other directors. When I call for places, I expect—"

"You're certainly not like anyone else I've worked with."

"—you to respond immediately." He finished his tirade as if she hadn't said a thing.

Patience is a virtue, she reminded herself. She recalled the proverb that advised that a soft answer turned away wrath. "I started on my way as soon as you called."

He looked at her, a lock of dark hair falling over his forehead. "Then perhaps you should take refreshment closer to the set next time."

"Pride, the weather is beastly hot. Muriel's been a good sport," Fred Fulton said.

Fred was sweet to jump to her defense like that. Movies were the perfect medium for him. The British accent coming out of the mouth of someone dressed to look like an Indian wearing buckskin clothes would ruin the illusion moving pictures sought to create.

From the red hue spreading across Rex's face, Fred had taken her defense a step too far. She put a hand on Fred's shoulder.

"I don't mind, Fred, truly. What matters is that I am here now. Let's not waste any more time. We need to continue filming while we have the light." She searched for the small pyramid of pebbles she had used to mark the exact spot where she awaited Killdeer's return.

"Not there. Don't you even remember where I placed you?" Rex said crossly. "Move a yard to your right."

The light had changed, that's all. Taking a deep breath, Muriel shifted her position.

"No, that's not right, either." Pride looked up at the unpredictable sky. "It's starting to cloud over. Benny. . ."

Muriel wished she had something to fan her face with. . .a page of script, a palm frond—not that palms grew in this desert—but Standing Corn held nothing in her hand. The slight breeze swirling from the clouds overhead provided little relief. Perhaps Benny would say the cloud cover wouldn't work for this scene, and she could escape until the sun came out again. But no, even from this distance Muriel could see that Benny assured Rex all was well. He drew in the sand, probably suggesting the placement of the actors.

"I say, fellows, you can't just leave," Fred said.

The extras had called it a day. They carried the props to the storage tent and set off at a brisk pace for their village. All around Muriel, people glanced at the sky and talked among themselves. After storing the props they left, their exodus streaming a mile long on the valley floor.

Lightning split the clouds, and thunder echoed down the walls of the canyon.

"Muriel." Sarah had changed back into her usual clothing. "You and the other white men must gain the heights. When it rains, the water will flood this place."

Deafening thunder rolled down the canyon. Frustrated, Rex waited for silence before resuming his conversation with Benny.

With a look at the sky, where dark-lined clouds filled a horizon that was clear only an hour earlier, Benny shook his head. "We have to wait. If we try to film now, it won't match what we've already done. Sorry, Rex."

Rex scowled at the sky. Everything was against him today, even the elements. "Let's hope they pass as quickly as they gathered. We'll wait out the storm and start again."

"You won't find that too easy." Benny pointed to the people scurrying in the direction of their village.

Rex cursed under his breath. Why had he ever decided to work with Indians? Edison and his *Indian Day School*, that's who inspired him to use the Mesa Verde setting for *Ruined Hopes*. But apparently they were more committed to filming a story about their children than to working as extras. If he were anywhere else, he could hire a thousand people off the street who'd be thrilled to have their faces immortalized on film.

But he had chosen this location. He was Rex Pride, and his pride pushed him to do more, to try outrageous stunts never done before. With the motion picture industry so new, he found exhilaration in exploring the possibilities, in pushing the limits of what the medium could do. They had only skimmed the surface.

"I should dock their day's pay. I hope what you have in the can works, that we don't need to use them again."

"Rex!" Muriel ran in his direction, sweat forming on her face, creating cracks in her makeup. She should know better. The Indian woman who had attached herself to Muriel followed behind. No emotions showed on her face, but Muriel looked panicked. What nonsense had the women whispered in the actress's ear?

"You there." Rex crossed the distance between them in two long strides. "You can tell your friends not to come back."

The woman, rather heavyset with no spark to make it onto a movie set aside from this project, didn't react to his threat. "The rains come."

He didn't need an Indian to state the obvious. "I know that."

"When the rains come, the canyon floods." She spoke slowly, as if to a child.

Rex gawked at the pair of them. "Flood? This place is drier than the Sahara."

"Rex, listen to her." Muriel almost dislodged the braids down her back when she shook her head. "This canyon is going to flood. You have to give the order to move. No one is moving without your say so."

The more she tried to cajole him, the more he resisted. "No one is to leave. We will resume filming when the storm passes over."

"There is no place else for the water to go." Muriel removed the bone necklace from around her neck. "I refuse to risk my life or the lives of the crew. I am through for the day." She tilted her head back calculating the ladder. "The third story should do it." Glaring at Rex, she called a warning to the others remaining on the canyon floor.

Sarah slung a bag over her back. She turned her dark black eyes on Rex one final time. "You will not have much time once the rain starts." Adjusting the pack, she put her right hand on the ladder and climbed behind Muriel.

"Miss Galloway, come back down here."

"Later." The word floated through the air while she continued climbing.

During the exchange, the sky had turned black. "We can't film any more outdoor shots right now, Rex. Might as well call it a wrap." Benny covered his delicate cameras and toted them away.

"Et tu, Brute?"

The clouds let loose at that moment, speckling the dry ground. Disgruntled, Rex lifted the bullhorn to his lips. "It's a wrap." The crew that hadn't heeded Muriel's warning scattered in a dozen directions, moving equipment and props into various apartments along the ground floor.

Rex ran after Benny. "Give me that camera. I want to capture this on film." He passed Fred as he headed for his tent. "After the rain stops, get Muriel and come up to my quarters. I'm hoping we can film your close-ups from after the hunt."

"Yes, sir." The handsome leading man headed for the same ladder that Muriel had already climbed.

The sound of yelling and men racing around the set, rolling dollies and dragging set pieces, joined crackling thunder that sounded like it had landed less than a mile away. Rain pounded the ground as hard as horse's hoofbeats. He wished he could capture the sounds as well as the look. But he shut out the activity behind him. Fin-de-siècle dress and invention had no place in his prehistoric drama.

Instead he focused the camera on the horizon. Over there, he could see sunshine. The rain fell like a sheet from the clouds. He smiled at the image. Water painted the canyon walls, turning rose rocks brick red and sweeping away the dust that carpeted the set. He frowned. With the rain changing the landscape, tomorrow's shoot wouldn't match today's. *Next time, stick to a studio.*

The water took on the sound of a rushing stream. He swung his camera, seeking out the source. Someone shouted behind him, but he ignored him. Lightning split the sky, sending a rumble through the ground. There. He swung his camera around.

"Rex. Come on." Benny grabbed the camera from his hands and ran to the ladder.

Rex stared at the expanding pool of water, spreading across the once dry plain.

"Move!" Benny yanked Rex's arm in the direction of the nearest ladder.

The water roared, heading straight down the canyon.

Rex found his feet. Water rushed behind him, urging him up, up, up. He raced higher and higher, past the second level apartment. Only a couple of rungs above him, Benny shoved the camera into the opening and threw himself behind it.

Muriel's head appeared above him, rain plastering her loosened braids to her face. "Hurry. You're almost here."

Did he hear panic in her voice?

Water surged below him, rising faster than he could climb. He reached up two rungs and hurled himself into the opening.

"Muriel, this might be a good time to pray to that God of yours."

The roar in his ears drowned his voice.

Chapter 2

". . .Pray to that God of yours."

Muriel added a word of thanksgiving for this break in Rex's rejection of all things spiritual. Then she returned to her entreaties for God's mercy to protect them. Surely the third story was high enough but when she had looked over the side, she had seen the water rise a rung every few seconds.

The prospect didn't appear to worry Rex. He grabbed the camera and approached the doorway. Unable to stand, he stayed on his knees and leaned precariously over the edge, half in, half out.

"Do something," Muriel pleaded with Benny.

Benny tugged at Rex. "Are you crazy?"

"Hold my feet." Rex refused to budge. "This is great stuff."

"It's like trying to film Noah's flood. Won't make any difference if you don't survive."

"If I remember the story right, Noah survived the flood."

The sound of the water subsided a fraction, making it a little easier to hear him. His voice bounced off the walls; no one else was talking.

Benny shrugged. "Guess I better do what the boss says." He planted himself against the wall and locked his arms and legs around Rex's right leg. Fred took the other one.

No one moved or spoke. Water gurgled close by, too close. *Lord, I should have done more.* She had hoped this film, in the remote corner of the country inhabited almost entirely by Indians who hadn't embraced the Gospel, would give her opportunities to share her faith. So far she hadn't done much except pray with Benny.

The familiar sound of the end of film running through the camera was followed by a curse from Rex, something he did with alarming frequency.

If she died tonight, she would also miss out on love, marriage, motherhood. Her eyes strayed to Rex.

The Indians weren't the only ones who needed the Gospel.

Lord, give me more time. And courage.

Rex wiggled back from the edge. "I got most of it." A wide grin spread across his face—Rex Pride, "King of Film", at his arrogant best.

"The water?"

"Oh, it's started going down."

"It will be gone by morning," Sarah said.

That meant they would spend the night on the cliff. How accustomed she was to her creature comforts. Muriel spared a moment to wish she could remove her makeup and brush her hair. Until she did that, she couldn't release her screen persona and return to herself, simple Muriel Galloway of Gardiner, Maine. With a deep, cleansing breath, she resolved to meet the resourceless hours ahead with cheer and faith.

As if following her train of thought, Sarah pointed to the back of the apartment. In a corner lay a stack of kindling, as if waiting for their use. "Fire."

"That doesn't do us any good, unless you know how to rub two sticks together."

With the closest thing to a smile Muriel had ever seen on Sarah's face, she opened the bag she had carried up the ladder. "Flint." Within moments a small flame illuminated the reaches of the cave.

"Now that beats all." Benny huddled by the fire. "Come on, Rex, come down to our level."

Rex spread out his hands over the flames. Long, slender fingers, that would have done a pianist proud, but he used them to point and shake and generally intimidate his crew. Seen in this setting, his dark hair flopping over his thick eyebrows and obscuring his startling blue eyes, grime coating every spot on his face, he looked like only a man. A handsome man. A man willing to do anything, to go to any lengths, to accomplish what he wanted.

She had to admit, she resembled him that way. All actors shared hubris. To perform night after night, they had to. Film was even worse, capturing her every movement and expression for all time.

Across from her, Fred's face reflected the same emotions she was feeling: fear, relief, discomfort. An overall trembling when he realized how narrow their escape was. The actress in her registered every expression, cataloging them for future use.

"I say, I don't suppose you have any food in that bag of yours?" Fred said.

Sarah had already opened a pouch of cornmeal and was mixing it with water from her canteen. "I will add pepper. It will warm you for the night." She took an innocent-looking green vegetable and chopped it into small bits.

Benny lifted weary eyes. "Do you have any jerky with you? We might have a feast on our hands."

A shadow of a smile graced Sarah's face as she unfolded a thin strip of something dark and stringy. "From sheep."

"You came prepared." Rex spoke with grudging admiration.

"My people have experience with this land."

"And we appreciate your help." Muriel spoke with her brightest stage voice. "Don't we, Rex?"

Rex stared at the clearing sky, wishing he could continue filming. What a waste of an evening. He couldn't view the day's rushes, couldn't go over the planned close-ups with Fred and Muriel. . . .

"I said, don't we, Rex?"

"What?"

"Sarah has been invaluable to us today." Muriel's dark eyes dared him to disagree.

He looked at the Indian woman, who was slapping thin pancake-looking circles on a rock set into the circle of fire.

Muriel's face threatened mutiny if he dared to disagree. "Look around you, Rex. Look below. Sarah cared enough to warn us and has provided us with fire and food. Everyone else has gone." She leaned forward. "Aren't you concerned at all about your crew?"

Fred scooted to the entrance and leaned out. Projecting with the stage voice that could reach the back row, he said, "Hello? Is anybody there?"

"Fred, is that you?" A familiar New England drawl answered. Abe Brent, the actor who portrayed Killdeer's best friend in the film, answered.

Voices called from up and down the cliff. Rex relaxed. His crew had survived, and that meant they could continue working with minimal interruption.

"Cecil Zimmer." Muriel pointed dramatically. "We haven't heard from Cecil."

"Zimmer." Rex repeated the name under his breath, trying to place the man.

"Cecil Zimmer, you say?" Fred said. He leaned out again. "Has anyone seen Cecil Zimmer?"

A chorus of "noes" came back. "I saw him." One lone voice answered, but they couldn't hear more

Details rushed through Rex's head. Zimmer. That was right. Short, redheaded, cheeky lad who refused to take Rex too seriously. Although he drove Rex crazy at times, his work was invaluable. And the equipment. . . He ran his hand through his hair and then looked at it. Grimy. He needed a bath, but he didn't think he would have a proper bath again until he left Mesa Verde behind.

"He's a good bloke. Always good for a laugh." Fred ran a hand across his forehead.

"Good at his job." Benny said.

"The food is ready." Sarah handed Rex a round golden cake and a strip of some kind of dried meat. He sniffed the cake. "What's in this? It practically singed the hairs off my nose."

"That would be an improvement on your appearance." Benny grinned. "Those green bits add flavor. Try it. You'll like it."

Rex sniffed it again. Benny rolled it like a cigarette paper, so he followed suit and took a bite. Fire exploded in his mouth and seared his throat. "What is that?"

"Jalapeño." Benny stuffed the rest of the cake into his mouth. "As good as the tortillas I had in Albuquerque."

"Wrap it with the meat." Muriel smiled.

"You're laughing at me."

"Not at all." But her smile widened. "Drink some water." She handed him a canteen that must have also come from Sarah's bag.

Rex turned to the woman. "I don't know whether to thank you for the food and water or curse you for burning my mouth. But I do appreciate all you have done today." He looked at Muriel, his gaze asking, *There, does that satisfy you?*

"Do you have another tortilla?" Benny had devoured his in seconds.

A smiling Sarah handed him one. Silently she held up a final. . . what did Benny call it? Tore-tea-ya?

"I'll pass."

Benny's second tortilla went the way of the first. They passed the canteen around the circle. "Does anyone want to join me in prayer?" Muriel asked.

Here she goes.

"Of course." Benny leaned over, his hands steepled in theatrical fashion.

Rex stifled a groan. He wouldn't work with these two fanatics if they weren't the best at what they did.

Fred joined Benny, willing to go along. Sarah sat back as if prepared to let them take the lead now that she had provided supper.

"Do whatever you want." Rex curled up against the wall, feigning sleep.

He couldn't shut out Benny's gravelly voice. The man thanked the Almighty for everything from the sunshine to the day's filming to the ridiculous rain "that refreshed the earth." Did Noah thank God for the supposed flood? These Christians could be crazy.

Next Benny thanked God for each person in the chamber—for

Sarah's warnings, for Fred's cheerfulness, for Muriel bringing Sarah's warning to their attention, and then. . .

"And I thank you, God, for Rex. For his vision of the film. For the creative gift You placed in him. Help him as he leads us."

So now this man was crediting God with Rex's skill? He could hardly keep his mouth shut.

Benny's rambling prayer ended with "Amen." Muriel prayed next. If only he could capture her voice on film. Listening to her ordinary speech gave him pleasure. When speaking in her natural accent, her broad vowels and dropped *r*'s sounded musical. Even if she read a parish record, he might enjoy it. She pleaded for the lives of the people, the Indians who had fled the scene before there was reason. She even prayed for the equipment and the day's films.

God didn't care about Rex's work. Did He?

After their prayer time, Muriel decided to investigate the apartment where they found themselves. She should be able to stand. At her full height, her head brushed the ceiling. The men wouldn't be able to straighten. Shadows from the flames danced on the walls of the chamber where they sat. Too bad they didn't have any torches handy so she could explore the other rooms hinted at by dark openings.

What were the people who lived here like? Why did they choose to live in rooms high above the ground? Today they had seen the wisdom of settling above the canyon floor, but they could have found other options. Thousands crowded together in prehistoric cities, faced with the same problems as all urban environments: food, sanitation, crime.

Bending her head slightly, she circled the room, glad for the opportunity to stretch her legs. It didn't take long. Sitting back down, she undid her braids. She ran her fingers through her hair in lieu of brushing out the tangles.

She caught Rex staring at her, and she blushed. He looked at her as if he had never seen a woman's hair before. She turned her back to him to preserve an illusion of privacy.

Sarah dug into her bag again. "Let me fix your hair." She gestured with a comb beaded along the edge.

"Thank you. You are a miracle worker." *I shouldn't have said that. A comb is not a miracle.*

The same fleeting smile appeared on her face, and Sarah sat down behind Muriel. Starting with the ends of Muriel's hair that dangled to her waist, Sarah tugged the comb through the strands. "Is the hair of all white women this soft?"

"Soft?" Muriel laughed. "At the moment it feels heavy with oil and dirt."

"If you come to my village tomorrow, I will arrange for you a bath." She paused. "In privacy."

Muriel grimaced as the comb broke through the tangles. God had opened the door for her to spend time among the Navajo. "That would be lovely."

Sarah lifted down a second layer of hair and gently worked the comb. "Your dress is not like what white women wear."

Muriel looked at the buckskin dress, lengthened to allow her modesty, although still uncomfortably short. Colored beads and fancy stitching covered the front. "The costume director wants to make me look like one of the Ind—one of the Old Ones who lived here years ago."

"It is a good thing you are showing this movie to others." Sarah's hand quivered as she tugged through a tangle, suggesting laughter rippling down her arms. "No Diné will recognize this as clothing we might wear."

Muriel looked at her dress—beautiful, intricate, designed to flatter her figure and draw attention. She hadn't noticed the difference from the practical clothing Sarah and the other Navajo had worn. "What would you suggest?"

"We wear clothing made from the wool of sheep. The Old Ones might have worn clothes from hunting and not from the field. But this dress is fancy. For a special ceremony. Not for every day." She glanced over Muriel's shoulder at her bare ankles. "I think they would wear shorter dresses, since they climbed up and down so often. Long dresses are not practical."

Muriel fingered the fringe that lengthened the design. Even this length was uncomfortable for her. Any shorter and movie theaters might refuse to run *Ruined Hopes.*

"I will ask the wardrobe mistress to speak with you. In fact, you would be a tremendous asset to the film. Would you be willing to come back? Advise us so we do things right?"

Muriel felt the shrug. Sarah worked on the crown of her head now, running the comb from crown to end with only little resistance.

"Muriel." Rex's voice boomed across the room. "Come over here. I want to discuss tomorrow's filming with you and Fred."

Sarah ran the comb through the rest of Muriel's hair then pulled it back with a tie. "I will braid your hair in the morning."

"Thank you." Muriel stood, bending over to make sure she didn't run into the ceiling.

"Anytime, Miss Galloway." Rex lifted a hand as if to forestall the objection she might make.

The three men sat in a circle. Rex grinned at her. They looked worse than she did, if that was possible. Stubble covered Rex's chin. Rain streaked the makeup coloring Fred's pale English skin. He had removed his heavy wig and light brown hair incongruously framed his darkened face. Benny had a grin that never changed. None of them looked their best, and her own bedraggled appearance no longer seemed so important. She sat down, pulling on her dress to cover as much as possible of her legs.

Rex ran his hand through his hair, so that it stood in spikes in places. "As soon as we can get out of this hole, we will view the rushes from today's shoot. I hope we have enough of the crowd scenes. Extras." He said the word with disdain.

"Different than the stage, I'll give you that." Fred crossed his legs with all apparent ease. He flashed a smile at Muriel. "That's what makes you so special, m'dear. Even in a crowd, even without that siren's voice of yours, you draw every eye." He saluted, and Muriel blushed.

"A lot of that is the magic of the camera." Muriel turned the praise aside.

Rex grunted, which came as no surprise. Muriel didn't expect praise from him.

She told herself she didn't want it or need it.

With her hair hanging loose down her back, Muriel looked almost fresh. Rex found himself smiling. A perfectly ordinary reaction to a beautiful woman, he told himself. He had never kidded himself about Muriel Galloway's beauty. In an industry where beauty was as common as the sunrise, she stood out.

He wouldn't have hired her to work on *Ruined Hopes* if she didn't. Between his reputation for great film and Muriel's star power, the film was assured success.

"We'll have to make some adjustments to tomorrow's schedule." Rex ran through what he hoped to accomplish in the morning.

"Before we film anything else. . ." Muriel lifted her hand like a child at school. "Sarah says our costumes are not believable. Anyone who lives in the area will laugh at us."

"Who knows what the old Indians wore. She doesn't have any photographs, does she?"

"Of course not. But what she said made sense. This dress is too fancy for every day."

Fred snorted. "People go to the movies to escape. They hope for better than what they have at home. The party dress is fine." He looked down at his buckskin shirt. "Did she have any suggestions for my costume? I'd love to hear whatever she recommends."

"Absolutely. In fact, Rex, I believe Sarah would be a valuable addition to the crew. We need someone who can set us straight about Indian customs and the like."

Rex's temper flared. "I've decided against working with the Navajo extras again. Today they showed how undependable they were."

She opened those wide brown eyes, eyes that drew audiences into the depths of her soul. "They left because they knew the canyon would flood. Do you expect them to risk their lives?"

"We escaped, didn't we?" On the set, his word was law. The quality of the film depended on it. "They had no business leaving before I dismissed them."

"That's why we need Sarah." Muriel wouldn't let it go. "We need someone who can help both sides understand each other."

"I say it's a good idea," Fred said.

Rex tilted his head and stared at the Indian woman. Impassive, she stared back. She nodded, as if accepting a position he hadn't yet decided that he wanted to offer.

"Very well. I will discuss it with her."

"Good." Muriel turned on the wide smile that invited the audience to laugh with her. "Now, have you given further thought to my request for a daily chapel for the crew?"

Chapter 3

Rex gritted his teeth against the anger he felt. He didn't want to unleash his feelings in this confined space. To paraphrase the old adage, give her a minute of time on film, and she'd demand an entire reel.

"We've discussed this already." Rex focused all his outrage into his voice. Rising to his feet, his head rammed into the ceiling, and he swore. Muriel winced. *Good.* He was a decent man, even if he occasionally let loose with words that expressed his feelings, and he didn't need any of that mumbo jumbo that she and Benny bought into. He sat back down.

"There are ladies present." Fred spoke into the silence.

"Miss Galloway knows my opinion on the subject. We are making a film, not holding a revival meeting. Not everyone shares her religious views."

Muriel looked at Benny, as if seeking his support. He obliged. "Neither one of us wants the chapel to be mandatory. God wants a willing heart."

"We only ask for a short time in the morning schedule to meet with any who wish to join us." She smiled that beguiling smile that worked so well on film.

"Look at it this way, chum." Fred winked in Muriel's direction. "These two do-gooders will work all the harder if they believe they have God's blessing."

That made Muriel laugh, something Rex knew his fussing never allowed. "Does that mean you will join us, Fred?"

He shrugged. "I might check it out."

Rex felt the eyes of all those gathered on him, including Sarah's taking in everything, revealing nothing. "Very well. As long as we take advantage of all the light possible." His eyes bored into Benny's, challenging him to disagree.

"We'll do that." The photographer grinned. "You're welcome to join us any time."

"That's not going to happen."

"We can always hope." Benny clapped him on the back.

"And pray. Thank you, Rex." Muriel's soft eyes reminded Rex of the prayer she had raised on his behalf earlier.

He huffed and turned his attention elsewhere. "You there. Sarah. Come on and join the party."

The woman stood—she didn't have to worry about hitting the ceiling, she could almost wear a hat and still fit—and shuffled her way to their circle. She took a place beside Muriel. Looking at her, Rex realized how different her clothing was from what they had designed for the cast. But what did it matter? *Ruined Hopes* was a fictional story about people who lived hundreds of years ago.

"Miss Galloway has recommended that we hire you as an advisor on the film. I have agreed to her suggestion. Tomorrow you can meet with the scriptwriter and wardrobe director."

Sarah stirred. "If I work for you, my brother must also come."

Rex sat back. This. . .native. . .was refusing his job offer? "My understanding was that you wanted the job."

"Yanaba is a hunter. He talked with me about the scene you filmed today. He will be a help."

Irritated at having his hand forced to hire not only one, but two, extra crew members, Rex frowned. "Very well. You and your brother can report for work tomorrow."

She nodded but said nothing further, earning a grudging smile from Rex. He valued a woman who knew how to keep her own counsel. She poked at the fire. "We do not have enough wood to burn all night."

Rex stared out the door. The neighboring canyon wall blocked most of the sky. "Then we'd best get settled for the night before the lights go out." He flashed a devilish grin. "I don't suppose you have any blankets in that bag of yours?"

Sarah shook her head once.

"Then good night, all." He stretched out with his head facing the opening, a light breeze stirring his hair, keeping it from being plastered against his face. He doubted if he would sleep a moment, not with the events of the day recycling through his mind time and again.

Muriel lay next to Sarah on the far side of the room, finding privacy in the shadows that turned into midnight blackness when the fire went out. Like the princess and the pea, she felt every pebble that had scattered across the floor under her. She folded her arms under her head, but she didn't know if that was an improvement over having the rock for a pillow. Was Jacob this uncomfortable when he took that trip so far away from home, when he saw the angels on the ladder? If she could spot a star, she'd imagine the ladder reaching all the way up to God. The thought gave her some comfort, and she drifted into sleep.

The next thing she knew, she opened her eyes to a sky turning a pale gray. Rex stood in the opening, leaning out far enough that he didn't need to bend. Her breath caught in her throat, afraid he might tumble to his death.

His shoulders squared, ready to take on everything the world threw his way. A leader among men, he would have succeeded in any place or any time. So much to admire about the man, so brilliant—so sad, without the Lord. Once again she asked God for a chance to share the Gospel with him, that he would be receptive to the message. A man like Rex would find it difficult to admit he needed anything, let alone salvation.

Muriel's stomach growled, and Rex ducked back into the room. "Fred?"

"It's Muriel."

"We should be able to climb to the canyon floor. I don't know how easily Cook can fix a meal for us, however."

Benny sat up and stretched. "No worries. Cook moved our

foodstuffs the day before yesterday. He was worried about animal predators, not floods, but it turns out it was the smart thing to do."

By the time they reached the canyon floor, the entire camp was stirring. Muriel expected the ground to be soaked, like the muddy morass of spring from her New England childhood. But aside from being a little soft underfoot, only a few hollows of water here and there gave evidence to yesterday's downpour.

Desperate for a bath, Muriel decided to find out what happened to Cecil Zimmer. She sought out Benny, where he was checking through equipment. "How does it look?"

"Not bad. A broken lens on one camera, but I have a replacement. No need to stop filming. Rex will be pleased."

Muriel laughed. "Has anyone seen the missing man this morning? Cecil?"

As she spoke the words, a cheer erupted from the crew. Zimmer had returned. Out of the corner of her eye, Muriel noticed Rex heading in his direction. *I have to head him off.*

She stretched her legs and reached Cecil at the same time. "We have been so concerned for you. You were in our prayers last night."

Rex snorted but didn't dispute her claim.

Muriel noticed wrapping around his arm. "What happened?"

"I got knocked around a bit climbing out the end of the canyon. Some of those Navajo folks helped me to their village and did my arm up proud."

"That's a blessing." Muriel touched his forearm. "How bad is it?"

"It will heal." He shrugged. "You don't have to worry about me, Mr. Pride. I can do my job, no problem."

"I'll get a doctor to take a look at it. Don't want to trust your future to a bunch of uneducated Indians."

"I'm sure it's fine. Nothing's broken, just a little sore."

Problem solved, Rex turned his attention to the day's work. Muriel could almost see the wheels turning in his head, calculating how quickly the daylight would disappear. He glanced at a piece of paper in his hand then looked Muriel up and down. "How much time will you need to get ready?"

She put her hand to her hair, wishing she could wash it, but Rex wouldn't allow that much of a delay. How much time did she need to freshen up and scrape off yesterday's makeup and grime and check her costume for damage? Speaking of costumes. . .

"Are we going to make any changes to the costumes?"

Rex scowled. "I don't know. Yates will be bringing me her recommendations by the end of the day. We will keep to today's schedule. If we change the costumes, we'll reshoot the scenes again later."

Muriel stifled a sigh. This was her job, after all. "I can be ready in an hour."

"Good." Rex flashed a smile at her. "I'll be in my tent looking at yesterday's rushes."

Rex went through the reel shot by shot. Not bad, but not great, until the scene where the women crossed in front of Muriel. The camera continued rolling, and his pulse quickened. He stuck his head out the tent flap. "Benny!"

The photographer glanced up from where he was overseeing the setup of the cameras and waved.

"You've got to see this. And bring Ernie with you."

Rex paused the film at a screen that showed the water cresting the first level of the cliffs, rustling the branches of the trees it rushed past. Moments later, Benny entered with Ernie Warner, the man responsible for coordinating stunts.

"What is it, boss?" Benny seemed untouched by the previous evening's excitement. He had found a basin to wash his face and shave his beard, and he was ready to go again. He glanced at the screen and whistled. "You got it."

In response Rex rolled the film back. "This is when the flood started."

Watching it from start to finish, Rex relived the moments. In some ways, it was like he was living it for the first time. While it was happening, he was too focused on capturing it on film to feel any terror. Seeing it, he wondered how they had escaped total destruction. His crew had done an amazing job protecting both life and equipment.

Muriel would give the credit to her God, not to the careful preparations and plans for emergencies Rex had put in place as producer and director.

When the film ran out, no one spoke for a moment. "We have to use this in the film," Benny said. "If you can shoot footage like that, you should be behind the camera, not me."

Rex smiled, accepting the compliment before he turned his attention to Ernie. "This is great, but I want a context for it. I'm thinking Killdeer rescues Standing Corn from the flood. I want you to arrange a stunt that we can superimpose on this footage." He backed up the film and pointed to an outcropping at the entrance to the canyon. "Here."

Ernie leaned forward, staring at the still. Then he opened the flat and stared down the canyon. "It's still the same. I wondered if yesterday's flood changed the scenery at all. It doesn't look like it." He shook his head. "I guess what is left is pretty sturdy."

"Like that shrub growing out of the rock over there." Benny nodded across the way. "I'll see if I can work that image into the film somewhere."

Rex grew impatient. "Can you do it?" He made a note in his diary to add it to the film schedule.

The tent flap opened, and Muriel poked her head in.

"Come in. We're discussing how to use the flood in the film. Ernie's cooking up a terrific stunt."

Muriel's eyes fixed on the screen. "You're crazy, you know that?" The tone of her voice expressed what her words did not. She was impressed, proud of what he had accomplished.

"Genius or fool, the two go hand in hand." He took a second

look: she had changed out of the costume she had worn yesterday and instead wore a longer wool skirt in an earthy rust color, the color of the rocks in this distant corner of the United States. She wore a matching linen blouse.

"Where did you get that outfit? I haven't decided on changing costumes yet."

Muriel lifted her shoulders in a delicate shrug. "My costume showed the wear and tear of yesterday's events. Sarah loaned these to me instead. If you wish to wait until my costume is repaired. . ." She blinked her eyes, eyes that needed little kohl to shine as black as an Indian's, and smiled.

Fred appeared at that moment. He had also changed into trousers of a similar material to Muriel's skirt. Benny stood and walked outside the tent. "We'd better get to work while the light is good. Sarah said these late afternoon rains are frequent, although it doesn't flood often."

"Next time, the studio." Rex stood and brushed down his slacks, which only succeeded in dislodging a clump of mud.

"That's what you say every time." Benny grinned. "But then you find a way to make it work."

Trust Benny to help Rex feel better. "That is so true. Let's get rolling."

❧

"Cut."

At Rex's call, Muriel accepted the chair Sarah pulled out for her in the somewhat cooler shade of the overhang, and handed her a glass of water. They had been filming for three hours nonstop, and the day had passed the midpoint.

"Sarah, if Rex hadn't already hired you as a consultant, I'd want you as my assistant." Muriel sipped the water in the glass. Cool, though not cold, liquid slid down her throat, and she emptied the contents in one long drink. Her stomach recoiled, and the muscles in her legs quivered.

"I will do both." Sarah refilled the glass. With a damp towel, she sponged the top of Muriel's head. Blessed relief flushed down her neck and arms.

"Be careful of my makeup." She didn't want to have to reapply it. The night had left her drained. She blinked her eyes against the stars wanting to dance in front of her eyes.

"Are you waiting in there all day?"

Sarah glanced at the spot where Rex stood, arms akimbo on his hips. "Does he always bark?"

Muriel laughed. "He often does. We have a saying in English. . . his bark is worse than his bite. Just do your best to ignore him. He appreciates excellence. And now I need to return to work. Thank you for the refreshment."

Muriel took her place in front of the camera. They were working on a love scene today.

"Muriel, you must make the audience believe you are in love with your Indian hunter. You must become Standing Corn and greet Killdeer with all the love stored in her heart."

Muriel counted under her breath. She was a leading lady of stage and film who had played romantic heroines to great acclaim. What more Rex wanted from her, she didn't know. She could say with all honesty that she didn't feel well, but Rex didn't abide excuses. Today she fought light-headedness. It was hard to act when she had to concentrate to stay on her feet.

"Take your cues from Fred. He burns with his passion for you."

She sighed. "I will try."

"Once we get this in the can, we'll break for lunch."

Muriel shut her eyes, focusing on what she needed to portray. Her failure was holding up a much needed break for everyone.

Once again Fred swept her into his arms. His eyes, darkened with tinted lenses, flamed with desire. His arm held Muriel's waist in a gesture that implied intimacy. His lips brushed hers.

Heat surged through Muriel at his touch. She sagged in Fred's arms, rendered lighthearted by his caress. Rex should be pleased. Blackness overcame her senses.

Something soft cushioned Muriel's head. Someone had loosened the strings on her blouse and cool air brushed her skin.

"Muriel?" Fred's face flickered over hers. "Are you all right?"

She blinked her eyes and stared at the sky overhead. "What happened?"

"You fainted. In my arms, actually. You didn't have to go that far for realism." Fred's smile was strained.

"Here. Drink."

Sarah hovered by her side. "It is not wise to go about in this heat. I told Mr. Pride, but he did not listen."

Heat had engulfed Muriel just prior to her faint, heat that had nothing to do with Fred's acting or her reaction but with their physical surroundings.

"I haven't heard that you were subject to fainting fits." Rex stared at her from the entrance to the tent.

"I'm not. Usually." When Muriel tried to sit up, dizziness swept through her again. She fell back against the pillow. "I'm sorry." She nodded at her aide. "Sarah has some ideas for dealing with the heat."

Sarah's dark eyes regarded Muriel. Without asking permission, she took a washcloth and began removing the makeup.

"Wait. We're not done filming."

"This powder does not allow her skin to breathe. Her pale skin does not like the sun."

With each gentle dabbing at her skin, Muriel felt herself ease.

"It is not wise to work in the heat of the day." Sarah finished removing the makeup. "You should eat and rest. I will come back later when it is cooler." With that announcement, Sarah walked away.

Trousered legs appeared by Muriel's side, and she looked up into Benny's smiling face. He dropped to a crouch. "Feeling better?"

"A bit." This time when Muriel sat, she was able to remain upright.

In a chair at the opposite end of the tent, Fred had removed his wig, and the makeup artist was removing the makeup. "That woman has a point. We all need a break."

Thank you. Muriel sent a silent expression of gratitude in Fred's direction.

"A siesta. It makes sense in this heat." Benny winked at Muriel.

"Very well." Rex squatted by Muriel. "You are better?"

Muriel thought she saw a glimmer of concern in his eyes. "I will be. I've never had this problem before." Heat rose in her cheeks, and Rex handed her a cup of water. Her face flamed even warmer. "I am sorry for causing such a fuss." Using the drink as a distraction from her blush, she looked down the canyon. "Perhaps the light will stay with us longer today."

"Can you guarantee no more storms?" He quirked an eyebrow.

"I prayed for sunshine today." She thought of it and almost choked on the water in her throat. "God gave me a little more than I expected."

Rex laughed outright. "If your prayers have that much power, I'll give you a shopping list for your chapel meetings."

"It doesn't work like that." But Muriel felt herself returning his smile.

"Let's go to lunch, shall we?" He held out a hand and helped her to her feet.

Muriel had expected the gruff director who barked out orders. She didn't know how to handle this kinder, gentler version of the same man.

Chapter 4

Rex didn't know if he believed Muriel's claims that she felt well enough to work again. Her strong work ethic had drawn his attention when he cast her, but continuing to film when she might faint again was counterproductive. Devoid of makeup, her skin still looked flushed. Sunburned, overheated, both?

His mind scrambled with possibilities. After two days of mishaps, the film schedule had fallen behind. Since Muriel appeared in almost every scene, any illness severe enough to keep her from working would set them back more than they were.

He was helpless against the draw of her warmth, the quality that made her so powerful on film. He could have hired another actress for less money, but he had wanted the best. Muriel's understudy, Helen Tucker, could take over for a few scenes, but why settle for second best?

He helped Muriel to a seat. "You stay here. I'll get your lunch." As he piled a plate with the side dishes Muriel loved, plenty of vegetables and fruit with the smallest sliver of a sandwich, he noticed the stares of the crew. When had he memorized her preferences in food? He set the plate in front of her and returned to a seat at the opposite end of the table, where the seats around him remained empty.

Helen Tucker, who played Standing Corn's sister in addition to replacing Muriel if she should have to leave the film, surveyed the table before approaching Rex. "Is this seat taken?"

Bother. "No, please join me." He held the chair for her, proving he did have manners when the mood struck him.

A natural blond, Helen's physical beauty equaled Muriel's. Once in makeup and costume, she could pass for Muriel at a distance. She was a competent actress, and made a point to agree with Rex even when he was at his most quarrelsome.

"If Muriel doesn't feel well tomorrow, I could stand in for her." She batted her eyelashes, long and curling, with the full effect of a makeup brush.

Her agreeable nature didn't quite hide her ambition.

"Muriel assures me she is prepared to return to work after our luncheon." He removed his notebook from his pocket. "Now if you don't mind. . .I want to go over the film schedule."

"Of course, Mr. Pride."

The woman's sweetness could be cloying. Rex glanced at Muriel from his lowered eyes. Muriel was a fighter, and Rex admired that in a woman. Her standards for perfection approached his own.

He flipped through the calendar he held in his hand. Storms, illness, extras, costumes. . .what further problems would this production encounter? Even with built-in days for unexpected delays, they were already running close to going over budget.

He drummed the calendar with his fork, a *rat-a-tat* sound. His planned film schedule allowed for eight to ten hours a day spent filming. Now they would lose an hour to two hours a day to a siesta. If Muriel could faint, so could anyone else. If more afternoon thunderstorms came, they'd have to shut down early again. With luck, they might average six hours a day.

He knew his math. Six days a week, ten hours a day, for eight weeks. . .480 hours. Adjust that figure to six hours a day, and he would need thirteen weeks—three months instead of two. Out of the question. Not only was it cost prohibitive, several key members of the cast and crew had back-to-back commitments and couldn't remain beyond two months. He'd have to reduce the number of takes of each scene and find extra pockets of time to film. If they cut out the religious observances, he'd gain an extra day each week. Without chapel, he'd have an extra hour a day to work with. That would come close to making up the difference.

He sneaked another glance at Muriel, who had bent over her now-empty plate with folded hands. Saying grace, he assumed. She would never agree to work on Sundays, but the morning chapel service was a different matter.

He was the director. He had the right to set the schedule at his discretion. Muriel would just have to live with it.

"Cut! And that's a wrap." Rex made a circular motion with his hand.

Muriel relaxed. The long, exhausting day had ended, and she had survived the afternoon hours without incident. Sarah plied her with water on their breaks more frequently than the morning. About the time Muriel reached the limit of her endurance, Sarah called a break. God had answered her prayer for more understanding from Rex.

"Do you still wish to come to my village?" Sarah followed Muriel to her tent. Without a word, she helped Muriel out of the clothes she had worn that day. The fabric scratched at her face as she pulled it over her head.

Muriel studied her reflection in a mirror. With the makeup removed, sunburn was evident in her red face. "You mentioned a bath?" Muriel slipped on her normal clothes, a light chiffon that provided some relief from the continuing heat of the day. "I almost wish it would rain. That cools the air somewhat."

"I have asked my mother to prepare a bath for you." Sarah helped with the buttons on her dress. "We will return in time for your church in the morning."

"Thank you. And I hope you will join us in our chapel service some time. It is open to all."

Sarah smiled in a way that Muriel had come to recognize as disapproval parading as agreement. *Lord, give me openings tonight. You know I wish to share Your love with these people.*

The shadow of a man's figure appeared outside the tent. "That is my brother."

"Oh, yes, you mentioned him last night. I'm looking forward to meeting your family."

A more sincere smile graced Sarah's face. "We do not often get to entertain a motion picture star in our hogan."

Her statement answered one of Muriel's questions. . .whether the Navajos had ever seen a movie.

Muriel tucked a small Bible into her purse, together with a night dress and a few other essentials. "I'm ready. Is it a far walk?"

"It will take about one hour. We are not in Colorado but in New Mexico, in the Dinetah. You will need shoes for walking." Her brief glance at Muriel's feet expressed everything she left unsaid about the Louis heels on Muriel's favorite pair of shoes.

"I have just the right footwear." Reaching for a pair of brand-new boots, purchased when she learned she'd be traveling to the remote Four Corners region, Muriel wiggled out of her shoes. Unfortunately, she hadn't broken them in yet. She changed to a heavier pair of stockings and dusted the insoles of the boots with baby powder before slipping them on. Sarah smiled in approval.

Sarah filled two canteens and handed one to Muriel, probably a habit ingrained in her since she was still too young to talk in full sentences. "Never travel anywhere without water." Next she handed Muriel a flat-brimmed hat with a red tassel tied in front. "Wear this while we walk. Your face is red like a pepper plant."

Muriel resisted the urge to rub at the irritated skin. Ducking back into her tent, she grabbed a vial of body lotion, although the alcohol might irritate her skin further. Back home in Maine, when Muriel's skin burned, Mother used to prepare a cool bath with baking soda and oatmeal. Maybe Sarah had some local remedy at her home.

They walked at a steady pace, Muriel's boots surprisingly comfortable. What point marked the boundary between the state of Colorado and the territory of New Mexico, Muriel didn't know. Unlike the Piscataqua River which separated Maine from New Hampshire, it was a manmade boundary determined by imaginary lines of latitude and longitude. Without her companions, she would have been lost within ten minutes in the monotonous desert landscape.

After an hour's walk, Muriel spotted conical images taller than the shrubs. "Is that your village?"

Sarah nodded. "My mother waits supper on us."

The prospect of a bath and supper hurried Muriel's steps. As they neared, she noticed more of the construction of the buildings. Made of brush and logs, each house opened in the same direction, to the east. Six to eight sides created an almost circular form. Smoke curled from the top of the roof, and she sniffed in appreciation of the meal to come.

What a supper it was. Blue-colored dumplings made from cornmeal, mutton flavored with celery and onions, squash, melons, goat cheese. Some foods she had never seen, but others were cooked and combined in ways she had never experienced. She might get a stomachache from so many new sensations, but she figured it was worth it. The flavors were a world away from the sea-inspired menus of her childhood, but seemed so much a part of this place.

Compared to her family, Sarah was a positive chatterbox. Her brother, who introduced himself as Charlie, hadn't said more than three sentences during their walk. A small girl of seven or eight dominated the conversation. Seeing the family together, Muriel could identify family traits: The same single swirl of hair on their right temple. The same straight nose with a slight hook to the left. Eyes incredibly dark that either sparkled with fire or joy and turned as opaque as obsidian.

When Sarah's mother accepted her offer of help in cleaning up, Muriel felt as though she had been accepted as part of the tribe. The woman showed Muriel everything that she needed to know without saying a word. When the last dish had been put away, she led Muriel to a low-lying table where she placed one of Muriel's publicity photos. "You sign?"

"What is your name?"

"Dibe."

Muriel stopped herself just in time from asking how to spell it. Not knowing the educational level of Sarah's family, she didn't want to embarrass her. "I'm sorry, I didn't understand. Could you say it again?"

"Dibe. D-i-b-e."

Muriel must not have succeeded in hiding her surprise, for the older woman smiled broadly. "I spent eight years in a government school."

Muriel shook her head. "I didn't know. In fact, I know very little about the Navajo. Only what I have read in books."

"Books only tell part of the story." She flashed a smile that reminded Muriel of Sarah.

"Your bath is ready." Sarah held a towel over her arm.

Muriel luxuriated in water warmed by the midday sun. She rinsed her hair once, then twice, until the water ran clear. By then the grime on her skin had loosened, and she was able to clean it off. After she finished, she stayed submerged in the water and drifted into sleep.

"Your bed is ready." Sarah's voice awakened Muriel. "And here is your gown." She laid out a few items on the ledge. "Call me when you are dressed." She disappeared into the darkness. She returned with a comb and a plant.

"This plant is good for burns. For your face." Sarah waited for Muriel to nod in acceptance. When she squeezed the leaf, a clear liquid poured onto her palm. When rubbed on Muriel's face, it brought instant relief.

Muriel lifted her fingers to her face. The liquid felt thicker than a body lotion, basically odorless. "I know women in New York who would pay a fortune for this."

"The desert holds many secrets."

Is this my opportunity? This woman understood the world God had created better than Muriel did. Close to creation, but not to the Creator.

Rex rejected both creation and Creator. In so many ways, he was more lost than Sarah and her family.

Sarah laid the comb to one side. "Shall I braid your hair?"

Muriel fingered her hair, treasuring its silky feel on her fingers. "It will save time in the morning. Yes. Thank you."

"And that will please Mr. Rex Pride. Work, work, work."

Muriel laughed. "That's Rex. We've had so many delays, he's getting worried." Why was she defending him?

"He is never satisfied. He is like a bird who drops the worm in her beak to reach for the beetle in the sand."

"If he thinks the beetle will make a better movie, you're right." Muriel smiled along with Sarah.

"You like him." Sarah finished the first braid and started on the second.

"I respect him. And I think he respects me."

She found that belief challenged when she arrived at the canyon in the morning. Rex had posted the day's schedule. Setup for the first scene was scheduled to begin at 8:00a.m.—the hour she and Benny had set aside for the daily chapel.

Across the set, she saw Benny engaged in a lively discussion with Rex. Good. She could count on Benny's support for the chapel time. Perhaps he was already arguing the point with their stubborn director. A glance at her watch indicated she had a quarter of an hour before eight o'clock. Deciding not to intrude on Rex, she stopped by the wardrobe tent. "Has Rex made a decision about the costumes?"

Daisy, the wardrobe mistress, liked to show off her talents in her personal dress. Today a necklace that could have been borrowed from a movie set in ancient Egypt adorned her neck. "Here is your costume." With the repairs, the dress shimmered with beads and glass. "Please be more careful with it."

Muriel dreaded putting the dress, heavy and hot with all the ornamentation, back on. "But Sarah said. . ."

Daisy sniffed. "You are not dressing like one of these Indians who live hand to mouth. You are a princess from an ancient culture, and your costume reflects that. Mr. Pride agreed with me."

Muriel fingered the dress, a rich sable-brown hide lit with flashing bits of yellow and red and blue. "It is beautiful." Even though the camera couldn't capture the richness of the color, the lights would bounce off the lens, creating an illusion of precious gems. She reminded herself this wasn't a lesson in history but a story. A story that sprang from Rex Pride's mind, about a time and place before recorded history.

"I will come back later to change." Muriel hung the dress back on a hanger. "I hope you can join us at chapel this morning." She had no idea whether Daisy would bc interested or not.

"Chapel? I didn't see that on the schedule." She spoke around straight pins she had in her mouth, working on a hem for a pair of men's trousers.

"Rex forgot to add it to the schedule." Muriel didn't blame Daisy for her raised eyebrows. Rex Pride didn't forget anything.

"Sorry, honey, but all that religious mumbo jumbo doesn't mean a hill of beans to me. Good luck with it." Daisy hung the costume on the clothing rack, right with Helen's less ostentatious dress of similar doeskin and the leggings and loose shirts the men wore. Just seeing them pulled Muriel into the story world. Maybe Daisy was right, image was more important than accuracy.

Muriel sped down the canyon to the spot behind the equipment tent they had designated for the daily chapel. They had looked into using one of the apartments. In candlelight, Muriel could almost imagine early Christians gathering in the catacombs. Now, there was an idea for a film. But they agreed they would rather meet in the tent.

Lord, let people come. She would hate it if only she and Benny attended. "'For where two or three are gathered together in my name, there am I in the midst of them.'" Jesus' promise gave Muriel comfort. God wanted to do amazing things on the set of *Ruined Hopes*, to give "beauty for ashes" and "the oil of joy for mourning" like the Bible said.

In spite of that reassurance, Muriel was secretly relieved to pull the flap aside and find half a dozen people gathered. Benny had made it before her, and she also recognized several crew members and Abe Brent, one of the supporting actors. "Good morning."

"So you made it back from the village." Benny grinned. "I wasn't sure if you could make it today."

"I wouldn't miss it for the world." Muriel beamed at the gathered people. "Thank you all for coming. Why don't we introduce ourselves and explain why you're here today? Benny, we'll start with you."

The curly haired photographer stood. "My name is Benny Gruber. I'm working here as principal camerist. While that's my job, I am first and foremost a soldier of the Lord Jesus Christ. When Miss Galloway suggested this daily meeting, I thought it was a wonderful idea."

Outside the tent something rattled, as if something had been knocked over. Rex's broad form filled the tent opening. "I thought so." Rage darkened his face. "All members of the cast and crew are expected to check the posted schedule. You are all in violation of the terms of your employment."

The crew members scattered at Rex's arrival. Only Abe Brent hesitated long enough to mouth *later* on his way out of the tent.

"Well?" Rex demanded. "Do you think you're too important to follow the schedule?"

"I thought perhaps it was an oversight. You did give us permission." Muriel turned to Benny for support. "When I saw you talking with Rex earlier, I assumed you were reminding him of the chapel."

Benny managed to look sheepish. "He told me he didn't need me while he ran through the scenes with the cast." He looked at his shoes. "I didn't expect you to come today."

Rex glared first at one then the other. "You didn't think you should discuss it with me before you flaunted my clear instructions?"

Rex knew he teetered on the edge of losing control. He had tolerated Muriel's religious practices. He had hired that Indian woman and her brother at her insistence. He had held his temper when she sent everyone scurrying at the first raindrops. He had allowed for a daily reprieve during the hottest part of the day.

He had given the film's leading lady everything she'd asked for, because he needed her for the film. She was the best for the part. Audiences would flock to see her. He even admired her on certain levels, although he had learned long ago to separate romantic entanglements from the workplace.

But no more. "Miss Galloway. The situation has changed since I agreed to your chapel observance. Due to circumstances beyond my control, or yours, we are losing film time every day. I have a responsibility to my investors to finish *Ruined Hopes* on schedule. We. Don't. Have. Time. For. It." He ground out the last sentence.

Muriel drew herself to her full height like the iconic actress she was. "You will make time, or you will make this film without me."

Chapter 5

I've had enough. When did you become such a prima donna? Effective immediately, Helen Tucker will take your place in the movie. If you choose to stay, you will be the understudy." Rex glared at Muriel, daring her to protest.

She froze, closing her eyes and moving her lips without making a sound. When she looked up, serious brown eyes regarded him. "I'm sorry. This film has been difficult for both of us."

Rex jutted his chin out but clamped his jaw shut without speaking. He didn't want to say something he could not take back.

"I have an idea." Benny came between them, his voice jollying them along. "Muriel, we need to take advantage of all available daylight hours. You know that as well as I do."

"But Benny." The look Muriel sent him could melt an igloo.

He raised a hand to forestall her objection. "So why don't we hold chapel in the evenings, after the day's filming?"

"Wait a minute. There is more to making this movie than time in front of the camera." Rex scowled. Control of the situation threatened to slip away from him.

Benny straightened his shoulders. "I personally will guarantee to work whatever hours are needed to cover my responsibilities. Muriel?"

Slowly she nodded. "That sounds reasonable to me." She turned those liquid brown eyes in Rex's direction, and something inside him wilted.

"A trial basis. For the remainder of the week."

The brilliant smile Muriel turned on Rex almost made his decision worthwhile.

The following Monday night eight people gathered for chapel.

"Welcome." Muriel greeted the newest member of their small

group, this time a young woman on her first job with the movies. "I'm so glad you decided to join us."

"I couldn't get away during the day. Now that you're meeting in the evenings, I can come." She took a chair next to the door. "I'm not sure I should be here tonight. I never knew we would be so busy."

Muriel and Benny exchanged looks. Tension had ratcheted up a hundred degrees over the past week, with tempers climbing even faster than the daytime temperatures. "That's why this daily chapel is so important to me. It helps keep my focus on the Lord, and off the frustrations of the day." Around her the others murmured their agreement. "Feel free to come and go as you need to."

"I appreciate that."

Benny turned to Abe. "You got a letter at mail call. How are things on the home front?"

The young man blushed. "My wife sent a picture of our baby." Shyly he handed Muriel a photo of a toothless baby with a bow in her hair.

"Isn't she sweet?" Muriel's heart constricted. Would she ever have a family to call her own? Actors had an easier time combining the happiness of home life and a satisfying career than actresses did. She was where God wanted her; she had to take comfort from that. God could bring the man of her dreams into her life tomorrow, even here in the middle of the Colorado wilderness.

The meeting fell into its usual pattern. A time of prayer, followed by any verses God had brought to mind. Either Benny or Muriel shared a devotional thought. Often one of them read a passage from *Practicing the Presence of God* or one of Charles Spurgeon's sermons.

The group came from a variety of backgrounds. Abe had come to know the Lord through one of Billy Sunday's revival meetings. Benny heard the Gospel at a mission in the Hell's Kitchen of his childhood. Muriel had grown up in the church, thrilling to accounts of missionaries who stayed at her parents' home. With her heart prone to faraway places and peoples, her decision to become an actress surprised everyone, herself most of all.

The meeting drew to a close. "Are you ready to call it a night?" Muriel asked Benny. He looked exhausted.

"No." Benny ran a tired hand over his forehead. "Rex handed me another encyclopedia of complaints at the end of filming today. I keep offering to meet with him—it would be easier than going through pages and pages of his scrawl—but he says he doesn't have time."

"Is it just my imagination, or is he avoiding us?" Muriel walked by Benny's side as they came down the canyon. "He hardly says two words to me, except to bark at me during filming."

"Perhaps we should count our blessings." Benny bared his teeth in a garish smile.

"The week trial period has passed, and he hasn't said anything about closing the chapel time."

"That's true." They reached the entrance to Muriel's tent. "Try to get some sleep."

"Don't worry. I will." This time Benny's grin was genuine.

In her tent, Muriel eased her feet out of her shoes and sponged off the day's grime. As usual, Sarah had laid out a clean nightgown for her and provided fresh water and a towel before going home. The woman worked silently, efficiently, anticipating everything Muriel might want or need. She had made these days in the desert heat bearable.

Lighting the lantern, Muriel picked up the script for tomorrow's shoot. Working with film presented unique opportunities and challenges. On the plus side, they could redo a scene until it reached perfection. And film could be manipulated in ways a live performance could never be.

But she missed the presence of an audience. Most actors did. She fed off their energy. Her timing allowed for their laughter or applause. Not to mention her voice, an actress's most important asset, which was useless on film.

She also found the sequence of filming disconcerting. Scenes were filmed by location, with no consideration of their placement in the story. Every night she spent time going over the following day's shoot, absorbing not only the scene but also its connection to the rest of the story.

Satisfied that she had prepared as well as she could, she called it a night.

Standing in front of the slate with tomorrow's schedule, Rex studied the calendar in his hand. They were still behind by two scenes. Tapping the piece of chalk against the calendar, he calculated the day's work. With grim determination, he wrote down act 2, scenes 3, 4, 5. The cast wouldn't be pleased.

Fred joined him in front of the slate board. "Pretty ambitious."

Rex grunted. "No costume changes necessary. If everyone is on their marks, we can do it." That was a big if. "Let's go."

Fred followed Rex into his tent and sank into the waiting director's chair. He shifted the pages of script to make a place for Rex to sit on the cot. Thumbing through the pages, he found the annotated pages for tomorrow's scenes.

"I don't expect to have much trouble with scenes 3 and 5. Scene 4 is the pivotal scene."

"I know," Fred drawled. "Killdeer wants to convince Standing Corn to wait for him while he goes on the big hunt. That he can prove himself to her father." Laughter lined his face. "Better than my personal life. Killdeer has a better chance with Standing Corn than I have with the lovely Miss Galloway."

Rex arched his eyebrow. "I didn't know you were interested." He glanced at the newspaper in Fred's hand. RUINED HOPES IN RUINS? "I didn't know you read these rags."

Color crept into his cheeks. "I like to keep up with the gossip. I'm always the last to know." He folded up the paper and tucked it beside him on the chair. "If you must know, I thought a budding romance would deflect interest from our other problems."

Rex laughed. "I like the way your mind works."

"But it won't work. She just brushes me off. Too much of a good Christian to engage in any dalliances." Fred drummed his fingers on the arm of his chair. "Beautiful, talented, principled—I could do worse."

Jealousy surged through Rex. He should have expected this development. Every man in America who had seen Muriel Galloway act felt in love with her. He had to guard against falling victim to her magic himself.

"Tap into that emotion in scene 4." Rex bared his teeth. "Be ruthless. Convince Standing Corn that you love her, that you can't live without her." He took the man step-by-step through the scene, suggesting gestures and expressions for each moment.

"A lot of this will depend on how Muriel responds. This would be more effective if we included her in the discussion."

Rex shifted on the cot. "How can we? She uses this hour for her precious chapel service."

"You haven't said more than two words to her except to yell directions at her since that brouhaha last week." Fred lounged back in the chair, but Rex didn't mistake his posture for a casual attitude.

"You think I'm being too harsh?"

"You could say that." Fred stood, slapping the pages of script against his thigh. "I've thought about checking out that chapel service myself. Why don't you come with me?"

Rex shook his head, but Fred's words stayed with him throughout the night as he reviewed the scenes for tomorrow, visualizing them frame by frame. His skill as a director lay in communicating what he saw so clearly in his mind to the camerist, wardrobe mistress, actors, and everyone else involved in the production. After one final review, he turned on his Edison cylinder phonograph. Bach's precise piano preludes and fugues helped order his mind and lull him to sleep.

In the morning, Rex headed for the chow tent to grab a breakfast tray. Muriel was there, her hair already hanging in braids down her back, with Fred at her side as well as several members of the crew—mostly men. The center of attention, she smiled and talked in low, musical tones that tickled his ears in spite of his efforts to block it.

"Rex." Her voice rang out, forcing him to respond. He paused by their table. "Take a seat and join us." Her eyes implied more than the simple invitation—an apology for their disagreement last week? Concern over the difficulty of the filming? He took a step in her direction.

"Good morning, all." Benny breezed past Rex and took the only remaining chair at the table, the spot next to Muriel. "Pull up a chair, Rex. We can make room."

Rex took a step back. "Not this morning. I want to review music scores for the film."

Disappointment flickered in Muriel's face. "Another time, then."

Rex hesitated long enough for a half-hitch in his step. "I'm too far behind schedule."

Behind schedule. Those two words summarized everything Rex had said to Muriel over the past week.

"Do it again. Let's get it right this time. We only have time for one more take before we start the next scene."

Muriel bit her lip. Rex had gone from one extreme to the other.

When they first arrived, they had taken two days to finish filming one scene. From problems with lighting to glitches in costumes to minute changes in facial expressions. . .every aspect, every detail, had to be precisely perfect.

Now he wanted the same perfection—after three takes, maximum.

"Bricks without straw." Benny mumbled under his breath as he rolled the camera into position.

Muriel laughed. "That's not quite the right analogy. At least Pharaoh gave the Jews the same amount of time to make the bricks, he just shorted them the straw."

When she laughed, Rex scowled at her. "What do you find humorous about your mistakes in the scene we're shooting?"

She took her place on the set. "I find a little humor lightens the load." She accepted a cup of water from Sarah, recognizing the value of drinking plenty of fluids. "I'm doing my best. We all are."

"Then do it right." Rex waited while they all took position. "Action."

Killdeer—it was impossible to think of the actor as the very English Fred when he was kitted out in full Indian garb, from the black wig on his head to the moccasins on his feet—crossed the field where Muriel waited among the waving grasses. His loping stride and open arms, expressed his eagerness to join with his beloved Standing Corn.

Muriel's eyes darted between Killdeer, entering from the left, to the stand of trees where her father sat with the village elders. His crossed arms and the glare on his face expressed his disdain for the hunter who wanted to capture the heart of the Indian princess.

Muriel slipped into Standing Corn's persona. She felt torn. On the one hand, her harsh but loving father demanded she act in accordance with his wishes. On the other hand, the handsome and brave Killdeer provided food for her people and fought their battles when necessary. She looked first one way then the other. She glanced at the sky, seeking direction. A single cloud appeared in the sky, blown by the wind in Killdeer's direction. Joy sprouted on her face, and she raced to embrace her warrior. She seized his arms, but he slipped to his knees before her, offering a seven-point buck with an arrow protruding from its neck. Overcome with joy, she clasped her hands together and swirled in a circle, inviting her father to inspect the proof of her lover's prowess.

"And cut."

With Rex's words, Muriel returned to the nineteenth century, to the camera honing in on her, and the paper-mache deer taking the place of Killdeer's trophy.

"Well done." Fred whispered. "That cloud in the sky was heaven sent."

The frown on Rex's face suggested he was less pleased than Fred with the outcome of the scene. He stalked in the direction of the village elders, the focus of the next scene, and her shoulder muscles relaxed.

Water in hand, Sarah hurried to her side. "I have your place ready in the chow tent, if you wish to rest during the next scene."

Within a week, Sarah had understood the rhythms of the film schedule better than some people who had worked in theater for years.

"I will in a moment, thank you." Muriel sought out Rex. He had struck one of his typical poses—one hand at his waist, the other gesticulating in the faces of the actors under the trees. Veteran actors all, they radiated tension as Rex took them to school for their performance.

It wasn't only those actors. Whenever Rex's shadow so much as passed over anyone, he or she darted a nervous glance at his face, fearful he would scold for some miniscule error. She had worked with tyrannical directors before—what actress hadn't—but Rex's drive threatened to cross the line from demanding to impossible.

With a short prayer for peace in the next scene—if Rex wasn't pleased with the result, they would all feel it—she followed Sarah to the chow tent and took a seat in the shade.

Sipping on the cool water, Muriel closed her eyes and tried to put herself in Rex's place. The success or failure of the film rested on his shoulders. With the motion-picture industry still in its infancy, he embraced the potential of the medium and threw himself into making it available to the public. He was brilliant, she'd give him that. If he demanded the impossible of his cast, he demanded more of himself. Like trying to find the right music for the score.

The Bach music he played at night, music she imagined running under her fingers at a piano, comforted her and reminded her of simpler times. But she didn't think it added anything to an ancient Indian culture.

Her mind cataloged the classical piano music she had known, trying to identify an appropriate style for the story. Not the precision of baroque, point and counterpoint. Not the frills of the classical period, Mozart and trills. He might find something in Beethoven's climactic chords or Schumann's sweet lieder. Did she dare mention her ideas, or would he resent her interference? She rubbed her temples and prayed about it. She must make the overture, whether or not he rejected her.

After dipping a towel in a basin of water, Sarah wrung it out and placed it over Muriel's head. Muriel moaned. "That feels wonderful."

"Your pale skin is not suited to the sun." Sarah held the towel in place. "My mother used to tell me about why people have different color skin."

Muriel's eyes opened. This might be the opening she was seeking to share the Gospel with the poor lost souls who were the descendants of people like Standing Corn and Killdeer. "I'd like to hear it."

"When Changing Woman created the first people, she fashioned the first man out of clay. . ."

"And the Lord God formed man of the dust of the ground, and breathed into his nostrils the breath of life; and man became a living soul." God revealed Himself through His creation, as the Bible said, so that all men were without excuse.

". . .She left the man in the oven too long, and he burned black like the Buffalo soldiers we have seen."

Interesting.

"She fashioned another man, but she took him out of the oven too soon. He was pale, not ready for the sun—people with pale skins like you."

"So we were mistakes." Muriel felt the tremor of Sarah's soft laughter through the towel she kept pressed to her head.

"Changing Woman fashioned one last man figure and placed him in the oven. She didn't take him out too soon. She didn't leave him too long. When she took this man out of the oven, he was a perfect brown color."

Muriel nodded in appreciation. The story offered an explanation of the differences among the races. The Bible was silent on the subject, unless you counted Noah's descendants. Because in Christ there was neither Jew nor Gentile.

"There are many wonderful stories in the Christian's holy book, the Bible. Stories that are true." She didn't ask Sarah if she believed the tale she had spun. "If you come to our evening chapel, you can hear some of those stories." She reached for her Bible and opened it to the picture of Adam and Eve at the front. "This picture is of our first man and woman."

Sarah touched the picture. "The man who was not in the oven long enough."

Muriel laughed.

"Of course Changing Woman did not make the first people that way. When she grew lonely, she created the Diné from skin rubbed off her body."

Muriel couldn't tell if Sarah truly believed it or not.

Chapter 6

Rex spread the phonographic cylinders in front of him. He had narrowed down his choices for a musical score to a handful of recordings. Tonight he must make a final choice. He worked the crank, ready to fill the camp with Schubert's melodies.

Before he started the machine, music stirred the still air in the camp, live voices raised in song. He assumed they were hymns, since the sound came from the tent where they held their daily chapel.

They sang in harmony, almost as if they were a trained chorale society instead of a film crew. Given the background so many of them had in musical theater, perhaps he shouldn't be surprised. Cocking his head, he concentrated on the music. He knew this one. "Amazing Grace." A favorite song at funerals, one that didn't need a thirty-piece orchestra to make it sound so good, beautiful in its simplicity. Straining, he could make out the words. "Through many dangers, toils and snares, I have already come. 'Tis grace that brought me safe thus far, and grace will lead me home."

Dangers, toils, and snares. Those words capsulized the difficulties they had faced during this filming. Rex scoffed. They hadn't made it this far by grace, but by his leadership and grim determination.

One voice, a high soprano, soared above the rest. Muriel sang with the voice of an angel; she could have been another Jenny Lind if she had chosen a different career path.

Rex couldn't tear himself away. They began a second hymn, and the words were harder to make out. Redeemed. He wasn't sure what it meant, but he hummed along. Waiting here in the shadows of his tent where no one could see, he could allowed himself to admit that something about Muriel's faith appealed to him. She would insist that her faith was the reason she was good at her job.

"Rock of Ages, cleft for me." Two voices joined in a duet, quieter, harder for Rex to hear. He recognized Muriel's voice, but not the man's. He came to the entrance to his tent and smiled at the number of people around the camp who had stopped the business of the night to listen. Fred grinned at him from across the way.

If someone from Edison's company were in the camp, they would sign up the pair for a recording contract. Rex's brain scrambled. Perhaps he could find a composer to write a love song, one that this pair could record and sell along with the movie. He had to discover who the second musician was. Resolutely he walked across the camp and opened the flap of the tent.

Muriel's eyes widened in surprise, losing a slight bit of voice control, before continuing. The man singing with Muriel was Benny.

I should have known. Those two did everything together, no wonder they sounded as if they shared a connection beyond their common faith. They had worked together on several films. Their friendship wasn't anything new.

The question was, was it only friendship, or something more?

Soured on his inspiration for music for the film, Rex left the tent, wishing he could slam a door behind him.

Schumann's music would work just fine.

Rex's unexpected appearance and abrupt departure had disturbed the spirit of the meeting. Even Muriel had held her breath, wondering if he was going to demand they stop meeting, that he had urgent tasks for them all to complete before heading to bed for the night.

Within moments of leaving the chapel service, music poured from Rex's phonograph. She and Benny managed to hold the duet together until the final "Amen," although she didn't know if anyone could hear them over the other melodies. Before sitting down, Muriel spoke to the gathering. "Let us join together in prayer. Does anyone have prayer requests or praises?" She smiled in welcome of new visitors, who included Sarah and Helen. "I'd like to welcome Sarah and Helen to our meeting tonight. We hope you'll join us again." She smiled in welcome.

"Do you think Mr. Pride will come back?" Abe Brent said. Uneasy laughter rippled across their small group.

Benny stirred beside Muriel. "Absolutely. I think Paul's words to the early Christians might be appropriate. Although he was talking about government and not an employer, he told the people in the Roman church to pray for those in authority and to obey the law."

"I don't know. It seems pretty appropriate." One of Benny's assistants grumbled. "Mr. Pride is the dictator in this part of the world."

Laughter, again. Muriel felt the need to speak. "This production has run into unexpected problems. We need to pray for Mr. Pride, for this film, for his salvation."

"That will never happen." Muriel didn't see the speaker.

"We should also pray for ourselves. We may be the only Gospel he will ever read. Let's remember that as we go about our daily business." Benny clapped his hands together. "Does anyone else have a prayer request?"

As the group went to prayer, Muriel opened her eyes and stared in the direction of Rex's tent. She caught Sarah staring at her, and she flushed. She squeezed her eyes shut and prayed not only for Rex, but also for Sarah and all the lost descendants of the ancient city. Sarah had come to chapel. Surely God had given Muriel confirmation of her calling to preach the Gospel to those who had never heard.

Benny spoke from the fifteenth chapter of Luke, on Jesus' three parables about lost things: lost sheep, lost coins, and a lost son. Muriel prayed for those whose faces indicated an internal struggle. Sarah's features remained as impassive as usual, and Muriel redoubled her prayers. To her chagrin, her aide left during the final remarks. *Let Your Word take root in good soil.*

Helen spoke with her before leaving. "You've given me a lot to think about tonight. Will you pray for me?"

"Of course." Wouldn't it be marvelous if this woman, who made no secret of her jealousy of Muriel, came to Christ?

Before Muriel could ask if she wanted to receive Christ right then and there, Helen slipped away. Muriel chastised herself. She had her mind focused on too many things. Overlooking the wheat that was ready to harvest while longing for the still fallow fields.

Soon she and Benny were the only ones left in the tent. "You look disheartened." Benny's face radiated concern. "It was a good night. We even received a look-see by the big man."

"I know." Outside the opening chords of one of Schumann's songs repeated. "I had some ideas on music for the film, if he's willing to listen."

Benny looked to the tent where Rex had secreted himself for the past week, only emerging during the hours of filming. "If you don't mind him biting off your head." He shook his head. "I shouldn't say that. What was I just telling the group, that we may be the only Gospel he reads. Go speak to him, Muriel. I'll be praying for you."

"Thank you." Sending a prayer heavenward, Muriel adjusted her dress, dropping the hem a quarter of an inch, and headed for Rex's tent. She hesitated outside the flap. Without a door, she couldn't knock. Then again, with the volume of the music, Rex might not hear a knock. With another prayer for courage, she pulled the flap open and ducked her head in.

"Excuse me? Rex?"

His head was bent over, his shoulders slumped, almost as though asleep. The phonograph reached the end of the song, and he put the cylinder away.

Muriel spoke into the ensuing silence. "Rex? May I come in?"

"Enter." His low voice was very different from his usual bark. But as she ducked under the flap and walked in, he squared his shoulders and stood. "How may I help you, Muriel?" A smile played around his lips, softening his expression.

"It was good to see you at the chapel service."

The smile disappeared. "I wanted to see what all the fuss was about. You were making an awful racket."

Peace, Muriel reminded herself. "The Bible talks about making a joyful noise to the Lord. He wants a whole heart, not happy harmony."

"Actually, it wasn't so bad." He cleared the script from a camp chair and gestured for her to take a seat. "Not Enrico Caruso, but not bad. But you didn't come here about that. Did you?"

"No." She shook her head. "I wanted to offer my help in choosing music to go with the film."

He arched an eyebrow. "Have I asked for help?"

"No. But you wouldn't." *Careful. Don't embarrass him.* "But I studied piano for years. If you are looking for music for the movie, I have some ideas."

"You have many hidden talents." Uncertainty flickered in his eyes. "I haven't decided. What do you have in mind?"

"I don't think it's been recorded. You haven't played it on this wonderful machine." She gestured at the phonograph. "I have to buy one of these for myself when I get home. Imagine. Listening to the Boston Symphony Orchestra in the comfort of your own home."

"It is a wonderful invention."

"One of many. I made a short list." Muriel reached into the tiny purse that carried her Bible and a notebook. She showed him the list she had prepared.

He looked at her suggestions. "You've been thinking about this for a while." He gestured with the notebook. "May I have this?"

"Of course."

He tore out the page and handed the notebook back. "These are good suggestions. I hadn't considered the American composers." His lips lifted in a lopsided grin. "You didn't have to do this."

"Why shouldn't I help? We both want the same thing."

"And what is that?"

"A good movie. What else?"

His lips curled in a full-fledged smile. "I'll leave that to your imagination."

"Can we call a truce between us?" She leaned forward, allowing a note of pleading into her voice.

"As long as you do exactly what I want." The smile on his face disappeared. "I will listen to any ideas you want to present. In private."

Peace descended over the production over the next few days, the tension between himself and the cast had lessened ever since his discussion with Muriel. More and more people went to the nightly chapel. They had begun to open the flap and set a few chairs at the entrance. Before long, she'd be asking for additional space.

Everyone seemed more at peace except for Rex himself. Early Saturday morning, he decided to take a walk with the dawn. Burbling water drew him, and he headed for the river, the same one that had flooded the canyon not so long ago. So far, a few late-afternoon showers hadn't caused a repeat of the day that had nearly brought total destruction to everyone involved in the film.

Leaves rustled nearby, and Rex realized he wasn't the only one headed for a cool drink before the heat of the day. A doe with a fawn by her side padded past him, their noses twitching at his unexpected presence. He changed his mind. Rather than heading for the river, which might only frighten the animals away. . .he went back to the cliffs and climbed to a spot where he could see the animals gathering at the watering hole.

With his bare eyes, he could see coyotes and deer, bobcats, too. Squirrels chattered in the branches overhead. He had heard tales of black bears in the region, as well as poisonous snakes, but they hadn't encountered any problems. From the sky a golden eagle swooped down on an unsuspecting chipmunk. He caught a glimpse of a turquoise-toned lizard skittering up the wall of the cliff. Another time he'd bring binoculars and look for small animals and birds. No, he'd bring Benny. See if they could add footage of the local fauna to the film. For all the challenges *Ruined Hopes* had presented, he was glad they'd come to Mesa Verde to make the film. He couldn't repeat the happy coincidences of nature in a studio.

Looking below, he saw smoke curling up from behind the chow tent. Benny stumbled out of his tent in the direction of the latrine. Rex cupped his hands together and yelled. "Benny!"

The camerist glanced around. Rex repeated his call, and he looked up. "Binoculars!" Rex made a sweeping motion to indicate he wanted Benny to climb up to him.

While waiting for Benny to join him, Rex watched the camp come to life. His eyes wandered time and again to Muriel's tent. A soft light flickered beneath the canvas. How did she spend her time when she wasn't filming, besides attending chapel? From time to time she received letters at mail call; he thought she had family in New England somewhere.

Had she formed any friendships with the crew? He knew the answer to that. She was friends with Benny and Sarah and more besides. Whereas he struggled to put names with some of the faces, men and women he had hired. People might find it easier to work for him if he put out a little more effort.

"You want these?" At the bottom of the ladder, Benny waved a pair of binoculars.

"Yes. Come on up."

Rex glanced at Muriel's tent one last time before Benny reached the top. Helen came by, and Muriel joined her before they headed toward the chow tent. When had the two rivals become friends? He almost wished it wouldn't happen. A frisson of tension between actors vying for the same part brought out an extra edge of excellence.

Puffing, Benny pulled over the ledge and removed the binoculars from around his neck. "Here you go."

"When did that happen?" Rex frowned down at Helen and Muriel.

"You won't like the answer." Benny brought the binoculars to his eyes and looked around. "I wish I had a camera that could bring images up close like this. Just think what I could do."

"Tell me."

Benny handed the binoculars to Rex. "Helen started coming to the chapel service. Muriel prayed with her, and now she's saved."

"I wasn't aware she was lost." Rex located the spot on the river where the animals had gathered. While the camp had come to life, the animals had come and gone. But he could still perhaps catch small animals on the ground or in the trees. He lifted the glasses to his eyes.

"'All we like sheep have gone astray; we have turned every one to his own way; and the Lord hath laid on him the iniquity of us all.' Another way the Bible describes it is that we're like an archer's arrows that miss the mark. The target is God's law, and we all fail to hit the bull's-eye from time to time."

"I suppose you mean the Ten Commandments." Rex zeroed in on a chipmunk with his pouches full of nuts, and then a chickadee fluttering in the branches of the piñon trees. A jay loomed so large in the lens that he took a step back. Taking the glasses away from his eyes, he could still see the jay with his bare eyes. "Look there." He handed the binoculars to his friend. "See the birds in the tree?"

"Let's see. Chickadees. Titmice. Nuthatches. And a squirrel."

"Is that a squirrel or a chipmunk?"

Benny squinted. "I think it's a squirrel, but I'm not sure. Hard to tell from this distance."

"There was a bunch of animals there earlier, stopping by for a drink before the bright light of day. Coyotes, deer, bobcats. I think I even spotted a turkey."

"Interesting." Benny eased the strap of the binoculars around his neck. "And you want to film them."

"If we can." Rex smiled as fire lit Benny's eyes. If anyone could do it, the camerist could.

"Why haven't we seen them at the river before?"

"I don't know. Maybe they stay away from the river during the day to escape predators and people. There are eagles here as well. Golden eagles."

Benny had the glasses at his eyes again. "Now, that's what I would like to capture on film. Look." He pointed Rex in a different direction, toward an outcropping of rock.

"What are they?" They were animals with shaggy coats like sheep, but they had horns worthy of an ancient musical instrument. Huge, gangly things.

"Bighorn sheep, I think."

"Rather obvious, but it works. But yes. Film it! Absolutely!" His imagination played with finding a pair of those horns for use as props.

"Maybe they could construct those horns if I get a decent photo?"

Rex chuckled. "You read my mind."

"Is that all?" Benny's stomach growled. "I want to get to breakfast before it's all gone." He grinned. "I work with this director who holds up lunch until we finish filming for the day."

Rex laughed outright. "Then by all means let's get down."

At dusk Rex tried to sneak up on the animals at the river. He must have sounded more like a stampeding elephant, because the banks had emptied when he reached them. He could see them running away as he approached. Perhaps Sarah's brother could give him a crash course in hunting. Maybe they could hunt a sheep together, so they'd have authentic horns for use as props. He shouldn't have any trouble convincing the Indian to work on Sunday, the only day not fully scheduled.

He hurried back to camp. Charlie had taken to attending the chapel service with Sarah in the evenings, so maybe he could catch up with him before he left for the night.

"I like the stories." Sarah sat with Muriel and Helen inside the chapel tent. Benny and Abe were busy talking with a member of the kitchen crew. God had done a mighty work tonight. "Was the story Benny told about the lost sheep true?"

Muriel's mind went back to the time when she had assured Sarah that the stories in the Bible were true. How to explain? "It was a story that Jesus told. He wanted us to know that God looks for everyone who is lost."

"Am I lost?" Sarah asked. Her face remained impassive, but her voice was strained.

"The Bible says we are all lost. We've all left the path God wants us to take," Muriel said.

"How do I find that path? Do I read the Bible?"

Helen smiled. "I never read the Bible until a few days ago. The good news is that when we invite Jesus into our hearts, God sets us back on the path, and we'll never lose it again."

Sarah looked from one woman to the other. "Even for the Diné? A Navajo like me?"

Yes, Lord, yes. God did have a special work for Muriel to do among Sarah's people.

"For everyone. For me, for you. Do you want to invite Him in?"

Sarah's face broke into a smile. "Yes."

Chapter 7

"Mr. Rex Pride and Benny should not be out in this sun." Sarah shook her head.

Muriel groaned. Both men had swarthy complexions; maybe that saved them from suffering from the heat. Not so for her. Each day seemed worse than the last. Today the heat hung heavy, threatening rain without delivering on the promise. The damp towel Sarah used to keep her skin cool dried almost before she set it on her head. "What are they doing now?"

"Benny is pointing the camera at the sky."

Storm clouds? Birds? Curious, Muriel looked up. A lone bird swooped before diving to the ground, lifting something in its claws as he rose in the air again. An eagle, perhaps, though not the white head of America's national bird. "He is probably chasing the eagle."

"I can show you pictures of the bird. Other pictures, too." Sarah moistened the towel again and replaced it on Muriel's head. "Your Mr. Pride might like to film them. They were made by the Old Ones."

"Cave paintings?" Muriel had heard about them.

"Not a cave. On the cliffs." Sarah pointed in the direction of her village.

"I'd love to see them. How far away are they? Can we walk there after chapel?"

Benny and Rex were walking back. "He'll probably want to start filming when he gets back here."

"It would be better if you come when you have the day. On Sunday."

Sunday. That was a good idea. Go to her village. Now that Sarah believed in Christ, perhaps they could begin a weekly Bible study. She'd ask Benny about that. "It's decided then. I'll come this week in the afternoon." Although they were too far from any town to attend church, Muriel set aside Sunday mornings for worship.

The two men walked down the canyon, laughing, talking, the most affable she had ever seen Rex. Benny was everything she could want in a man—a Christian, wholeheartedly devoted to the Lord, to spreading His word, a camerist whose passion for the new medium of film equaled her own, who was still single without a sniff of scandal attached to his name. At least not since he had come to know the Lord.

So why were her eyes drawn to the irritating Rex Pride, who derided her faith at every opportunity? She sent up simultaneous prayers: *Lord, save Rex and Lord, protect my heart.*

Rex paused long enough to take a peek through his binoculars. With any luck, Benny had caught some good footage of the eagle soaring in the sky today, talons extended. Magnificent bird. To think Benjamin Franklin had once wanted to make the turkey the national bird of the United States. He shook his head, glad better heads had prevailed on that issue.

But those sheep with the magnificent big horns that seemed as much a part of this wild mountain country as the junipers and piñon trees that brushed the sky remained maddeningly elusive. He'd pin down Charlie for a time to go hunting. Put the actors in costume and capture them on the hunt. That could work. . . .

"You've had an idea." Benny panted beside Rex, carrying the heavy camera over his shoulder.

"Sorry, I got lost there for a minute imagining our actors going on a hunt after those bighorn sheep."

Benny lifted his eyes to the rock faces surrounding them. "They're hard enough to climb even when we have ladders."

"How would you film it?" Rex looked sideways at his camerist. Benny relished challenges.

The two men craned their necks to study the bare rock soaring above them. Rex's foot encountered a rock, and he lurched sideways, knocking into Benny. His arms jerked like a windmill, and he fell. Rex reached out to help, but succeeded only in saving the camera from the same fate.

"Don't worry about me. You rescued the equipment." A grinning Benny attempted to stand, but his ankle buckled beneath him. "The dangers of filming in the wild. Give a fellow a hand, will you?"

Rex stretched out his right arm and helped Benny to his feet. He winced when he put weight on his left foot.

"Is it serious?" Rex hefted the camera over his shoulder. "Can you walk back to camp?"

"It's just a sprain, but I aggravated an old injury." A single step, and Benny almost toppled over. "I can make it back to camp if I can borrow your shoulder."

Rex kept from cursing the lost film time as Benny hobbled back into camp.

Would they not get through a day without drama? Knowing he was the one who'd wanted to film the eagles didn't help his mood.

"No need to look so glum." Benny's hold on Rex's shoulder tightened. "This ankle has been injured so often, I bring a pair of crutches with me when I go out to do a shoot like this. I won't hold us up."

Rex scowled, and Benny added, "Perhaps I should say it won't keep me down much. Getting those eagles on film was worth it." He grinned, his trademark insouciant smirk. "I bet I can even get those shots of the bighorn sheep that you want."

Rex laughed at that. "You're as bad as I am. You stop at nothing to get the shot you want."

"Nope. Not with my incredible talent"—Benny pointed to himself—"and the Lord working everything for my good, I can't lose."

"There you go again. You talk like God is in charge of every pebble on the desert floor."

"That's because He is. 'He is before all things, and by him all things consist.' He keeps the earth spinning on its axis."

"Then why didn't He blow the rock out of your way to keep you from falling over it?" Rex kicked a small stone with the toe of his shoe.

"God gave me eyes, didn't He? He doesn't say He'll save us from our own stupidity or bad choices." Benny hopped along another couple of steps.

"So if something goes well, God gets the credit. And if something goes wrong, you take responsibility."

"Would you rather have a deity who made all your choices for you?" Benny shook his head. "No, God wants us to love Him by faith. Not because He's some kind of magical Santa Claus who grants our every wish."

Rex considered that. "Faith in some invisible God that won't reward good behavior. I'll stick with doing things for myself."

Benny stopped his forward momentum, causing Rex to halt with him. He looked at Rex with serious blue eyes. "Sooner or later you're going to run into something you can't control. I pray you turn to God before you face that test. But whether sooner or later, whenever you turn to God, He'll be there to catch you." He placed his hand on Rex's shoulder and started moving again.

"Is the sermon over for the day?"

"For now." Benny grinned.

"Good. Back to the sheep—I hope I can convince Charlie to take us hunting on Sunday."

Benny hesitated. "But. . ."

"Sundays are the only days we can get this done. We don't have any other blocks of time." His desire to demand Benny's cooperation fought with recognition that he couldn't command the man's conscience. Benny's strength of will, his drive to make something as good as possible, rivaled Rex's own. Destroy that, and he might lose his unique skill behind the camera.

Rex was forced to do something completely opposite to his nature: beg. "What? If you skip church one Sunday, do you think God will send a thunderbolt from heaven? Or maybe another flash flood?"

"There's the sheep again." Balancing on one foot, he pointed to the rocks. "They're beautiful."

"It's just one week." Rex allowed a wheedling tone to come into his voice. "Will you do it for me? For the film?"

Benny gazed into the distance, uncertainty stamped on his face.

"I was thinking maybe you could tell the parables from Luke 15 again. The idea of lost and found, of being so precious to God, resonated with Sarah." Muriel hadn't stopped chattering about the opportunity before them since Benny had returned from his afternoon expedition.

"Muriel." Benny's arms crossed over his chest. He couldn't look her in the eye. "I promised Rex I would go with him to film the sheep he's chasing." Hunching his shoulders, he raised a stricken face to Muriel. "Just one week. I didn't think it would matter. I thought maybe we could talk about God while we were climbing around. He actually listened to me today."

"You're going to evangelize Rex by forsaking basic Christian values?" Muriel was angry enough to bite the head off a rattlesnake and live to tell about it. She held her tongue in check. She would process her anger later. "I can't believe you made that choice. And what message does it send to these people who need to hear the Gospel so desperately?"

"I'll tell Rex I can't do it. That I've changed my mind." Benny waved a crutch at her. "I have a good excuse."

"How did you expect to get around?" The image of Benny using the crutch as a ladder to climb the mountainside brought a smile to Muriel's face. Even Jesus would need a miracle to climb a mountain with a sprained ankle.

"It'll be better by the weekend." He tapped the ankle bone with the tip of his cane. "It goes out on me off and on. I know my limits."

"You've spent too much time around Rex." Muriel stared at the high cliffs around her. She couldn't imagine climbing to make a film, and yet some people did it for fun. Mountains were beautiful to look at, but she preferred New England's gently rolling hills.

Then again—on a second glance—she hadn't seen such wild beauty anywhere. *Ruined Hopes* would bring this ancient beauty to wider audiences. If only the film could convey the golden glow of the cliffs at sunrise, the purple mountain majesty that Katherine Lee Bates immortalized in her song, the greens from sage to spruce to spring. "Capture this cathedral of God's nature on film, Benny. Do it as best as you can. Bring this testimony of God's creation to the world." She wagged a finger in his face. "Just be sure you don't make a habit of it."

He turned his attention in the same direction Muriel was staring. "I'll do that. Pray for me, that I don't lose my way. I don't want to be the poster boy for 'the path to hell is paved with good intentions.' "

"Of course. Always."

"Are you two going to stop lollygagging and come back to work?" Rex called from the spot where he was talking with Fred.

Benny glanced at Muriel, and they both smiled. "I'll double my prayers for him. He's more closed than anyone I've ever met." He gave her a friendly pat on the shoulder. "You've found your mission field, Muriel, in the middle of this sparsely populated wilderness."

"I'll tell my parents what you said. They prepared me for a quiet life in Maine, and I do the unthinkable and go into theater." She shook her head, and her braids flapped against her shoulder. "God leads us down strange paths."

"That He does." Benny hitched the crutch under his arms and pushed the camera tripod ahead of him.

As they neared the set, Rex's brooding stare burned brightly. His gaze flickered between Muriel and Benny. "I'm glad the two of you decided to leave your tête-à-tête and join the party."

He's jealous. A tiny shiver of pleasure scurried up Muriel's spine, and she hurried her steps to the staging area. Then he returned his attention to Fred and Irving Sampson. Irving was a dear, an aging leading man who had made a successful transition to splendid old man of the stage. He oozed authority and dignity as the chief of his people. Rex motioned for Muriel to join them.

"I was telling Fulton and Sampson that I'm giving the story a new slant." Rex scowled.

Muriel refused to be intimidated. "It is just now time to start filming for the afternoon. What do you have in mind?"

He glowered but didn't comment further on her lateness. "I am expanding on the Romeo-and-Juliet theme. Gruber and I are working on footage of local animals and we're going to name the different families after those animals."

"Benny mentioned eagles and bighorn sheep." Muriel wanted Rex to know that she was abreast of current developments. "Will you try to get some others?"

"Those will be the primary clans. We're going after those deer we see everywhere. I've heard stories about black bears."

"But I said I don't want to get close enough to one of those critters to get his picture," Benny said.

"It's still under discussion." Rex glared at Muriel and Benny in turn, and she no longer felt quite so pleased about the jealousy. Not if he became even harder to work with.

"I'll let you take over the camera for all the black bears and rattlesnakes you want." Benny grinned. "I'll even point them out to you."

"My clan will be the Bighorn Sheep. Big and strong. We are working on a model of the horns." Fred flexed his muscles. "Be careful of my wrath." He turned to Muriel. "And you, my dear, are part of the Golden Eagle clan."

"Where we will soar above everyone else." Irving sketched a bow. "Of course, we look down on the earth-bound sheep, who rely on brute strength."

"So no matter what Killdeer does, my father won't approve." Muriel nodded. "I see. I like it."

"Good. I'll sketch out the changes to the scenes tonight."

The group split up, but Rex held Muriel back. "Your contract calls for approval over all changes to the script."

Muriel nodded. She demanded it, so that she didn't end up appearing in a production of questionable moral values.

Rex shifted his feet then turned his fierce gaze on her. "Thank you for your support." His mouth twisted in a half smile.

The great Rex Pride was thanking her? Warmth flooded her, followed by skin-tingling chills. "I want the same thing you want, a movie that tells a great story. A film that will lift up the audience." She met his gaze, and something akin to respect flashed in his eyes.

Muriel was never so glad for her experience at masking emotions as she was in that moment. Otherwise she would have melted into the ground, leaving her heart on a platter ready for him to scoop up in his capable hands.

Chapter 8

Muriel wished she were wearing Standing Corn's dress instead of the skirt that dangled so close to the ground. She didn't realize that the visit to the paintings would involve climbing up rocks as impossible as Rex's quest for the bighorn sheep.

"We are almost there." Ahead, Sarah paused. The way she climbed, she could have had the same clattering hooves as those bighorn sheep instead of normal human feet.

Grabbing ahold of a rock outcropping, Muriel pulled herself up to Sarah's level.

Her friend stood with her back to the wall, looking in the distance. "I come up here when I want to be alone."

Fighting a wave of dizziness, Muriel forced herself to look down and around. From her vantage point, she marveled anew at the ingenuity of the ancient cliff dwellers. No one today would have patience for such an undertaking. The time, strength, and ingenuity involved in building an entire community with such primitive tools seemed impossible.

But the community built out of rock faded in comparison to the natural backdrop. And God spoke the universes into being, in six short days. In addition to majestic mountains, the cliffs reflected the colors of sand and dirt and blood, blasted by centuries of wind. Other places she saw heaps of loose, gray rock. Green carpeted the canyon floor, more green than she expected in such dry country. Yellow dotted bushes, like drops of sunshine. A fierce beauty, one that would take a sturdy people to survive. She looked at Sarah with renewed admiration.

A gigantic circular hole in the earth, reinforced with thousands of rocks, stared up from the ground like an unblinking eye. She had never seen it before. She was pretty sure Rex hadn't ever spotted it either, or else he'd make it a center point of the film. "What is that?"

"A kiva."

Kiva. She tried the strong syllables on her tongue. "What is it, exactly?"

Sarah hesitated. "Come with me. I will explain it to you when we reach the painting." She handed Muriel a canteen. "Drink. We will take a break after we look at the paintings."

Muriel gathered her skirts above her ankles, deciding at this height, no one would notice. She should have taken Sarah's advice and changed her clothes.

"It is right there." Sarah pointed to a ledge a little ahead of them.

Muriel looked up. She saw paint, what looked almost like scribbling. An ancient Navajo alphabet? But she didn't think Navajo was a written language. Curiosity sped her steps.

Abruptly Sarah stopped moving. "Here it is. There are others, but this is one of my favorites."

Faded white paint gleamed on gray rock. White that reminded her of the whitewash Tom Sawyer conned his friends to splash on his aunt's fence. But these were no paintings of a Mississippi boyhood. She wanted to reach out and touch the surface, to physically connect with a piece of the past that might be as old as Europe's castles. Older, even. She leaned forward, and rocks slid beneath her feet. The pebbles underfoot had once been rock as solid as the cliff face. She settled back, unwilling to risk destroying it. Benny would love to photograph it.

The painting was nothing like any art Muriel had seen hanging in museums. It reminded her more of a child's chalk drawing, but its power still touched her. A bird with wings and talons that suggested an eagle, proud in flight. Sheep with horns that curled around and around, alongside a spiral that reached down to the ground, like it climbed out of the bowels of the earth. Other animals crawled and sprang to life. They danced and pranced as if meant to tell a story.

"I recognize the animals, but what is that spiral? It looks like, I don't know, a cave, or a spring of water, or. . ."

"It is our creation story. The first people climbed out of the earth, the Towering House, One-Walk-Around, and Bitter Water clans. I am of the Towering House clan and for the Bitter Water clan." Pride laced Sarah's voice. "The Bible you gave me says that God created all the animals that crawl and walk on the earth on the same day. And that He made one man and one woman." She hesitated. "It is different."

Muriel thought of the story of the Tower of Babel, when God separated the people of the earth. The Navajo had confused story with truth to the point where they couldn't distinguish between the two. Maybe here was a way to connect the Navajo way with the truth of the Gospel. "That reminds me of a Bible story. I'd like to share it with you and anyone else who might be interested. Can you arrange that?"

Sarah looked at the painting, then at Muriel. At length she nodded. "I will do as you ask."

Muriel had the impression Sarah had more on her mind, but she didn't add anything. God kept opening doors. Surely He would also open their hearts.

She sat on a rock and stared at the wall. Rex might not believe the first people crawled out of a hole in the earth, but he was just as lost. She would just have to pray that God would open his eyes as well.

"More mountains to climb?" Rex resisted the urge to reach down and rub his sore leg muscles. He and Benny had spent sunup to sundown chasing after the sheep, which scampered ahead of them whenever they got closer than a hundred yards.

"You have to see them. I'm sure you'll want to include them in the film."

"Benny won't be doing any more mountain climbing anytime soon." Rex touched his ankle in sympathy. "His ankle has swollen to double its normal size. For all the good our expedition did, he should have stayed at camp." Rex tapped down impatience at the thought.

He needed Benny working at full capacity. Of all the members of the crew, the camerist carried the most responsibility, almost more important than the actors themselves. Without his eye behind the camera, his expertise and instinct with the equipment, *Ruined Hopes* would be hardly better than a comic strip.

Muriel tilted her head to one side. Her hair, loosened from the braids that she wore on set, threatened to spill out of the loose knot on top of her head. What would the dark tresses look like lying loose down her back? His breath caught at the thought.

"I haven't seen rushes for days. I would love to see what Benny has captured on film."

Benny again.

She fluttered her long eyelashes. "I would like to incorporate some of the eagle's characteristics into Standing Corn's gestures."

Coming from a lesser actor, such a statement would sound ludicrous. But Muriel Galloway could probably pull it off. "Very well. I will schedule a viewing tomorrow night right after dinner."

"That's when we hold chapel."

"You can either hold it later or skip it for one night. Your Benny missed one week of church, and the world didn't come to an end."

Muriel's lips thinned. So, there was trouble in paradise. His desertion had troubled her. But she based her protest on something else. "Sarah has been coming to our service. I don't want to make it any later for her than it already is."

Rex tamped down on his temper. "I don't run this film on the need's of one person. Invite her to spend the night with you if she wants. Invite her brother, too. I want to talk to them about acting as guides."

"To take you to see the cliff paintings?" A smile curved her lips. "You can film it, even if Benny can't make it up the mountain. He says you're nearly as good as he is behind the camera."

Rex scowled. "I'll ask them about it." Back in his tent, he spent time splicing different scenes together into a coherent story. They had large chunks of the story in the can. Sitting in the dark, watching flickering images on the screen, he could admit his admiration, even attraction, to his leading lady. She dominated every scene, made Standing Corn both an ancient princess and a modern woman the audience could understand. When he added the film he had captured of the flood, *Ruined Hopes* grabbed a visceral part of his emotions and carried him far away.

The footage they had taken of the animals was laughable, but he wasn't ready to admit defeat. He spliced them in with the scenes showing the different clans, marking the spots where the final shots would go.

Word of the viewing spread, and on Tuesday evening, every member of the cast and crew gathered in a hastily arranged amphitheater. Rex cranked up his phonograph and put on the recording of the music Muriel had helped him choose, and nodded for Benny to start the reel.

Rex slid into a chair next to Muriel, where he found himself watching her profile, every nuance of her facial expression, instead of the film. He could tell she was carried away by the film. When they reached the flood sequence she gasped, together with everyone in the audience. To a person, the cast and crew loved the power of film. Even a story they knew as intimately as *Ruined Hopes* had the power to carry them away. Their enthusiasm spoke volumes about the success of their endeavor.

The minutes with the eagles on screen soaring in the sky brought a few *oohs* and *aahs* and even more puzzled expressions. When the sheep appeared far away, mostly shots that captured either the gigantic horns or the fluff of their tails as they ran away. Muriel's lips twitched, and laughter rippled through the crowd. On her other side, Sarah shook her head once.

When the viewing ended, Muriel brought her hands together in a clap, and soon the circle rang with cheering. When at last the din died down, Rex thanked everyone for attending. Muriel stood before he had a chance to speak with her privately. Of course. She'd be anxious to get to her Bible study. "I suppose you're headed to your chapel service."

"Yes." She smiled before adding, "Why don't you join us tonight?"

When she looked at him with those chocolate eyes, he would agree to anything.

❧

" 'The Lord is my shepherd, I shall not want.' " Muriel tried to focus on the words, but they slipped out by rote, one of the first Bible passages she had ever memorized. She'd fallen in love with the beauty and poetry of the language. In fact, she had won her first speech contest with a recitation of that psalm.

But she should focus on God's Word, on His message to her, not on the man sitting next to her. She had been walking several inches off the ground ever since Rex had accepted her invitation to come to their service. The side where he sat tingled from head to toe with awareness. He was staring at Benny, who had taken a seat at the center of the circle.

"That's from the twenty-third psalm, if any of you want to mark it in your Bibles," Benny said.

On Muriel's other side, Sarah turned her Bible to the middle, as Muriel had taught her to do when looking for the Psalms, then looked through the chapter numbers.

"But today I am going to share from a different place the Bible talks about sheep. Turn to John chapter ten." Muriel opened her Bible and offered to share it with Rex. He slid his left hand under the book, and her fingers warmed where they touched.

"I couldn't help but think about what the Bible says about sheep after my adventures on the mountain. I discovered sheep are contrary creatures."

"They didn't want the likes of you chasing them, that's for sure." Brent grinned.

A few people tittered, casting nervous glances at Rex. To her relief, he laughed along with them.

"Jesus said, 'I am the good shepherd.' Did he care for sheep, as David did? Not that we know of. He probably worked as a carpenter alongside Joseph until He started preaching." Benny grinned. "But He knew a lot more about sheep than I do."

More laughter rippled across the room.

"No, Jesus is a shepherd to people." Benny expounded on the subject, looking at the qualities of a good shepherd from Psalm 23. "God leads us through the worst times, even when we're facing death. When the waters we travel by aren't as quiet as we would like. Think about the flood we saw on the film tonight. God protected us all. We had one minor injury, when all could have been killed." He nodded in Sarah's direction. "He sent Sarah to give us a warning. We were as dumb as most sheep are, unaware of the dangers we faced."

Benny leaned forward. "From the stories in the Bible, sheep are stupid beasts. They get caught in thorns. They wander away from the flock and get lost and can't find their way home."

"That is true." Sarah nodded. "Sheep require a lot of care." She fingered her wool skirt as if a reminder of her knowledge of the animals the wool came from.

"Jesus is saying people are like that, too. Isaiah said it earlier. 'All we like sheep have gone astray; we have turned every one to his own way.' Left to our own devices, we get into one scrape after another. We need a shepherd."

Rex let go of the Bible and sat back in the chair, crossing his arms. He might as well have put his hands over his ears.

" 'The sheep follow him: for they know his voice.' They listen. They follow. Won't you listen to the voice of the Shepherd today?"

Muriel's heart sank as Rex shook his head. The service ended shortly after that, and he slipped out without saying anything. Her heart twisted. Why was it that with each passing day, she found herself more attracted to a man who refused to give God an inch?

"He does not yet know the Shepherd's voice." Sarah stood, waiting for Muriel to join her. "But he will."

"I pray that's so." Once again, Muriel thanked God for the quiet strength of the woman beside her.

The strains of the music Rex had chosen for the film filled the air as they made their way back to Muriel's tent. Perhaps Rex needed the phonograph to shut out that other voice he didn't want to hear. The thought encouraged her. Whether a whisper or earth-shaking shout, God's voice couldn't be ignored.

That Sunday, Benny accompanied Muriel to Sarah's village.

"I told Rex he was on his own to film the cliff paintings. He knows how to operate the camera, and it's not like he's filming live action. The paintings aren't going to jump off the rock face."

"I only wish he didn't want to go today." Muriel frowned. "I was hoping Charlie might join us at the Bible study this morning, and instead, he's running around with Rex."

"I bet Sarah is sharing what she's learning with her family." Benny didn't seem upset. "I've never run across anybody so hungry, so excited for God's word as she is."

Sarah said very little about her family, or anything personal in nature. She occasionally asked for explanations of some of the archaic English of the Bible. In the Bible study, she made comments that showed how much knowledge she had stowed away in such a short time. "I wish you were telling the Bible story today."

"You're an experienced actress. You'll do fine."

The Navajo didn't need second and minute hands to keep time. Rather, they gathered silently about midmorning, while the air still carried some of the cool of the early day. All of Sarah's family came, as well as a number of others with weathered, lined faces and children who sat cross-legged at their parents' feet.

One of the elders came forward and addressed Muriel. Although she couldn't understand the words, she gathered she was being welcomed to the village. Sarah translated into English, ending with "We are ready to listen to you."

Muriel stood, more nervous than she had ever felt in front of a camera. Benny winked at her and folded his hands in prayer. Emboldened, Muriel spoke of the way God created the first man and woman from the dust of the earth, and how, when they were so proud they thought they could build a tower that would reach heaven, He changed their speech and divided the peoples of the world. "So some people spoke English, and some Spanish, some Navajo and Hopi and Apache and Chinese." She didn't directly challenge the myth of people emerging from underground, but prayed they would understand the truth of God's Word.

Their expressions didn't register any emotion as Muriel spilled her heart. When the elder thanked her for sharing her story with them, she invited him and the others to join them at the film site on Sunday afternoons for a Bible study.

Sarah's expression said it all. No one was interested.

Chapter 9

Charlie didn't say much as he guided Rex to the site of the cliff painting, which suited Rex fine. With a guide, he was free to observe his journey, the fresh perspective of the canyon spread below him.

"Will we see any sheep going this way?"

Charlie shrugged.

"Another time, I'd like to film the sheep. Could you get me close?"

"Next week."

Charlie knew how to pace the trip, but even so, Rex was panting before they reached the destination. Perhaps it was the higher altitude. Whatever the reason, when they reached a point where the canyon stretched out below them, a wave of dizziness hit him, and he stumbled back against the wall.

"Drink this." Charlie handed him a canteen with lukewarm water.

The water slid past Rex's sputtering lips. He held his handkerchief against his forehead, and gradually the dizziness receded. He hadn't had any problems with the heat before, and it wasn't even afternoon yet.

While he rested, Charlie handed him a handful of nuts and dried fruit of some kind. Rex stared at it, unable to identify any of the ingredients, but ate it anyhow. He washed the mix down with more water. His head cleared. "I'm ready. Let's go."

"We are close." Within minutes they rounded a corner and came upon the paintings.

Muriel had described the paintings, but she hadn't communicated their impact—full of life and power, vibrant with the life of a people who had lived in this harsh environment. The figures danced before his eyes. He could see Killdeer and Standing Corn pledging themselves to each other in front of the rock, adding to the stories portrayed there. Not that he would try to haul the entire film crew up the mountainside, but they could achieve something similar on ground level. He took the camera Benny had grudgingly entrusted to his care and filmed the painting from all angles. Up close, back at a distance, turning in the other direction to take in the panorama stretched before them. At length the end of the reel of film fluttered out of the camera. "I've done all the damage I can do."

"I brought food. We will eat before we return."

More nuts and fruit?

Charlie took pear-shaped fruit with spines on it from his bag. He dug a knife from his pocket and peeled the spines away before cutting it in half. He handed a piece to Rex.

Rex examined it. It was more gelatinous than pulpy, reminding him of a melon in appearance. He brought it to his mouth—refreshing, sweet, tasting a little like watermelon or strawberries. "This is good."

The hint of a smile played about Charlie's lips. "It is the fruit of the cactus."

Rex almost choked on the words. "Cactus?" He reached for the peel, but the spines jabbed his skin. "I wonder how anyone figured out they could eat it."

Charlie answered with another wordless shrug. He offered Rex a chunk of dried meat and a piece of flat bread. Although he wasn't familiar with any of the items, he ate with gusto, enjoying dishes that were delicious, filling, and fitting to the environment. He wasn't like the English in India, who expected tea and cakes at their usual time regardless of the setting. The fruit of the prickly pear fruit moistened his mouth, and he finished it off with a long drink from the canteen.

"What is the story of the painting?" Rex said.

Charlie's natural storytelling skill revealed a good grasp of the English language and surprised Rex. So far removed from the hustle of his everyday work, Rex relaxed. Sighing, he lifted himself from the rock where he had taken a seat. "Let's get back down the mountain."

When he reached the foot of the trail, he spotted Muriel and Benny returning from their day at Charlie's village. Since Benny hadn't been able to walk any distance, they rode on horseback. They waved in greeting. Some of the joy leaked out of Rex's day.

"Your camp is that way." Charlie nodded at the plainly marked trail. "I will take you to see the sheep next Sunday."

"I'm looking forward to it." Rex started toward their camp, but Muriel's voice stopped him short.

"Rex! Wait up."

He turned around and gestured to remind them he was on foot, and continued walking. By the time he reached the outskirts of the campsite, they caught up with him. "Rex, can we get together tonight? I want to hear what you thought about the paintings."

"Sounds good. Give me a few minutes and come to my tent."

She hesitated, probably questioning the wisdom of meeting with him alone in his private quarters.

He hurried to add, "Both of you." He gestured to include Benny in the invitation. "Fred, too. I have ideas for the movie."

She smiled broadly. "Of course you do. I want to freshen up." She gestured at her dress, although it looked perfectly fresh to him. "Half an hour?"

"I'll arrange for refreshments. Maybe Cook can provide some lemonade or tea."

"I'll settle for anything, so long as it's cool." She laughed. As she urged the horse forward, she looked over her shoulder. "I'm looking forward to it."

"Of course we'll have to figure out what to use for paint. I suppose some kind of brush made of bristles from one of these bushes. Don can figure it out, I'm sure. Anyone who could construct fake deer. . ."

Muriel kept her eyes trained on the floor, not wanting to disappoint Rex with her initial reaction.

"I say, those paintings are certainly primitive, aren't they?" Fred blinked his very blue eyes. "I'll have to practice my brushstrokes."

"An ancient wedding certificate." Benny tapped his chin. "I like it. I'll get together with Don to figure out how to re-create the setting down here, safe on flat ground."

"That leaves you, Muriel. What do you think?"

She hesitated. "It fits with the story of the film. It makes a picturesque ending."

"I hear a 'but' coming." Rex sat back in his chair. "Let me have it."

"It's not their story, the story that goes with the painting." She waved her hands around.

"You knew that when you suggested I go take a look at the painting." He sounded skeptical, and she didn't blame him.

"I know. I don't know what I was thinking. It just seems disrespectful. As if someone said the Mayflower sailed from Gibraltar or Cape Horn instead of England."

Rex scratched his head. "Who cares?"

"They will care. Sarah. Charlie. Her people."

"Charlie told me the story today. They know story and imagination. I'm sure they'll understand." Rex turned to Fred. "Brits don't think Shakespeare's *Henry IV* tells the true story, do they?"

"History teachers don't use it to teach about the Tudors, if that's what you mean."

Rex spread his arms as if to say, *See what I mean?*

I'm grasping at straws. Muriel let the subject drop, uncertain why the idea bothered her, and they discussed how to fit filming the key scene into the schedule. When the others filed out, Muriel stayed behind. Rex was already bending over his phonograph, ready to broadcast his nightly serenade. "Do you mind if I stay a few extra minutes?"

Rex glanced up, the cylinder still in his hand, an unguarded expression sprang to his face. Unlike his usual impatience, this looked like. . .hope. "No." He settled the recording back in its place and took his seat. "You're not still upset about the wedding scene, are you?"

"Not exactly." Now that the two of them were alone, as alone as anyone was in this camp where wind could whip the tent flap open at any moment, she felt a little shy. "I spent the day at Sarah's village. I find their community very interesting."

"I feel a story coming on." Rex smiled. "Tell me all about it."

Muriel went into detail about the day, describing everything from the intricate weave of their baskets and blankets to children at play.

"Charlie gave me some fruit from a cactus." Rex smiled. "It was quite tasty."

"Did you know they abandon their homes—they call them hogans—when someone dies for any reason except old age?" She thought about the house where her parents lived, built for her great-grandparents during the Federalist era. The home was the heart of her family's history. "And yet, the family, the clan, is at the heart of their lives."

Rex settled back. "Did you get the sense that there is rivalry between the clans? Is it possible for someone from the Beaver clan to marry an Eagle?"

Muriel lifted her shoulders in a delicate shrug. "I don't know. And I don't think they have a Beaver or an Eagle clan."

"So what happens in the film is possible."

"About as likely as my fancy costume and the rest of it." She laughed. "It's a good story." Taking a breath, she plunged ahead. *Lord, open his mind and heart.* "I found their explanation for the different clans fascinating. I don't know if it's their explanation for different races or not. It reminded me of the Tower of Babel in the Bible. People wanted to reach heaven. Pride. The same sin that got Lucifer kicked out of heaven."

"Pride." Rex arched an eyebrow.

"Pride, yes. They wanted to be God. So God made them speak different languages. They went up the tower speaking one language and came down speaking something entirely different."

"Too bad I didn't have that when I went to France. Would have made learning a foreign language a lot easier." Rex laughed. "I couldn't film the Christian version. Hard to show different languages when there's no sound."

"Wait a minute." He must have caught her expression. "You believe that's what happened. Of course you do." He planted his hands on his knees and leaned forward, his eyes alight with sincerity. "I don't have anything against the Christian faith. In fact, I admire it. It's the most superior moral code the earth has seen. Hard to argue with the Ten Commandments."

"Oh, Rex. I don't believe in a moral code but in a person." Muriel sighed, despair lacing her heart. "Without God, all our good works are not any better than dirty linen."

"Can't you accept the areas where we agree and let the rest go?"

"How can I? When the rest is the most important part?"

The light in Rex's eyes died. "So you say."

Muriel blinked back the tears forming in her eyes. Why, oh why, was she so attracted to a man so blinded to the eternal truth of the Gospel?

After Muriel left his tent, Rex turned the phonograph as loud as it would go, substituting the sound waves vibrating the air for the howls that wanted to escape from his throat.

Why did Muriel have to be so obstinately narrow-minded? He had admitted his admiration for the Christian faith. Its influence permeated western art, government, music, history, the foundations of the United States. He figured God gave them the directions, but He left it up to people to act on them.

If Muriel wanted more than that, she was free to choose, but why did she insist the rest of the world feel the same way? As much as Rex liked her, as much as he suspected she liked him, the question of her faith would always stand in their way. Unless he could change her mind.

If they could spend time away from the atmosphere of the film set, as man and woman—more than director and actress—maybe she would relax enough to see he wasn't such a bad fellow.

At mail call later that week, Rex received a local newspaper. Fire danger remained high. Good thing they took care of fires around camp. It didn't take a native to see that things would burn quickly in this dry country. He surveyed the canyon, envisioning how they could escape if fire balled down the narrow valley. He shook his head. The fact was, they probably wouldn't.

Other articles, about local politics and plans for a celebration of the new century in a few months' time, didn't offer much interest. By January, he would be back in civilization in Denver. The new year seemed so far away, and he had so much to do between now and then, he couldn't generate much enthusiasm, even for the once-in-a-lifetime event.

At the bottom right-hand corner on the first page, he spotted a short paragraph. A new sandstone marker had been placed at a remote location described as the "quadripoint," or "four corners" in simpler language. Rex reviewed what he remembered about the map in this part of the country. Colorado joined the Union in 1876, during the centennial of the United States. Utah became a state shortly after the Civil War. They formed the southern boundary of the United States, adjacent to the only territories left in the United States, New Mexico and Arizona. On a map, they all looked like big, square dabs with little to differentiate between them. Of course their citizens would probably disagree.

Four right angles met at a geographical pinpoint, and someone had commemorated the location with a marker. "Four Corners." It had a certain poetic ring to it. He checked the map—not all that far from the film site. It would make a good addition to the film, tying the past and the future.

That's it. At the beginning of filming, Rex had built a week's break from filming to coincide with the Fourth of July holiday. Perhaps he could convince Muriel to spend part of that break at the Four Corners. He could film it himself. Muriel would insist on a chaperone. Perhaps

Sarah would agree to come.

He folded the paper to showcase the article. Striding into the chow tent, he scanned the room. As usual, half a dozen people surrounded Muriel. He could have his pick of a seat at any other table, but he wanted to invite her right away.

"Hey, Rex. I'm done here. Take my seat." Benny waved him over.

Rex couldn't help but notice the strained looks passed between the other people at the table, his reward for being a harsh taskmaster. It wouldn't change overnight, but he wouldn't let that rob him of the pleasure of Muriel's company.

In her hand, Muriel held a piece of plain white stationery with a faint scent of lilacs clinging to the paper. Her eyes scanned the page, and she folded the letter and tucked it back in its envelope.

"News from home?"

"Mother says the blueberry harvest is excellent this year." Muriel stared at the peaches that came from a can on her plate. "The food here is excellent. But I would love just one dinner of lobster, roasted corn, and blueberry cobbler."

"Point me in the direction of the nearest ocean, and I'll be happy to oblige."

Her laughter tickled his ear. "Which way is west?" She leaned over and glanced at the paper in Rex's hand. " 'Four Corners Marker Replaced.' What's that about?" She read the brief paragraphs.

Rex could see that her interest was piqued. "How would you like to see it? It's some distance away. I thought a small group of us could travel to see it over our break from filming. Get some footage of the marker. I might use it in the film or sell it as a news story. I'll find a use for it."

She cocked her head. "I was going to spend the week at Durango." She drummed her fingers on the table. "Enjoy some comforts of civilization for a few days. But I'll admit, I'm intrigued." Her hand twirled the braid on her right shoulder. "Who else is coming?"

This was the tricky part. "I'm still inviting people. I thought perhaps Sarah could come with you. She knows that part of the country better than any of us do."

"If she's willing to give up her days off. I'll ask."

"Is there anyone else you would like to come?"

"I'll ask around." She smiled. "I'll let you know by Friday night. Does that work?"

She didn't say no. Rex's heart skipped ahead as he dreamed of the week ahead.

Chapter 10

Sunday morning the film crew relaxed in the miniature city they had created in the Colorado wilderness. Cast and crew alike took advantage of the day off to take care of personal errands, catch a little rest, or take in some of the countryside.

Rex and Charlie had returned to the mountains, chasing after bighorn sheep. Muriel prayed they found them, so he would stop hounding Benny about giving up his Sundays for "just one more thing." This time, her friend had resisted the invitation. At the urging of the chapel group, they had decided to hold a Sunday service. Benny dubbed their gathering The Church of Renewed Hope.

"I wonder how many people will come today." Muriel set the planks in rows as Benny brought them out. "Some people might want to sleep in on their only day off."

"You might be surprised. People who don't see the need to meet every night of the week might welcome a Sunday service. Well, look who's here."

Muriel shaded her eyes against the midday sun. "Fred?" Fred wasn't as vocal about Rex in his disdain of the Christian faith, but neither had he ever expressed more than minimal interest. But the actor, looking very colonial in his white linen suit and hat, approached with Helen on his arm.

"Good morning, Helen. Fred. How wonderful that you could join us."

Fred flashed the trademark grin that made women the country over swoon. "I try to attend Sunday services when I'm home. If you're going to the trouble to hold church right here at the camp, I figured why not give it a shot." He patted Helen's arm. "Helen invited me."

Whether Fred was motivated by spiritual hunger or the obvious admiration in Helen's eyes, Muriel welcomed his attendance. With both major actors and the principal camerist in attendance, others might check it out.

Benny's prediction came true. More people joined them, women dressed in their best, men scrubbed a little more closely than usual. They crowded the planks to the point where a few latecomers had to sit on the rocks close by. She could count on one hand the people missing from the service, including Rex. She refused to let thoughts of that man distract her from worship.

Muriel led in singing hymns, mixing old standbys that everyone knew with newer music that she hoped would appeal to those unused to a church service. Their voices echoed across the canyon floor, as if the mountains themselves joined in praising God. Benny made a clear presentation of the Gospel. Muriel's gaze wandered, willing Rex to reappear and hear at least a part of the message. He didn't, of course, and the service drew to a close. Although no one responded, she prayed that the Word would land in good soil.

"Good service, Muriel. I'll plan on making a habit of attending as long as we're filming." Fred tipped his hat to her and escorted Helen to the chow tent, where cold cuts awaited them in a serve-yourself buffet.

Good soil, indeed.

After the morning, Muriel held high hopes for the afternoon service. Through Sarah, she had sent an invitation for the people of her village to join them for Bible stories and discussion.

Muriel's heart was burdened for the Navajo. Most of the film crew would return to cities where the Gospel was preached from a local pulpit on a regular basis, but she had seen no evidence of a Christian presence among Sarah's people. She hoped, prayed, they would respond. Sarah was the first fruits; surely more would follow.

More excited and nervous than she was before the first night of a new play, Muriel barely touched her lunch. She kept sneaking glances at her watch, her gaze wandering to the front of the chow tent, wondering if she would catch a glimpse of Indians arriving.

The gap remained frustratingly empty.

After the lunch crowd dispersed, Muriel walked slowly to her tent for a brief prayer and a moment's respite from the heat. Not only had no one appeared in the chapel area, but she also saw no one approaching on the horizon. She tamped down the worry rising in her throat. Indians didn't keep time the same way they did. They would come. Eventually.

She tied a wide-brimmed hat on her head—remembering Sarah's advice to protect herself from the sun—and joined Benny on the planks. Unlike the morning, they were devoid of occupants.

"Don't worry. I'm sure it's just a misunderstanding." Benny's voice didn't convey the comfort he tried to offer.

"There's someone now." Muriel leaped to her feet then subsided back onto the bench. "It's Rex. And Charlie. And they're not here for Bible study." She started to cry.

"Aw, Muriel, God is still in control." Benny tucked her head against his shoulder.

"I so hoped—"

"I know."

A traitorous part of Muriel's heart wished Rex was the one holding her and comforting her. She must root out the ridiculous and foolish wish, since Rex didn't share her faith, let alone understand her passion for sharing it with others. Benny was a rock, and she appreciated having a big brother to fight her battles.

"Don't you two look cozy." Rex's sardonic voice jarred Muriel out of misery. She lifted her head in time to see the disappointment on his face.

This day was going from bad to worse.

"Buffalo Bill's Wild West Show come to life." Rex surveyed the streets of Cortez. On one corner he saw an Indian who only lacked the feather headdress to take Sitting Bull's place in the show. Over there, he spotted men with ground in dirt in their clothes and a gleam in their eyes that announced them as prospectors. Several saloons dotted the main thoroughfare. Cowboys abounded, faces shaded by the rolled-brim hats they favored.

Did Muriel know what she was getting into when she booked a room here? This looked as much a set piece as a lobster-trap-covered dock from a Maine fishing village.

"A setup shot of a street like this would set the tone for an entire movie." Benny held his hands before his eyes, probably envisioning the street through a camera lens. "It looks crowded. Lucky we got a room."

"I just hope the Last Chance Hotel is better than the name implies." Rex glanced down at his clothes, his usual working attire of black twill trousers and beige shirt unbuttoned at the collar. If he had worn a suit, he would be branded as a dandy.

"Buck up. It's bound to be better than a camp cot. Come, lad, let's go." Benny gestured to the porter who was hauling their luggage and camera equipment to the hotel.

Rex couldn't come up with a reason to leave Benny out of the expedition, not after Muriel invited him. He couldn't decide if they were anything more than good friends, if a hint of romance sparked between them. Last Sunday, when he had returned from filming the bighorn sheep with Charlie, he found them nestled together. Muriel looked so comfortable, her head resting on Benny's shoulder.

No, Rex couldn't take back the invitation. The Rex Pride people knew relished in pushing his crew to give up their free time and pour everything into the current production. Charlie joined the expedition, making a total of five.

Charlie jogged alongside the porter, making sure the equipment received gentle treatment. Rex followed at a slower pace. The sight of a theater down a side street sent a thrill up Rex's spine, like the first time he had set foot in Times Square. What would the people of Cortez think if they knew the great Rex Pride, the one who had brought them *Sherman's War* and the popular *Love's Idyll*, strode their streets? Would they hound him, demanding his autograph? Beg him to give them a part in his next picture? Or ignore the whole pursuit as a child's game?

Looking at the mountains rising steeply to the east of the town, Rex wondered why people would lock themselves in a dark theater when they could be outside enjoying the ephemeral beauty of the town. He sidestepped a pile of horse droppings and held his breath. That offered one explanation.

"Rex!"

His head snapped to attention at the familiar voice. A wide smile curved Muriel's generous lips. Dressed today as a modern American woman and not an ancient Indian princess, she took his breath away. The people of Cortez might ignore Rex Pride, film director, but they would flock to the first lady of stage and screen. He increased his pace and joined them moments later.

Rex recognized the gleam in Benny's eye. "Go ahead and film it if you want to. We might use it in another movie."

Benny's eyes wandered to the camera case standing to his right side. "Not unless I want to start a stampede." He sighed. "Some people still object to still cameras; they won't want me following them around. They may not have even heard of moving pictures."

"There's a—" Muriel started.

"I saw a theater down one side street." Rex supplied the information. Trust Muriel to have found it already. "You're right. I would prefer to remain incognito for the time being."

After they settled their equipment in a room for the night, the five of them went to a restaurant that Muriel recommended. "Plain cooking, and plenty of it. Not quite like home, but then again, my mother has different ingredients to work with than here in Colorado. The pot roast is excellent."

"What are Rocky Mountain oysters?" Benny asked. "Do they have oysters packed in ice and shipped here from the sea?" He shook his head. "No, that can't be it. Then they wouldn't be called Rocky Mountain oysters."

Muriel blushed, and she dabbed at the corner of her mouth as if to hide her embarrassment. She recovered enough to say, "I asked the same thing my first night. They're not exactly oysters. . .they're from. . . oh dear. From bulls that have been made into steers." She grabbed the menu and hid her red face behind it.

Benny's expression told him he was working as hard as Rex was to contain his laughter. Once he knew he had control of his voice, he said, "I believe I'll stick with the pot roast. That sounds like a safe bet."

The meal was as delicious as Muriel had described. While they were eating, one of the prospectors Rex had noticed earlier on the street, hardly recognizable after a two-bit haircut and shave had removed most of the mop of red hair on his head, came in and ordered the most expensive item on the menu.

Even with five of them present, the well-set table with dancing candlelight was the most intimate setting Rex had ever shared with Muriel. She sat to his right, between him and Sarah. A part of him celebrated the fact she did not sit next to Benny. After the waitress served the first course, Benny, Muriel, and Sarah bowed their heads. Rex hurried to follow their example. All three of these people professed to be Christians; if he didn't watch out, they'd convert him before they returned to Mesa Verde. He blanked his mind while Benny said grace, and raised his head when he said Amen.

Conversation flowed naturally, that of people who knew and respected each other and felt no need for pretense. Even the taciturn Sarah contributed a story or two, displaying a droll sense of humor he had never suspected lay beneath her quiet exterior. Rex said little, remained quieter than usual, satisfied to enjoy Muriel's company.

As he kept her profile in sight, he registered the variety of people wandering in and out of the dining room. Compared to the crowds he had seen on the street earlier that day, most of them had taken some effort to spruce up for the occasion. Someone in town must be aware of current fashion trends. Women sported a wide variety of hats, from straw boaters that perched on top of their heads to elaborate creations, complete with feathers and bird's nests and such. Their clothes ranged from prairie homespun to outfits that wouldn't look amiss among Denver's elite.

But Muriel exuded a simple elegance that made every other woman in the room fade into obscurity. In an industry where the lines between the stage character and the actress could get blurred, she stood out as the most genuine person he knew. She exemplified everything he admired about the Christian faith.

"You're not saying much tonight." Muriel turned to face him full on. Her skin glowed with health after her summer in the sun.

He cleared his throat. "I was thinking how you are three of the best people I know." Which was true, even if he was bowled over by Muriel's beauty. "And that all three of you claim to be Christians." He turned his gaze from the affable Benny to the quiet and steady Sarah to the luminescent Muriel. "You may be the only true Christians I have ever known. You live what you preach."

Sarah cast her eyes downward. Benny gaped at him for a moment before nodding, a smile crossing his face.

Rex turned his attention to Muriel, hopeful that she would blossom in the wake of his words of praise. Instead sadness clouded her eyes as she shook her head. "I'm no one so special. I'm only a sinner saved by God's grace."

The chasm between them only widened. He might not be perfect, but he didn't need saving. By anything or anyone.

"You are sad." Sarah stood behind Muriel where she sat in front of an ornate oval mirror. She ran a brush through Muriel's hair, and it fell in gentle waves down her back. "Is it Mr. Rex Pride?" She looked over Muriel's head into the mirror, a challenge in her eyes.

"You know me too well, my friend." Muriel blinked away tears. She didn't want salty tear drops to mar the pampered beauty regimen she had enjoyed this evening. "He thinks it's enough to admire

Christian teaching. He doesn't think he needs God—or anybody else." Her voice caught.

Sarah paused in mid-brushstroke. "He admires you. I saw him watching you tonight. His eyes were as bright as the stars at night." She continued with the brush gently separating a tangle. "Or is he a man who admires many ladies?"

"Sarah." A giggle hid the shock in Muriel's voice. "I don't think so. He doesn't have that reputation. That is one of the reasons I agreed to do this film. He makes us work hard, but he doesn't chase women. I wouldn't work with him if he did." She heard the smugness in her tone and cringed.

"Then it is you he likes. Something about you draws him. Perhaps it is the Lord Jesus." Sarah parted Muriel's hair and began brushing the other side.

"I don't think so." Muriel stared at her fingernails, which she had kept short during the filming of *Ruined Hopes*. "I so long to lead people to the Lord, but it's not happening. Except for you." She smiled at Sarah in the mirror. "You don't know how thankful I am for you."

She picked up a nail file and began smoothing a rough edge. "I was so disappointed when no one came to the Bible study last Sunday." *Not even you.* Twisting in her seat, Muriel looked up into her friend's face. "What am I doing wrong?"

Sarah's cobalt eyes bore in Muriel's. She set the brush on the marble countertop. "My people think Jesus is the white man's god. One more way the white man tries to change us. You call me Sarah and my brother, Charlie. Those are names given to us in the white man's school."

Apprehension dawned on Muriel, and she shivered. "What name did your parents give you?"

"My name is Nascha. The Owl." Pride vibrated in her voice.

"And your brother?"

"He is Yanaba."

Muriel stood and extended her arms to her friend. "The name

suits you. You are truly as wise as an owl, and I was too blind to see. Can you forgive me?"

"Of course. Is that not what our Lord Jesus teaches us to do?" Sarah—Nascha—stepped into her embrace. This time, Muriel let the tears flow.

Chapter 11

"So this is the famous Four Corners."

Muriel couldn't blame Benny for his disappointment. The landscape stretched for miles in every direction, barren desert dotted with cacti and scrub brush, far more desolate than Mesa Verde. Never had the artificial nature of manmade boundaries been more evident.

"Not even as dramatic as when two country lanes intersect, is it? Well, do what you can with it." Rex walked around the marker. "Hey, I just walked through four states."

Sarah stood to one side, not saying much. Her faint smile seemed to say *These white men and their artificial lines in the earth.*

"It is a crossroads of sorts." Muriel closed her eyes to orient herself.

She pointed back the way they had traveled. "Colorado. Mining towns. Boom or bust." She swung to the west. "Utah. And I confess I know next to nothing about these so-called Latter-day Saints. But imagine. A salt lake in the middle of the continent!" She thought back to their discussion about "oysters." What kind of fish lived in that Great Salt Lake?

She spread her arms to encompass all the land south of them. "New Mexico and Arizona. Even the names remind us of their ties to Mexico. And how can we forget that before the Europeans came, this all belonged to Sar—Nascha's people?" And hadn't she heard of other Indian tribes? Wasn't Geronimo from somewhere around here? She shook her head. She knew less about the native peoples of America than Nascha did about Europe.

"And before that, people lived in the cliff dwellings where we're filming." Benny tightened his eyes as if envisioning the procession of history.

"We could put that in a storyboard. 'At this spot, where four territories and states meet, paths of people have crossed since before time began.' That kind of thing, and tie it back to *Ruined Hopes*." He nodded his head. "That's good. Be sure you get the countryside here. It's forbidding." His cocky grin was infectious. "We'll discourage anyone from ever visiting, and keep it to ourselves."

Muriel laughed. Sarah's smile was strained, and Muriel reminded herself that this was her home. For her, there probably was no place on earth where she would rather live.

Benny and Rex roamed the area, using up a roll of film, while Nascha and Muriel set up camp. The camp where the film was located was just as removed from town, but with all the adaptations they had made while staying there, it felt like New York City compared to this spot. "Out here, I can almost imagine I'm Abraham, wandering the desert."

"Abraham, the man who was married to Sarah?" Nascha smiled. "Me?"

"That Abraham, yes. Whenever I'm tempted to doubt God, I think of Abraham. Wandering around without a permanent home. Waiting twenty-five years for God to give him the son He promised. Sarah was ninety when she had Isaac. Can you imagine?"

"Ninety winters?" Nascha shook her head. "Do white women still bear children at that age?" She sounded incredulous.

"Certainly not. Not that many people live to be ninety anymore, although it was more common in Bible times than now. It was a miracle. When it was impossible for man, God made it happen."

Her gaze shifted to Rex. "A God who can make an old woman give birth can change that one's heart, I think."

"That's what I'm praying for." Out here, it seemed more possible.

The men spread out their bedrolls under the stars while the ladies retired to the tent they had brought with them. Muriel appreciated their consideration of her modesty, but she almost wished she could spend the night in the open air. In spite of the filling supper and several days' strenuous riding, she found herself unable to sleep. She blamed it on the excellent coffee they had consumed by the potfuls throughout the evening hours. Slipping on a dressing gown and her walking shoes—no soft slippers for this rugged terrain—she left the tent, determined to walk no farther than she could see by the dying embers of the fire.

Sitting down on a smooth rock face, she looked up into the sky, and began praising the God of creation. "'When I consider thy heavens, the work of thy fingers, the moon and the stars, which thou hast ordained.'" No wonder a poetic soul like King David was drawn to write of Creation and the Creator after spending so many nights watching over his sheep. She listened to the sounds of the night, the hoot of an owl—Nascha. She sent up a prayer for her friend.

"Mind if I join you?" Rex's quiet voice startled Muriel.

"Please, take a seat."

In pajamas, Rex looked the most informal of all the times she had ever seen him—almost ordinary. She suppressed a grin. Rex Pride was many things, but ordinary wasn't one of them.

"A penny for your thoughts."

Your pajamas. Muriel shushed the thought. *God.* Rex wouldn't want to hear that either, and she didn't want to push him away by sounding religious.

"Is it a difficult question?" He sounded amused.

"Oh, it's only that I was thinking about how the skies remind me of God. And I didn't think you joined me to hear another sermon." She tilted her head back. "So let's talk about the constellations. I like the Big Dipper—mostly because I can always identify it. That and Orion's Belt."

"Let me point out some of the others to you." Rex leaned in and put his arm over her shoulder, pointing with his hand. "There is Cassiopeia—the seven sisters."

Muriel counted under her breath. ". . .five, six. . .where's seven? Oh, there she is." She settled against Rex's chest. It felt so good, so right.

"And there is Aquarius and Lyra and Pegasus." He continued

pointing out various groups, and somehow, through his keen eye, she could see the shapes that had eluded her before.

Their conversation died down, and they sat in a comfortable silence. "There's one you missed."

"Not possible. Where is it?"

She pointed to the east, to the bright white globe hanging in the sky. "The moon." Her voice came out in a hoarse whisper. "It's beautiful."

"Yes, it is." But Rex wasn't looking at the sky. He was staring at her face. He leaned forward. Muriel knew she should jump up, leave, at least pull away. But instead she leaned in, accepting his caress.

And it felt like the most natural thing in the world.

I never should have kissed her. Rex repeated it to himself for the hundredth time since they had returned from their expedition to see the Four Corners marker. Ever since that night, Muriel had distanced herself, pulling back when he wanted to push forward.

But oh, that kiss. . .a man could do a lot of dreaming on that kiss. For those brief moments, they were one man, one woman, as it was meant to be. As God, if He cared about such things at all, intended.

He knew the kiss had awakened something in Muriel as well. Now in her love scenes with Fred, she brought a depth he hadn't seen before. This film might represent the best work of an actress already renowned for her extraordinary abilities. From time to time, when she thought Rex wasn't looking, he caught her licking her lips, as if reliving the feel of his lips against hers.

During their trip back to Mesa Verde, he put down her silence to the difficulties of the trail. Back at the camp, he attributed it to a return to the hectic pace of filming. Nearly every minute of her day was accounted for, and he was even busier, skimming his sleep to a maximum of six hours a night.

But as the days dragged on, she didn't speak more than two sentences to him on any given day, aside from pleasantries at meals and necessary dialogue regarding the movie. Something precious had slipped through his grasp, and he didn't know how to get it back.

To distract his mind from disappointment, Rex threw himself into finishing. Scene by scene they built the film. As he had seen happen in previous productions, filming took on a life of its own as the actors became their characters and needed less and less direction.

"You should be pleased with today's rushes." Benny set up the projector in Rex's tent after the nightly chapel service. "Muriel and Fred lit up the screen."

The camera loved Muriel, or maybe it was the man behind the camera, but he wasn't alone in that feeling.

Fred ducked into the tent. "Mind if I join you?"

The film's leading man was another man enamored of Muriel. The deeper he sank into Killdeer's character, the more solicitous the Brit became of Muriel. Rex reminded himself that no whiff of scandal had ever attached itself to Fred, who was a devoted family man. He channeled his emotions into good acting, nothing more.

Images flickered on the screen, accompanied only by the whir of the film feeding between reels. Rex kept a notebook and pen ready to take notes, as did Benny, but his hand didn't move. The story carried him away, something that rarely happened in an art form created by camera angles and lighting and gestures that could be controlled.

Sometime midreel, the tent flap rustled and Muriel entered. When the film ran out of the reel, she brought her hands together in a single clap. "That was good."

Rex turned to greet her, unsure if his mouth had twisted into a frown or a smile. "The film is going well."

"Coming from you, that's high praise indeed." Muriel had tucked her hair into a loose bun at the back of her neck, which managed to look both cool and elegant. Fred vacated his chair and took a seat on Rex's bed. Muriel accepted the seat. "Are we still on schedule to finish filming next week?"

"We have a few scenes to do over."

A smile hovered on Muriel's lips.

"But yes, I expect us to finish."

"The biggest scene ahead of us is that paint scene. Don has come up with white-limestone paint that looks quite realistic. He's also fashioned your paint brushes."

"Do you expect us to actually paint? I can't even draw a straight line." Fred looked from Rex to Muriel. "What about you?"

"Artistic talent passed me by."

"You're acting like I'm asking you to do your own stunts." Rex picked up the pen and tapped it against his notebook. "You don't have to do much except dip the brush in the paint bowl and dab some on the rock face." He explained his plans for the scene.

"So the wrap party will be next Friday." Muriel nodded with satisfaction. "We'll hold our final chapel service on Thursday night, then. We'd love to see you all there." Her invitation included everyone, but she directed her gaze at Rex. There he saw the longing, the passion, he had felt in their single kiss. She cared more for her God than for a mere mortal.

No flesh-and-blood man could hope to measure up. "I'll add it to the schedule." He uncapped his pen and made a big deal of writing it down. "I'll be busy splicing the reel together for the wrap party."

Her shoulders deflated. "Thank you for putting up the announcement." With a quiet good night, she left the tent.

The paintbrush made out of spruce needles bound together by vines scratched against Muriel's palm. How had the ancient inhabitants of this city managed to create art out of such primitive materials? But they had. They must have told stories around the campfire and perhaps acted out the adventures of the hunt. The descendants of Jubal and Tubalcain, the first musician and worker in bronze. Art, whether Beethoven's symphonies, Rembrandt's paintings, or Shakespeare's plays, was part of what stamped God's image on man. That ability to create.

She stared at the brush again, feeling the weight of it in her hand. She thought of the men Moses appointed to sound the trumpet for the movement of the Israelites. Once she asked herself how slaves who had spent their days making bricks had learned how to make music. But they had, on instruments made of animal horns instead of the intricate instruments of wood and string and brass enjoyed in the nineteenth century.

She was blessed to live in an age where her performances could be recorded to be played over and over again. But if she had lived in the times of ancient Greece, she would have donned a mask and taken part in one of the tragedies. She understood the drive that made people create art with whatever means they had at hand very well.

During the filming, she would pretend to mix the paint. But for this practice, she only wanted to conquer the movement of the brush and try her hand at creating a spiral.

"They're uncomfortable things, aren't they?" Beside her Fred grimaced at the brush in his hand.

Nodding, she straightened and touched the brush to the rock. Streaky lines of white paint appeared, but didn't drip. "The paint's a good consistency. No drip."

He imitated her motions, a good swatch with his first swipe. "I wonder if they had colors. What might they use? People used plants and such to dye clothes, after all."

"I don't know. I've only seen the white." She passed her brush over the patch several times to get a solid white color. After several tries, she had a thin line that wobbled as she tried to form a spiral. "The needles don't hold the paint very well." Next she tried an eagle, but it looked more like a flattened *v* than a bird.

Out of the corner of her eye, she spotted Rex in his typical pose, perusing their efforts. That man knew exactly what he wanted and headed straight for it—brimming with confidence that appeared as cockiness. That kind of man could woo any woman he wanted, but he didn't. He was, in so many respects, a very moral man, puritanical in his work habits.

Her lips tingled as she remembered their kiss. They hadn't ever discussed what had happened that night at the Four Corners. In the days since, she spent hours on her knees, asking for forgiveness—and pleading for strength to withstand Rex's magnetism. God answered her prayer by keeping Rex at a distance, which had the unfortunate result of making her miss him all the more. She decided she had practiced enough, and walked in Rex's direction with her paintbrush in hand.

"What do you think?" She kept her voice as neutral as possible, only her acting skill holding back the warmth she felt. "Will we get the result you want?"

"I only need the suggestion of you painting. The focus will be on you and Fred, on the marriage the painting represents." Rex gestured to their props director, who had come up with the paint and brushes. "Don said there was no way to get something that would match the ancient painting, and I believe him." He gave a rueful laugh. "There goes my wonderful climax."

"You mean you do have limits?" Muriel flicked her hand, and paint flew in Rex's direction. Dropping the brush, she put her hand over her mouth. "I'm so sorry."

"Better my shirt than that lovely frock you're wearing."

Muriel looked down at her dress, a pale green dress she wore often as her coolest outfit. So he noticed. She fought the pleasure the thought brought her. To hide her confusion, she bent over to pick up the brush and carried it to Don. Returning to Rex, she said, "I should at least wash it for you."

His lips formed the shape to say no, but what came out was "I'd like that."

"Do we have time now?" She reached out to trace the splash on his shirt. It started at his third button and trailed down nearly to his waist. "Before the paint dries."

"You want me to give you the shirt off my back." A smile played around his lips, and he started unbuttoning the shirt at the top button.

"That's all right. Bring it to me when you've changed."

His laughter followed her as she scurried away in the direction of the wash tent.

Chapter 12

Why not? Rex smoothed out the shirt Muriel had laundered, bleached almost white after so many washings, and put away his dress blue. She should appreciate the gesture. Eight weeks and countless hours later, cast and crew of *Ruined Hopes* would celebrate the end of filming. He still had months of work ahead, shaping the rough footage into a seamless story, adding subtitles and storyboards and working with a composer to arrange the music he had chosen and integrate it with original compositions.

However, on this night, everyone would relax and enjoy their accomplishments, including him—including Muriel. Smiling, he tied a red bow tie around his neck, the only dash of color with his shirt and white linen slacks. What would Muriel wear tonight? Sensible walking shoes or heels? Evening dress or one of her day dresses? No matter what she wore, she would be beautiful.

Through his tent flap, he heard a popular song playing on his phonograph. Whistling the tune between his teeth, he checked himself in his mirror one last time and joined the party. Muriel stood talking with Helen and a couple of the minor actors in the film, her hips gently swaying in time to the music, sending the shimmering lavender fabric of her dress in motion. He poured himself a cup of lemonade and sauntered across the yard.

At his approach, the actors fell silent.

"Rex." Muriel turned a brilliant smile on him. "I was beginning to think you were avoiding your own party." She eyed the lemonade in his hand. "You should get some cookies to go with that. Cook has made some amazing shortbread cookies."

She held it up to his mouth, and he took a bite. Rich with butter and sugar, it melted in his mouth. "A man could become addicted to these." He took a sip of lemonade and his mouth puckered. "A good contrast to this stuff."

A smile hovered around her lips.

"Come with me while I get some more cookies?" She accepted his arm for the short walk to the refreshment tables. In addition to the shortbread cookies—the nearly empty tray testifying to their popularity—he found a three-tier yellow cake and berry and buttermilk pies. He took a piece of each but left his lemonade cup on the table. "Coffee will go better with these sweets."

Muriel chose to stay by Rex's side all evening, the last night the crew would spend together. She wanted to spend this one night enjoying the company of the man she had come to admire—to love, even if she only admitted it to herself. There was only today, no future for them, she knew that, since the man remained as stuck in his refusal to see his need for God as ever.

At the last chapel service the night before, a dozen people and more shared testimonies of how God had changed them over the summer. Muriel's heart rejoiced, but she kept looking, praying, hoping for a sign of the person she most wanted to appear. He remained away, having only visited chapel that one time.

No, Rex wouldn't change, and she would avoid working with him in the future to protect her heart. But for one night she pretended her dreams could come true.

All too soon the night drew to an end. Rex walked her to her tent and lingered, his eyes fixed on her face. "The moon is beautiful tonight." He leaned forward.

He's going to kiss me. With her last ounce of courage, Muriel took a single step back. "It's been a lovely evening, Rex. Good night."

The next morning, Muriel rose early to say good-bye. Almost everyone was leaving today, heading in the direction of all four winds. Cook would stay as long as Rex chose to work on-site. Benny would check out the last of the film before he left.

As for Muriel, she sent a letter to her family with the people departing today. She had planned to take a vacation before returning to New York for George Bernard Shaw's play, *Mrs. Warren's Profession.* Instead, she would visit with Nascha in her village and assist her as she started a Bible study among her people.

Fred, as unflappable as ever, stopped by on his way to the waiting wagons. "It's been a pleasure working with you. I hope we can do it again? Perhaps on another Rex Pride production?"

She nodded, afraid tears would choke her voice. She accepted his hug. "The same to you, Fred. Do you think I would be welcome in London?"

"For you, dear. Always!" He kissed her on the cheek. "I'll see you at the premiere, then." He waved and climbed onto the wagon. They pulled away, leaving only empty sand and flattened bushes where they had lived and worked for the past two months. Dust swirled behind the wagons, obscuring her view of the people who had been closer than family for that brief span of time.

Rex stood by her side, watching them leave. "And you'll be leaving tonight?" He had stuffed his hands in pockets.

She nodded. "I'll spend a few weeks with Nascha."

"Trying to convert the heathen, I suppose." He kept his voice light, but she heard the puzzlement.

"It is my hope to help Nascha share the Savior, who died for all people, with her village." *Oh, Rex, please tell me you're wanting to know more.*

"It certainly seems to make you happy."

"Happy? Maybe not." She felt anything but happy at the moment. "But peaceful, yes. And joyful."

"Joy and happiness are different?"

"Joy is permanent; happiness is temporary." She decided to take one last gamble. "Do you want that kind of joy, Rex?"

"You're about to tell me the plan of salvation, I suppose." He put his hands on her shoulders, willing her to look at him. The same despair she felt in her heart was reflected in his eyes. "Look, we both know whatever we have between us wouldn't work out. Don't worry about me. I do okay."

"Oh, Rex." She lifted her hand to his cheek, unable to resist that last caress. "I promise I will always pray for you. There may come a time you will realize you need it." Hiding her tears with a laugh, she dropped her hand and took a step back. At the edge of the clearing, she saw Nascha waiting. "Good-bye, Rex, and God go with you."

I must like pain. Rex could think of no other reason for accepting Benny's invitation to visit Sarah's village after his painful good-bye with Muriel. He'd have to find a way to let the extras know if the film came to Cortez.

"I suppose you want me to attend that Bible study Sarah and Muriel are starting."

"I wouldn't object." Benny flashed bright teeth at him. "Or you might visit with Charlie and ask him about the shots you want to get. Up to you."

When they arrived at the village, Charlie welcomed Rex with a quiet manner he had come to recognize as friendship. They walked through the village, Rex taking in the unusual structure of the hogans. He itched to include it in a film. Maybe he would return.

"Are you available to come with me this afternoon? I want to get some more local color."

Charlie thought for a minute before answering. "I can go tomorrow. Today I go to the study of the Jesus book with my sister."

"Tomorrow then." Rex accepted the inevitable. Muriel came with Sarah to draw water from the well. After a warm welcome, she had stayed too busy to visit. He was curious to see how this Bible study differed from the one they held on the set. How many people would attend?

For Muriel's sake, he hoped they would have a good showing.

An older Navajo woman, unmistakably Sarah and Charlie's mother, offered Rex a seat on the only stuffed chair in the home. He tried to demur, wondering how he could refuse since he didn't know her language.

She gestured again. "Please. Take this seat. You are our guest." That answered one question: at least one person spoke English. A hope stirred in him that they would speak English at the meeting.

Mrs. Begay led Benny to a hard-backed chair next to Rex's. "Do they all speak English?"

Benny shrugged. "Not unless they have to."

Rex knew a smidgeon of other languages: high school Latin, enough French to get around, a bit of Spanish. But Indian languages had never come up on any curriculum he had studied. When Muriel came in with Sarah, both Benny and Rex stood and offered their seats. "I will sit here." Sarah took her place across the fire pit from the men.

Rex turned to Muriel. "You at least will sit here." Rex heard the demand in the words, and scrambled to compensate. "No American male can take this comfortable chair while in the presence of such beauty."

In spite of the smile that indicated her appreciation of the compliment, Muriel shook her head. "Mrs. Begay gave you the place of honor. I will not dishonor her—or you—by trading places." She took a seat next to Benny.

"Do you know if they'll be speaking English?" Rex feared that a steady diet of unintelligible speech might lull him to sleep. Maybe not. He pulled his favorite notebook and pencil from his pocket. People watching had often provoked new ideas.

"I hope not." She must have seen his surprised expression. "I am praying that these people will realize Jesus is for everyone, not just for white men. They need to hear that in their own language. In fact"—her eyes narrowed in concentration—"I need to find out if anyone has translated the Bible into Navajo. I want to get a copy for Nascha. All people deserve to hear God's word in their own tongue."

"And what would be my tongue?" He found himself asking.

Muriel didn't laugh but tilted her head before offering an answer. "American English with a generous helping of cockiness and every term in the theater lexicon."

Benny laughed at that. "You nailed our Mr. Pride, all right."

Voices at the door indicated the arrival of guests, and Rex followed Muriel's gaze at the doorway. Two older gentlemen followed by one elderly woman entered. This man should have had Rex's seat, he realized. Dark eyes regarded him and nodded in welcome. The elders of the village, perhaps? A couple of young women about Sarah's age entered, followed by a few children. Men came in, nodding greetings to Charlie. All in all, about twenty people had gathered when Muriel returned to her seat, and silence fell on the gathering.

Charlie stood behind Rex.

Rex waited for the meeting to begin. No one chattered the way they had at the film site; not a single person held a Bible. Not even Sarah had a Bible, although Rex was pretty sure Muriel had given her one.

Sarah began speaking. She said their names, and he realized she must be introducing them. She paused and gestured in their direction. Muriel smiled and waved a greeting to the group, as did Benny and Rex.

After the introductions, Sarah began a long tale. She used more words in that one afternoon session than he had heard her use through the entire film shoot. Rex understood none of it, although now and then he thought he heard something that resembled "Jesus."

Her voice rose and fell in the cadences of a natural storyteller, and her face lost its usual impassive expression. Grief and guilt and joy all flittered across her face. He didn't need an interpreter. The story of her decision to believe in Jesus as God read like an open book.

So much so that when Sarah broke into English, he was almost surprised.

"My friend Muriel told me about Jesus. She showed me that Jesus is for all people. She is a good friend. Muriel, would you like to say a few words?"

"Thank you." Muriel stood. "I have much to learn from Nascha, as well. She reminded me that Christian doesn't mean being white or American. I confess, I was too proud to see that for a while. Please forgive me. I look forward to learning from all of you as well."

Her voice throbbed with all the pathos he had heard her evoke on stage, but he knew genuine emotion lay behind her words. Here she exuded fulfillment and peace. This was her world, in a way *Ruined Hopes* or any Pride production never would.

Instead of resenting it, of wishing he could abolish or redirect her drive, for the first time, he found himself wondering what it would be like to share it.

Back at camp, Rex cranked up the phonograph, seeking something to fill the vacuum created by the departure of the crew. The quiet enjoyment he experienced at the end of filming was missing. With every rattle of pebbles or snapping twig, he looked up, half expecting to see Muriel appear. He needed to get her out of his head.

Cook had left with Benny yesterday, so he was on his own with simple rations. It was time to get back to Denver and finish putting the film together. Go on to his next project. Stay busy and get Muriel out of his head and heart, before he turned into one of those Christians himself.

He tipped his head to see the highest of the apartments in the cliffs. If he could get up there, he could pan the entire canyon with the camera. That, plus the animal footage he had captured when he went out with Charlie yesterday, would finish what he needed. He scanned the cliff with his binoculars, seeking the best route. He had been climbing Colorado's mountains since he was a boy; he'd strap the camera securely to his chest, and he could do it. Determined to finish that day if possible, he gathered his equipment and headed for the ladder.

He was passing the first level when he thought he heard a shout. That wasn't possible. He kept climbing.

"Rex."

Muriel. What was she doing here? He chanced a glance down and waved. A squirrel skittered by his other side, knocking his arm loose. He reached back with his hands but grasped at air. His back bent, and he fell, arms and legs flailing in empty air.

"Rex!" Muriel sprinted for the cliff. Her shoes caught on her hem, and she stumbled. *Lord, help!* Straightening and picking up her hem close to her knees, she ran as fast as she could. Even so, Rex reached the ground before she did.

Oh, God, please don't let him die. She dropped to her knees. Check his pulse? See if he was still breathing? While her mind raced with choices, he moaned. *He's alive. Oh, thank You God!*

His eyes fluttered open. "Muriel. You're here." Then he closed them.

"Oh, God, what do I do?" She couldn't leave him to go find help. The camp appeared deserted, and no one ever came by this way. Didn't Rex have a gun? She looked around, her brain scrambling. He must keep it in his tent. She whispered in his ear. "I'll be right back." She ran to his tent. In other circumstances, she wouldn't touch his things, but in other circumstances, she wouldn't be there. Prying his trunk open, she found a revolver.

Let someone hear and understand. She remembered what her father had taught her about guns, chambered the round and pointed it in the air, pulling the trigger. Once, twice, three times. *Let Nascha or Yanaba hear and understand. Keep Rex alive. Give me wisdom.* Those prayers and other wordless cries poured from her as she raced back.

Rex had shifted a fraction, and his chest moved up and down with reassuring regularity. His left leg lay at an odd angle, and his left arm draped over his head. Broken bones at the least. She could only pray there was no internal damage.

Rex's eyes fluttered. "You came back." His right hand reached for hers, fingers tightening on hers. "I want what you have. I'm not ready to meet God."

Chapter 13

Tears streaked Muriel's cheeks. Rex closed his eyes and drifted off again. *Don't die on me now, now that you are ready to live.* She lost track of time as sobs shook her shoulders, prayers pouring from her soul in wordless supplication. Brushing back his hair from his forehead, she allowed herself to study his features in a way she had never allowed herself before. Her fingers traced his strong chin, clean-shaven, even though he was alone in the camp with no one to please but himself. The coating of dust on his hair did nothing to tame the waves. She leaned over and kissed his forehead.

She pulled herself out of her daze and glanced at her watch. Half an hour had passed since she had ridden into the camp just in time to watch as Rex flew to the ground from two stories up. Ten, fifteen minutes maximum, had passed since she'd fired the gun. So far no one was riding to the rescue.

His breathing was labored. Had he broken any ribs, or had he injured his lungs? The longer he lingered without medical help, the greater the risk of permanent damage grew. Chewing her lip, she debated her options. Fire the gun again? Since no one answered the first shot, probably no one was in the vicinity. Ride back to the village? That would mean leaving Rex alone, vulnerable to sun and animals and who knew what else. Move Rex to a safer place before she left? Even if she could carry him, which she doubted, she knew better than to move someone with this kind of injury.

All the options involved risk. She decided to try the gun again and wait five minutes. Removing herself a distance from Rex, she fired three more shots. If no one came this time, she would have to find a way to bring Rex back to the village with her. She looked around the camp for materials she could use. Only Rex's tent remained. She didn't even see a wagon. Perhaps he had sent instructions with Cook to send it back. Perhaps she could use the sheets from Rex's cot. She hated to think of the damage that could do.

When the minute hand of her watch crept past four minutes, she stood to go into the tent. In the distance, she saw two figures on horseback, racing in her direction: Nascha and Yanaba, Charlie's Navajo name as she had learned since staying in the village.

She lifted her face to the heavens. "Thank You!" She gestured widely with her arms, urging them forward. The speed of their horses increased, and she moved back to wait with Rex.

"We heard the gunshots. What has happened?"

Yanaba had already dropped to his knees beside Rex. He ran sure hands over his body, and Rex stirred, moaning.

"He fell from up there." Muriel looked up the cliff. "About two stories, from where that bush juts out by the door. I'm pretty sure he broke his left arm and leg."

Charlie ran his fingers over Rex's left ankle. "He also broke this bone." Running his hand under Rex's head, he brought them out and measured his fingers about two inches apart. "A bump on the back of his head about this wide, which may be why he is not awake."

"He's opened his eyes a couple of times."

Charlie grunted. "That's good."

"Can you tell about his ribs?"

"I'm not sure. His back isn't injured. He should heal."

Thank You, God. "How are we going to move him? And where?"

Yanaba and Nascha glanced at each other. "There is a man in our village who is skilled in these matters. But he knows nothing of the white man's medicine."

These people had survived in this environment for hundreds of years. The medicine man—or whatever the Navajo called him—was a good choice, the only choice. "Yes. The sooner, the better."

"Does Mr. Pride have blankets in his tent?" Nascha said.

"I'm sure he does. He definitely has sheets." Muriel surveyed the now empty campsite. "Everything is in his tent. They packed out the rest of it when the crew left last week."

"We will come right back."

Muriel continued praying as Yanaba worked on making a litter. Each second increased her concern, as Rex sank deeper into unconsciousness. She held his hand, as if that physical touch would keep him tethered to the physical world.

Charlie chopped down three branches of a piñon tree and dragged them to the place where she waited with Rex. Nascha came out of the tent with a couple of blankets, as well as a length of rope. Quickly they lashed the branches together in an isosceles triangle and fastened the blankets to the pole. Yanaba checked the strength of the construction. "It's ready." Another length of rope attached the litter to one of the horses before he placed gentle hands under Rex's body and shifted him to the litter with no seeming movement.

"You can ride behind me." Nascha invited Muriel to join her on the back of her horse, and they left at a pace that minimized the bumps over the ground.

Rex woke in a dark, enclosed space filled with smoke. Or maybe the smoke was in his head, brought on by the fiery pain searing his bones. Someone waved a bright light in his face, and he tried to move his arms over his eyes. Pain scored down his left arm, and he cried out.

"You have awakened." The speaker was a man with plaited gray hair and a weathered face who reminded Rex of photographs he had seen of Navajo chief Manuelito. He carried a bowl with steam rising from it that seemed apart from the smoke in the room. "Good. Eat a little." He raised Rex's head with one hand. Dizziness flushed his body, and he blinked against the nausea.

"I will help you." The man held a spoon to Rex's lips and tipped it in. He tasted corn, onion, and garlic in a meat broth. After the first taste, he ate it greedily, as if he hadn't eaten for days.

"What day is it?" He looked at the man who was tending to him—obviously Indian. "Where am I?"

"Rest. Answers later."

Rex fought to demand an answer, to concentrate, but his thoughts grew fuzzy and his eyes drifted shut as he sank against the pillow. Off and on he awakened. Each time, the same ancient Indian fed him soup. He thought he dreamed that the man rubbed ointments into his legs, arms, head, rewrapped the limbs. When he came fully awake again, the smoke in the room had dissipated, and pale light filtered through an opening overhead. "You're awake."

Relief flooded Rex at the sound of Muriel's familiar voice. "What happened? Where am I?" He tried to sit but his arm collapsed under his weight.

"Did you hurt yourself?" She bent over him, her hair shining around her shoulders like a dark halo.

"Aside from feeling like a hundred bees stung my arm, I'm fine. What happened?"

Instead of answering, she said, "What do you remember?"

"I was spending an extra couple of days on-site to get some final shots. You had left. I was alone." He turned his head side to side, trying to make sense of his surroundings. Moving his head was slightly less painful that leaning on his arm. "Where am I? What day is it?"

"It's Sunday morning. You're in Nascha's village."

"That's not possible. It was just—" His brain reached for the weekday.

"What's the last day you remember?"

"Wednesday, no Thursday. I got up and. . ." His mind went blank. "I don't know. How was I hurt?"

"Sani said you might not remember. And that I shouldn't tell you, but I should let you remember on your own."

"Who is Sani?" Memories of an elderly man hovering over him, spoon-feeding him and tending to his wounds, surfaced. "Who's been taking care of me?" Rex stirred in the bed, forcing himself into a sitting position from his right elbow.

"Sani. He's the one the Diné—that's what the Navajo call

themselves—go to for medical help."

So it wasn't a dream. He didn't know what happened. And this—charlatan—refused to let Muriel tell him.

"He's been by your side the whole time, until today." Muriel continued, oblivious to his mood. "He said you were getting better, and agreed that I could sit with you."

"Tell me what happened."

She smiled. "You'll remember when you're ready."

"Why should I listen to some Indian medicine man?" Rex's voice gained volume. "I want to see a doctor. A real doctor."

"You shouldn't move." The man, shorter than Rex remembered but who radiated compacted power, entered the room.

"You must be Sani. So you think I'm doing better?"

"Yes. For a few days I was afraid you would die. Now you will live. If you don't do anything that will make it worse."

The words sent shock waves through Rex. "If I was that ill, why didn't you take me to a hospital?"

Instead of answering, the man unwrapped the bindings on Rex's arm where he had pushed into a sitting position. Humming a sing-song melody, he also checked his legs. "You are not a prisoner here. You can leave if you want to." He folded his arms across his chest. "But if you do, you will not walk again."

❧

Muriel's heart broke when she saw the fear in Rex's face at Sani's words. "*I'm not ready to meet your God.*" Did he remember saying that? She had never prayed as constantly as she had for the past three days, while Rex slipped in and out of consciousness. Would his admission—I need God—count as a deathbed confession? Or did he need a fuller understanding of his sin and Jesus' provision?

For now he was alive and likely to remain that way. She prayed his heart would remain open.

She leaned in. "Sani has been taking excellent care of you. When you"—She stopped short of saying "fell." Sani said it was best for him to remember on his own—"when we brought you here, you were in bad shape. I've been praying for you."

Rex winced at that statement.

"Healing prayers and healing hands. God has kept you alive. Now let Him finish His work on your legs."

"You're a strange woman, Muriel Galloway. God and Indian medicine. Quite a combination." He closed his eyes. "I'll get out of here after I rest a little longer." Soon his chest raised and lowered with the rhythm of sleep. Sani left the room.

"You do that." Muriel spoke to his sleeping body. "Rest and heal." She followed Sani outside. "I apologize for what he said."

A smile let Muriel know Sani held no grudge. "I do not mind. Many of my people do not trust the white man's medicine either."

Muriel laughed. "I never thought of it that way. I'm sure there is much you could learn from each other."

He waved his hand dismissively. "Tell me. Do all white men believe as you do, that your God will heal a broken body?"

With all her heart, Muriel wished she could say yes. "No, they don't. But the Bible teaches that God created us. Jesus healed many people when He came to earth."

"Nascha has spoken of these things. That Jesus put mud on a blind man's eyes, and he could see again. That He healed a man who couldn't walk. Like Mr. Rex Pride. Have you prayed for that?"

"Of course."

"Then why is he not walking?"

Muriel felt confused. "Because he is still recuperating."

"You say you believe God can make lame men walk. But then you do not think He can do the same for your friend? I don't understand." He bent over the cook fire and stirred the pot.

Muriel's mind sputtered, but she couldn't come up with an answer for his question.

"I will ask Nascha. Perhaps she can explain."

Muriel felt properly put in her place.

"Stir this pot from time to time. When Mr. Rex Pride awakens, feed him as much as he will eat. I will fix him some mutton to strengthen his bones when I come back." Sani straightened and handed her the spoon. "Someone should stay with him at all times. Do you wish to stay?"

Muriel gave a fleeting thought to the Bible study Nascha would lead that afternoon. But Rex needed her, and Nascha could handle the Bible study on her own, perhaps even better, than if Muriel was present. "I will stay. And if something happens, I will ask someone to find you."

He nodded and walked away, a low hum streaming from his lips.

Muriel took a seat by Rex, wishing she had her Bible with her. At times like this she relied on the scripture passages she had memorized over the years: some for contests, some for public recitation, and some just for the beauty of the words. *"Seek those things which are above, where Christ sitteth on the right hand of God."* One summer when she had started to achieve success on the stage, she had committed the entire epistle to the Colossians to memory. Knowing that if she didn't keep her mind centered on God and His will, she could lose herself. The discipline had served her well, and she brought the verses back effortlessly.

Grasping Rex's right hand, she focused on the floor and moved her mouth with whispered words. " 'That ye might walk worthy of the Lord unto all pleasing, being fruitful in every good work, and increasing in the knowledge of God.' " What was a life worthy of the Lord? She fell so far short, but pleasing Him, that came by faith.

Only today an unbelieving Indian healer had challenged her faith, yet God had used her in spite of her less than perfect life.

But Rex. . .dear Rex. How she prayed he would come to the Lord.

A soft, feminine voice murmured words. Comforting, soothing, pleading words. They washed over Rex and teased him awake.

"Dear Rex."

The words brought Rex to full wakefulness. Struggling for comprehension, he added up memories. He was injured, broken left arm and leg, holed up at the Navajo village under the care of a medicine man.

Muriel.

He kept his eyelids closed, not wanting to interrupt, feeling like an eavesdropper, but wanting to hear her heart. Had she really said "dear Rex?"

"You know how much I care for him, Lord. And You have kept him alive. But he needs You. For his broken body. For his broken spirit." Her voice broke.

Rex could hardly contain himself. Her voice rang with pain and sincerity and—dare he hope?—love. She continued praying, her words flowing over him like a soothing ointment. He could lie all day listening to her voice. In fact, he didn't have a choice. He couldn't move without help. His left arm itched beneath the wrapping, and he wished he could scratch it. A single twitch of the muscles sent shards of pain up his shoulder, and a groan escaped.

Soft fingers massaged his temples. "I wish I could give you something for the pain."

He opened his eyes and stared into Muriel's beautiful dark eyes, inches away from his. A smile lifted his lips in spite of the pain. "Looking at you is all I need, unless you have a stiff whiskey on hand."

"You charmer, you."

"Charmer. No one has ever called me that before." He turned his head side to side, grimacing as his right side hit the pillow. "Ouch."

"You have a nasty bump back there. That's probably what knocked you out."

Rex wanted to reach up and touch it, but he couldn't. He still couldn't believe he was stuck in a primitive dwelling with a medicine man instead of a doctor who specialized in whatever broken bones and other problems he had. "Get me out of here. Please."

She shook her head. "Not until you can walk out on your own

power. But since you're awake." She smiled, a mischievous glint in her eyes. "Sani said you could sit up for a few minutes and get a bite to eat."

"A reprieve." When he struggled to sit, he broke out in a groan.

"Let me help you." Muriel put an arm around on his weak side. "Here you go."

Sweat dotted his brow when at last he reached an upright position. He felt like he had climbed a mountain.

A mountain. . . The memories clicked.

"I fell off the cliff. Didn't I?"

Chapter 14

Yes, you did." Fear rippled across Muriel's face at his words. "What else do you remember?"

Memories washed over him. He wanted to climb to the top tier. Halfway there, he heard Muriel's voice and waved. A squirrel darted by, knocking his hand enough to send him flying. He flailed at the air, helpless, for the few seconds it took him to plunge to the earth.

"I remember the climb, the fall. . .nothing after that. I don't know what would have happened if I had been alone. I guess I was lucky. You came back."

"That wasn't luck. That was God. He's not done with you yet."

"There you go, preaching at me again." But his protest was half-hearted. She had saved his life.

A frown flickered on her face. "Do you remember waking up at all?"

He shook his head. "It's a blank until I woke up here."

She stepped back. "Think you can stay by yourself for a few minutes? Sani said you should eat."

"I can handle it. I'm a big boy." He watched her walk to the door, dressed in a skirt and blouse similar to what Sarah wore, her hips swaying gently. No matter what she wore, even if it were a dress made from flour sacks, she drew his eye. She was beautiful, inside and out. He wasn't sure which side he loved more.

She brought in a bowl of the same steaming soup that Sani had given him before. When she brought the spoon to his mouth, he tried to lean forward to swallow the liquid, but the back of his head protested. She tipped the spoon over his lips, and half of it fell down his chin.

Handkerchief in hand, she cleaned his skin. "I apologize. Can you tell I haven't had much experience doing this? Although I did play a nurse in a movie one time."

"Practice makes perfect?" They made it through another ten spoonfuls, her aim improving with each swipe. "What does a man have to do to get real food around here?"

"Sani said he is bringing you some mutton later."

"Mutton. . .like lamb chops?"

"Sheep. I've had it. It's delicious."

"Steak. Rare. Baked potato. Apple pie." He accepted more soup. "I was looking forward to some city food when I got back to Denver this weekend. Are you sure I can't leave?"

She shoved more soup into his mouth to quiet him. "Can you walk out of here yet?"

"I think I hear an echo."

"Sani says you should be ready to start exercises in a day or two. And I won't leave until you're better. I've already written to the director of the play I'm supposed to appear in next, explaining the situation."

He swallowed a few more mouthfuls, then pushed away the spoon, feeling full. "No more. You don't have to do that, you know. Stay here."

"I know I don't." A smile played around her mouth. "I want to."

By the time Muriel had put away the bowl, Rex had closed his eyes. She lifted his shoulders and laid him down against the pillows. Bristles covered his chin, the beginning of a good beard, together with the mustache growing over his lips. Too bad he spent all his time behind the camera; he'd look good on the screen. The thought brought a blush to her face.

Her stomach growled, and she realized she hadn't eaten since early that morning. She brought in a bowl of the same corn soup and quickly spooned it down. Some of their flat bread would sop up the broth. She had rediscovered her appetite since she had arrived at the village. If she stayed here much longer, she would find herself needing to lose a few pounds.

Nascha headed in her direction, together with four other people.

"Ya'ah'tee." Muriel had learned the familiar greeting. Hoping to

cram as much information as possible into her time in the village, she asked the words for various everyday items. The first step in communicating God's love must involve speaking the same language.

Nascha came forward, Bible clasped in her hands. "Since Mr. Rex Pride cannot move, I asked Sani if we could come here. I knew you wanted to take part in the Bible study. He said yes." She nodded, and Muriel sensed her friend came not only for Muriel's sake but also for Rex's.

"That's thoughtful. You caught me while I'm eating. But Rex just fell asleep. I'm not sure—"

"Sani said he should stay awake."

Yanaba followed, together with a couple of the young women who had attended last week, as well as one of the elders. Disappointment fluttered in Muriel's stomach when Sani didn't return. In spite of the smaller attendance, she took heart from the presence of the elder. She searched her memory for names as she finished up the soup. Doli, Kai, Mosi, Ahiga, Ashkii, Bidziil. Something like that.

Did the people present share Sani's doubts about the truth of the stories Nascha had shared last week? She shook her head to clear the doubts. God was here, and He was at work.

She took a seat by Rex's bed. His eyelids fluttered open. "What?"

"Nascha brought the Bible study here, so I could attend."

"Wasn't that nice of her." Mirth danced in Rex's eyes.

"And Sani said you should stay awake. Do you feel up to sitting again?"

His nod stopped halfway, settling back into his pillow. "Maybe later."

Taking the chair beside him, Muriel realized the room had quieted, everyone waiting for her. Nodding, she acknowledged their consideration, and smiled to encourage her friend.

Nascha opened her Bible about three quarters through, somewhere in the New Testament, Muriel guessed, and spoke briefly. Was she translating as she read? Muriel didn't know. In the mail she had sent out, she had included an order for a Navajo Bible.

"Is this all going to be in their language?" Rex whispered. "She's telling quite a story."

Muriel nodded, showing him the Bible. "She's talking about the time Jesus calmed a storm." She pointed to the relevant words. After he read them, she passed the Bible to Yanaba.

Nascha added actions to her words, as if she had been taking acting lessons from Muriel all summer long. Her gestures suggested the raging storm, Jesus' calming words, the surprise and awe in the disciples' faces when they said, " 'What manner of man is this, that even the winds and the sea obey him?' "

"Help me sit. I want to see."

After she helped him sit, he leaned forward, watching. When Nascha reached a break in her narrative, the elder spoke. He held up the Bible and pointed to a picture of Jesus on the cross. He appeared to be asking a question.

Muriel prayed while Nascha answered his question. This time, the others interrupted her, asking questions, shaking their heads. Muriel sensed their shock at the awful torture that crucifixion represented. But would they understand the meaning behind His death? She could only pray.

After a while, Nascha surprised her by switching to English. "One of the things I liked going to the chapel at the film was the time they spent in prayer. These people shared their lives. They talked about things that made them angry, sad, or happy. They talked about their families, about missing their children or their spouses. They talked like a family, and then they talked to a God they couldn't see about their problems." She smiled at Muriel. "I learned that God answered their prayers. I wanted to be part of their family. To know the God who was their father." She stopped. "I will pray today. We will pray for Mr. Rex Pride. We will pray for Muriel, who is missing her family. My mother's back is hurting. Does anyone else have something they want to pray about?"

No one spoke for a moment, and Muriel prayed that God would use this prayer time. Beside her, Charlie stirred. "The corn needs rain. If Jesus can stop rain, He can make it rain, too."

Nascha nodded and waited to see if anyone else would speak. As the silence lengthened, Muriel fought the urge to fidget in her chair. Then Nascha spoke a few words and closed her eyes, folding her hands. God listened to different languages all day long. Muriel knew the Bible wasn't written in English, of course, but she had always heard God's word in English. Once again she thanked God that Nascha could share the good news of Jesus in their own language.

A week later, Rex got into a chair before the Bible study. Sani promised he could start walking on crutches this week. Sitting in a chair was a welcome first step.

From his seat he could see out the door. Sunshine baked the air with golden hues. The rest of what he could see out the opening looked like it had come from the same artist's palette: brown dirt, beige sand, rust rock. If only film captured color, he could bring the stern beauty of the landscape to life.

"Look at you." Muriel entered the room, a wide smile on her face. "It is good to see you doing better."

"What? Are you tired of me yelling at you about getting out of bed?"

"Where's that echo?" She cocked her head. "It's getting softer. Pretty soon I won't hear it at all, as soon as you're up and about."

"You won't get any argument from me on that score." Muriel had been a saint. She hadn't let his bad moods, complaints, or occasional curses keep her away. Day-by-day, she demonstrated the depth of her faith, her commitment to live by the word she professed.

Over the past week, he had come to a better understanding of why Muriel kept insisting "I'm not a good person. I'm a sinner saved by grace."

She didn't always hide her distaste of the dishes served at meals. Once she had displayed a flash of anger when Rex tried to stand before

Sani had given his permission. She still came out ahead of most people he knew, but she wasn't perfect. And according to what he heard, that's what God demanded: perfection. Never telling a white lie, never feeling envy, never disobeying your parents. No one lived up to that standard.

"Nascha offered to teach in English today, for our sakes. I told her I would enjoy that." She gestured with the slim volume she held in her hand. "I brought my Bible, in case she wants to borrow it. We got her Navajo Bible this week, but she might want to read from the English."

The group had grown by one person this week, a man about Charlie's age. When Sarah read from her Navajo Bible, the group leaned forward, as if drawn by the magnet of the words.

"Muriel, please read the Bible in English."

"I'll let you do the honors." She handed Rex the Bible, pointing to the passage. "Verse sixteen."

Rex peered at the words, wishing he could plead bad eyesight. "Verse sixteen?" At Muriel's nod, he read aloud. "'For God so loved the world, that He gave His only begotten Son, that whosoever believeth in Him should not perish, but have everlasting life.' " He got the basic meaning, although "only begotten" confused him a bit. Begotten suggested fathering a child—God's only child. Perhaps it was clearer in the Navajo Bible. Too bad he didn't speak Navajo.

Nascha began speaking. "I have told you some stories about this Jesus. He was a good man, a powerful man. He did things only God could do. He taught people to love each other."

Exactly. Rex had never argued with the Christian religion or their moral tenets, started by one of the greatest men who had ever lived. Maybe Sarah understood the truths behind her faith better than Muriel did.

However, Sarah didn't stop there. "But Jesus was more than that. The verse Mr. Rex Pride read says He is God's only Son. He came to earth because God loves us."

Rex's leg hurt, and he focused on Sarah's words to keep his mind off the pain. The themes of sin, punishment, salvation, and God's free gift sounded different coming from her lips. With her new approach to old truths, they conveyed meaning that had escaped him before.

"When we pray in a few minutes, I will say words that will help you ask for this gift if you want to."

He found himself mouthing the words as Nascha prayed. But when he reached the part where she said, "I know that I am a sinner, that I have done wrong things," something in his spirit balked. A God who loved everyone wouldn't condemn a man who did the best he could. He would reward someone who tried. Someone like—Rex. He closed his heart against the stirrings Sarah's testimony had in him. Once he got away from this forsaken corner of the world, he would regain his sense of balance. No need to change his whole way of life because of a few weeks in the desert.

Even though she kept her eyes open, Muriel prayed throughout the entire meeting. Rex drank in every word; she sneaked a glance at him during the prayer and saw him mouthing the words with Sarah.

Her inner "praise God" halted when his lips stopped moving. He shoved his right hand under his left arm and leaned back in the chair. "Almost thou persuadest me to be a Christian." Like King Agrippa, he came so close but stayed so far away. But five others in the hogan needed Christ, and she prayed with renewed fervor.

After the Amen, Charlie stood. "I accepted this Jesus and His gift of salvation."

His friend—a first-time visitor—also stood. "I have also."

Nascha let the silence linger. The elder shook his head, and Muriel felt another sting of disappointment. If he took the step to receive Christ, others would follow his example.

Nascha prayed, thanking God for the new believers, and the group broke apart. She spoke with Charlie and his friend, offering them her Bible. Muriel smiled. Her English Bible would return to her friend's hands. Perhaps she should order a dozen Bibles in faith that God would continue working among the people of this village.

"Do you think Sani will fuss if I lay back down? I overdid it, and my legs hurt like. . . Well, I won't say it here."

The angry, complaining Rex had returned. The possibility that he fought God's conviction only brought Muriel small comfort.

Chapter 15

"Now that you don't need to stay with me all day long, Sarah can hold the Bible study in her own home. After all"—he tapped the wrapping on his left leg—"Sani says I can leave this week."

"Very well." Muriel didn't move. The Bible study wouldn't start for a while longer.

A week had passed since Rex had rejected God's conviction. Muriel wanted to rail against his decision. Today might be the last time he would hear the Gospel. Of course, God wasn't limited to her presence in Rex's life. Still, a small piece of her died because she might never know the outcome. They would go their separate ways, further apart than when they first met, in spite of everything they had gone through—or perhaps because of it.

Like Paul, Rex kicked hard against God's pricks. Remembering that, Muriel strove for patience whenever he barked at her. She remained firm when he questioned Sani's wisdom. She practiced a loving attitude when he sneered at something she or Nascha said about the Lord.

With each effort expended, her burden of guilt grew heavier. If she and Rex had agreed to film scenes in the top cliff dwellings, Rex might not have climbed that fateful day. In the privacy of her bed at night, she cried. She had hoped God would do the impossible, bring him to faith, so the path would be cleared for romance between them.

She was glad Rex had turned back into a harsh taskmaster. It made it easier to leave him behind.

"I'm going for a walk." Rex stomped out of the hogan, his crutches hitting the ground in a regular rhythm.

Muriel followed him. "Can I get you something?"

"I'm good. I don't need you to wait on me hand and foot anymore."

She would welcome someone who could string more than two civil sentences together in a row.

"What are you staring at? Get on to your Bible study before you're late. Come back when you've finished your hallelujahs."

Muriel had had enough. "I accept that you don't believe the way I do. Show the same respect to me that I show to you."

His mouth twisted in what she could only describe as a sneer. "That's expecting too much from an old reprobate like me."

"We'll pray for you today. That you will continue to recover and leave as you want to."

"Can't wait to get rid of me, can you?"

She paused, holding her breath and counting. She couldn't win this argument. Letting him have the last word, she left without saying anything more.

"Can't leave you alone for five minutes without you getting into trouble."

Benny ambled along beside Rex. No matter how fast he wielded his crutches, he felt slow, awkward. Face it, he would stay grouchy until he could walk unaided. He measured his progress by how far he could walk before needing to rest. He had worked up to three homes. "Plain and simple, I was stupid."

Benny guffawed. "The great Rex Pride can admit that he is less than perfect. I never thought I'd live to see the day."

Rex managed to walk past one more house, to a rock that served as a convenient resting place. His right foot caught on a pebble, tipping his ankle ever so slightly. Growling, he plopped down on the rock. "I've had to live with a lot of things I don't like for the last few weeks."

Benny squeezed next to him. "The truth is, if I had been there, I'd have been climbing the cliff with you. We both do whatever it takes to get the shots we want. I thank the Lord I was well out of harm's way when you tried the impossible."

There he went with the God talk. In so many ways, Benny was unlike Muriel. A risk taker and a visionary, he had a wild reputation in his youth. He fit Rex's perception of a "sinner," yet he had changed.

He didn't say any of that. "There'd be no point in both of us getting banged up. Everybody climbed the ladders when the canyon flooded. I didn't figure another level or two would be any different."

"Like I said. I'd have been with you." Benny swung his hands between his knees, studying the landscape. "This place is incredible. Peaceful."

Rex understood. However, after weeks filled with words he couldn't understand, Bible stories he didn't want to hear, and food that left him hungry for a good American meal, he wanted to leave. "Try staying here for as long as I have, and you might not feel that way."

Using the crutch as a pointer, he turned Benny's attention to the desert surrounding the village. "I keep thinking I wish we could capture this in color. The quality of light is unlike anything I've ever seen. Black and white doesn't do it justice."

"Someday."

Benny and Rex sighed at the same time. "Add it to your list of devices to invent."

Benny opened his canteen and took a deep swallow. "I had begun to forget how dry it is out here."

"I'm almost used to it. I'll probably feel cold back in Denver."

A swish of skirts announced the approach of women. Rex still had a hard time twisting his limbs to look over his shoulder, but Benny didn't have any such problems. "Hello there, Muriel, Sarah—or is it Nascha?"

Feet tapped the ground, and Muriel burst into his line of vision. "When did you get here? Rex didn't tell me you were coming." Her eyes burned into Rex, challenging him.

"I figured I could help him get back to Denver. Even after he's okay to travel, he's going to have a hard time."

Benny hugged Muriel, and Rex turned his face down, not wanting to see their comfortable camaraderie.

"It's good to see you. That explains the film reels in Rex's room. I was wondering if he had been digging in his things."

Rex decided to insert himself into the discussion. "Sarah, would the"—he stopped himself from saying "Indian" in the nick of time—"people like to see the film? Benny's setting it up for me to see it, but we could find a place everyone could see it."

Sarah nodded. "That would be good."

Muriel felt the tension radiating from Rex. Since his accident slowed him down, Benny had taken on the task of splicing the film together. No director liked to leave that crucial step to someone else. At least he would do the final editing.

"It will be fine."

Her attempt at reassurance failed. He turned flat eyes on her before curving his mouth in a smile that didn't quite reach his eyes. "I'm always like this before I see it all together the first time."

"Fear always seizes me every time I go on stage." She took a seat next to Rex, careful of his legs. The way he shifted his legs and rubbed his shins told her they bothered him, although he would never admit it. The dear, sweet, impossible man. She took his hand in hers while the screen flickered, and the low hum that buzzed among the gathered people silenced.

Ruined Hopes, a Rex Pride Production. When the words appeared on the screen, he tensed again, his leg jerking and straightening. The credits rolled, and a small frisson of pleasure rolled down her arms when she saw her name. Nascha Begay—bless Benny for getting that detail right—showed up far down on the credits, as "assistant to Miss Galloway." Muriel wished she were sitting next to her, enjoying this moment of recognition.

But Nascha had chosen a seat with her family. Of course. She wanted to share this night with those closest to her. Muriel felt an infrequent pang of homesickness.

The credits finished rolling, and the Four Corners marker appeared on the screen. "At a place in an isolated corner of the far west, two states and two territories meet at a single point. Long before the first white men crossed the Atlantic, these four corners were the crossways of an ancient people. The Old Ones lived in the high desert. They built homes for themselves high along the cliffs. An entire city. . ."The words scrolled by before moving into the first scene. Standing Corn and Killdeer embraced, hiding in a corner of the canyon, away from the eyes of her father.

Muriel forced herself to think of the figure on the screen as the Indian princess Standing Corn, not as herself.

Soon they came to the scene after the hunting party, where the Diné had appeared as extras. People pointed when they saw themselves on the screen. Laughter rumbled around the circle. Rex relaxed as the scene rolled past, tracing his fingers over the back of Muriel's hand. Even the paper-mache deer and horns looked realistic, the way Benny had captured them on film. "It's beautiful," she whispered in Rex's ear. He pressured her hand, and she smiled. If only all their time together could be this simple.

At the climax, when Killdeer and Standing Corn married and added their painting to the cliff wall, Muriel lost herself in the love shining from Killdeer's eyes, laying Rex's chiseled face over Fred's strong features. Closing her eyes, she let her imagination take flight, adding the soundtrack of the music they had chosen, humming it to herself. She sneaked a glance at Rex and saw him directing the music with his pointer finger.

The film rolled to the end, but no one moved. Benny stood. "That's all, folks. I understand a feast has been arranged, and I for one can't wait."

Rex struggled to his feet. Muriel wanted to help, but knew he would resist her assistance. Once he had the crutches under his armpits, he swung to face Muriel. "May I escort you to the feast? More mutton and corn and fried bread?"

"Certainly." She laced her fingers over Rex's on the rung of the crutch as they made their way to the tables set up in the center of the village. "The film turned out well. You've created an amazing story."

"It was easy to do when I was working with such an amazing actress."

His words surprised Muriel. He dispersed a minimum of compliments to anyone.

Benny had taken a seat with Nascha and her family. He made people feel comfortable, whatever the circumstances.

Rex didn't have that skill. His skill lay in teasing, demanding the best from people around them. How she longed to see his strength dedicated to the service of God, instead of fighting Him.

Enjoy the night. Be at peace. God loved Rex, and He was at work. She couldn't change a thing by worrying about it.

If only all Rex's time with Muriel could go this well. When it came to the power of theater and film, they shared the same passion. While watching the motion picture, he could forget about the things that separated them.

He studied Muriel's profile, committing the details to memory: the slope of her nose, her trembling lips, her eyelashes fluttering against her cheeks, pink with health. The uncuffed sleeve of her dress fluttered in the slight breeze, showing a glimpse of creamy pale skin.

Rex grabbed another piece of fry bread and added a dollop of honey—not quite Mom's apple pie, but it was delicious. Arching his eyebrows, Benny lifted the last of his bread to his mouth and stuffed it in. "Delicious." The words came out muffled. After he swallowed, he dug in his pocket for a handkerchief and wiped the sticky residue from his hands. At Benny's nod, Charlie rose to his feet.

"I have spent many hours with Mr. Benny Gruber this summer. You may not have seen him. He stays behind the camera, taking pictures. He brought the movie for us to see. He has asked to speak to us."

People settled back, prepared to give him an audience.

"He also asked me to translate, for those who do not speak English." Charlie spoke in Navajo.

For a man who spent most of his time behind a camera, Benny looked at ease in front of an audience. He walked to a spot where he could see everyone around the tables. Charlie took his place beside him.

After clearing his throat, Benny started speaking. "Thank you for listening to me. We couldn't have made *Ruined Hopes* without your help. We never would have gotten the pictures of the bighorn sheep without Charlie's help, or found the cliff paintings or gotten close to a deer or any of a dozen other things. You made this the best experience I've ever had working on a film."

Charlie translated, and their audience nodded and smiled.

"I was poor when I was a child, poor as white men measure wealth. I worked hard until I had everything that represents success to the white man. Education, things, money. But something was still missing."

The audience didn't react as Charlie translated. Rex wondered what point Benny wanted to make; a single glance at the village showed they valued other things more than money and might not understand.

When Benny continued, he made the same point. "You might care about different things, like honor, courage, family. No matter who you are, Diné or white, we all make something the goal of our lives." One of the elders, the one who had been attending the Bible study, nodded.

The words sank into Rex's heart. He didn't value money or things, although he had them. But he craved respect, insisted on independence, challenged anyone who threatened his opinion of himself as a self-made man.

"I got everything I thought I wanted. But I was still miserable."

Rex had achieved all his goals, but what had he gained? At the end of the day he was lonely, tired, and restless until the next challenge presented itself. He who took pride in everything he possessed in reality had accomplished nothing on his own.

Without Muriel's unexpected appearance at the film site the day he'd fallen, he would be dead. Without the care of a man he derided for his lack of education, he wouldn't be walking, even on crutches. He wouldn't even have a film if not for Benny's intervention. He wouldn't even have survived the filming if not for Sarah's warning the day of the flood.

Benny was still talking. "One day a man, a janitor at the building where I had my photography studio, introduced me to the one true God. Right away I knew that Jesus was what I had been looking for all my life."

Was it as simple as that? No matter how hard Rex worked, his accomplishments left him empty. In fact, he was nothing without the God Muriel and Benny worshipped. But after all the times he had told God no, God wouldn't take him now. He'd blown his opportunity. Tears prickled behind his eyes, and he didn't even wipe it away as a single teardrop slid down his cheek.

"Rex?" Muriel took his hand. "Are you all right?"

He turned tear-filled eyes at her. "I need your God. If He will still have me."

Chapter 16

Rex?" Muriel reached for his hand. The man who never showed weakness, who bristled at the suggestion he needed help, who scoffed at any mention of God, was crying in public?

"I need your God. If He still will have me."

Muriel hesitated a second too long. Like the time God got Peter out of prison, she couldn't believe God had answered her prayers.

Tears cascaded down his cheeks. "I've been a fool."

No one looked directly at Rex, but Muriel sensed the sideways glances. "Let's take a walk." She kept her voice low.

"But Benny—"

"Benny will understand. Let's go."

They walked until Benny's voice was only a low rumble in the background, pausing whenever he needed to rest a minute. He led her to a rock on the outskirts of the village where he sank with a sigh. "God has been talking to me for a long time."

She joined him on the rock, lacing her hand with his. "I know. I've been praying for you." She laughed, somewhat self-consciously. "Do you have any questions?"

He looked straight ahead, not meeting her eyes. "Is it too late for me?"

"It is never too late, as long as you're still breathing. Have you ever heard of the thief on the cross?"

Rex screwed his eyes shut, as if envisioning the scene at Calvary. "There were three crucifixions the day Jesus died, right? He was one of those men?"

"Yes. The thief was a criminal, maybe something serious to warrant that kind of execution. But when he hung on the cross, dying, he said, 'Jesus, Lord, remember me when thou comest into thy kingdom.' "

"What did Jesus say to that?"

"'Today shalt thou be with me in paradise.' He went straight from his deathbed to the presence of God."

"The original deathbed confession." Rex's tone took the sting out of the flippant words. "So you're saying I still have time."

"As much as you need, although the Bible also says 'Behold, now is the day of salvation.' Are you ready to open your heart to the Lord?" She heard the pleading note creep into her voice. "Can you admit you can't save yourself?"

Laughing, he circled his crutch around. "I haven't done such a good job of that lately. Yes, I'm ready. So what do I do?"

"You just tell God what you're feeling. Admit you've sinned. Tell Him you believe Jesus died for your sins. Accept His forgiveness." With someone else, she might have led him in a sinner's prayer. But with Rex, he had to reach this decision on his own. She didn't want to put words in his mouth, like a movie script.

"Do I need to do anything special? Temple my hands, close my eyes?"

"It doesn't matter. Do whatever makes you feel comfortable."

His gaze grazed the sky. "It's hard to talk to someone you can't see." Looking at her, he said, "I'll close my eyes, then. So I'm thinking about God and not about you.

"God, I don't know much about how prayer works. But I guess You already know that. I'm used to being the one giving directions. Do this, go there. But I finally realized I can't do it on my own. I can't make up for the bad things I do by being good. I need a Savior. I need Jesus."

Muriel's heart melted as Rex talked to God in his direct fashion. He sounded like an actor talking over the day's filming with his director, accepting the director's right to make decisions for him.

When at last he raised his face, light beamed from his eyes as brilliantly as Edison's light bulb. "I feel. . .strange."

"You're a new person. 'Therefore if any man be in Christ, he is a new creature: old things are passed away; behold, all things are become new.' "

"There you are." Benny hustled in their direction. One look at Rex's face, and he let out a whoop. "You finally did it. Welcome to the family, brother." He threw his arms around Rex's shoulders.

Rex arched his eyebrows. "Is it that obvious?"

Benny looked at Muriel, and they both laughed. "You'll find out. The time will come that you'll sit down at a table filled with strangers, and you'll know which one is a Christian. Without"—Benny raised a hand in self-defense—"anyone saying a blessing over the food."

"I guess I have a lot to learn."

"But you're not doing it on your own. Not anymore."

Like a little boy on his first train ride, Rex kept his nose pressed to the window. Muriel stood on the platform, hand raised in a good-bye wave, her face frozen between joy and sadness. Now he was a Christian, the greatest barrier between them had dissolved. But he knew it was too soon. Like a child with a new toy, he was almost afraid that it would break if he played with it too much. He shook his head; this "toy" came with a book of operating instructions. He had purchased a Bible as soon as he'd arrived in town the night before.

The train started moving, the rhythmic motions of the wheels knocking him off his balance.

"Take a seat. You don't want to hurt that leg now that you've finally escaped." Benny patted the seat beside him. "Besides, you'll see her again. At the premiere."

Benny helped him into the seat, an awkward process between the swaying carriage and his cast. He pulled the slim Bible out of his carpetbag. "Where should I start? At the beginning?"

"Genesis is wonderful. The word means 'beginnings' and it's all about beginnings—of the world, of man, of the Jews. You'll learn about Abraham, the father of our faith. And the start of Exodus is full of excitement and drama, Moses and Pharaoh, plagues and grand confrontations."

"You make it sound like movie fodder."

"It is a great story. But after they arrive at Mount Sinai—let's just say it's slow going for a while. The law."

"The Ten Commandments?"

"And the temple, sacrifices, the priesthood, how society should work. That's getting into Leviticus. Important, all of it, but my annual attempts to read through the Bible falter before I reach the end of Leviticus."

Rex laughed. "So maybe I'll start with, what is it called, the New Testament?"

"Good idea. Start with Matthew, read on through Mark and Luke and John. By then you'll know a lot more about the Lord, not only what you've heard all your life. You might be surprised."

Rex looked at the table of contents and located the page number for Matthew. Hmm, well toward the back of the Bible. He started reading. " 'The book of the generation of Jesus Christ, the son of David, the son of Abraham.' "

He became caught up in the words. Several times he noticed that it said "As it is written." Probably referring back to passages from the Old Testament, which he had yet to read.

By lunchtime, he had reached the halfway point of the book, chapter fourteen. He set the Bible beside him in the dining car. Over the meal, overdone pork chops with lumpy potatoes, his eyes kept straying to the Bible.

Benny laughed. "Go ahead and read. I'm so glad to see you like this. Hungry for God's Word. If someone had told me when I arrived at the village that you would be reading the Bible all the way back to Denver, I would have laughed. But I'm so glad I was wrong."

"If you're sure you don't mind." Rex slipped his finger at the spot where he had stopped and started reading again. "I've heard about this before. Palm Sunday, right? When Jesus rides into Jerusalem on the back of a donkey? Great pageantry for a movie." He gave a self-deprecating chuckle. "I've got to stop reading this like a director."

Benny set down his fork and pushed the plate away. "That's not all bad. God gave you the gifts that make you so good at what you do. Just remember this is truth, not fiction."

"I'll try." Rex settled into finishing the unfolding events of the last week of Jesus' life on earth. Hours later, he reached the end of the book. " 'And, lo, I am with you always, even unto the end of the world. Amen.' " With a satisfied sigh, he closed the Bible. "You couldn't write a better ending. Dead leader, does the impossible, comes back to life, and gives a stirring speech to the troops. And yet it's all true."

"Pretty amazing, isn't it."

The waiter appeared with slabs of pie.

"Do you have any questions?" Benny took a bite of pie. "You ought to try it. It's the best part of the meal."

Rex considered. "Not yet. I'm going to close my eyes and think about what I've just learned."

Over the next few months, he discovered he had a lot to learn. He devoured the New Testament twice over, then went back to Genesis and looked for those verses quoted in Matthew. Benny came over several times a week, encouraging him, eager teacher to an even more eager pupil.

He had persevered, putting the final touches of the film together and making arrangements for its distribution. A month ago he had thrown away the crutches.

As busy as he was, Rex should have found it easy to keep his mind off Muriel.

He tapped the envelope in his hand against the table. An engraved invitation to the premiere of *Ruined Hopes* was addressed in his best schoolboy script to *Miss Muriel Galloway, c/o 20th Century Theater, New York City, New York.*

He kissed the envelope and sent up a prayer. "Lord, let it be."

Muriel stood at the window of her room at the Brown Palace Hotel. Traffic bustled up and down Broadway. *Broadway.* The view looked nothing like the Great White Way she had left behind in New York for this premiere.

She had arranged to take off time from the play for the movie's premiere—it was written into her contract—and took the train to Denver. Benny had picked her up at Union Station; she had run into Fred as well as several of the other actors over dinner. Of Rex, she had seen no sign. Benny said he was busy with last minute details regarding the film.

Muriel wanted to see Rex, to reassure herself that the fears that he had slipped away from the Lord when he returned to his usual environment were unfounded. To look into his eyes and convince herself that whatever she thought she had felt for him was a result of hours spent together in an isolated setting.

Because it couldn't be anything else, at least not on Rex's side. Why else had he maintained silence for all this time?

Why was he ignoring her now that she had arrived in Denver?

She looked at the sky. Gray and overcast, as if it might snow soon. From what she had heard from Rex over the summer, weather in Denver varied wildly, going from shirtsleeve weather to snowfall in the same twenty-four hours. She didn't want to spend the day cooped up inside the hotel, even one as beautifully appointed as this one. Settling her cloak over her shoulders, she headed for the stairs.

As she passed the front desk, a clerk called, "Miss Galloway!"

She pulled the hood of her cloak over her features, as she often did when in public. Then she let it fall back. This wasn't New York. She approached the window at the desk. "Yes?"

"You have a message. I was just going to send it up to your room." He beamed.

Muriel turned the envelope over in her hand. Addressed to "Miss Muriel Galloway" in a strong hand. Fine quality linen paper. Could it be. . . Her fingers fumbled at she slipped her nail under the flap and opened it.

Dearest Muriel,

Benny tells me that you have arrived safely.

I hope you find your room at the Brown Palace to your liking.

I would like to meet you tonight, beneath the beautiful stained-glass ceiling at the Brown Palace. I have much I wish to say to you, but pen and paper will not suffice.

Please join me at the hour of seven o'clock in the lobby.

Truly yours,
Rex Pride.

The sight of his bold signature brought a smile to her face. Seven o'clock. She didn't have much time. She turned to speak to the clerk. "Can you recommend a hair salon?"

A couple of minutes before seven, Muriel paused at the bottom of the stairway. She touched her hat and looked at her dress. Would Rex think the tiered skirt, complete with ruffles and lace, too dressy? She had worn practical clothing while on location. She touched her hair uncertainly, scanning the room for a sign of Rex.

The door flew open with the force of the wind behind it, and Rex strode in. The wind had curled his hair into comfortable peaks. He was dressed in a suit but ignored a tie, instead leaving the top button unbuttoned. Gladness filled her heart, broadening her smile and filling her senses. She couldn't hide her happiness at seeing him if she wanted to.

Most marvelous of all, the expression on his face said he felt the same way.

"Muriel." Rex's tongue swelled, thick in his mouth. "You're beautiful."

"Thank you." She glanced shyly away. "You look fine yourself." Her eyes searched his face. "You have changed. I can tell." Her hand reached for him then dropped without reaching his face.

"Have you seen the ceiling up close? It's beautiful."

She craned her neck to look. "Who's the artist?"

He told her what he knew about the stained glass while they walked the stairs.

She asked, and he talked about the past few months, about what he had learned and what he had yet to learn, about how excited he was with his Christian faith while they circled the railing that looked down on the lobby.

"I had something else I wanted to discuss with you. If it were spring, I would have taken you to Elitch Gardens but given the snowfall. . .I asked you here. Walk with me?"

Dark eyelashes fluttered at him as he took her arm and walked her to a quiet spot at the end of the hall, overlooking the snow-shrouded street below. Taking both her hands in his, he turned her to look at him.

"Muriel, I know a vain, foolish man. He was so eaten up by pride that it almost cost him his life—both eternal life and physical life. Can you accept the love of a man like that?"

"Oh, Rex." She swung his hand and dropped it. "If that man has received Christ, he's a new creation in Christ. The old man is gone forever." Bringing his hand up again, she took a step closer. "And if you're talking about Rex Pride, yes, I could love a man like that. I do love a man like that."

He lifted her hands to his lips, kissing each knuckle, then pulled her into an embrace. "May I make a double announcement tomorrow night? Introducing you as the future Mrs. Rex Pride?"

Happiness shining from her eyes, she said, "Yes."

He pulled her into a close embrace, claiming her lips—and her heart—with a kiss.

Bestselling author **Darlene Franklin**'s greatest claim to fame is that she writes fulltime from a nursing home. She lives in Oklahoma, near her son and his family, and continues her interests in playing the piano and singing, books, good fellowship, and reality TV in addition to writing. She is an active member of Oklahoma City Christian Fiction Writers, American Christian Fiction Writers, and the Christian Authors Network. She has written over fifty books and more than 250 devotionals. Her historical fiction ranges from the Revolutionary War to World War II, from Texas to Vermont. You can find Darlene online at www.darlenefranklinwrites.com.